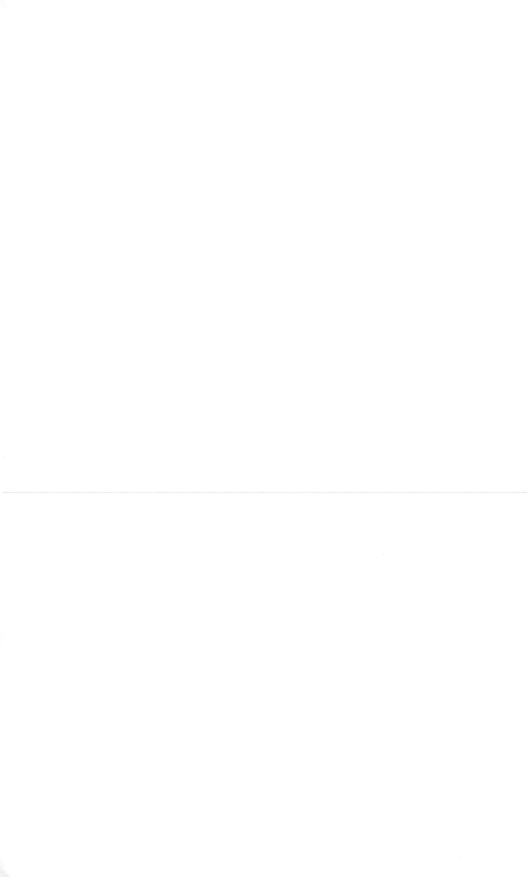

A Valley Wedding

ANNA JACOBS

A Valley Wedding

Backshaw Moss Saga Book Three

HODDER &
STOUGHTON

First published in Great Britain in 2022 by Hodder & Stoughton
An Hachette UK company

1

Copyright © Anna Jacobs 2022

A CIP catalogue record for this title is available from the British Library

Hardback ISBN 978 1 529 35356 3
eBook ISBN 978 1 529 35357 0

Typeset in Plantin Light by Manipal Technologies Limited

Printed and bound in Great Britain by Clays Ltd, Elcograf S.p.A.

Hodder & Stoughton policy is to use papers that are natural, renewable
and recyclable products and made from wood grown in sustainable forests.
The logging and manufacturing processes are expected to conform
to the environmental regulations of the country of origin.

Hodder & Stoughton Ltd
Carmelite House
50 Victoria Embankment
London EC4Y 0DZ

www.hodder.co.uk

Dear Readers,

I hope you enjoy reading this last story set in the Ellin Valley. I have very much enjoyed writing the four series. *A Valley Wedding* is the 14th book set in my imaginary valley – which sometimes feels a very real place to me.

When I first started writing seriously, I was also working full-time and we were raising teenagers, so it took a while to polish my skills to a professional level. I had just turned fifty when I heard the news that one of my books had been accepted after years of trying.

The first novel published was *Persons of Rank,* which won a $10,000 prize in Australia – and that paid off our mortgage. I was thrilled to be published and literally didn't sleep all night, just lay there feeling joyful. My economist husband was thrilled for me, and just as thrilled that this lump sum paid off our mortgage. He keeps my feet on the ground, thank goodness.

I remember thinking that if I wrote steadily, I might get as many as 10 novels published before I made my final exit. Shows how good I am at foretelling the future, eh? *A Valley Wedding* will be my 100th book published.

I still love telling stories as much as I always have and I'm not considering giving up writing or even slowing down. It's my favourite activity. I'm already planning my new series, but I shan't give you any details about it yet. I'll just let you know that my publisher was so pleased by the basic idea that they accepted my suggestion for the new setting after a two-sentence description of it. As a consequence, they have contracted me to write three more historical novels and set them there.

As for the characters who will be involved, they are lively enough now to have woken me several times in the middle of the night to 'show' me scenes. Well, that's what it always feels as if they do. I usually think about a series long before I start working on the stories which take place there.

And finally, on a personal level, I'll share with you my joy that this September will mark our 60th wedding anniversary. Something to celebrate big time. Dave and I have had a wonderful life together. In addition, he deals with the business side of my writing, so he's an integral part of the writing team. And it does take a team to turn a story into a book and sell it to the world.

Thank you for reading my story. I hope you enjoy it as much as I enjoyed writing it! I'll now go back to working on the next one.

All the best
Anna

A Valley Wedding

I

Lancashire, 1936

As Gwynneth Harte was getting her basket and purse ready to go shopping in town, the post arrived. She picked up the letter that had dropped through her door. It was addressed to her youngest son. Well, letters usually were. She turned it over and let out a muffled groan at the sight of the sender's name stamped on the back.

Lucas had already been to a week-long course at this workers' college and had come home thrilled to pieces. Apparently he'd done so well they'd found a private benefactor who would pay for him to go to Manchester University and become a doctor. It was something he'd wanted since he was a small child, caring for an old teddy bear and 'mending' its broken limbs.

She wished he was at home to open the letter and put her out of her misery about when he'd be leaving. She shouldn't begrudge him this chance and she didn't, but these people would take him away from her, she knew they would, and things would never be the same.

Three sons she had, all of them over thirty, and none of them had produced grandchildren for her to love. Well, during the past ten years when times were at their worst and little steady work available, how could they have married? As a widow, she'd often depended on their support.

Then, as life improved slightly and they were getting on their feet again, she'd fallen ill and nearly died, costing them a lot of money for an operation. Now, however, her two eldest sons were in employment and married, so surely there was hope that they'd start families?

She'd tried to introduce Lucas to suitable young women, but he'd told her bluntly that he didn't intend to get trapped in marriage because he was determined to become a doctor. That would take him years, so he wasn't likely to marry till he was at least forty, if then.

She'd known her youngest lad was clever, but no one she knew had ever had a son go to a university. What would happen to him there? Would it change him, make him look down on the rest of the family? She paused, head on one side. No, not their Lucas.

She was working as a part-time housekeeper and lived in the flat at the rear of her employers' house, but she hated the thought of living there on her own.

She mopped her eyes and blew her nose, telling herself to pluck up. She caught sight of the clock, snatched up the basket and hurried off to take the bus down the valley into Rivenshaw. What couldn't be cured must be endured, and best do that with a smile or you'd drive folk away.

Biff Higgins walked into the seedy pub in the poorer part of Rivenshaw, keeping a careful eye on the men sitting there, some of whom looked ready to cut your throat for twopence. He doubted anyone drinking in the middle of the day had any sort of job.

He walked up to the bar and asked the chap behind it for a half pint because in his experience as a private investigator, people who worked in pubs were usually more willing to talk to you if you bought something. He'd decided to lose the slight Irish accent he'd pretended to have last time he visited this town.

He paid for the drink and put a further shilling down on the counter, keeping his forefinger on it. 'I'm looking for Arthur Chapman. I was told he comes in here regularly.'

'What do you want him for?'

'I have some good news for him.'

After a searching gaze, the man said, 'The poor sod definitely needs some good news, for a change. He's the one in the corner by the fire.'

Biff turned to stare in that direction and saw a scrawny, sad-looking man of about the right age, who looked chilled through and was holding his hands out to the fire. Nodding thanks to the barman, he pushed the shilling across the counter, not surprised at how swiftly it vanished.

As a private detective, he'd found the heirs to the other two properties left by Miss Jane Chapman and her nephew, and now, hopefully, he was about to find the heir to the final house.

He sat down in a chair across the tiny table from the man, who seemed to be drinking lemonade, or was it water? If so, the barman must have taken pity on him and given him a drink so that he would have an excuse to stay and warm himself.

'Are you Arthur Chapman?' he asked quietly.

He got a suspicious glance in response. 'Who wants to know?'

'Biff Higgins.' He extended a business card.

After a slight hesitation the man took it, read it and dropped it on the table. 'Has she set a detective on me now?'

'She?'

'Don't pretend. That Mrs Hicks will do anything to keep me from my granddaughter.'

'I've never met or communicated with anyone of that name. I've been sent by Mr Albert Neven, a London lawyer, to find Arthur Chapman who has been left a bequest by a distant relative.'

That was greeted by a frown. 'That's my name, but who'd leave me anything? I've got no close relatives left.'

'It was a Miss Sarah Jane Chapman.'

After a moment's thought, he snapped his fingers. 'Ah. Dad's second cousin on his father's side. He allus spoke well of her. I didn't think she knew I existed, though.'

'She must have done, because she's definitely left you something.'

Arthur shook his head, clearly baffled.

Biff realised that the men sitting nearby had fallen silent and were trying to listen to their conversation. 'How about we go somewhere more private to discuss it, Mr Chapman? I could buy you a meal at the Star hotel. They're open for luncheon and I'm hungry, even if you aren't.'

'Well, I could certainly do with a good meal, so I'll thank you kindly for that offer.' He stood up, leaving the rest of his drink, so Biff left his beer. It had served its purpose and he didn't enjoy drinking in the daytime anyway.

At the hotel, the waiter glanced at Arthur and showed them to a table in the corner, away from the better-dressed folk.

Biff's companion seemed to relax a little once they were seated. 'Eh, it's a long time since I've been in a posh place like this.'

'They do excellent food. Let's order, then we can talk.'

When he nodded across the room, a waitress came to their table, smiling at him. 'Nice to see you here again, Mr Higgins.'

After she'd taken their order, Arthur asked abruptly, 'What has the old lady left me, then?'

'A house and its contents.'

Arthur gasped, then spoke in a shocked, croaky whisper, '*A house?*' Then he scowled. 'You're mocking me.'

'I'm not. It's the simple truth. She left houses to three of her distant relatives who'd fallen on hard times, people she thought deserved a helping hand.'

Tears came into Arthur's eyes and he blinked furiously. 'I don't deserve anything. I've made a mess of my life in the past two years. Yes, a right old mess, and all my own fault.'

'Well, now you've got a chance to sort things out.'

'As long as it's not too late.'

'What do you mean?'

'My wife died two years ago, an' I started drinking. I let myself get cheated out of what savings I didn't spend on beer. I'd talk to anyone, buy them a drink rather than go home to an empty house. I missed my Susan that badly I could hardly think straight for the first few months. We'd been wed since we were eighteen, you see, courting since we were fourteen.'

'Grief can do strange things to people.'

'Aye. I turned into such a drunken sot my son wouldn't speak to me an' I don't blame him.'

He was speaking in such a bleak monotone, Biff's heart went out to him.

'Then my daughter and her husband were killed in that big railway accident down south a few months ago. Her husband's widowed mother, who is a mean old devil, took my granddaughter in and got the minister of her church to speak for her as being a proper guardian. As if he knows her, he's a new man to this town, that one is!'

He stared into space for a few seconds, then said in a husky voice, 'She's not let me speak to my little Beatie since, not once, and has threatened to bring down the law on me if I go near them, even though I've give up the booze.'

'Could you not have hired a lawyer to help you?'

'I might have if I'd any money left. Or a job. Only I haven't got either.'

'Ah. I see.'

'What upsets me most is that my granddaughter looks unhappy since she's gone to live with Ruby Hicks. Beatie may be warmly dressed and live in a comfortable house, but she's downright miserable there if you ask me. It fair breaks my heart to see her in the street. She used to be such a happy little lass, skipping along an' chattering away.'

'How old is she?'

'Just turned nine.'

Their meal was served and Arthur proved how hungry he'd been by clearing his plate rapidly. He looked across the table apologetically as he laid down his knife and fork, because Biff's plate was still half full. 'Sorry for my poor table manners. I were famished.'

'Have a piece of apple pie for afters, then. They do a good one here.'

His companion gave him another of those wry, twisted smiles. 'I've not been eating well for a while, so I couldn't fit anything else in. Thank you for the offer, though. That were extra kind of you.'

Biff finished his own meal then pushed away his plate. 'Can you prove who you are?'

'Aye, easy. I've lived in the valley all my life. There's a dozen folk in Rivenshaw who've known me since we were childer together.'

'We'll go and see Henry Lloyd straight away then. Do you know him?'

'I'd recognise him by sight. Folk speak well of him.' Arthur closed his eyes, murmuring, 'I hope I don't wake up and find this is all a dream.'

Henry Lloyd studied the man Biff Higgins had brought to see him. 'You don't need to prove who you are, Mr Chapman. I used to see you around town when you worked for Sam Redfern. After you lost your wife, you seemed to vanish, and when I wanted to find you, I couldn't.'

'Well, it's good that you can identify him yourself,' Biff said. 'That'll save me one job. What do we need to do next, Mr Lloyd?'

'I'll contact Mr Neven and we'll get him to send us the key to the third house.' Henry turned back to Arthur, and added,

'Miss Chapman said those houses weren't to be opened up again until the heirs had been found, just kept weatherproof. So I'm no wiser about the contents than you are.'

'It's a strange business altogether,' Biff said.

'But kindly meant. Both Miss Chapman and her nephew were very pleasant people to deal with. Now, where can I contact you, Mr Chapman?'

Arthur flushed, looking embarrassed. 'I don't have proper lodgings. You could leave a message for me at the church hostel in East Rivenshaw. I earn my night's shelter there by doing some cleaning, and they let me leave my spare clothes in the cellar, but no one can stay there during the day so I never know where I'll be then.'

Biff had seen unemployed men both here and in London walking the streets in the daytime come rain or shine, some carrying bundles, some without any possessions.

Mr Lloyd nodded. 'I'll do that.' He glanced at the clock. 'Now, if you two will wait in reception, I'll telephone Mr Neven and see if we're in time for him to send the house key here by the overnight express service.'

He came out to join them again a few minutes later. 'They've just got time to catch today's post, so the key will arrive in Rivenshaw late tomorrow morning. Perhaps you'd like to check tomorrow that it's arrived, then bring Mr Chapman to meet me at the house at one o'clock in the afternoon, Mr Higgins, then we can hand everything over?'

Both men nodded, then Biff turned to Arthur. 'There's something else I need to tell you, Mr Chapman. Because of the difficulties the heirs had last time, with Higgerson trying to bully them to sell him the properties at a knock-down price, Mr Neven has hired me to keep an eye on you for a week or two and help you settle in. Will that be all right with you?'

Arthur looked from one to the other in puzzlement. 'Higgerson wants my house?'

Mr Lloyd nodded. 'Yes, and you know what he's like. You'll definitely need to be on your guard, Mr Chapman.'

Biff knew what he still had to tell the heir would give him further difficulties, so he tried to think how to cheer the poor fellow up. As they left the lawyer's rooms, he asked, 'Would you like to see your house from the outside today?'

'I'd like to, of course I would, but it depends where it is. I can't afford bus fares, and my shoes have holes in the soles, so I can't walk very far. I put fresh cardboard in them every morning, but it soon wears through, especially on rainy days.'

He saw Biff's pitying expression at this admission and added, 'I made a vow after I stopped boozing to tell the truth – when it doesn't hurt anyone but me, that is – so I'm not pretending about how broke I am.'

'Well, I have my car and was expecting to drive you there and back. I'll need to give you some more information after you've seen the house. You'll understand better then why I'm here.'

He shrugged. 'I'll do whatever you and the lawyers think best. Where is this house exactly?'

'Backshaw Moss.'

Arthur looked disappointed. 'If it's in that slum, it can't be up to much – though anything's welcome, of course.'

'It's quite a nice house, actually, the end one on Daisy Street, so not in the bad part of Backshaw Moss. What's more, the council knocked down the row of slum dwellings that was on the other side of the street at that end, and they've built a row of new houses in their place. They've worked quickly, and the new places are almost finished. So where your house is situated is being transformed into a respectable area.'

'Eh, that's a relief. I've had enough of living in slums this past year, I can tell you. Thank you for that offer to drive me there, Mr Higgins. Once again I'm grateful to you, an' I won't forget your kindness. I can't wait to see the house. Maybe even that Hicks woman will let me see my granddaughter now.'

And maybe, Biff thought, he could help him with that as well. He could try, anyway. Not being from the valley, he didn't know who this Ruby Hicks was, but he'd make it his business to find out and get a look at her and the child, who clearly meant so much to her grandfather.

Arthur sat in the car as he was driven slowly up the hill to Birch End, enjoying the comfort of this means of transport. He wondered what he had to be warned about. Whatever it was, he'd cope. Life wasn't always easy, but if the house was even halfway decent, he'd do it up gradually. He was good with his hands.

Surely he could find a job of some sort to earn the money for that? Especially if he didn't have to pay rent. Maybe he could take in a lodger or two as well? No, they'd need someone to prepare meals for them, and he wasn't a cook.

As they slowed down to go through the village centre of Birch End, they passed a couple of women standing chatting. Biff had to slow down just then to let an old man cross the road, and waved to one of them. She waved back, smiling.

'Nice woman, Gwynneth Harte. Do you know her?'

'I don't think I've ever met her, but she looks friendly.'

'You'll be bound to meet her now because as well as visiting her son, who lives two doors away from your new home, she lives just down the road in Birch End.'

Arthur turned his head to take another look at her. She was about his own age, he'd guess, and had a lovely warm smile. Comely was the word that came into his mind to describe her. It was old-fashioned, but it suited her, some-how. He always judged people by their smiles. His wife had had a lovely one.

He forgot the stranger as the car drew up at the very end of Daisy Street. He hadn't been up to this part of the valley since before his wife died. If he remembered correctly, a huddle of tumbledown old houses had once stood on the other side of the street, as if signalling the entrance to a slum. They were gone now, and a row of brand new terraced houses were standing there, giving a completely different impression to those who passed by.

As he opened the car door, he could hear the sound of hammering coming from inside one of them, and there was a lovely smell of freshly sawn wood. He turned his head slowly, hardly daring to look at his inheritance in case it was a tumbledown place. But it wasn't! On this side of Daisy Street there were three larger houses. He'd passed them a few times, but hadn't taken much notice of them until now. He sucked in a sharp breath. His inheritance couldn't be one of those, surely?

As Biff got out of the car, he pointed to the end house. 'That one is yours. Number 25.'

It felt to Arthur as if the world had stopped turning and he with it. When he did manage to put a few words together, all he could say was, 'But it's a big house!'

'Bigger than the average dwelling, yes.'

'It can't be mine!'

Biff smiled at him. 'Well, it is, thanks to Miss Chapman and her nephew.'

'I don't deserve it, 'deed I don't!'

'She thought her bequests might help her descendants to pull their lives together, and it has done with the other two. She would be so pleased about that. I'm sure this one will do the same for you.'

Biff waited, but Arthur still said nothing, so he continued to offer information in a gentle flow to give him time to get used to his inheritance. 'These houses are very soundly built, but you'll probably find that yours needs modernising inside, as the others did. They've been empty for over a decade, you see, and all that's been done in that time is maintenance of the exteriors.'

Arthur put one hand on the roof of the car, as if to steady himself, and said harshly, 'I have only a few shillings in the world. How would I do any modernising at all?'

'Miss Chapman will probably have left you a way to do it, with a bit of effort. She was a great believer in working hard if you wanted something. We'll find out more tomorrow when we see the interior.'

'What were the other houses like inside?'

'Number 23 had been divided into flats, with some very badly behaved tenants needing throwing out. The owners have done a lot of modernising, and they have a couple of good tenants living there now, so maybe you can do that too. The whole of Number 21 was crammed so full of larger furniture, you could hardly walk through it.'

'Why would anyone leave it like that?'

'Miss Chapman had inherited two other houses when she was old and failing in health, so she had just had the furniture from them dumped inside to be dealt with later. I gather she had expected to recover and live to a ripe old age like most of the Chapmans. Sadly, she didn't.'

He waited, but Arthur just nodded.

'I have no idea what we'll find inside yours, but probably some things to help you set yourself up.'

'Anything would be a help, but I'll sleep on the bare boards and use sacks for blankets if I have to.'

Biff nodded acceptance of this. He'd have been the same. Owning your own house was an impossible dream for most people. 'Shall we walk around the outside and peep over the wall into the backyard?'

Arthur nodded, following him past the side of the house along which ran a side street where the better village of Birch

End began. They could just see into the backyard if they stood on tiptoe. It contained the usual outhouses and was paved with big square flagstones.

They studied it in silence, then continued.

When they finished their circuit, Arthur stared at the house again from the front, muttering, 'Eh, it's a fine building. I don't deserve it, 'deed I don't.'

'Then you'll have to make sure you do deserve it by the time you get things sorted out.'

Arthur stared at Biff and nodded slowly, as if that remark had hit home.

Biff gave him a little more time to stare, then said quietly, 'I'll drive you back down the valley to Rivenshaw now. Can you meet me at half past twelve outside the town hall tomorrow and we'll drive up to meet Mr Lloyd?'

'Yes, of course. I'll be grateful for the lift. Thank you.'

As they got out of the car, Biff slipped a ten-shilling note into his hand. 'To help you smarten up a bit.'

Arthur stared down at it then nodded thanks. This was no time to stand on his dignity.

He watched the car drive away and walked slowly along the street to the hostel to do the cleaning job that would earn him a night's shelter. On the way there he bought a second-hand pair of shoes from the pawn shop. The uppers were a bit scuffed, but the soles were sound, which was the main thing.

He also spent sixpence at the public baths that evening, taking his one spare set of underclothes in with him to wear afterwards so that he could wash the others in the bath water. He could dry them overnight at the hostel.

Sitting in the warm water, he bent his head forward and wept for both joy at the prospect of owning a house and sorrow that Susan hadn't lived to move there with him.

★

When he raised his head, he felt cleansed in more ways than one, and utterly determined to make full amends for his recent mistakes and stupidity. He didn't know how he'd do that, but he'd find a way.

He didn't tell anyone at the hostel what had happened, though. Time enough for that later.

2

Gwynneth was glad to be going into Rivenshaw. It'd take her mind off her worries to do some shopping and maybe meet a few people she knew and chat to them. The village shop in Birch End supplied everyone's basic needs, but it didn't stock much beyond essential groceries.

She had a quarter of an hour to wait for the bus, but there was a bench behind the bus stop and she enjoyed watching people. Today she saw a little lass she'd noticed before walking sedately along the street, accompanied by a harsh-faced old woman.

Other children of her age skipped along and chatted to their companions, but this one always walked sedately. She'd have been bonny had she not been dressed in funereal black, with her hair dragged back into a tight single plait.

The stern-looking woman seemed to be scolding the child. Why was she not at school? Ah, that was a bandage on her wrist. Perhaps she'd been to see the doctor.

The child's face bore an expression of what looked like the stoic calm of utter despair to Gwynneth, a way to hide her real feelings. Such a young creature to be so guarded and unhappy. She couldn't have been more than about nine or ten.

It tore at Gwynneth's heart to see her. She'd have given anything for a grandchild of that age to take for walks, chat to and make clothes for.

The old woman's expression remained grim. Once, when the lass started to move in a pattern of steps to avoid stepping on the cracks between the paving slabs, she cast a quick, furtive glance around and slapped her young companion good and hard on the back of the head. From her expression, she enjoyed doing it.

The blow was so hard it sent the child tumbling to the ground, and when the poor little thing got up, she was cradling the arm with the bandage on it. That didn't stop her getting scolded for not walking properly. The bandage was now trickling blood.

The woman's shrill voice carried clearly in the damp air. 'You stupid fool. Look what you've done to yourself now!'

Gwynneth knew better than to intervene, but she wanted to. Oh, she wanted to very badly! It was heartbreaking how some folk treated those weaker than themselves.

That particular day, the woman must have got a stone in her shoe, because she stopped suddenly, pointed to one end of a park bench, and snapped out a command. Sitting down at the other end, she pulled her shoe off and shook something out.

The child didn't attempt to sit down, just stood motionless next to the bench while the woman bent to put on her shoe again. Gwynneth winked at the little girl as they started moving again and walked past the bus shelter, giving her a tiny wave with her hand lowered so that the woman didn't see it.

After a quick look of shock and a glance to check that the old woman wasn't watching her, the lass gave a tiny nod and a flicker of her fingers in response.

Gwynneth jerked in shock when someone spoke to her. 'Did you see that, Mrs Harte?'

She recognised the voice and looked up to smile at Sergeant Deemer, who was standing nearby, half-concealed behind an evergreen bush. Had the policeman been watching the woman too?

'Yes. And it's not the first time I've seen her hit that poor child, sergeant. I think she's the grandmother.'

'Yes, she is. The child's parents are dead, and she looks after her, but I'm starting to worry about what's going on. My constable's seen the woman hitting poor Beatie several times when they're out in the back garden because his beat takes him past it. Mrs Hicks must think she can't be seen there.'

They both sighed at the same time.

'It's one thing to slap a child for being naughty, another to beat them regularly,' the sergeant said. 'I wonder how Beatie got that injury?'

'Who knows? There's nothing we can do, though, is there? People are allowed to chastise their children.'

Deemer scowled. 'That doesn't mean beating them black and blue.'

As the bus came into view in the distance, a thought occurred to Gwynneth. 'If something really bad happens and you need a place for the child to stay in an emergency, Sergeant Deemer, I'd be happy to take her in and look after her.'

He studied her face. 'Are you sure about that, Mrs Harte?'

'Yes. Definitely. I love children, and I don't have any grandchildren yet.'

'I'll bear it in mind.' He nodded and moved on.

Gwynneth sighed as she got on the bus. She couldn't get the memory of that poor child being knocked to the ground out of her mind.

And here she was with all that love to spare. Life could be so unfair.

In London, Albert Neven called his clerk into his room. 'Good news!' he said by way of a greeting. 'That phone call was from the lawyer in Rivenshaw. Mr Higgins has found Arthur Chapman.'

'Oh, jolly good, sir.'

'Yes, Penscombe. But the poor fellow is apparently in a sorry state. He lost his wife, then his daughter and son-in-law within the space of a year, and fell to pieces.'

'Those were some hard blows.'

'He's pulled himself together during the past year and stopped drinking, but is living in poverty. *Respectable* poverty, Biff says, so he will be allowed to inherit.'

'Good to know, sir.'

'Can you please send the key to Number 25 up to Mr Lloyd by overnight express? He'll take Higgins and Chapman to the house and hand it over. It'll be interesting to find out what it's like inside, won't it? Miss Chapman and her nephew had some very devious plans for their heirs, if you ask me, and they knew how to keep their plans secret.'

'Their ideas worked well for the first two houses, did they not? Jerked both of their relatives out of ruts and into happier lives. Let's hope this final heir can also benefit from their generous if eccentric actions.'

3

Arthur arrived outside the town hall ten minutes early the following day, so eager was he to go inside the house. *His* house! He had to keep reminding himself that he owned a house now, it seemed so impossible. He came from a poorer branch of the Chapman family and no one on his side had ever *owned* a house before.

He'd spruced himself up as much as possible for this first visit, but that wasn't much. These might be his best clothes, but they were threadbare, only used for going to church – and he hadn't done much of that since Ruby Hicks had taken his granddaughter away from him and joined that strange little church in Birch End. No one looked happy as they came out of it, certainly not the subdued group of children.

He looked down and brushed away a speck of lint. At least his clothes were clean now. Maybe he'd be able to find a full-time job too. He still had the necessary skills and was gradually living down his bad reputation as a boozer.

He was one of the fortunate ones. There were still some chaps who'd never be fit enough to hold down a job after being injured in the Great War. He'd been lucky; he'd come out of the fighting whole, physically at least.

It seemed a long time till Mr Higgins drove up, so Arthur went to read the public notices. They were still showing the tribute to the old king, who'd died and been buried in January. The new king was the eighth to be called Edward.

Arthur sniffed in disapproval at the official photo of the latter. This one sounded to be a bit of a playboy, if you believed the newspapers, and he didn't like the snooty expression on the fellow's face.

Arthur read a lot of newspapers, usually ones a few days old that he acquired for free after they'd been discarded. Once he'd become sober again, he'd taken up his old habit of trying to understand what was going on in the wider world.

Then he forgot about kings as Biff stopped his car beside him, smiling and beckoning to him to get into the front passenger seat.

'Excited?'

'I don't know how I feel to tell you the truth, Mr Higgins. I'm all of a tozz-wozz, as my mother would have said.'

'That's very understandable.'

As he set off again Biff looked in the rear-view mirror and frowned. A couple of minutes later he pulled in by the side of the road and looked once more, muttering under his breath, beginning to worry. He set off again.

'Is something wrong, Mr Higgins?'

'That car seems to be following us. Do you recognise it? Or its driver?'

Arthur twisted around. 'Yes. It's Jem Stanley driving Mr Higgerson's new car. He's been working for him since he came out of prison.'

He let out an involuntary chuckle. 'Everyone's still laughing at the way that Dobbs fellow, who used to arrange for Higgerson's dirty work, ran off with his boss's car.'

Biff smiled too. 'Sergeant Deemer told me the police haven't found any sign of Dobbs or the car, but I'd guess he hasn't tried all that hard, knowing how he feels about Higgerson.'

'He's a wicked man, that one is. Done near as much harm to folk in this valley as the war did. We've had villains before, every place does, but not usually as bad as him. Why, even his own wife ran away from him.'

They both fell silent for a few moments, thinking of poor, pale Lallie Higgerson.

'I hope she stays safe,' Arthur murmured. 'She gave me sixpence once when she was out shopping, said I looked hungry. I was. I'd not eaten for two days.'

As they left the town, the other car stayed behind them. 'I can guess why Jem Stanley is following us,' Biff admitted.

Arthur twisted his head round again. 'Because of the house.'

'I don't understand how Higgerson could have found out so quickly that you're the heir to Number 25.'

'Someone will have reported seeing you and me together looking round the outside of the house yesterday. He'll have put two and two together.'

'Why would he be interested enough to be keeping watch on you, though?'

Arthur scowled. 'Higgerson likes to think he's king of the valley. I refused to do a job for him last year because I *don't* steal or hurt people, and ever since then he's been trying to get at me. He's lost me a few temporary jobs that I know of.'

'If he bears a grudge against you, you'd better be more careful than ever before from now on. He tried to get hold of the other two houses Miss Chapman had left, and not by honest means, either. Mr Neven is worried he might go after your house too, though why the man's so keen to get hold of any of these houses is more than either of us has been able to work out. Most of his properties are in the slums, bought cheaply and nearly falling down because he skimps on maintenance.'

'He's even had extra cellar rooms dug out on a few of them,' Arthur said. 'You should have seen the mess it made.'

'But that's dangerous! How the hell does he get away with it?'

Arthur couldn't hold back a sigh. 'Eh, who knows? I just hope I can keep out of his way from now on.'

'Don't forget that I'm available to help you. I could stay with you for a while to help you settle in.' He saw the regret on his companion's face and added quickly, 'Don't worry! Mr Neven is paying me to do that as part of his duty to ensure that the final bequest is passed on smoothly. It won't cost you a penny.'

'Oh. Well, I'll appreciate any help you can give me, Mr Higgins, I definitely will.'

'Since we'll be working together, why don't you call me Biff from now on?'

'Biff it is. And you should call me Arthur.'

They turned right off the main road that continued to the top of the valley, and drove through Birch End, stopping where it ended at Daisy Street.

Jem Stanley drove slowly past them, hooting the car horn and making a rude sign. After stopping about a hundred yards further along the street, he got out and leaned against his car, watching them openly. He was a big, lumpy man with an ugly face, whose nose had been badly broken at some time.

'He's only been out of prison for a few months,' Biff said. 'We'll stay in the car until Mr Lloyd arrives. I'm not afraid of Stanley or his master. I can look after myself in a fight, believe me. But I always prefer to avoid trouble, if possible.'

'So do I. I used to be able to stand up for myself when I was younger. Well, you had to where I lived as a kid. What I'm worried about now is being outnumbered and then beaten up. Mr Higgerson has no scruples about hurting folk if they've upset him. He might not do the beating himself these days, but he knows others who'll do it for him.'

'Well, there are two of us at the moment, which makes it a bit more difficult for them.'

Arthur was grateful, but couldn't help wondering what he'd do after Biff left the valley and he was on his own again. Then he got angry at himself for being so timid. Use your brain, Susan would have told him.

He stared at the house, thinking hard. If he made a will as soon as the house was his, leaving it to someone honest and with a bit of power like . . . like Mr Lloyd, Higgerson would have no way of getting hold of the house.

That idea made him feel a bit better. He still had a brain. It was just a bit rusty.

The lawyer arrived at Daisy Street five minutes later and got out of his car straight away, smiling at them till he noticed Jem Stanley, who was lurking next to a car further up the street. It was all too obvious that he was there to watch what they were doing.

Mr Lloyd's smile vanished and he led the way towards the front door at a brisk pace, asking in a low voice, 'Has that fellow been causing any trouble?'

'Not so far. But Higgerson must have sent him to report on what happens here today. How did he even find out enough to think us worth following?'

'Sergeant Deemer told me a while ago that our so-called builder sends out word asking for information about people he's interested in and pays sixpence for anything useful. But we can ignore Stanley today because he won't be able to follow us inside. He won't find out anything about what's in the house from me afterwards, I promise you.'

'Don't you have any idea about what's there?' Biff asked.

Mr Lloyd hesitated, then admitted, 'Not much. I've been given some guidance, since I have a part to play in what happens next, but there's nothing else I can tell you at the moment.'

He stopped at the front door and pulled a large, old-fashioned key from his pocket, holding it out to Arthur.

'Perhaps you'd like to open the door of your new home and go in first, Mr Chapman?'

Arthur took the key, staring down at it, then tried to put it into the lock. He had trouble getting it in at first because his hand was shaking. They must think him a fool.

Then the key slid in suddenly and he unlocked the door. Taking a deep breath, he turned the tarnished brass knob and pushed the door open, staring inside.

The hall was dusty and bigger than the main room in the terraced house where he'd lived with his wife and two children for many years.

He forgot the others and walked to the centre of the space, turning round slowly on the spot and marvelling at the huge window that took up most of the upper part of one side wall, shedding multi-coloured light on the staircase, which led up to the next floor. He noticed the exquisitely carved bannisters and also that they needed a good polish. He'd like to get his hands on them, bring that wood to life again.

The glowing jewel colours in the stained-glass patterns brightened the whole space, even on a late winter's day. The tinted light was reflected across the hand he stretched out towards the nearest shaft of sunlight that angled across the space. It felt as if the house was greeting him.

It was so beautiful! So elegant! Or it would be, if properly cared for.

A thought came from nowhere, taking him by surprise. He'd need a wife to help him look after his new home. Even Susan would tell him to find one. That was partly why people got married, she'd always said, to help one another through life, and if either of them died, the other should marry again.

For the first time since his loss he felt the need to move on with his life, though he would never stop feeling glad for the wonderful years he'd had with Susan.

Was it possible for a house to do that to you when you owned it? Make you see its needs as well as your own?

Time enough to think about that later. For the moment, there were several closed doors waiting for him, and he was eager to see what lay behind them. He walked across the hall to the right and opened the nearest one.

Biff was still standing at the front door, watching Arthur, when he heard footsteps crunch on the gravel of the path behind him. He spun round to see who it was, anger rising in him when he saw that Stanley had moved through the gate and was part way down the path, craning his neck, trying to see into the house.

'Get out, you!' He walked quickly along the path, fists clenching instinctively. He wasn't as tall or as muscular as Stanley, but he was furiously angry. After one look at his expression and the lawyer frowning at him from the doorway, Stanley took a hasty few steps back on to the footpath.

Biff slammed the gate shut on him and said slowly and clearly, 'Do not set even one foot on my client's property again or I'll report you to the police for trespassing! Your sort are not welcome here.'

Stanley squared his shoulders and shook himself, looking as if he was debating whether to fight.

Biff watched him steadily. He didn't feel nervous or hesitant about defending Arthur and the house.

After a couple of moments, Stanley shook his head, like a dog shaking off water. 'You're going to find out differently soon whether I'm welcome here or not, Mr Bloody Higgins, so you'd better make the most of the house while you can.' He jabbed his forefinger towards the building. 'That drunken sot won't be staying there for long, that's for sure. Mr Higgerson will make certain of that.'

Biff didn't respond, merely turned and followed Mr Lloyd back into the house, removing the door key from where Arthur had left it on the outside. He closed the front door behind him and used the key to lock it from the inside.

He was thoughtful as he moved across the hall. Clearly Higgerson was planning something. He must really want these houses. What the hell could he do to get hold of this last one? Even he couldn't just take it off Arthur.

Ugh! He had only to think of Higgerson to feel disgust roil inside him. The man claimed to be a respectable businessman and he had even managed to get elected to the town council, but he was an out-and-out villain and should be locked away instead of let run loose to harm those weaker than him.

Mr Lloyd was now standing at the open door of the sitting room, watching the heir, who had lingered a couple of paces inside to stare round. Biff joined the lawyer and gave him a quick, whispered summary of what Jem had taunted him with.

'We may have to hire more guards, as we did with the other houses. Don't say anything to Chapman yet. Let him have his first tour of the house in peace. He's looking so happy.'

Arthur began to walk slowly round the room, but the others stayed where they were, letting the new owner touch pieces of furniture and pause to stare up at the paintings on the walls. He was fairly glowing with joy. It was lovely to see.

After a circuit of the room Arthur went to stand by the fireplace, bafflement slowly replacing the initial joy as he stared round again.

Biff looked round too, giving the room more than a cursory glance this time as he tried to work out what was puzzling the heir.

The room contained several substantial pieces of furniture and some smaller tables and stools. He suddenly realised that though every single piece was of good quality, most of them were damaged in some way. Chairs stood lopsidedly, a small side table was propped up by a pile of books, with the missing leg lying on the floor beside it. Some of the stuffing was coming out of the seat cushions of a sofa.

He watched the heir move across to the small table and run gentle fingers over the dusty carving at the curved tops of the three intact legs, then pick up the fourth one from the floor to examine it.

'This was beautifully made,' Arthur said suddenly. 'It could be repaired, and so could the other pieces. I don't understand why everything has been left in such a sad state. There isn't a single piece of furniture in this room that doesn't need some attention. If I had my tools, I could do a lot of the work myself, but I pawned them when I was at my lowest point with the drinking. The tools will have been sold by now, because I've never had enough money to retrieve them.'

'Are you sure you're skilled enough to do any necessary repairs?'

'Oh, yes. Most of the ones needed by the furniture anyway. I'm not good enough at French polishing to do justice to pieces this good, and if there's plumbing needing doing elsewhere in the house, I've no experience of that. It's wood I like working with. I'm not trained, because my parents couldn't afford to pay for an apprenticeship. They needed my wages as soon as I could leave school, but Mr Redfern used to say I had an instinct for it and I learned a lot from working with him.'

Well, if Redfern said it that boded well, Biff thought. He ran a respected cabinet making business in the valley.

Arthur stroked another piece as he spoke, not even seeming aware that he was doing it. 'Eh, I've never handled such fine work in my life.'

4

Biff found it touching to watch Arthur's reaction to his inheritance, but he saw Mr Lloyd surreptitiously pull out his watch and peek at it, so he knew they'd have to get through this preliminary tour more quickly.

He moved across to Arthur. 'Let's go and look in the other rooms now. We can study the details later, but it'll be better to get a sense of the whole house first, don't you think? You can look your fill after you move in.'

Arthur nodded happily. 'Aye, I mustn't keep a busy man like Mr Lloyd for too long, must I? I'll have plenty of time to look at everything later.'

'Maybe somewhere we'll find a clue as to exactly what Miss Chapman's nephew wanted you to do with the house. You'll not only need to repair the pieces of furniture but bring the whole place up to date and install modern amenities.'

It upset him to see the bright smile fade.

'I don't have any money at all. I couldn't make even a start on that.'

'There may be provisions for helping you in the will itself.' He glanced at Mr Lloyd, who gave a slight nod.

'Do you think so?' Arthur asked.

'I doubt she'd leave you without some means of looking after your inheritance. Come on.' Biff led the way across the hall into what turned out to be a dining room. There was a big table there, but it lay in several pieces. The beautifully polished mahogany top leaning against the wall showed it had been a good table in its day.

Arthur bent to examine the other pieces. 'These don't look damaged. Someone's just pulled it apart and left it. Why would they do that?'

'To move it from one house to another, perhaps?'

The heir didn't look convinced and the lawyer was deliberately staring out of the window.

After that Biff only gave Arthur time to peer into the other two nearest rooms and work out what they'd been used for: a small sitting room and what looked like a cosy study behind the dining room. It was immediately clear that they too contained several broken pieces of furniture, so he chivvied the heir along.

'Let's find out what's at the back of the house on the other side.'

Mr Lloyd gave Biff another slight nod of approval when Arthur wasn't looking.

The last door at the rear of the hall led to the kitchen and related work areas. There was more damaged furniture there, but the cooking equipment didn't appear to be harmed and was of a high quality, even though it was as dusty as everything else.

Arthur stopped suddenly in front of several sets of crockery set out neatly on shelves. 'Why would anyone need all these dishes?'

'When these houses were built, there would probably be a housekeeper and at least one maid, as well as the family,' Biff told him. 'The servants would use the cheaper crockery and cutlery.'

'Well, I can't even support myself properly, let alone hire a maid, so no one except me will be using any of these pieces.'

He took the initiative again, making his way across to the scullery, which led off the rear of the kitchen, and relaxing visibly at what he found. 'Eh, look! My grandma had an old-fashioned slopstone made of sand-coloured stone exactly like this one, with a cold water tap over it.'

'So did mine.' Biff smiled at the fond memories it brought up.

'The modern white ceramic sinks are a similar shape to this one, but they're much easier to keep clean. Why, there's not even a gas geyser here to heat the water. Didn't my relatives have enough money to keep up to date?'

He was about to move on when he noticed an envelope propped against the lower corner of the window addressed to 'Arthur Chapman, Esq.' in large black handwriting.

He did nothing, staring at the envelope as if expecting it to bite him.

Mr Lloyd gave him an impatient glance. 'It's addressed to you, Mr Chapman. Why don't you pick it up and find out what it says?'

Arthur stretched out his hand, but still hesitated to touch the envelope. It was such a posh one, and the handwriting was really fancy. But it was definitely addressed to him so he picked it up, blew the dust off, then tore open the top as carefully as he could.

He found two sheets of paper inside, covered with the same black handwriting. It took him a while to work his way through it, given the fancy, unfamiliar style of writing. He was uncertain of the exact meaning of a few of the words, too, but didn't like to ask for help and show his ignorance. Anyway, he was pretty sure he could understand the main points being made, and the letter was very friendly.

Dear Arthur

Welcome to your new home. I hope you'll be happy here.

I know about your lapse into drunkenness and the sad reasons for it. The fact that you have stopped drinking and are trying to remake your life in a better mode has prompted me to give you this chance to do something with your future.

This house originally belonged to my aunt, Sarah Jane Chapman, a distant cousin of yours. I know she would approve of you inheriting it. She wanted all three properties to go to relatives who needed a helping hand, you see.

It will take a lot of sheer hard work to turn this house into a real home again. And I'm told that you have good practical skills, especially with woodworking.

I know you don't have any money, so once you've moved in, a set of basic tools will be supplied by the hardware store. You must collect these in person, and there will be £5 credited to you there as well to spend on screws and the like.

There is also £100 in an account at the bank which will be transferred to your name as soon as Mr Lloyd gives them the word. I hope you will use this to start modernising the house.

There isn't enough money to bring it fully up to scratch, what with the need for a sewage connection, electricity, and a bathroom, but there's enough to make a good start. It'll be up to you to work out how to finish the job.

Please hire Mr Tyler to do any building work for you. He can be trusted. Others in the valley can't.

With warmest wishes for your success.
Your distant cousin.

James Barker

Arthur gaped at the pieces of paper and laboriously squinted his way through the letter again, after which he held them out to Biff with one shaking hand, tears welling in his eyes. 'It's as if my family has reached out from beyond the grave to help me, as if I'm not alone any longer.'

The detective read the pages quickly, then asked, 'Are you skilled enough to work on the furniture and house?'

'I can do some of it, aye, now that I'm sober again.' He held his hands out in front of him, palms upward. 'These seem to know how to make or mend wooden objects, but I might as well tell you now that I have a bit of trouble with reading and writing, especially when I'm tired. My teacher said I needed glasses but my family couldn't afford them. And even if I'd had some, we lived in a rough area and the other lads would have enjoyed breaking them. Glasses wouldn't have lasted a week. And I've been too busy scraping a living to bother about reading and spectacles lately.'

The lawyer spoke, changing the subject slightly. 'Well, Mr Higgins will make sure you get some glasses. How did you manage to acquire your woodworking skills, Mr Chapman?'

'Bit by bit. On the job I'd watch the men who'd hired me to run errands and do whatever else they needed, and I'd try to copy them on throwaway scraps of wood. I made my mum a few platters and such.' He sighed. 'I had to leave school at eleven, half time, you see, to help put bread on the table. Kids could do that in them days, work half a day and attend school the other half. Mornings one week, afternoons the next. You have to stay on full-time till you're fourteen nowadays.'

Biff couldn't stop himself from reaching out and putting one hand on Arthur's shoulder in a gesture of unspoken comfort. 'Doing this house up should suit you down to the ground, then.'

'Yes, if—' He broke off, staring blindly into the distance.

'What is it? Tell me.'

'If Higgerson doesn't find a way to prevent me. He's got a lot of power in the valley.'

'I keep telling you: we won't let him do that. I won't leave you on your own until it's safe, I promise you, and there's money been left to hire watchmen as well, till things settle down.' He hated to see the happiness fade still further, and had been dreading telling him Higgerson's interference had been expected.

It was at that moment that Biff realised something about himself. He liked this valley and, against all the odds, he felt he'd found a home here. He liked the plain-spoken northern people, and there was no one waiting for him in London now, after all. He was tired of travelling all over the country, hunting for missing relatives or spouses, many of whom didn't want to be found again.

He even had an idea about how he might be able to earn a living in a different way here: by setting up an employment agency. His former employer had sent him on an investigation for one a few years ago, and he'd found it interesting seeing how they did that sort of work. He'd dealt with other agencies since then, after opening his own private investigation business. He had a fair idea of how to organise an employment agency, yes, and do that more efficiently than most of the ones he'd seen.

In the modern world there were better ways to find workers than at the labour sections of markets or fairs that they'd used in the old days, or by asking around at the pub, as still happened. If you advertised in a newspaper, you had to wait for replies, and interview people to see if they were suitable. An agency could often provide a worker more quickly, sometimes within an hour or so.

Here in the valley they were not quite as forward-thinking as they were in the south and he felt that would be an advantage for him. He suspected it was partly because of a lack of jobs since the Great War. You don't need an agency when there's little or no work to be had. But the work situation here was improving all the time.

It surprised him when he looked back over his life and thought how the world had changed. More affluent people now had all sorts of labour-saving devices in their offices, as well as their homes. Telephones were so useful and saved a lot of running around, especially as towns were growing larger. And offices could be equipped with typewriters, adding machines, Gestetner copying equipment, all sorts of gadgets, and more being invented all the time.

He should be able to sell his little detective agency on the outskirts of London to give himself some start-up money, but he was tired of the work and ready to move on.

He jerked to attention, realising he'd been ignoring his client, but Arthur too had been lost in thought.

He looked at the third member of their trio, who was being very patient with him and Arthur. 'What do we need to do next, Mr Lloyd?'

'Go to my office and complete the paperwork, after which I shall send it by express post to Mr Neven in London. Only he has the power to hand over the inheritance officially. We can't take you to the bank and introduce you till we hear from him. Anyway, it's past three o'clock now, so the bank will be closed for the day, but if we bustle, we can still put the envelope on the train to catch the evening express post from Manchester to London.'

'The money will be very important to our client, given his circumstances,' Biff said quietly.

'Of course.' Mr Lloyd started moving towards the front door, talking to Arthur now. 'It'll be up to you to sort out how you go on after I've handed things over, Mr Chapman, with Mr Higgins' help at first, of course, but don't hesitate to contact me if I can assist you in any further way.'

As they went outside, Biff saw Jem Stanley standing near his car further down the street, still looking at them with that sneering, confident smile on his ugly face.

He was quite sure Higgerson would have some nasty tricks brewing, but he'd do his best to prevent trouble.

He'd taken a liking to the heir, who seemed a gentle, honest soul, and he also liked the idea that his final job as a private investigator should consist of helping a man climb out from the pit of despair to make a respectable place for himself in the world.

Biff kept a careful watch on the other vehicles as he drove into Rivenshaw. As he'd expected, Stanley followed them into town. He drove past them when they stopped near the lawyer's rooms, slowing down to give them another of those rude signs with his forefinger before driving off down the street.

And good riddance to bad rubbish, as the saying went, Biff thought as he followed Mr Lloyd into the building and watched him guide Arthur through the necessary paperwork.

They also made a quick, simple will – only a few lines long – in case anything happened to Arthur, but the lawyer insisted on Biff being the beneficiary not himself. He hoped it'd never be needed.

After that Biff took Arthur to the upper storey of Charlie Willcox's bigger pawn shop, where they sold better quality second-hand garments. They found some surprisingly cheap but decent clothes there.

Biff paid for them himself, but pretended he'd been given some money by Mr Neven before he left London to cover necessary expenses like these. And if he was being soft doing that, too bad. You should help decent people who were in trouble when you could.

As they came out of the shop, he asked, 'Where are you sleeping tonight, Arthur?'

'Ah. Well, I hadn't thought. The hostel, I suppose, but I'll have to get back there quickly and do some cleaning to earn a bed.'

'Hmm. I'd rather you don't move around town alone from now on, not till I'm sure you're safe. Let's go to the hostel to pick up your things, and then I suggest we set ourselves up with somewhere to sleep in your new house. Would that be all right? It'll be easier for me to make sure that you're safe there than at the hostel, where anyone can come in for a night's lodgings.'

'There were mattresses at the house, but the bed frames need sorting out, and I didn't see any blankets,' Arthur said dubiously.

'Well, it won't matter to me if we have to sleep on mattresses on the floor, and I'm sure I saw some blankets in that big cupboard next to the scullery. We can light a fire in the sitting room and give everything a good airing, then sleep on the floor in front of it.'

He'd got it all worked out, because Arthur seemed too bemused by his good fortune to plan anything. 'On the way back to Daisy Street, I'll have to pop into my lodgings to let my landlady know I'm leaving, and collect my possessions. It'll be all right if I stay with you for a week or two, won't it?'

'Of course it will. I'd welcome the company, actually. I'm really grateful for what you're doing for me.'

Biff shrugged and changed the subject. 'We'll get some fish and chips and have an early tea before we leave town, then buy some basic food and tea-making stuff from the shop in Birch End.' He grinned as he added. 'We can sit in the car and eat our tea with our fingers while it's still hot. Fish and chips always taste better hot from the shop, wrapped in greaseproof paper and newspaper, and slathered in salt and vinegar.'

'Ooh, yes. It's ages since I've had any.'

'Tomorrow we'll come back into Rivenshaw and let Mr Lloyd introduce you to the bank manager, if the paperwork has been sorted out.'

But before then Biff had one more job he intended to do now he'd seen Higgerson's henchman following Arthur around: hire a couple of men to help keep watch over the house and its new owner at all times from tomorrow onwards. He'd had to do the same for Maisie when she inherited Number 23 next door to Arthur. Mr Neven really had supplied him with the money for further protection.

If Rob and Phil Becksley were free, he'd hire them again, because they hated Higgerson, who'd tried to make their lives difficult after they had also refused to do his dirty work. Biff had found them decent and reliable, and they lived in a nearby part of Birch End.

Luck was with him. When they were leaving the village shop with the tea-making materials, plus a loaf, a pat of butter and a jar of jam for breakfast, they ran into Rob's wife just coming in. Biff stopped her to ask if her husband was working at the moment, explaining his need.

She beamed at him. 'That'll suit my Rob down to the ground, it's so close to home. And I happen to know Phil has just finished a little job for Mr Tyler. Shall I send them both to see you? They'll enjoy stopping that horrible man causing more trouble.'

'Yes, please. Tomorrow morning will do. No one will know we're there tonight. Thank you.'

'It's me as should be thanking you, Mr Higgins.' She frowned at him. 'Didn't you have a bit of an Irish accent last time we met?'

He beamed at her. 'I did indeed. I put on that accent as a sort of disguise, but I don't need to do that any longer.'

She looked a bit surprised but didn't question what he'd said.

All in all, things were going as well as could be expected at this stage. He'd do his very best to see that they stayed that way.

When they got back to the house, they used Biff's torch to light their way to the kitchen, where they lit two of the candles they'd bought and fixed them into old-fashioned portable holders, then searched the house for suitable beds. Unfortunately there were no bed frames that were intact and Arthur said he'd rather do the repairs by daylight.

They did find mattresses, so lit a fire in the kitchen and hauled them downstairs, putting everything to air in front of the fire. Then they made themselves cups of cocoa.

Biff thought regretfully about his comfortable lodgings as he snuggled down among the chaos. At least he was warm enough, but this was a lumpy old mattress. Tomorrow they'd sort out proper sleeping accommodation and get some oil lamps set up for the evenings.

On the other mattress, Arthur heard his companion sigh into sleep, but couldn't follow his example for a while.

He didn't mind lying awake and mulling over the day. He was still coming to terms with his good fortune, and working out what to make a start on repairing as soon as it was light. Chairs to sit on and bed frames, he decided.

He'd been given this chance to improve his life, and he wasn't going to waste even a second.

There was hope singing through him now, and that felt so good.

5

After he saw the two fools going into the lawyer's office, Jem Stanley drove back to see Mr Higgerson. His employer had been staying later at his office since his wife left him. Jem loved driving and wished he didn't have to go back to him. It'd been good to drive around the valley in the new motor car today without a sharp voice criticising him or yelling orders from the rear seat.

He knew why Mr Higgerson had been in such a bad mood lately. Well, the whole town knew that, which only added to his boss's fury. His wife had run away, and he hadn't been able to get her back, and everyone knew it.

Even worse, Lallie Higgerson was staying with the son who'd also run away a year or two previously, and Higgerson hadn't been able to get him back either. No one wanted to live with such a cruel, bad-tempered sod, it seemed to Jem.

He didn't really like working for Higgerson, but he enjoyed the money, enough of it for his wife to build up some savings for the first time in their lives. She wasn't letting him waste it on booze, said she'd leave him if he did.

Well, it was Higgerson's own fault. He shouldn't have bashed his wife. It stood to reason that if you thumped your wife she'd not be on your side. And Mrs Higgerson had been a frail-looking little thing, too. It'd have been like bashing a baby.

Jem always made sure his wife had nothing like that to complain about. He might not be the best provider, but he'd never thumped her, and he'd looked after her as much as he could, just as she looked after their two sons. She'd even stood by him while he was in prison, sending him a couple of food parcels. Good lass, his Callie.

'How could you have missed the chance to see inside the house?' Higgerson yelled at him suddenly.

Jem continued doggedly between such interruptions to report what had actually happened.

Thump went a fist on the desk. 'You were just along the street from it. You could have *pushed* your way in.'

'I didn't see inside it because that detective chap was guarding the gate.'

'He's smaller than you are.'

'He's a good fighter.'

'How do you know? You didn't even try.'

'I don't have to fight him to know just by watching him, and by the way he holds himself as he looks round. And anyway, it was broad daylight and people were nearby. They'd have called in Deemer if I'd attacked him, and I'd have got arrested.'

That stopped the complaining. Higgerson always trod carefully around their police sergeant, Jem had noticed.

'We'll have to break into the place one night, Mr Higgerson. If I do anything openly, I'll get sent back to prison. How would you manage without me now? I'm in the middle of sorting out quite a few things for you.'

Higgerson looked at him in surprise, opened his mouth, then snapped it shut again and scowled down at his clenched fists as Jem continued talking.

'With that house next door, the so-called detective hired men to keep watch night and day. I bet he does the same with this one. I'll go and check tomorrow, if that's all right with you.'

Higgerson stared into the distance, as he often did when thinking, so Jem waited in silence for him to give permission.

'Yes, do that. We'll have to work out how to get rid of the heir, or discredit him.'

'I could set a fire in one of the outhouses. That'd upset them.'

'Don't be stupid. I want to use that house, not turn it into a wreck. There has to be a way to get hold of it, yes, and the two others as well eventually. I'll sort it out. I always get what I want in the end, one way or the other. Those houses are perfect for my purpose.'

Jem had worked out what that purpose was even though his employer hadn't been specific. It baffled him as to why setting up a fancy brothel had become so important to a respectable man, then abruptly, he remembered that Higgerson's wife had left him, and smothered a desire to grin. He wanted a woman at his service, but not any old woman from the streets, and he wanted to provide the same service for other gentlemen, and charge highly for it.

But why did he want to keep making more and more money? You'd think he had enough now to sit back and enjoy the rest of his life.

Still, not for him to quibble at his master's orders, as long as they didn't put him in danger. Jem had been lucky to get this job, and he knew it. He didn't intend to lose it, whatever it took.

'You can drive me home now. Come round to the back of my house after you've put the car away. You've given me an idea. There's something else I've been waiting to do. People have to be reminded that they don't get away with messing me about. I've been waiting to pay back Wilf and Stella Pollard for refusing to sell to me. And don't forget to bring me the keys to the car and the garage.'

Jem didn't smile at that till he was out of sight. Dobbs had kept the keys all the time, and been able to drive away when the time was ripe.

He went to see Mr Higgerson in his fancy room at the back, but was shocked at what he was told to do. It seemed so stupid for Higgerson to hold grudges against people and take risks to pay them back for going against his wishes. No one could win all the time, not even this man.

He opened his mouth to protest, then shut it again. He couldn't keep refusing to do the things his master wanted. He had to tread carefully with this job. Best to do this himself so that no one could betray him, though it was a waste of time and effort.

Higgerson jabbed a finger at him to emphasise his next instructions. 'And tomorrow morning you'd better check on the new basement room that's being dug out in Clover Lane. Tell those lazy sods to hurry up with it.'

'Yes, Mr Higgerson.'

That made two jobs that Jem would rather not have done.

He frowned as he walked home. It seemed to him that Higgerson was getting rash and careless, far too sure of getting away with anything he decided to do. All he wanted was money, more and more of it, the way a drunkard went after booze.

And as for digging out an extra basement room in two of the worst houses in Backshaw Moss, it was asking for trouble. Those houses hadn't been built on good foundations in the first place, and to dig out an extra underground room with only the scantiest bracing around it was just plain daft. All for a few more shillings a week that the man didn't need.

Jem wouldn't like to live in one of those new rooms, by heck he wouldn't. He hated the shut-in, airless feeling that any cellar gave him, and these were going to be bad places. He'd never feel safe in them, never.

But some folk were so desperate for a roof over their heads, somewhere cheap and out of the rain and cold, they'd live anywhere they could afford.

That night Gwynneth went to bed early. Lucas had left for Manchester that morning, suddenly called to start his new work early. Only it wasn't like real work, being a student, was it? Fancy getting paid for reading books!

She was proud of him for being supported by a benefactor, of course she was, but she'd shed a few tears after waving him goodbye. She shed more after she went to bed, sad at spending a whole evening all alone.

She had trouble falling asleep, even though she was worn out by all the rush of getting her son packed and off. She tossed and turned, then suddenly realised she could smell smoke. She sat bolt upright in bed. Lucas usually put the fire out last thing at night and checked that everything was safe.

Could she have left a live coal that might have rolled out of the grate and set the rug alight? She had to check.

She switched on the light and ran into the living area, but there was nothing wrong there. The smell of smoke was still strong, however.

She followed her nose, which led her outside at the back of the house. Not only was the smell coming from the main house, there was a glow at the far corner of the building. A flame shot out, licking the air hungrily, and she squeaked in shock, freezing for a moment before starting to shout for help at the top of her voice.

She didn't wait to put her dressing gown on, but switched on the outside light and went to get the hosepipe they used to water the small garden at this side. Only, the hosepipe was missing, nowhere to be seen. How was that possible? She knew it had been there earlier because she'd tripped over one of the coils that had come loose.

Oh, no! Someone must have taken it, and that meant the fire had been lit on purpose. She shouted even more loudly, calling on the neighbours for help, and screaming the dreaded words, 'Fire! Help, fire!' at the top of her voice.

Lights came on in the main house and Wilf burst out of the back door in his pyjamas, stopping dead when he saw the fire.

He went looking for the hosepipe at his end of the building. Only that one wasn't there either.

'Have you taken the hosepipe?' he called.

'Someone's took them both!' she yelled back.

'Fill some buckets.' He too began to roar for help at the top of his voice, alternately shouting to his wife to get the kids out of the house.

Gwynneth ran into her flat for her buckets, filling the biggest one at the outside tap where the hosepipe should have been. Still yelling for help, Wilf snatched it from her and went to hurl it on the flames, by which time she'd started filling the other one.

She saw Stella bring the two children out to stand at the far end of the garden, then go back inside their house. She appeared at the window filling a bucket at the kitchen sink. Flames were now licking further up the corner of the house, but the walls were thick, and if Stella was still working to put the fire out from the inside, it couldn't have spread far into the house yet.

To Gwynneth's relief, neighbours had now come running out of nearby houses in their nightclothes, some also bearing buckets. When Wilf told them what had happened, one man ran back home for his hosepipe, panting back a couple of minutes later with it looped around his arms. He connected it to the tap outside Gwynneth's flat and started dousing the flames.

She continued to fill buckets at the outside tap and the kitchen sink, the full ones being snatched and replaced immediately by empty ones brought back by neighbours.

'Where's your hosepipe gone?' the neighbour who'd brought his asked.

'Someone's took it,' Gwynneth told him. 'Mark my words, that fire was set deliberately.'

'No! What's the world coming to?'

They all knew what each other's houses and gardens were like. Hosepipes didn't vanish into thin air. He cursed fluently, something he'd never normally do in front of a woman, and she couldn't help wishing that the dire retribution he was calling down on the villains really would happen to whoever had set the fire.

Buckets filled at the houses next door and across the street were now being passed along lines of willing helpers, and didn't stop coming till the fire was out. Thanks to their ability to work together, they'd caught it in time to save the main house, though the back corner and scullery had been badly damaged by smoke and water.

Sergeant Deemer had been called, and arrived just before the last flames were being extinguished.

The helpers left several full buckets of water 'just in case', then stopped filling more. Stella went to bring her children to stand with her as she joined the people gathered around the sergeant.

He listened to their tale. 'I'll find whoever did this,' he said in a harsh voice, unlike his usual quiet tone. 'But I need to know every detail you can remember. Everything. Starting with you, Mrs Harte. I gather you're the one who found the fire, and thank goodness you did.'

Gwynneth went through it, stopping to answer questions, though she didn't feel she knew anything that might indicate who had done it. She'd not heard any strange noises. It had been the smell that caught her attention after the fire had been set.

'Hosepipes can't just vanish,' he said. 'And there was a distinct smell of paraffin near that end of the house. I've got a good sense of smell.'

There was a gasp and a ripple of shocked murmurs as this confirmed their fears.

'Why?' someone asked. 'Why would anyone do such a thing? They could have killed Wilf and his family but for Gwynneth sounding the alarm.'

'I don't know why … yet.' Deemer let that sink in for a moment or two, then said, 'We can't do much in the dark, but can some of you keep watch for the rest of the night? And please try not to trample on the soft earth of the garden. The intruder might have left footprints in it.'

'The children went down to stand at the far end, so they'll have left prints,' Stella said. 'And so would I when I fetched them back.'

'Their footprints will look different from a grown man's.' He glanced down at her feet. 'And you're barefoot.'

She looked down in surprise at her muddy feet. 'I never even noticed.'

'Well, you should try to rest a little, but you won't want to go into that end of the house. It stinks of smoke. Besides, we'll need to make sure it's safe. We don't want you encountering any other nasty surprises. Can you and the children stay with Mrs Harte, perhaps?'

One of the neighbours from across the road said, 'Mrs Harte's flat is only small. Shall I take the children back with me, Stella love? They can sleep with my two. And you won't need to worry about them. You know I'll look after them like my own.'

Stella's voice wobbled. 'Thanks. Yes, please.'

Sergeant Deemer nodded approval and turned to Gwynneth. 'Perhaps you could make her a cup of tea, Mrs Harte? I'd like to have a word with Wilf and the other men.'

'Yes, of course.' She could see shock setting in with Stella. Well, she was feeling a bit shaky herself, and was also embarrassed to have been seen in her nightdress, not even her best nightie, either. Thank goodness it was made of nice thick flannel with long sleeves and a high neck, and didn't show any of the body inside it!

'Come through into my part of the house, Stella love. It's escaped the worst of the smoke. I'll make us both a cup of tea, shall I?'

When they got into the flat, Stella began shivering and suddenly burst into tears. 'S-sorry. It's just that I lost my first husband in a house fire. It's brought it all back – such terrible memories. And – someone has tried to burn this house down before, only they didn't even get started then. They more than got started this time, didn't they? Who can hate us so much?'

Gwynneth was certain she could guess who'd done this, or at least arranged it. There was only one person in the valley wicked enough. She didn't say anything though. They'd work it out for themselves. She guided Stella to a chair and put the kettle on, grateful that the gas was still working.

She found clean dishcloths for the two of them to wash their smoke-blackened faces with, then she got out a large man's handkerchief left behind by one of her sons for Stella to continue mopping her tears.

It had to be Higgerson's doing. Had to be! How could even he do such a thing with two small children in the house?

***

Sergeant Deemer was asking himself the same question and coming to the same conclusion about who'd caused the fire as he drove home. Why had Higgerson done this now, out of the blue? He'd been quiet for a while, but had started to cause trouble again, and in bigger ways than before. And if that man didn't realise that people would guess who was behind it, he was getting stupid as well as careless as he grew older. Or perhaps he thought he was powerful enough to be untouchable.

It was strange, because he was usually extremely cunning.

Deemer sighed. Whatever the reason, wasn't there enough trouble in the world without causing more? One wicked man was creating wholescale mayhem in Germany, and those in the know were worrying about him starting another war. Now another evil man was causing upsets in the valley, just as times were at long last getting better.

The sergeant had a strong sense of impending trouble. He'd applied several times for an extra constable to be appointed, given the increase in population in his valley. He'd apply again, of course he would, but would the authorities give him another man even now?

It had been hinted to him that someone with influence was preventing such an appointment. Did Higgerson have a way of pressuring someone with power in the county?

Deemer was worried sick, definitely couldn't do any more with only himself and one young constable to look after the whole valley. He had to find a way to get more help, not just the special constables you could call on in an emergency, but full-time help.

6

In the morning, just before dawn according to her little bedside clock, Gwynneth woke with a start. Well, she hadn't slept soundly, had she? It was not only the fire, but the fact that she had guests. Stella and Wilf were sharing Lucas's bedroom, but they could only have got an hour or two's sleep, so probably wouldn't get up for a while yet.

However, when she tiptoed into the kitchen area, she found the fire burning brightly in the grate, and Wilf sitting at the table hugging a mug of tea.

He gave her a faint smile and a nod. 'Stella was upset last night and it took her a while to drop off. I couldn't sleep at all for worrying, so when it started to get light, I came up here to let her have a bit more time in bed.' He gestured to the teapot. 'I hope you don't mind me making myself a cup. It's only a few minutes old, so the tea won't be stewed yet, just a bit stronger than usual.'

'I don't mind at all. Do you want a piece of toast?'

He looked faintly surprised. 'I do actually.'

She poured herself a cup and got out the loaf and bread knife. She could guess what was coming. As she was getting dressed, she'd reached the conclusion that she'd have to move out of the flat and let the four of them use it while the main house was being repaired. They were the owners, after all, and there were four of them. Their kitchen and living area must have been badly damaged by smoke, and there was only one of her to re-house.

He was looking uncomfortable, and that'd be why. Well, he was a kind man, wouldn't turn her out lightly, so she said it for him. 'It makes sense for me to move out. Let alone, you own this place, you'll want somewhere to live while you do the repairs.' She cut a slice of bread and reached for the toasting fork.

'I hate to turn you out of your home, Gwynneth.'

'It was already feeling empty without Lucas. Anyway Gabriel and Maisie will have room for me in their house. I shan't want to stay there permanently, but it'll give us all breathing space.'

She hesitated, then threaded the bread on the toasting fork. 'It'll be Higgerson's doing, don't you think? He hates you, and he always tries to hurt people who have upset him, even if he has to wait to do it. He's a bad man.'

'He's more than bad. I think he's crazy. But surely he wasn't always this bad?'

She held the bread out to the heat of the fire. 'I don't think he was. He's grown a lot worse since his wife left. It's as if her escaping made him feel he has to prove himself to the world – as if he's showing he's still a force to be reckoned with. I'd not like to be in her shoes. He'll go after her and catch her one day, for sure.'

'She's in another town. It's harder to get at people from a distance. And Sergeant Deemer told me that the man about to become her son's father-in-law is very clever, and has people working for him who'll keep her safe.'

'Let's hope that's true.' She turned the toasted side and held the other side out to the fire. 'I'll walk round to Daisy Street to see our Gabriel in an hour or so about moving in with them. I'll give him and Maisie time to get up first. I can be out of this flat by teatime, probably earlier. I'll have to find someone to cart my things, and—'

'I'll see to that. You just do the packing, Gwynneth.'

'Thank you. I'm so sorry this has happened to your lovely house.'

'So am I.'

She buttered the toast and handed it to him without bothering with a plate, then started toasting another piece of bread. He gobbled the first one down and stood up.

'I'll have something else later. I want to look round the outside of the house now that it's light, and start assessing the damage. The sergeant had said not to touch anything till he's checked it all, but I can see how bad it is.'

Gwynneth watched him leave, then wept into her apron briefly. She didn't let herself dwell on feeling vulnerable for long, and forced herself to stop. It hurt to think of losing her home, but it was no use crying. She was old enough to know that life hit you with nasty surprises every now and then. You just had to find a way to carry on. At least she was sure her son would welcome her into his house.

The trouble was, she'd much rather have her own home and run it her way. She *liked* housework and keeping things nice, had taken a pride in this flat, small as it was, and in the housework she did for Wilf and Stella to pay for living there.

She helped out other people from time to time too, for free if someone was sick or had a crisis, for payment otherwise. She was sure she'd pick up more cleaning jobs once it was known she'd lost her main job. She didn't intend to be a burden on Gabriel, or on anyone else if she could help it.

How lucky that his wife had inherited that lovely big house in Daisy Street. The new man who'd been left the end one was lucky too: Arthur Chapman. She'd heard that he'd had some bad things happen, but she only had a vague idea of what they were because he'd lived down the valley at the other side of the town.

No doubt she'd find out when she moved in with Gabriel and Maisie. She just hoped Mr Chapman inheriting a house hadn't upset Higgerson because she'd be living two doors away from that house from now on, and didn't want to get caught up in anything else involving *that horrible man.*

Now, enough of that. She had to go and catch her son before he started work. She put the bread and other things neatly out at one side of the table. She wasn't hungry, but Stella might want some breakfast and Wilf would definitely want more later.

Gabriel answered the door, looked at his mother, and held his arms out. 'Whatever's upsetting you, we'll find a way to sort it out.'

She hugged him and managed not to burst into tears. 'You heard about Wilf and Stella's house being set on fire?'

'Yes.'

'They're going to need somewhere to live while they're repairing the damage, and the flat is the obvious place, with only me living there now. So . . . I have to find somewhere else to live.'

'And you're coming here, naturally.'

'Will Maisie mind?'

Her daughter-in-law joined them, giving her a quick hug. 'Will Maisie mind what?'

Gwynneth explained, and Maisie said, 'Of course you must come here. We've got rid of a lot of the excess furniture that had been left in the house when we moved in, thanks to Charlie Willcox, so we can fit yours in easily.'

'Thanks, love. Wilf said he'd get it brought over today.'

Maisie nodded. 'It's the least he can do if he's turning you out. Come and have a cup of tea with us and we'll decide which room you should use and where to put any spare pieces.'

'Anywhere will do. I won't stay for tea now, if you don't mind. I need to start packing my things.'

Gabriel exchanged glances with his wife but didn't say anything. 'We've got a few empty cardboard boxes, Mum. I'll drive you back and you can use them to make a start, then I'll check that Wilf can come for everything with Mr Tyler's van later this afternoon.'

Gwynneth had expected her son and his wife to take her in, and she knew they'd be kind to her, but she still didn't like the idea of living with them. That might be ungrateful, but she couldn't help it. She valued her independence. It had been hard earned.

Trouble was, she knew only too well that older women on their own had trouble finding decent places where they could live independently, so she had no choice. It'd probably be months before Wilf and Stella got their house repaired, and would they even want her to move back? They'd said they'd ask her to do some cleaning for them once the house was repaired and cleared up a bit. In the meantime, she'd have to try to find some other work because she didn't want to be a burden on her son.

Oh, who knew anything? she thought, as Gabriel drove her the short distance to her flat.

She waved goodbye to him, forcing a smile. Well, she hoped it looked like a smile. It didn't feel like one.

Ah, just get on with it, you fool, and stop worrying about the future, she told herself as she walked inside.

It took her until mid-afternoon to pack all her things, and some had to be stuffed into pillowcases. There were also the items Lucas had left behind. He wouldn't want to lose his precious collection of books, she knew.

While she was waiting for Wilf she wrote a quick postcard to Lucas telling him not to try to come home yet. His things would be safe in his brother's house. It was a good thing she always kept postcards and stamps handy. She gave a neighour's child a penny to drop it in the post box near the village shop.

Wilf turned up later in the afternoon with another man sent by Mr Tyler to help out. They wouldn't let her help carry the heavier articles, like her bed, table and chairs, so Gwynneth had nothing to do but stand and watch them.

When they got to Gabriel's house she took the men upstairs and showed them where to put her bed. The other larger items went into the fancy dining room, which Maisie and Gabriel weren't using.

While he went off to pick up the rest of his mother's furniture and possessions, she chatted briefly to Maisie, then went to stand by the front door enjoying the early spring sunshine.

While she was there, two men drove up and went towards the end house, the nearest one to Birch End. Biff must be bringing the new owner of Number 25 to see his inheritance. Eh, imagine inheriting your own house like her son's wife and this man had done. Wouldn't that be wonderful? No one could throw you out, then.

The stranger would be quite good-looking for an older man – well, he would if he weren't so thin – and he had a nice, if rather shy smile. You could usually judge people by their smiles.

Gabriel came back just then with Wilf, and the two of them went across to say hello to the new owner and beckoned Gwynneth across to be introduced properly. 'My mother has come to live with us because of the fire at Wilf's house.'

'My family need to use the flat till the main house can be repaired. The downstairs isn't liveable, and the whole place reeks of smoke. We'd not have turned her out if we didn't know she could come here,' Wilf said.

'Any idea yet who set the fire?'

'We can guess. But there's no proof.'

Mr Chapman was standing next to Gwynneth. 'Hard to lose your home like that,' he said quietly. 'I hope you'll settle in comfortably here.'

She didn't intend to appear weak, so she said as firmly as she could manage, 'Thanks. I'm only staying for the time being till

I can find another job as housekeeper somewhere. I know Wilf will give me good references.'

He nodded. 'I certainly will.'

Gabriel put his arm round her shoulders. 'No rush to do that. We're happy to have you here with us, Mum.'

Mr Chapman shot a quick glance at her and she thought from his understanding expression that he must have guessed how badly she wanted her own home again.

She gave them another nod and followed her son into the house, forcing a smile to her face.

'Do you think they'll find out who set that fire?' Arthur asked Biff as they went inside Number 25.

'From what I heard in the shop, everyone's sure it's Higgerson, but of course they won't be able to prove it.'

'He's a wicked man, that one. Causes a lot of harm and unhappiness.'

'I won't let him hurt you,' Biff said, not for the first time.

'I won't just cower in a corner if someone attacks me – or you.'

It pleased Biff that Arthur was already sounding as if he was pulling himself together.

Arthur hesitated, looking as if he wanted to say something but was unsure about it.

'Just say it,' Biff told him.

'All right. No offence, but I'd like to walk round the house on my own, if you don't mind. Get to know it a bit. You sometimes get feelings when you go into new places, don't you?'

'Yes. Shall we make a shopping list before you do that, then I can nip out and buy some food for today?'

'No need for a list. I don't mind what you get. I'm not fussy.'

'All right. You'd better lock the door while I'm out. Don't let anyone inside, and don't go outside on your own. That Stanley brute might still be lurking nearby.'

'Yes. I'll be careful.'

When he was on his own, Arthur walked slowly round the ground floor, mentally working out which pieces of furniture would be easy to repair. They'd need a kitchen table and chairs first, he decided, and set the chosen pieces out. He could easily put these right once he had some tools. After Biff had brought back the groceries, he'd suggest going to collect the set of tools waiting for him at the hardware store.

He smiled at the kitchen. He didn't want to waste another minute in getting started. In fact, he'd not go and look round the upstairs yet, but sort out the things down here which he could easily repair for their daily needs. He'd seen several comfortable chairs scattered here and there.

He looked round and soon found two that'd be simple to repair.

'Thank you Sarah Jane Chapman,' he whispered as he took them into the kitchen. He stared towards the ceiling as you seemed to do when talking to those dead before you. 'I won't waste this opportunity, I promise you.' They could make this room their headquarters, and keep nice and warm.

He glanced out of the kitchen window, and it occurred to him that they hadn't gone outside into the yard. Once Biff got back, he'd suggest taking a quick look at the outhouses. Who knew what was in them?

He hadn't needed Biff's warning. He wasn't stupid enough to go out of the house on his own yet, not with that Jem Stanley turning up everywhere.

It was half an hour before Biff got back, judging by the crooked little kitchen clock, which had one foot missing but still managed to produce a happy-sounding tick. Arthur made sure who it was before he opened the door, and put the idea of buying a chain lock for the door on his mental list, so that he could partly open it and have a chance of shutting it quickly if he didn't like the looks of someone.

Biff was accompanied by a lad with a home-made trolley full of brimming paper carrier bags. When they'd unloaded them all, Arthur saw him slip the lad sixpence, a generous payment when threepence would have brought the same service.

It took the two men a while to put the food away, because they had to work out where they were going to keep each item, then wipe down the shelves.

When that was done, Biff suggested going to collect the tools from the hardware shop in Rivenshaw. Arthur nearly agreed, but then suddenly wondered if there were any tools in the house. There might be some in the cellar. It'd be worth checking.

His stomach let out a growling sound and he realised he was ravenous. He'd got his former appetite back with a vengeance, was feeling better than he had for ages. It'd have to wait, though.

When they got down into the cellar he gasped in both surprise and pleasure.

'This is set up as a workshop, a really good one too, and there are a few tools left. Look at that workbench. Lovely wood it's made from. And there are even wooden offcuts piled up over there ready to use.'

He stared at the bench and how it fitted against the wall, then frowned and bent closer.

'Something wrong?' Biff asked.

'I'm not sure.' He ran his fingers over the rough wooden panel behind the workbench. 'This isn't quite— Look, the grain of the wood doesn't match. Why put in a new piece at the bottom corner?'

He ran his hands over that area again, stopping at one edge, which seemed slightly raised, and pressing it. The wood moved slightly and when he pressed harder there was a loud click, and the whole back panel and bench top moved, just a little.

'Why would they build a workbench that comes loose?' He tugged at it and exclaimed in surprise as the whole workbench then slid to the left, giving a space just big enough for one person to squeeze through. Below the space were steps leading down into utter darkness.

Arthur ran his fingers over the edge of the panel. 'This is very skilfully done! It takes two movements to open it. I reckon it's the work of a master craftsman.'

Biff whistled softly. 'What next? This whole house is puzzling. Let's find out where it leads.'

He was about to start down the steps, but Arthur put one arm across the gap. 'Have you got a torch?'

'No. Why?'

'We don't know what's down there – or who – or even if the panel will stay open. No use going down there without getting a torch and finding something to prevent the panel closing behind us.'

Biff looked at him with new respect. 'You're right. I think there was a torch in the scullery, but I don't know whether it had any batteries in it.'

'Probably not, after all this time.'

Biff's stomach rumbled suddenly. 'Let's get something to eat first. I'm famished.'

'So am I.' Arthur turned to leave, then swung back. 'I think we should close this again and put a few pieces of wood on the surface.' He bent to check the lock more closely. 'I'd guess when this piece is fitted into place at the side, it'll prevent anyone coming in from below. I'm not sure, though. I'll need to check the other side more closely, but it's very dark down there so I won't be able to make out the details.'

Biff was still peering into the hole. 'There's not a sign of light coming in from anywhere else down there.'

'None at all. I wonder what's beyond the bottom of those stairs.'

'Let's go and find that torch.'

They shut the panel and went back up to the scullery. There was indeed a torch standing on the windowsill, but it had no batteries in it.

'This is the most frustrating house I've ever been in,' Biff said. 'Nothing's ready to use. And most of the stuff is broken.'

Arthur's voice was soft. 'It could be such a lovely house. If I can keep it, I'll bring it up to scratch again, however long it takes.'

'You do that. Let's grab some food quickly, then go to the hardware store in Rivenshaw. We can buy some torch batteries at the same time.'

'Yes, let's. It used to be one of my favourite shops.'

Arthur felt disappointed not to have found where the stairs led straight away. But that was only one of the many things he needed to investigate in his new home. He still had trouble believing this house and its contents belonged to him.

Eh, he wished Susan were still alive. She'd have loved this house. And it'd need a woman's touch as well as his to bring it up to scratch. Women seemed to notice and deal with the details of daily life much better than men.

He remembered again how Susan had several times said if she died, he should marry again, because he'd need a wife. He'd got angry at that, but when he'd told her he'd never be able to replace her, she'd said gently that no one could replace another. It'd simply be a different type of partnership, and nothing wrong with that.

Maybe she'd been right. She'd been such a wise person, even as a child.

Of course he'd need to meet a woman he at least *liked*. You couldn't marry someone if you didn't find them easy to get on with. But he could see already that he'd need a wife to manage a big house like this.

And why was he thinking about that now? He and Biff needed something to eat.

Besides, what decent woman would want to marry someone who'd been one of the town drunks only a few months ago?

After they'd eaten some thick slices of buttered bread and a piece of soft, crumbly Lancashire cheese, they drove into town and called in at the hardware store.

Arthur checked out the set of tools that had been paid for and compared them mentally to the few tools in the cellar. He asked diffidently whether he could swap one or two for others that he preferred to work with, and explained that he had a few tools already.

'Of course, Mr Chapman. You can have anything you like as long as it comes to the same value in total.'

It was the first time anyone had called him 'Mr' for a couple of years. The term of respect made him straighten up and square his shoulders.

He'd make Susan proud of him, he vowed. And maybe one day his son would start speaking to him again.

He didn't let himself dwell on that sadness, concentrated instead on checking out each tool he was offered, changing a couple of them for better quality pieces, and adding a few smaller tools. He also chose a basic collection of screws, nails and a glue pot, enough to start him off.

'You enjoyed doing that, didn't you?' Biff said with a grin as they carried the two full boxes out to the car. 'You were very impressive, clearly knew your stuff.'

'It'll be good to get tools in my hands again. I won't lose this lot, I can tell you.'

Back at the house, Arthur repaired a couple of kitchen chairs and the table, by which time the short February day was coming to a close, but at least they had somewhere to sit and eat.

Biff said quietly, 'Well done. That was a good day's work.'

'Thanks for your help.'

The two Becksley brothers turned up just then.

'Are you sure it's necessary to hire them?' Arthur was worrying now about how much it was going to cost to have two men keeping guard.

'It was necessary with Maisie's house, believe me. One of them will do days, and one nights for a week or two, but they'll both sleep here. They'll keep a very careful watch, believe me. Once Higgerson sets his mind on acquiring something, he'll play any nasty trick there is to get it. You and I need our sleep if we're to stay alert as we settle in.'

When his companion still looked dubious, he realised why. 'Don't worry. You won't be paying for this.'

But Arthur did worry. How could he not?

7

Sergeant Deemer strolled along the street, still worrying about the fire at Wilf's house a couple of days ago. He could guess who had arranged for it and why? Did Higgerson think he was fooled? What worried him was what that fellow would try next.

But he hid his feelings, nodding and smiling as usual to people he knew. He took note of more than most of them realised, though, as he walked along. He always kept an eye on the various goings-on in his town.

He saw Judge Peters strolling towards him and slowed down. The judge was a capable man, a decade or more younger than Deemer, and folk reckoned he was going to rise high in the county's legal circles one day. He'd been working in London for a while and hadn't been back in the valley for long.

Peters also slowed down, smiling a greeting but waiting to speak until there was no one nearby. 'Can you make it to an extraordinary meeting this Sunday, Gilbert?'

The sergeant nodded, not needing to be told what sort of meeting, let alone who would be involved or where it would be held. 'Happy to.'

'About nine o'clock in the morning?'

'Fine by me.'

'We'll drive there together.' The judge raised his voice as a woman came towards them, 'And do please give my regards to Mrs Deemer.'

The passer-by gave the sergeant a half-smile and hurried past them, her shopping basket bobbing about on her arm, her mind clearly on her imminent purchases. The two men waited till she was out of hearing, however, before carrying on their conversation.

'On another topic, I found out that you've made several applications for another constable to be appointed in the valley and they've all been turned down. I was surprised at that. If a man of your experience says you need more help, Gilbert, then I'm quite sure you genuinely do need it. I can see two reasons for it myself even after only a short time back, one being the increase in population round here, but the other is Higgerson. It hasn't escaped my notice that he seems to be growing more active again.'

'Unfortunately he is, and yet he's as slippery as ever. I haven't been able to pin anything on him.'

'He had the nerve to invite me to lunch with him at the inn yesterday.'

'I'd as soon lunch with the devil in hell.'

Peters smiled. 'I made it very plain that I wasn't interested in ever spending any time with him socially, and said it loudly enough to be overheard by several people. I don't think he'll risk asking me again. Anyway, re your request, I had a word with a couple of chaps I know who have some influence in this region, and they've been making sure the new officer you've asked for will be assigned. The people who'd been blocking the appointment were, I think, also warned about making decisions without consulting others.'

A sigh of relief escaped the sergeant. 'I can't tell you how grateful I am, my friend. I've been finding it . . . well, rather disheartening to be under-manned, and to tell you the truth, I've been feeling over-tired lately. I'm not getting any younger. My wife says I've been doing too much for a man of my age.'

'Thinking of retiring?'

'I'm not quite old enough yet. And I certainly won't go until I've put an end to Higgerson's criminal antics.'

'The valley's lucky to have a man of your calibre in charge of policing it. You should have been promoted years ago.'

'They did offer me a promotion, and more than once, but I prefer to be involved with people. I don't enjoy paperwork and meetings, not to mention political to-ing and fro-ing, which seems more like childish bickering to me half the time.'

'That doesn't surprise me. Anyway, someone will be phoning you to say your new man will be starting work here next Tuesday. It's a promotion to senior constable for him, and well deserved. He's a capable chap, should go far: Mike Grafton. Do you know him?'

Sergeant Deemer beamed. 'I've not worked with him, but I've heard good things about him from a couple of chaps who have. Did he want to come here? We're a bit out of the way for those who are likely to climb high in the service.'

'He got married recently and his wife grew up round here. She wants to move closer to her family for a while because she's expecting their first child.'

'Even better. I'm sure Grafton will fit in.'

'Yes. And I'm sure you're the right person to help him on his way up the ladder of promotion by polishing his skills at managing situations and people. At the same time he'll supply you with some younger legs to run around the valley as needed. Oh, and he's also a very good driver if you need to get anywhere fast.'

Gilbert nodded and suppressed a sigh. He resented the limitations of growing old, and simple things galled him these days, such as not being able to run as fast as he used to. Only you didn't get much choice: slowing down as you got older came to everyone. He felt he still had a lot to offer, though. The age of retirement for police officers in his local force was sixty, lower than for the average citizen, who had to wait till sixty-five to retire under general government rules.

He remembered when old age pensions were first introduced in 1908. It had been a measly five shillings a week after age seventy, means tested, yet his grandfather had blessed the government for even that small amount. Eh, how times had changed! The sergeant would receive half his salary as a pension, and he'd already saved hard and bought a cottage for when he and his wife had to leave the police house they currently occupied.

He could apply to retire later than sixty, and he might do that, because he was still in good health and enjoyed his job. Besides, if it was humanly possible, he was determined to catch Higgerson before he left the police force.

'Will your present constable resent someone being brought in over his head?' Peters asked.

'Bless you, no. Cliff is well aware that he still has a lot to learn. He'll probably enjoy having someone younger to work with instead of an old fogey like me though.'

'The police could do with more old fogeys like you, Gilbert. Experience is a valuable commodity. Anyway, I can't stand here all day chatting. See you on Sunday.' He offered his hand and they shook warmly before parting.

That was done deliberately to show anyone watching how highly the judge regarded their police sergeant, Deemer guessed. Well, the respect was reciprocated.

As he went on his way he noticed Jem Stanley on the other side of the street haranguing a chap who looked terrified. The thug poked him in the chest so hard he staggered backwards and thumped against a wall.

The sergeant changed direction abruptly and started to cross the road. Unfortunately, by the time he'd waited for a slow-moving lorry to pass, Stanley was striding away so fast he was almost running, and his victim was making a hasty escape down a nearby alley.

The sergeant didn't call the fellow back, but he knew the man and didn't have to wonder why he was being bullied. He lived in one of Higgerson's run-down houses, and had most likely fallen behind on the rent.

Deemer had been surprised when Higgerson employed Stanley, who wasn't nearly as clever as the previous henchman had been at this sort of thing. Dobbs had known how to hide what he was doing most of the time; Stanley went after people like a bull at a gate.

Most of his victims declined to lodge a complaint against him, even after he'd given them a thumping. But Stanley would make a mistake soon, Deemer was sure. And he'd be watching out for it, ready to pounce.

He let out a happy sigh. Only this morning he had been feeling down in the dumps because he simply didn't have the manpower to keep a proper watch on Higgerson. There were, after all, only twenty-four hours in a day, however cleverly you used them.

Now, after his conversation with Peters, he was feeling much more optimistic. Things were going to improve, he was sure of it.

And he'd be waiting to seize the moment where Higgerson was concerned.

Sergeant Deemer set off early on the Sunday morning, leaving the young constable to hold the fort in the valley. Even his wife didn't know exactly whom he was meeting or where, it was so hush-hush. He'd told Cliff he was visiting a sick acquaintance who lived outside the valley, so the constable was to stay on duty at the police station and answer any calls for assistance.

Deemer considered the meeting extremely important. When the Great War had broken out, the country had been caught napping, with outdated equipment and horse-based approaches to fighting in a world where vehicles were taking over transport at an increasingly rapid rate.

Sadly, it looked as if war was brewing once more, however much the authorities denied it. Mr Churchill had gone against the current government's pacifist approach, calling publicly in newspaper articles and at meetings for better preparations to be made in Britain this time.

The present government consisted of a bunch of short-sighted weaklings in Deemer's opinion, but he and many other people who'd lived through the Great War had a lot of respect for Mr Churchill and took that man's warnings seriously. The articles were well written, with cogent arguments for being better prepared.

It was partly as a consequence that some people had formed groups to make sure unofficial preparations were made in their area of the country for resistance, even allowing for the worst that could happen and Britain be invaded – 'just in case'. You were a fool if you didn't recognise that Hitler was gathering together a much cleverer group of men than had been in command in 1914. It seemed obvious that he had his eye on the parts of Europe near Germany, but dictators rarely stopped their rampages once they got going, and who knew where he'd turn after that?

The people in the local group were making preparations even while hoping that they'd never have to put these measures into operation. Fortunately there was an abandoned quarry just outside Rivenshaw, to the south-east of Birch End. The workings had been extended over a century ago by those labouring in it, to connect the natural caves and tunnels nearby with the town and villages in the valley. This had been done on purely selfish grounds, to give themselves a safe and dry journey to and from work in inclement weather.

Only a few of the older generation knew exactly where these tunnels were these days. The group Deemer was working with had renovated and extended them, while at the same time spreading rumours that they were being blocked off because they were dangerous.

Given that there were natural tunnels, the work had not been arduous. It meant that people could leave or enter the valley secretly by various routes. This would in turn allow them to access a national system of concealed routes and refuges. No one in the country knew the details of the whole system, only their own part of it and how to get in contact with nearby groups.

If there were another war and, heaven forbid, an invasion of the country really did take place, the government might be caught napping again, but others, deeply loyal, would be able to lead a loosely organised resistance.

No true patriot believed the country would ever allow itself to stay occupied for long. 'Rule Britannia' was more than just a song; it was a deeply held belief for most inhabitants of the country.

The sergeant felt honoured to have been invited to join the local group, but prayed that another generation of their best and bravest lads – yes, and lasses too these days – would not again have to give their lives to keep their country safe.

When he and Peters arrived at the quarry, they found the usual man on guard. Its so-called caretaker was a genial fellow who was reputed to make a good living selling chunks of rock for the owner, a gentleman in London, and also selling a few on the side for his own benefit.

That had given him the excuse to set up a stout gate across the entrance and keep it locked except during opening hours when he would be there to deal with bona fide customers. There was another way into the tunnel system on foot, again not known to many except a select and trusted few.

The gate was open at the moment, though with a wheelbarrow parked sideways to block the entrance. The caretaker moved it to the side so that the sergeant could drive through and park his car out of sight of the road, then the wheelbarrow was put back across the space.

The two men got out of the car and walked round to the far side of the quarry in silence, going along a narrow tunnel to the large cave a little further inside. The entrance was so low they had to bend uncomfortably to get inside, but as they turned the first corner out of sight of the road the ceiling quickly became higher.

Lanterns guided them into a larger cave where most of the people in the group were already assembled. Nodding to the others, the two men found places to sit on rocky ledges or on large chunks of fallen rock and chatted quietly with the nearby people they rarely met other than here.

The leader of the group waited for the last few to arrive, then stood up and everyone fell silent. He was an imposing figure, tall and still handsome in spite of his silver hair, as well as highly respected by everyone who knew him.

'Thank you for coming today, ladies and gentlemen. I'll get straight to the point: I have some bad news for you. There is a traitor in Rivenshaw, who has been making overtures to a certain minor political party whose members would support a fascist invasion and takeover of our country. This man has told them about our group's existence, though he doesn't know any details yet. He guarantees to stop us taking action against them *when* the invasion happens—'

There were involuntary gasps of shock and anger at this.

'—but he wants their guarantee in return that he'll be appointed as the local officer in charge of this part of Lancashire after Hitler takes over our country.'

This was followed by dead silence as all those present considered the information. It was the last thing they'd have expected to hear today or any other day.

'How did anyone else even know about us, Your Lordship?'

'That's what I want to know,' he said grimly. 'Fortunately, this chap doesn't seem aware of the full details or wider connections our group has, and thinks it consists of only a few men, myself included.'

'Do you know who the traitor is?'

'Not yet. I heard of this from a man who is in a position elsewhere in the country to pass us further information – when he can do so safely. The initial contact has been made by the traitor very tentatively, it seems, and he's taking great care to conceal his identity. I brought you here today as soon as I heard about this. I felt it was important to make you aware of the situation and ask you to keep your eyes and ears open.'

'We'll find him,' someone muttered.

'And eliminate him,' someone else added and no one disagreed.

'I didn't want to put anything in writing or even mention it on the telephone in case an operator was listening in. If you hear anything, even if you're not sure whether it's true, please take the same precautions and let me or one of our two deputies know in person.' He inclined his head to another man and a woman as he said this.

He waited until the ongoing buzz of speculation and anger had died down, not surprised to hear the name Higgerson mentioned several times.

When someone said bluntly, 'It has to be Higgerson. Who else would betray our country?'

'I don't think that fellow is clever enough to do this, or interested enough in politics. Higgerson's personal god has always seemed to be to make money, not gain political power.'

'Nonetheless we'll keep an eye on him. How the hell did anyone find out about us?'

'My guess is that the information has probably come in the first place from one of the workmen we employed to extend the tunnels. I know those of you involved in that vouched for the men you gave the work to, but pressure can be brought to bear on even the most loyal people, especially if they fear for the safety of their loved ones. Or someone could simply have spoken carelessly.'

He shook his head sadly, gave them a little longer to murmur to one another, then continued in his usual quiet tone, 'I think it might be best for you to form pairs, or at the most, trios, chosen according to location. You should share every single piece of information about your area, however minor, so that if one person is attacked the other can spread the word about where to look for the traitor or traitors. Perhaps you'd like to decide now whom you could best work closely with?'

There was a quiet buzz as they sorted out their partnerships and contact arrangements.

It was clear that Sergeant Deemer and Judge Peters would be able to form a suitable alliance, but the two of them also chatted to the people who lived closest to Rivenshaw and the Ellin Valley. Peters knew them all, had done for years, but Deemer had not moved in the more elevated social circles, so didn't know nearly as much about them, except as a police officer.

There had been no snobbish treatment offered to him when he joined this group. Their leader was one of the shrewdest men in Lancashire, and His Lordship had chosen his working partners very carefully indeed. They'd been told to use his title and not the rest of his name when working on this venture. If a man of his calibre valued people enough to choose them, the others felt they could rely on his judgement.

As Sergeant Deemer drove back, the two men were mainly silent.

'It's worrying to have a leak,' Peters said after a while.

'I know who my first suspect is and some of the others seemed to feel the same.'

'If you're thinking of Higgerson, Gilbert, I'm in agreement with His Lordship. I doubt it's Higgerson. I checked and he got out of fighting in the Great War for genuine health reasons, some heart problem or other. No, it must be someone else, a newcomer to the valley perhaps.'

'I shall certainly keep my eyes open.'

'You're probably in a better position than me to do that. No one knows our valley folk as well as you do. But don't hesitate to call on me if I can help in any way, and I shall, of course, keep my own eyes open and share any information with you.'

'I shan't hesitate to ask for your help if needed, Dennison. And if you don't mind, I'll tell my wife the broad details and say that if I'm not available and she feels suspicious, she can call on you for help and trust you implicitly.'

'Of course. I've heard nothing but good of her.'

That pleased Deemer greatly. 'I've not told my wife any details so far, but she's not stupid, and has no doubt guessed that we're involved in some secret work for our country. I would trust her with my life any time.'

'You're a lucky man. I lost the woman I loved in the Great War. She was a nurse, working in France.'

'I'm sorry to hear that. And you're right: I am indeed lucky in my wife.'

He didn't say anything else, was a bit embarrassed at having confided so much to Dennison, but he hadn't met many men he liked and trust as he did this one.

In fact, after a slight hesitation, he confided another worry to Peters.

The judge was shocked. 'Are you sure?'

'Yes. But I don't have any proof.'

'I can't act without it.'

'I know. I'm getting rather worried about the safety of the child, though.'

8

That same week Ester Goodsal found herself a job in another town. She'd been looking around for a while because she couldn't stand to work as Mrs Hicks's general maid any longer. Having to stand by helplessly while that poor, orphaned child was beaten and harangued tore her apart.

She didn't give her notice because she didn't trust her mistress not to do something terrible, like accusing her of theft. She felt it'd be safer simply to vanish and forfeit the pay owing. She didn't want to leave Beatie without anyone to keep an eye on her, though, so on what she'd decided would be her last day at that unhappy house, she got permission from the housekeeper to slip out in her midday meal break supposedly to do some urgent personal shopping for Kotex sanitary towels.

The housekeeper was old-fashioned, and grimaced at the thought of buying such items publicly. She had several times told the maid she could save money and make do with rags that she soaked and washed, as women had done for centuries. But in the end she gave in and let her go out.

Instead of shopping, Ester went searching for Sergeant Deemer. Her grandparents knew him and, when she'd confided in them, they'd assured her that he'd believe her. They had been shocked at the tales she'd told them over the past few months.

She was lucky enough to catch him at the police station and, after a hasty glance around to make sure none of her mistress's acquaintances was walking along the street, she slipped through the door.

He was behind the counter and looked up in mild surprise at the sight of her coming in so furtively. 'What can I do for you, Ester lass?'

'It's what you can do for that poor child I look after sometimes, sergeant. If Mrs Hicks goes on beating her like this, she'll kill her. I can't stand by and watch helplessly any more.'

He stiffened. 'Beatie Hicks, you mean?'

'Yes. Are you aware of what's going on?'

'I'm aware of what I *think* is going on, but I can't do anything to stop the woman officially till I can prove it. People are allowed to chastise their children, after all.'

'But not beat them till they bleed. If you take a doctor to examine the child today, you'll find evidence of her being severely beaten – the poor little thing can hardly sit down. And it was for nothing, as usual. She was supposed to have been looking at her grandmother "cheekily". Just looking!'

'Tell me the details.'

He listened carefully, then said, 'Will you sign a statement to say what you saw happen?'

'Yes. But I'll have to do it today and quickly, because I've found myself another job and I'm leaving tonight without giving notice.'

'Come through to my office and I'll take your statement down, then young Cliff can witness it.'

'You won't do anything till after I leave?'

'We'll see how it goes.'

When she'd finished, he looked at her regretfully. 'Eh, lass, I have to act straight away on something as bad as this. We can't let that child be killed or maimed!'

She stared at him in mute dismay.

'Can you get your possessions out quickly? If you leave them in the laneway behind the house, young Cliff will pick them up and fetch them here.'

'I have them packed already. I deliberately broke the lock on my trunk and said I was sending it to be repaired last week, but I sent it to my grandparents instead. It was full of my possessions and my summer clothing. I think I can get the rest out without being seen.'

'I can bring you here for questioning if she tries to stop you leaving, then let you slip away with your luggage, since you've already signed a statement. Have you got somewhere to go?'

'Yes, straight to my new job, and my grandparents have got a friend who's going to drive me there. The minister at their church knows my new employers and gave me a reference. They've already sent me a train ticket. I can't go to my grandparents because it's the first place Mrs Hicks will look. They're giving my trunk to their friend today.'

'You've got it well organised. I'd appreciate knowing your new address, just in case I need to ask you something else.'

'I'd rather not. I don't want *her* to have any way of finding me again.'

'Will you be able to live with your conscience if that child dies? I may need you to act as a witness to keep her from being sent back to her grandmother.'

Ester couldn't hold back a sob. 'No, I couldn't bear that. She's such a loving little lass given half a chance. I wish there was somewhere for her to run away to as well.'

The sergeant hesitated, then said, 'There's another person worrying about her. Do you know Mrs Harte?'

'The one who lives in Birch End?'

'Yes. Turns out she's seen that woman thump Beatie more than once when they were out in the park. She's already told me she'd take in the child if she needed a refuge.'

'Really?'

'Yes. She's just moved into 23 Daisy Street, in Backshaw Moss. You could tell Beatie to go there if she ever needs to escape.'

'I'll do that, and make sure Beatie knows where it is. She really isn't safe at Mrs Hicks's, Sergeant.' Ester whispered her new address, vowing to tell Beatie to run away as soon as she could.

'Thank you. I'll call in to the doctor's and we'll go and check the child's injuries out together later today. I'll try my hardest to get her away from that woman, believe me.'

Ester worried all the way back about whether Mrs Harte had meant it, and decided that if the sergeant believed in her offer, she must have done. She'd definitely tell Beatie to run away and go to her as soon as she could. Who else was there for the child to turn to? She didn't trust the grandfather to stay sober.

Beatie lay on her bed, her body aching and sore where she'd been beaten with a cane. She wasn't going to stay here, whatever the minister at her grandmother's new church said about it being her duty to obey her grandmother. He'd also said these beatings were for her own good, to teach her right from wrong. Only, she knew she hadn't done anything wrong, couldn't understand why her grandmother hated her so much.

She had somewhere to run away to now, though, because Ester had sneaked in to see her while her grandmother was having her afternoon nap. The nice lady who'd smiled at her in the park had offered to look after her. She knew exactly where Mrs Harte lived now, because Ester had made her memorise how to get there in case she ever saw a chance to escape.

She wasn't going to wait for a chance to happen. She was going to find her own way of escaping and do it straight away to take them by surprise.

It was a risk to expect a complete stranger to hide her till she could find out how to contact her grandfather, but she had no one else to turn to. And surely a lady with such a nice smile wouldn't lie about helping her? Ester said the sergeant seemed sure Mrs Harte meant it. He had a nice smile too.

Her grandmother had told her that her mother's father had died, but Beatie had immediately recognised that as a lie because her grandmother's face got a certain look on it when she was fibbing. Her nose wrinkled and her eyes stared at you even harder than usual.

Her grandmother always said when she thumped her that she wasn't having Beatie giving in to the bad blood on her side and behaving as wickedly as him, and that was why she hit her. That was so unfair. Beatie knew her grandfather wasn't wicked, and nor was she, but she'd decided that her grandmother was a horrible woman.

She lay in bed till the house was quiet after the evening meal, then put a pillow under the bedcovers to look as if she was still there. She was wearing two layers of clothing to keep warm, and had crammed some underwear and a change of clothes in her school bag so that she'd have some spare clothes.

As she crept downstairs, she stopped just before she got to the bottom. Yes, she'd timed it right: Ester wasn't in the kitchen. The maid often had a sit-down in her bedroom with one of her magazines at this time of day, and Mrs Garton went into her own little room just off the kitchen to eat a second piece of cake.

Beatie crept across to the back door, feeling her back prickle with fear of being spotted, but no one came into the kitchen. She closed the door gently behind her, then slipped across and through the backyard gate, closing that carefully too, but of necessity leaving it unbolted. She hoped no one would notice that till it was too late to fetch her back.

It was dark now, and since she had no money of her own, she couldn't catch the last bus but had to walk up the hill to Birch End. Anyway, if she'd got on a bus, someone would have seen her.

It took her a long time to get there. Whenever a car passed her she continued to walk steadily, and no one stopped to ask what she was doing out at this time of night. With a scarf over her head, she thought she looked like a maid going home after a day's work, because she was quite tall for nine years old.

Sergeant Deemer phoned Dr Mitchell as soon as Ester left and found to his dismay that he was out attending a difficult home birth and wouldn't be back for a while.

He left a message with the doctor's wife for her husband to contact him urgently as soon as he returned, and sat in the police station to wait. The time seemed to pass very slowly.

It'd be no use going to see the child till he had a witness whose word would be believed in court about her injuries.

It was late when Beatie reached Birch End, but Ester had told her exactly where to go, so she continued to plod along through the village. It hurt to walk, though. It hurt so much.

She couldn't help letting out a low groan of relief when she found the three big houses in a row, all alike, just as she'd been told.

She had a moment's panic when she reached the one furthest away from Birch End and raised her hand to the knocker. Did she dare do this? She had to.

Taking a deep breath she banged the brass knocker good and hard.

When a man answered the door, she nearly ran away, but he spoke gently and had a kind expression on his face, so she gathered her courage together. Anyway, she had nowhere else to go, had she, and she was exhausted.

'Is Mrs Harte here, please? I need to see her. It's really urgent.'

He turned his head and yelled, 'Mum, it's for you.'

There was the sound of footsteps and the lady from the park came to join him.

For a moment, Beatie couldn't form a word, then she managed to say what Ester had told her: 'Sergeant Deemer said to come to you if I needed help.'

She couldn't stop herself from bursting into tears. What if they sent her back to her grandmother?

Before she knew what was happening, the lady had pulled her inside and was holding her close, patting her back. 'It's all right, love. It's all right. *Shh* now. I told the sergeant I'd look after you if you ever needed help, and I meant it. I'm really glad you came to me.'

As Beatie let go of the mountain of anxiety and terror that had been weighing her down, everything seemed to spin around her.

'Eh, the poor little thing's fainted. Pick her up quick, Gabriel love, and I'll shut the door.'

He did as she told him, but asked, 'What are you doing this for, Mum? You'll get yourself into trouble if she's run away from home.'

She led the way to the kitchen. 'I'm doing it because that child's grandmother's been beating her for no reason. The sergeant and I have been really worried about her safety. You'll let her stay, won't you? I'll show you why.'

Maisie came towards them.

When they saw the side of the child's face in the brighter light of the kitchen, they all exclaimed in shock. She had a huge bruise on one cheek and, as Gwynneth pushed up her sleeve, more bruises showed on her arm. Not a time for modesty, so she lifted the child's skirt, guessing there would be other marks. She hadn't realised how bad it would be, though. All three of them gasped at the mass of old and new weals near the child's bottom, and the streaks of blood.

Gwynneth let out a sob. 'She's been caned even more viciously than I'd expected. Who would do that to a child this young?'

Maisie stared in horror. 'Only a very wicked person. Look how thin she is. Has she been half starved too? Well, we've plenty of space here, and she's welcome to stay. She can have a nice room of her own till we can work out what to do with her to keep her safe.'

'I think she'd probably rather sleep in my bedroom. She's bound to be frightened of her grandmother finding her.' Gwynneth looked at them fiercely. 'I can't bear to see children beaten and hurt. I'll run away with her if anyone tries to force her back to *that woman*.'

'No need. If we have to hide her while they search the house, we can take her down into the tunnels,' Gabriel said.

Gwynneth looked at him and Maisie, tears welling in her eyes. 'Thank you.' Then she looked at them in puzzlement. 'What tunnels?'

Gabriel looked at Beatie. 'I just have to show my mother something. You'll be safe here.'

She nodded, huddling under the blanket they'd given her.

He took Gwynneth down to the cellar and showed her how to get in and out in case anyone came looking for Beatie. That warmed her heart. She'd expected her son to offer help, but hadn't been as certain of her daughter-in-law, because the two of them hadn't been married long enough for her to know Maisie well.

When she came back she sat down on the sofa and couldn't help planting a kiss on Beatie's cheek. 'You're safe with me, my little love.' Another kiss landed haphazardly.

The child clutched Gwynneth's sleeve. 'I'll be good. I'll help in the house. I won't be a burden.'

'Children are never a burden to me. They're a pleasure. And I especially like cuddles.'

Beatie nestled closer and shut her eyes, sighing softly.

Gwynneth turned to her daughter-in-lw. 'Could you heat up some milk, please, Maisie love? I bet she hasn't been fed properly today. And I'll need some warm water to wash her injuries.'

She didn't wait for an answer but continued to hold the child, trying to make her feel she was not only safe but wanted.

She wasn't even going to tell Sergeant Deemer about the poor child being here yet because he had to follow what the law dictated, and that would probably force him to take her back to her grandmother.

Over my dead body, Gwynneth vowed.

Just after midnight, the phone at the police station rang and Sergeant Deemer was relieved to hear Dr Mitchell's voice.

'My wife says you need to see me urgently.'

The sergeant explained what he'd been told and ended, 'Can I pick you up and take you to examine the child straight away? I think it's a case of the sooner the better.'

A sigh was his answer.

'I'd not ask you to do this, but I've seen the woman at the park hitting the child for no reason I could tell. We don't want a child's death on our hands.'

'Is it that bad?'

'Could be. I'm not risking it.'

'Very well. But I'll come in my own car and meet you there.'

They met outside the comfortable house near the park where Beatie lived with her grandmother. There were no lights showing, but the sergeant didn't hesitate to hammer on the door.

Lights came on in the upstairs and attic windows, but it took a while for someone to open the front door. Were they hiding something? he wondered.

It was the elderly housekeeper not the young maid who'd spoken to him earlier, whose job it should surely be to answer the door. Had Ester left already?

'We need to see young Beatie.' He used his sternest tone.

'Beatie? But she—'

A harsh voice interrupted from inside the house, 'What on earth do you need to see her for?'

He looked up to see Mrs Hicks standing part way up the stairs, wearing a fancy velvet dressing gown. The woman was plump, clearly didn't stint on her own needs, but even he had noticed that the child's clothes were too small for her and she was thin and hungry looking. 'I'll tell you after I've seen her.'

She glared at him, then called to the housekeeper, 'Where's Ester? It's her job to answer the door.'

'I don't know, madam. She wasn't in her bedroom, so I thought it more important for me to answer the door than go looking for her.'

That maid has definitely left, Deemer thought.

'Well, she must have slipped out to meet a man. I shall dismiss her for poor morals.'

'And Beatie?' the sergeant prompted.

'If you insist. This way, Sergeant. Who's that with you?'

'Dr Mitchell.'

'There's no one ill in this house.'

'We've been told there is, and we need to check.' He moved up the stairs and was past her before she could stop him. 'Which is Beatie's room?'

She looked puzzled, but pointed. 'At the end of the landing.'

He opened the door she'd indicated. It looked as if someone was asleep in the bed, but if so, why hadn't they been woken by the noise? When he went across and tugged the bedcovers away, it showed him only a couple of pillows – and something else. 'Dr Mitchell, could you please come and look at this?'

The doctor walked along to the room and this time Mrs Hicks came too.

'That looks like blood to me,' the doctor said.

'The child cut herself today,' she said quickly.

Dr Mitchell shook his head. 'That's not the way a single cut bleeds. Those smears are spread out, come from a much wider set of injuries, I'd guess.'

Sergeant Deemer turned to the housekeeper. 'Come and look at these, please, so you can bear witness to what we've found.'

She hesitated, casting an anxious glance at her mistress, then came across, gasping at what she saw.

He waited for her to study the bloodstains, then said, 'Can you come round the house with me and help me look for Beatie? I'm really worried about her safety. And we'll check for Ester while we're at it.'

The housekeeper shot another glance at her mistress, but Mrs Hicks folded her arms. 'Do as he says, you fool.'

The housekeeper stiffened, looking angry now.

Neither the child nor the maid were anywhere to be found, and they searched every room, including the cellar. Ester's things were all missing from her attic bedroom, but most of Beatie's things were still there. He was surprised at how few there were, and no toys at all.

When he came back downstairs, he found that Mrs Hicks had gone to sit in the breakfast room and got the fire blazing again.

'Neither Beatie nor Ester are there. Do you have any idea where they could be, Mrs Hicks?'

'Of course I don't. The maid must have run away, but she'd not have taken Beatie with her. The child is probably hiding somewhere. She'll reappear when she's hungry enough.'

'Your housekeeper and I have searched the whole house very carefully and there's no sign of her. I'll tell you now that your maid came to see me earlier today and said she was intending to run away because she couldn't bear to see you ill-treating your granddaughter any longer. She said you'd beaten her severely today.'

'Rubbish. No one's been ill-treating that child.'

'Then why did we find blood on her sheets?'

She shrugged. 'How should I know? She must have fallen over and grazed her knee.'

He exchanged worried glances with Dr Mitchell, then turned back to Mrs Hicks. 'I am giving you warning now, madam, that since you can't tell me where that child is, I shall have to take her disappearance seriously and report it officially.'

'Rubbish. I'm sure it's just a child's naughtiness.'

The housekeeper looked from one to the other, then said abruptly. 'I'm giving notice too, Mrs Hicks. I've seen you beat that poor little girl more than once, and I've had enough of it.'

'You'll sign a statement saying that?' Deemer asked quickly

'Yes, Sergeant.'

He got out his notebook and scribbled in it, holding it out to the housekeeper. 'Is that correct? If so, please sign it.'

After she'd read it, nodded, and scribbled her name, he held it out to the doctor. 'Will you please sign this to say that she signed of her own free will?'

'Happy to.'

Deemer put the notebook away. 'Do you have a telephone, Mrs Hicks?'

'No. Why would I want to be annoyed at all hours of the day and night?'

He turned back to the doctor. 'I shall have to stay here in case Beatie returns, but I'll let you get back to your bed now. I'd be grateful if you could please phone my wife when you get back and ask her to contact my constable to tell him to join me here as soon as it's light?'

'Certainly.'

Deemer caught Mrs Hicks's eye and watched her open her mouth to protest, then shrug and say, 'Well, I'm going up to bed. You're making far too much fuss over a naughty child.

And you can be sure I'll complain about this intrusion to your superiors.'

She didn't wait for an answer, but walked out of the room and could be heard going slowly up the stairs.

The housekeeper waited till they'd heard a door close overhead to ask, 'Would you like a cup of tea while you wait, Sergeant?'

'I'd be very grateful for one.'

'I'll make you one, after which I shall pack my things, ready to leave once I'm sure the child is safe.' She hesitated, then added, 'I'm a light sleeper and I'll leave my bedroom door open so that I can hear if Mrs Hicks comes out of her room. If she does, I'll call you. She may have got poor Beatie locked in a cupboard somewhere, though I didn't think we'd missed any.'

'Does she do that as well?'

She nodded and left the room.

He held his hands out to warm them at the fire, which was now blazing nicely. What on earth had happened to that child?

Could she have gone to find Mrs Harte? He hoped so.

In the early morning Cliff turned up at Mrs Hicks's house just before it got light, and he helped the sergeant search the house again from attics to cellar. No sign of the child, and this time they checked every cupboard thoroughly.

Where on earth could she have gone? Surely her grand-mother hadn't killed her? There had been blood on the sheets, but not enough to indicate a mortal injury. In the end, he sent Cliff off to the police station and gave the mistress of the house strict instructions to let him know if Beatie turned up.

'Why?'

'Because otherwise I might think you'd killed her,' he said bluntly. That shocked her, at least.

When he left the house, the housekeeper left with him, which was a surprise. 'Do you not want to wait for your wages?' he asked.

'No, Sergeant. Truth to tell, the mistress has been getting very strange lately, ever since she started going to that new church. I'd not like to be left alone in the house with her. I've seen her eavesdropping outside the kitchen, and I even saw her coming out of my bedroom one morning. My drawers had been rifled. I know how I leave my clothes, and it wasn't like that.'

'And you've really no idea where the child could have gone?'

'No. But I hope it's somewhere a lot kinder than here.' She hailed a shabby man passing by and asked him if he had time to fetch her a taxi, holding a sixpence at the ready.

'Happy to, missus.' He ran off at once.

After she'd left, Sergeant Deemer drove home and lingered over a hearty breakfast, telling his wife what had happened and hoping that Ester had passed on his message about Mrs Harte being willing to take in the child.

He wasn't going there to find out during the daytime, in case he gave away her hiding place, nor did he intend to telephone. There were too many people in Rivenshaw at the moment poking their noses in where they shouldn't.

9

The next morning Arthur took the tools he'd bought down into the cellar and set them carefully on the hooks and shelves. It felt good to be putting order back into his life.

What he would do to protect his property once the money from the London lawyer ran out he didn't know, but he'd worry about that when it happened. One step at a time.

After he'd finished he stood back and looked round in satisfaction, then turned to Biff, who'd been watching from the top of the cellar stairs with a slight smile on his face.

'That looks good, Arthur. Now, shall we find out what's down that hole?'

'Definitely. If you get the torch ready, I'll slide open that secret door.'

When he'd done that, Biff held the torch out to him. 'Take it. It's your house, so you should lead the way.'

It felt strange to be the leader, but he moved down into the space at the bottom of the steps. It looked dark and forbidding till he shone the torch down and around the area at the bottom. The open space there was bigger than he'd expected. Well, such solidly built steps didn't usually lead nowhere, did they?

He took a few cautious steps, leaving Biff to position the two pieces of wood he'd nailed together so that they prevented the opening from closing up behind them. 'There's quite a wide tunnel leading off to the right.'

When he took a step towards it, Biff grabbed his jacket and pulled him back. 'Don't go any further yet. I know we've got the wood preventing the panel from closing, but anyone could remove that. I'm going to fetch one of the Becksleys to guard it and then we'll explore a bit further together.'

'You're always very careful.'

'It's my job to make sure you're safe. And I must admit, I'm rather fond of staying safe myself.'

It felt strange to stand in a tiny island of torchlight surrounded by shadows. Arthur shivered and decided to follow Biff to the top of the stairs. *Coward!* he told himself. Or was he just being sensible?

When Phil joined them, they showed him the steps leading to the lower cellar and promised to let him go down and explore later, then left him to guard the entrance.

'Let's check first that there's no concealed tunnel or opening to the left.' Arthur didn't wait for an answer, but moved in that direction.

They found nothing except a dead end, so set off to the right, moving slowly, checking every step of the way.

After a few steps Arthur stopped. 'I don't know where this tunnel comes out at, but we're heading past the other houses. Do you think they have secret entrances too?'

'How can you tell where we're heading? The darkness makes me feel disoriented.'

'I've always had a good sense of direction.'

After about twenty yards he stopped again. 'Look, there are some more steps leading up and they're exactly like ours. I bet they lead to Maisie's house. We've come too far along for the middle house. So two of the houses lead down here. I wonder why?'

'We won't try to go up the other steps today. We'll count our paces going back, then pace it out above ground in the street after we close the tunnel entrance. That'll show us roughly where the other steps lead. For the moment, let's carry on a bit further and see where we get to.'

They moved slowly and carefully, stopping every few paces to shine the torch up and down at each side. They didn't want any nasty surprises.

'I think the section near our house must have been dug out fairly recently,' Arthur said suddenly.

'How can you tell?'

'The walls in this part look . . . I don't know, slightly different from the ones near our house, older and dried out.'

'Do you know about the existence of tunnels? I never had anything to do with them till I came to the valley. I've spent most of my life in cities.'

'I used to play in some tunnels which led out of the old quarry when I was a lad. I should think these are an extension of them. My granddad told me about the tunnels from the quarry and showed me how to get into them once I was old enough to have a bit of sense. They were my secret hiding place. Not many people knew about them then, and even fewer know they're there these days.'

'Well, I think we should go back now and try to find out more about the old tunnels before we go any further in our explorations. There must be some reason for extending the passages if you're right about our part being recent. I reckon Sergeant Deemer would be the best person to ask. If anyone knows what's going on here in the valley, it's him.'

'Why would anyone want to make new ones?' Arthur wondered. 'They can only lead to the old quarry and no one uses it any longer.'

'I don't know. Let's go back now.' Biff shivered. 'I don't like it down here, to tell you the truth. If anything goes wrong with our torch, we'll be in real trouble. Anyway, sorting out the house is more important at the moment, don't you think?'

'I suppose so, but we can still ask the sergeant. There's so much to do to set the house to rights, I hardly know where to start.'

'Now you've got some proper tools you can start by mending some of the furniture properly. There's enough of that to keep you busy for a while.'

'I shall enjoy doing it.'

He stopped walking, head on one side. 'I've had a more careful look at the stuff in the dining room and I think some of the pieces are quite expensive, even though they need putting together again. Maybe if I can mend them properly, I can sell them. I'm going to need money to pay the council rates, not to mention the household electricity and gas bills once it's been modernised, aren't I, however frugally I live? The money I've been left will give me a start, but it won't last for ever.'

'How about we ask Charlie Willcox to come and take a look at the furniture? He'll be able to give us some idea of what the better pieces might be worth if they could be repaired,' Biff suggested.

'Good idea. He's a kind chap. He bought me a loaf more than once when I was at my worst. Eh, I was such a fool.'

'Well, you've come out of that patch now and you're sounding more alert all the time.'

'Good food helps, but most of all it's hope that's buoying me up. I didn't have hope for anything good after Susan died, especially when my daughter was killed and I was kept away from my little granddaughter. My son hasn't spoken to me since then. Perhaps, if I continue to pull myself together, he'll forgive me. I doubt that horrible woman will ever grant me permission to see Beatie though. She always was a spiteful old devil, and how she got such a pleasant son, I don't know. He really loved my daughter, made her happy in their marriage till the accident.'

'You might have to ask Judge Peters to make an order allowing you to see Beatie.'

'I'll need to prove myself sober and respectable again first, so I can't do it yet. I'm worried about my little lass, though.

I'd not give a dog to that woman to look after, let alone a grieving child. I've only seen Beatie in the distance, but she looked so unhappy.'

'I've not actually met this Mrs Hicks.'

'You don't want to. She's like the wicked witches in the storybooks I used to read to Beatie.' After a moment of scowling into the distance Arthur turned and led the way back, surreptitiously brushing away a tear or two.

Biff didn't say anything but he was glad to hear Arthur making sensible plans for the future. 'We're agreed to bring in Charlie Willcox, then? Apart from anything else, he loves to be the first to find something out, so I reckon he'll jump at the chance of seeing inside this house. He'll be able to tell you if anything's worth selling. He came to look round Maisie's house and gave her some good prices for the best pieces of furniture.'

'Well, if he can sell some of the stuff for me, it'll be a big help, and I won't waste the money, I promise you. But I'll still have to find a way of earning a living in the future, won't I? It costs a lot of money to run a big house like this one, more than I can earn as a carpenter's assistant – always supposing anyone would give me a job now.'

'You don't want to sell the house and buy a smaller one?'

Arthur gazed round, shaking his head. 'It'd break my heart to do that. I love the place already. Besides, Miss Chapman wanted me to have it.'

'I bet Higgerson tries to buy it. He did with Bella, though he offered a ridiculously low price. Don't sell to him, whatever you do. He'd make the other heirs' lives a misery.'

'I hate to think of him even coming inside here. He's . . . evil, spreads misery. Even his own wife and older son ran away from him. He went after me when I refused to work for him. I had to hide at night for weeks till his men stopped trying to beat me up.'

'What did he want you to do?'

'Bully folk who fell behind with their rent, hurt them to remind them to pay their debts. But I couldn't have done that to folk down on their luck, not even at my worst.'

Biff didn't let himself smile. He couldn't imagine Arthur doing anything nasty. The man was a bit of a softy, really, but it was good to see him starting to pull himself together.

That was what Sarah Jane Chapman had wanted her bequests to do.

The man who'd been sheltering from the cold wind in the gateway of a yard across at the other side of the back alley managed to hear some of what they were saying when they walked round the yard, because sounds seemed to carry further in damp air.

What he'd heard surprised him. Fancy an old drunk like Arthur Chapman inheriting such a big house!

If he went and told Mr Higgerson about what he'd overheard, like there being valuable furniture in it, there might be a chance of getting sixpence or even a shilling as a reward.

He knew Mr Higgerson collected information and put it together to make money. The man was clever about things like that.

The listener tried not to let anyone see him leave the alley, then made his way to the rear of Higgerson's house. He found Jem Stanley cleaning the car in the garage, whose doors were open, whistling cheerfully as he dipped a cloth in a bucket of soapy warm water and rubbed off the mud splashes.

He explained why he was there.

'I'll go and ask Mr Higgerson if he's free to see you. Wait there and do not touch a single thing.'

He didn't touch anything, but he did hold his cold hands out over the warm air rising from the bucket of hot water.

Jem came back a couple of minutes later and beckoned. 'He'll see you. Make sure you remember all the details.'

'Yes, Mr Stanley.'

As he led the way, Jem hid his satisfaction at how cringingly polite the man had been. Working for Mr Higgerson was a big step up in the world. He watched his master as he listened to what the man told him, asking questions and frowning in thought.

Then Higgerson fumbled in his pocket and brought out a little coin purse. 'I'll give you a shilling for that information. Do not tell anyone else what you heard or that you spoke to me about it. If you find out anything else about Arthur Chapman, there could be another little bonus for you.'

The man went away beaming.

Jem waited, but his master didn't share his thoughts.

He'd noticed that Higgerson had brightened considerably at the news the chap had brought. Something was brewing and it was to do with those houses. Jem was sure he'd find out what was going on sooner or later, and benefit from it.

It puzzled him why there would be a lower cellar hidden under that end house. No place he knew had been built with those, and he thought his master was mad having extra cellars dug out under the Clover Lane houses. Even going there to check on the progress of the new cellar gave him the heebie-jeebies.

He smiled at that word, which exactly described how he felt. He'd first heard it at the cinema. People were thinking up some comical new ways of saying things these days. Heebie-jeebies was one of his own favourite words now.

'Go and finish cleaning the car!' Higgerson shouted suddenly. 'Are you asleep? I've told you twice.'

'Oh, sorry, sir. Just thinking about the new cellar in Clover Lane. It's going to need more bracing on the walls.'

'Then get some, but only the smallest amount you need. I'm not made of money.'

Jem shook his head as he went back to finish off the car. Higgerson said that regularly, acting as if he had to be careful with every penny, yet by most folk's standards, he was rich.

Now that Jem had started to follow his example and let his wife watch where their money went, every single farthing, it felt good to have some coins put by in case of bad times. He was surprised at how it was mounting up. They'd never managed to save money before, and it put her in a very good mood.

Biff left Arthur mending a beautiful little corner wall cupboard with Rob Becksley patrolling the house, keeping watch. He strolled along to the end house to ask if he could use their phone to call Charlie Willcox because there were no buses down the valley at this time of day.

To his surprise, when Maisie opened the door, he caught a glimpse of a little lass running up the stairs and tripping up.

Maisie said quickly, 'I'd be grateful if you don't mention my young guest to anyone.'

'Of course not.'

He waited for her to explain, but she didn't, so he decided to mind his own business. She showed him the phone on the hall table, and when he tried to give her twopence for the call, as folk did at the village shop, she waved his outstretched hand away.

'It's a poor world if neighbours can't help one another. How's Mr Chapman going on?'

'Enjoying his new home, busy mending some broken furniture at the moment.'

She smiled. 'I remember how I felt when I first found I'd inherited this house, so wonderfully happy.'

'He wants Charlie Willcox to come and value a few things, as he did for you.'

'Mr Willcox is very knowledgeable. He's sold quite a lot of things for me already. He's a very nice man, too. Someone was telling me he's the favourite to become mayor next time there are local elections.'

'He'd make a good mayor.'

'An honest one, too, unlike Higgerson's friend, who's also going to stand.'

'I'm a bit out of touch with local gossip. Folk around here regard me as an outsider and are a bit wary about what they say to me.'

She chuckled. 'They did me at first, though they started to soften a little when I married Gabriel.'

Maybe he should find a local lass to marry once everything settled down. Why not? He had been getting on very well with his landlady before he moved in with Arthur. She was a very cosy armful and an excellent cook, fun to chat to as well.

He jerked himself back to the present and made the phone call, not surprised when Charlie said he'd be there in about an hour.

Maisie had told Beatie to run up to her bedroom and stay out of sight whenever someone came to the house, but she was feeling very lethargic today after her long walk up the hill last night, and she tripped on the stairs.

She realised the man had seen her when she looked back and caught him staring. But Maisie waved to her to carry on, and Beatie heard her ask him not to tell anyone. Maisie had smiled when she saw who was at the door, so he must be a nice person.

Hardly anyone ever came to her grandmother's house, and they certainly weren't greeted with smiles. Her grandmother didn't visit other ladies, either, and when she passed them in the street, they just nodded to her and walked on quickly, never stopping to chat. Her mother had had lots of friends and often chatted to neighbours.

Beatie went into the bedroom, which was at the back of the house, and decided to watch what was going on outside.

Out of habit she sat concealed by the edge of the curtain and when she saw a man creeping along the back alley, she stiffened. He looked sneaky, kept glancing over his shoulder as if to make sure no one was following him. What was he doing? Was he a burglar? Or had he come looking for her?

He didn't try to go into any of the backyards, but stood in the alley mostly concealed by the sagging edge of a shed near the end house, the one her Auntie Gwynneth said a new man had just inherited.

The stranger looked dirty, as if he never washed himself, and his clothes were ragged. What was he doing there? She'd better tell someone about him, just in case.

She ran down the stairs without thinking, calling for Auntie Gwynneth, but stopped dead when she saw the visitor just putting the phone down in the hall. She'd forgotten about him. Would they be mad at her for not staying hidden?

Maisie came out of the front room. 'Your auntie has nipped out to the shops. What's the matter, dear? Can I help you?'

'There's a man staring into the backyards from near the end house. He looks as if he doesn't want to be seen. Has he come after me, do you think?'

'I don't think so. You're quite safe. No one can possibly know you're here and I'm sure Mr Higgins won't tell anyone.'

The stranger stepped forward. 'I certainly won't. But I'm living in the end house, and he may be spying on me and my friends. Can you show him to me without him seeing us, do you think?' He looked at Maisie. 'Would that be all right?'

'Of course it would.'

'You can see him best from my bedroom.' Beatie led the way back upstairs and gestured to the window. 'If you walk round the sides of the bedroom and stand behind the curtain, he won't see you.'

The visitor did that and stayed perfectly still, watching.

She looked at Maisie and got another of those lovely reassuring smiles. No one in this house seemed to get annoyed at her, let alone smack her suddenly for no reason. She loved being here.

'It's all right, love. Mr Higgins is pleased that you noticed that man. Shall we sit on the end of the bed and wait? We'll be out of sight there.'

Biff frowned as he watched. 'I don't know that chap's name, but I've seen him at a pub where ne'er-do-wells hang around. I wonder what he's looking for.'

He watched for a few more minutes then said abruptly, 'I think I'll creep up on him from behind and find out what he's doing here. Thank you so much for coming to tell us, Beatie.'

When he left the bedroom, Maisie said, 'I'll see you out, Biff. I won't be a minute, dear. Wait for me here.'

At the front door she said in a low voice, 'You won't tell anyone that the child is here, will you? She's been badly beaten and run away to Gwynneth. Her parents are dead, you see.' She deliberately didn't tell him Beatie's name.

'Of course I won't. Thank you for letting me look.'

She called up the stairs after he'd gone, 'Do you want to finish eating your scone now, Beatie?'

The child came down, still looking hesitant. 'I didn't do anything wrong, did I?'

'Good heavens, no.'

She let out a huge sigh of relief. 'So I'm not in trouble?'

'Not at all. In fact, you did a good thing coming to tell us about that sneaky man. If you see anyone else sneaking around, come and tell someone straight away.'

Beatie took the hand Maisie was offering, walking with her into the kitchen, feeling so safe here. She could have as much food as she wanted, second helpings of anything. The others ate second helpings too, so her grandmother was wrong saying only people with no manners ate like pigs.

★

Biff crept around the houses and managed to take the watcher by surprise. 'Looking for someone?'

The man tried to shake the hand off his jacket and failed. 'Just sheltering. It's a cold day.'

'Go and shelter somewhere else. If I see you around here again, I'll report you to Sergeant Deemer and ask if there have been any burglaries.'

'I'm not a thief!'

Biff let go of him and called, 'Give my regards to Higgerson!' after him as he ran away.

The man slowed down for a moment and turned a startled look in his direction, so he knew he'd hit the nail on the head with that guess.

What the hell did Higgerson want? He'd not managed to buy the other two houses, and he wouldn't get his hands on this one, either, if Biff could help it. This area was coming out of being a slum. Higgerson would only push it back towards crime and misery.

10

Half an hour later someone knocked on the front door and Biff went to answer it, relaxing and opening the door fully when he saw who it was.

'Is it like the other end house, full of furniture?' Charlie Willcox asked before he'd even stepped inside.

'No. It's different again. There's a reasonable amount of furniture, but nearly every piece is broken and it turns out mending furniture is a job Arthur's skilled at.'

He looked over his shoulder, then whispered to Charlie. 'It's obviously been done on purpose to stir him up. He turned to booze after his wife died.'

'Yes, I remember him, poor chap. He might have gone to pieces, but he never stole from anyone that I heard, or committed any acts of violence either.'

Biff nodded, glad to know that others also found Arthur a basically decent chap. He took Charlie through the house to the kitchen, where the man in question was busy screwing a couple of chair legs back on. They stood quietly in the doorway, watching him work so intently that he didn't notice them till he'd finished dealing with the chair legs and stood up to stretch.

'Why, it's Mr Willcox! Sorry I didn't see you standing there. How kind of you to come so quickly.'

'My pleasure. I'm dying to see what this house is like inside.'

'Why don't you show Charlie round and point out the pieces of furniture you think are more valuable?' Biff suggested. 'You know far more about that sort of thing than I do.'

'Happy to, but I don't know as much about the expensive furniture as about the everyday stuff. Just a tick.' He set the chair upright, made sure it didn't wobble, and sat on it, patting the chair back as he stood up again. 'That's better. Please come this way, Mr Willcox.'

Biff tiptoed after them, standing at the back of the hall to check that Arthur didn't need his help and smiling as a few exclamations floated across to him from both men. They were soon deep in discussion as they examined the pieces in the dining room.

Arthur, in a shocked whisper, 'Is it really worth that much?'

Charlie, voice booming as usual, 'Easily. If you can mend it, that is?'

'Oh yes. That won't be hard. There's not a lot wrong, actually. It's a lovely piece, isn't it? Look at that patina.'

More exchanges followed, with a few more shocked exclamations from Arthur as the two men continued to look around.

Pleased with how it was going, Biff went back into the kitchen and filled the kettle. Arthur definitely didn't need his help when it came to furniture.

About an hour later, after he'd heard them go into and out of all the downstairs rooms, he poked his head into the hall to catch them before they went upstairs. 'Anyone for a cup of tea?'

'That'd be champion,' Charlie said at once.

Arthur nodded. 'I'm always ready for one.'

When they came into the kitchen Biff waved their visitor to a seat, and Arthur to one next to him. 'While I finish making the tea you two can carry on with your conversation.' He winked at Charlie, who took over.

'If you repair the small table and the carved hall chair first, Mr Chapman, so that I can see you know what you're doing, I'll sell them for you at around the price I suggested, more if I can get it. I take ten per cent of what I get for the better furniture, plus whatever it costs me to do that, mind.'

'That's very fair. I wouldn't know how to begin selling things. I shall enjoy doing the repairs, though.'

'Can I see the rest of the house after we've had our cuppa?'

'Happy to show you round if you can spare the time.' He turned to Biff. 'Some of those pieces are worth more than I'd expected, a lot more. Isn't that marvellous?'

Charlie beamed at Biff, clearly enjoying his visit. 'Why don't you come with us?'

'I'd like that. I'll just tell Phil to keep an eye on the front door.'

Their visitor stopped dead for a moment. 'You're having the house watched even in the daytime?'

'Better safe than sorry.'

Charlie shook his head sadly. 'I don't know what the world's coming to, but I know one of the causes.'

When the three of them went round the upstairs bedrooms, taking the time to look in every corner, these provided more surprises, beautiful antiques standing cheek by jowl with everyday furnishings.

Then they went up to the attics where there was a similar jumble of smaller pieces.

Charlie moved towards one of the windows. 'I bet you get a good view over this part of the valley from here.' He jerked back and his smug look vanished. 'What's that sod doing watching your house?'

'Who are you talking about?' Arthur went across to peep out. 'I recognise his face but I don't know his name. I couldn't prove it, but I'm sure he picked my pocket one night and took all the money I had left that day. It was my own stupid fault for getting drunk, but still – he preyed on me after I'd treated him to a drink. What sort of person does that?'

'Harry Caxton wouldn't hesitate to do it. He's a real lay-about and one of the most skilled pickpockets in the valley.

Take a look at him for future reference, Biff lad, but be careful he doesn't see you.'

'I've only just sent away another chap who was watching the house,' he said indignantly. 'Why has this one taken his place?'

'Higgerson must have sent him.'

Arthur let out an angry snort. 'I suppose Caxton thinks he can benefit from my stupidity again. Well, he's got another think coming. I haven't had a drink for months.'

Charlie sighed. 'You might have frightened the other chap away, Biff lad, but Caxton doesn't frighten easily. If he saw me arrive, he'll be reporting that to Higgerson, who will guess that there's some valuable stuff here.' He stared into space for a minute or two, then added, 'I'll mention it to Sergeant Deemer next time I see him. He has no time for Caxton. It'd make his day to get that sod put behind bars.'

He studied his fancy modern wristwatch. 'I'd better get going now. Let me know when those two pieces are ready, Mr Chapman, and I'll send someone to pick them up.'

Biff saw Charlie out, and then went to find Arthur, who was standing near the kitchen window, staring blindly into space.

'Will you be able to repair those two pieces for Charlie?'

He jumped in shock but nodded. 'Eh, I was miles away then. Seeing Caxton reminded me how bad I got for a while. I'm deeply ashamed of it.'

'If it helps, you're not on your own this time.' That won him a faint smile.

'No, I'm not, am I? I'm very lucky to have you helping me, Biff lad. Don't think I don't appreciate what you're doing, more than you were hired to do sometimes, I reckon.'

Biff gave an embarrassed shrug. He had more money than they realised, thanks to a nice little inheritance recently.

'But I have to learn to stand up for myself, don't I, can't rely on you for ever? I need to be more self-reliant and alert than ever before. Thieves and other villains didn't pay me much attention when I was just a rough working chap, but they will now I own this lovely house. They'll think I must have come into a lot of money as well as the building.'

'I'm sure you'll find a way to earn a decent living and look after this house.'

'I have to, if I'm to see that little lass of mine again, and win back my son's trust.'

Sergeant Deemer heard that his new constable had arrived in Rivenshaw the day before he was due to start work, and wasn't surprised when Mike called into the police station to introduce himself in the late afternoon.

The sergeant beamed at him. 'You're extremely welcome, lad. We have an interesting situation going on here, but I won't bother you with that till tomorrow, when I'll tell you and my other constable about it at the same time. More important for the moment, do you and your wife have somewhere to live?'

'Yes, thank you. We're staying with her parents for a few days till a nearby house they found for us becomes vacant, then they'll help us move in. Our own furniture is in storage till then.'

'It's not one of Higgerson's houses?'

'Definitely not. I know the name already. My in-laws once rented a house from that man and found him to be a terrible landlord. They haven't a good word to say for him.'

'Neither do I. Anyway, that's for tomorrow. Good of you to call in.'

'I've come out partly to stretch my legs and partly to let my Delia and her mother have a good old natter about people I've never heard of. I thought I'd take a stroll round Rivenshaw to renew my acquaintance with the town centre and start getting my bearings.'

'Why don't I come with you? There's nothing like a stroll for keeping you up to date with what's really going on around you. I try to get out and about regularly. Since you've heard of him already, I'll tell you that Higgerson is our main problem. These days he's gone far beyond what he used to get up to. I shall catch him out if it's the last thing I ever do. Anyway, let's not spoil a fine day by talking about him.'

As they walked the sergeant introduced Mike to some of the people they met. He was pleased to see the younger man act automatically to stop a young boy from running into the road chasing after his ball, and saw that he knew exactly how to tease a group of little girls about their skipping skills and set them giggling and blushing at the attention. A policeman was there to serve his community and needed their willing help to keep order.

Mike also spotted the fact that some people turned off the street in order to avoid meeting the sergeant, and commented on it quietly.

'You've got sharp eyes, lad. There are minor villains everywhere, and I suppose there always will be. You'll gradually get to know our home-grown ones.'

'Just a minute, Sarge,' Mike moved quickly to help an old lady who was having trouble crossing the road, making her laugh by giving her a sweeping bow as they reached the footpath on the other side.

When he came back, the sergeant said, 'Nicely done, lad. That old lady has just turned ninety. She still manages to look after herself and get around the town centre, but she isn't very good with modern motor vehicles, doesn't seem to understand how fast they can go.'

A little further on, he asked, 'Have you ever been up the hill to Birch End and Ellindale during your visits, lad?'

'No, Sarge. When we're here, we usually spend the time with Delia's parents, and they prefer to stay at home and chat, or stick to a gentle amble around the town centre. She's their only child and they miss her greatly.'

'I'll take you for a drive up and down the valley tomorrow, then, so that you can see the framework for what's going on. We have our own fizzy drinks factory at the top, and I'll treat you to a glass of the best ginger beer you've ever tasted. At the other end of the scale, I'll show you our worst slum on the way down, Backshaw Moss, which is just beyond Birch End.'

'How bad is it?'

'Parts of it are about as bad as a slum can get, but the council is making a start on clearing it. Trouble is, Higgerson is trying to prevent that, via the council and by any other means.'

'Have you got any police vehicles?'

'Just one police car, a nice little Morris. Hasn't let me down yet.'

'Must be hard for both of you to get around the valley quickly sometimes, with only one car. It's the coming thing to have more police vehicles.'

'Yes, I know. I doubt local finances can stretch to that, but I've been wondering whether to get a motorbike now you've joined us. I've been tipped the wink that money could be found to fund and run one. We have a shy chap living in a big house near Ellindale who donates to good causes occasionally. Have you had any experience of riding motorbikes?'

Mike chuckled. 'I own one and brought it with me. It's just a small Triumph and—' He noticed the lack of comprehension on the sergeant's face and broke off without going into further details. 'Do you know anything about motorbikes, sir?'

'Not really, and I reckon I'm too old to learn to ride one. But having one might help you and Cliff in your work. And in fact, I might be able to pay you a bit extra if you use yours on the job, as well as our little team having one of our own.'

'It can certainly come in useful being able to get to the site of a problem quickly.'

'Well, now we have someone who understands motorbikes I'll make a bit more effort to get one. We're quite isolated here in the valley, so we have a better case for needing our own transport than places with plenty of regular bus and tram services.'

All in all, Deemer liked his new senior constable even more than he'd expected to. There was a steadiness to this young man, an inner strength, but a kindness too. You needed kindness to deal with some of the situations the police had to face. Well, you did if you cared about people, some of whom had had very hard lives.

Deemer would brief him in more detail about Higgerson tomorrow before they started driving about. Then another day, he'd send the two constables out to patrol the town together. He felt it important to make sure his officers knew one another well, and the two younger men would probably learn to pull together better without their sergeant overhearing every word they said.

He intended to brief them both about the possibility of a traitor making plans in the valley, but would have to get permission before he could do that.

He wondered how Mike felt about the political situation in the country. Many people, especially the younger ones, believed that war wasn't really going to happen again, but Deemer was sure it was inevitable, sadly. During the last war, he'd had to kill ordinary chaps who spoke a different language but weren't all that different from himself in order to save his own life, and hadn't enjoyed doing it.

He recognised the telltale signs of another damned war looming, by hell he did.

He hadn't understood such signs before the Great War began, few people had, but if you couldn't learn from what had happened in the past, you were pig stupid or wearing blinkers.

Sergeant Deemer pointed his new constable in the right direction to get back to his relatives' house and called in on Judge Peters, pleased to find his friend at home.

'I've just been making the acquaintance of my new senior constable. Nice young chap, Mike Grafton, and unless I'm much mistaken, as shrewd as they come. He's a motorbike enthusiast, and I feel we won't be able to make the most of him unless we police officers become more mobile and, well . . . ' He hesitated.

'And you're wondering whether there is any way I can help you get funding to buy a motorbike for your police force.'

'Having one as well as a car could be a good way to provide better communications for our group as well, in an emergency,' he said pointedly.

'It will indeed, and I'm sure that will help get your request funded, Gilbert.'

'And I think I should tell my constables about the group, to prepare them in case they have to take over from me.'

Dennison looked surprised. 'Are you retiring after all?'

'No. But a friend of mine just dropped dead, two years younger than me, he was, and it makes you think.'

'Oh. Well, we can't do without you, so don't you dare follow his example.'

Deemer grinned. 'I'll do my best to stay on the right side of the grass. I could tell my officers the bare details without names to start with, well, maybe just a couple of nearby contacts fully named.'

'I'll check with His Lordship, if you like.'

'Thank you. You know him better than I do. There's also Mike's own bike. He'd be happy to use it for work if we refund him for petrol and any damage incurred. It's a cheap way for us to get more transport.'

Dennison looked thoughtful. 'Finn has kindly offered to fund any areas the council isn't covering. Maybe I could ask him. It'll sound better coming from me.'

'Good idea. We have to move forward and use modern equipment. The smarter criminals do, that's for sure.' Deemer felt relieved that he hadn't needed to beg for this sort of help. 'The world is changing quickly, isn't it, Dennison? Modern inventions are transforming life, even here in the wilds of Lancashire.'

'It needs to be transformed in some ways.' He paused, then asked, 'Any progress with finding out if Higgerson is our traitor?'

'Not yet. I'll take my two lads into my confidence about what he may be up to, as well as what I know for certain he is up to already.'

'We'll catch him one day,' Dennison said.

Gilbert scowled. He'd expected to catch him by now, but it was taking longer than he'd hoped. He'd never give up while there was breath in his body.

But you didn't always win your battles in this life, however hard you tried.

Deemer walked home enjoying the exercise after spending so many hours sitting in a car or his office. He had always loved being out in the fresh air.

Suddenly, two men rushed out of the darkness caused by a broken street lamp, and attacked him from in front and behind, taking him by surprise. He fought back, of course he did, roaring at the top of his voice for help. But they were younger than he was, and much bigger, and he'd have no chance of holding his own against them for long, he knew.

Then two lads ran out of an alley and chucked cobblestones at his attackers, knocking one of them sideways and distracting them from the attack. The lads must have had the wit to scrabble at the edges of the alley for loose stones, and they were smart enough to run away almost immediately.

This distraction gave Deemer time to get his whistle and blow it for help, hoping desperately that there would be someone within earshot who understood what that particularly shrill call meant. He tried to grab his truncheon too, but failed because the attackers were on him again.

Only, once again stones were hurled at them by the lads, and he managed to land a couple of return blows.

Then a punch sent him to the ground and the nearest man kicked out at him. He rolled away and was only struck a glancing blow, but that was enough to make him double up with pain.

Before either of them could get in another blow, there was the sound of yelling coming closer, and footsteps pounding along the street. A woman was screeching for help at the top of a very loud voice.

When voices yelled out from the other directions as well, one of his assailants called, 'Leave it now!' and they ran off.

Surrounded by his rescuers, Sergeant Deemer lay back and watched two men chase after his attackers.

He had to leave it to others to keep him safe while he fought for breath, wincing with pain when he moved his upper body where they'd got him in the ribs.

'You all right, Sergeant?' a woman whispered.

It was Gwynneth Harte. 'More – or – less.' If he wasn't mistaken they'd not only bruised his ribs but made his forehead bleed, and his right eye was blurring as blood ran down into it. 'Can you – help me – to stand up?'

As she bent to offer her arm, a man came to his other side, her son Gabriel. With their help Deemer managed to heave himself to his feet. It was a struggle not to moan, so painful was it, and he had to lean on them.

'The sergeant needs to be taken to the doctor,' she called out.

He recognised some of the other helpers too by the light from a street lamp further along, good folk all of them.

The two men who'd chased after his attackers came back, shaking their heads.

'Sorry, Sarge. They were fast runners,' one said regretfully.

'What's the world coming to when a policeman gets attacked on a public street, and in one of the better parts of Rivenshaw too?' another asked.

The sergeant was thinking the same thing. This was usually a quiet, law-abiding area, or he'd not have walked through it alone at this hour.

He hadn't been able to see his assailants clearly because they'd had knitted hats pulled down over the tops of their heads. They hadn't sounded local, though, had spoken with a markedly different accent. Where had they come from and why had they attacked him?

He could only think they'd been brought into town for that very purpose. He shook his head sadly. It must have been Higgerson's doing, because who else would want to put him out of action? Was he getting paranoid about the fellow? Or was the sod growing steadily more dangerous?

He let Gabriel help him into a van and drive him to seek medical help.

Dr Mitchell was as horrified as everyone else at the attack. He strapped the sergeant up and told him to take a few days off work to recover.

Sergeant Deemer didn't argue, but he wasn't going to do that, because it'd show whoever it was that they'd come out from the encounter victorious. He reckoned he'd need his new constable to drive him round for a while, though, because it hurt to move too suddenly – hurt a lot, damn those sods to high hell.

He accepted an offer from Gabriel to drive him home, and was told that someone had already let his wife know he'd been attacked.

The pain was enough to make him say, 'Drive as smoothly as you can, lad.'

'Of course.'

Deemer closed his eyes and leaned back, trying to think of other things to take his thoughts off the sudden jolts of pain, which set his mind losing its focus.

On his visit to Dennison earlier in the evening, they'd been talking about the dark forces gathering in their world, in Europe particularly. What had Shakespeare called those forces? *The dogs of war*, that was it. Which play was that from? *Julius Caesar* perhaps? He couldn't remember for sure, but he would once his head had stopped aching. It was an apt phrase not only for the wider troubles brewing over in Germany and the nearby nations, but here in the valley.

'You'll need to rest for a few days to give your body time to recover, Sergeant.' Gwynneth's soft, musical voice from the rear of the van jerked him out of his thoughts.

'I'm not going to take time off work, because I won't give the one who organised this attack the satisfaction of putting me out of action. He's not getting the better of me.'

Gabriel joined in. 'You sound sure of who planned this, Sergeant.'

'I can guess. I bet you can too.'

'He's a blight on our valley, that one,' Gwynneth agreed.

The sergeant sat as still as he could. The doctor had given him some aspirin tablets, which seemed to be gradually taking the edge off the pain. He'd take more later when these wore off, as the doctor had suggested, because his whole body was protesting at being ill-treated.

'We've arrived, Sergeant.' Gabriel's voice made him realise they'd stopped in front of his house.

He accepted help getting out of the van and into the house, then his kind helpers left him to his wife's ministrations.

She helped him undress and put his pyjamas on, then brought him a hot-water bottle, trying not to let him see the tears she was shedding over his injuries.

'I'm all right, bonny lass,' he told her. 'It's only bruising.'

'What if they come back and kill you next time?' She clasped his hand for a moment.

'I won't let them take me by surprise again, believe me.'

'Let's get you up to bed and I'll fill our other hot-water bottle.'

As he lay in bed his pain subsided a little, but his mind still wandered.

'I'll sleep in the spare bedroom,' she said. 'I've put some aspirins beside the bed and some water. You'll need some more later. You've only to call out if you need anything.'

'Thanks, love. But I'd rather have you beside me.'

'Are you sure?'

'Yes. I daren't cuddle you, but I prefer to know you're there beside me, safe, and you could hold my hand at least.'

'I'll get ready for bed then.'

As he waited for her to come back from the bathroom, he stared at the white shapes of the pills on top of the chest of drawers next to the bed and they set his mind off leaping around again. He'd needed aspirin tablets during the Great War, when they'd first come into common use, and a real godsend they'd been. But he'd never needed them as badly as he did tonight.

His wife came back and got into bed beside him.

'Wake me in the morning at my usual time, love.'

'What? You're surely not going to work! Gilbert, no! You need to take a few days off. I'm sure the doctor didn't say you could go straight back to work.'

'I need to show whoever it is that I'm not going to be easy to stop. But I shall leave Cliff and Mike to do the running around for a few days, I promise, and they can take it in turns to drive me here and there. Will you phone Cliff first thing in the morning and ask him to hand the car keys over to Mike? I'll walk about indoors under my own steam, but I'll definitely need to be driven around whenever I go outside, for a day or two anyway.'

'You're a stubborn man and I don't know why I love you so much.'

'I love you too.' He smiled and closed his eyes, comforted by her love. Then, as she drifted into sleep, he distracted himself by trying to think who the two lads had been who'd come to his assistance. He'd recommend them for a commendation by the mayor. He'd need to . . . need to think out how he could . . . organise the next day or two. He'd just close his eyes for a minute or two to gather his strength.

He didn't wake till morning and his wife had already got up. She must have been listening and the minute he stirred, she refilled the two hot-water bottles to comfort his poor aching body and followed up with the treat of a cup of tea in bed, plus two of his favourite chocolate biscuits and then two more aspirins.

And he took the day off, couldn't summon up the strength to go to work. Eh, he felt his age sometimes these days.

When Gwynneth and her son got home, he went round to ask Biff and Arthur to join them, then told everyone what had happened.

Maisie clutched her husband's arm. 'Who were the attackers, Gabriel love? Did either of you recognise them?'

'I only caught a glimpse of them. They're not from the valley by their accents,' Gwynneth said.

Her son's indignation spilled over again. 'Two against one, it was, the cowards! Actually, I think someone brought them here deliberately to attack our sergeant.'

Dead silence greeted this, then Gwynneth said, 'And there's only one person wicked enough to have done that, as well as having enough money to pay them. Two attackers wouldn't come cheap.'

'Higgerson will have been somewhere public at the time it happened and will pretend to be shocked. It's what that man always does whenever he arranges an incident,' Arthur said.

'Who does he think he's fooling?' Gwynneth let out a little growl of irritation.

'I doubt he cares about fooling us, just about not giving anyone proof that he was involved,' Biff said.

'Well, we need to protect Gilbert Deemer. You couldn't get a better police sergeant than him. I'm going to speak to a few people tomorrow about setting up an informal watch over him for a few days,' Gabriel said. 'He's a good man, but he's not young.'

Arthur gaped at him. 'You don't think they'll try to attack him *again*, surely?'

'They shouldn't have dared do it once, but they did, and if it hadn't been for the people nearby rallying round, who knows what they might have done to him?'

'Deemer said there were a couple of lads who helped hold them at bay by throwing stones and rubbish at them till others could come to his aid,' Gwynneth said. 'I'm going to speak to some women friends. We can keep our eyes open too, especially us older women. We might as well be invisible half the time. Some people just push past us in the street.'

'If there's another attack, don't you even think of fighting back, Mum, just run away! If they can hurt Sergeant Deemer so badly, I don't think they'd hesitate to bash a woman.'

'I'd never try to tackle them on my own,' she said quietly. 'I'm not stupid. But they aren't all as tough as they pretend. Some are slower to hit women.'

'Even if you have several friends with you, please don't get involved. These men are ruthless. And for goodness' sake, don't let Higgerson know you're watching him.'

She smiled slightly, which left him worrying. His mother could be very determined when she felt something was the right action to take. She was a very special woman, who'd worked hard all her life, brought her three sons up with loving kindness, if not always enough to eat, and he was proud of her.

And now, she was caring for another child, one who desperately needed love and feeding up.

12

When Mike and Cliff went into the police station the second day after the attack, they found Sergeant Deemer already there.

'Should you be at work yet, Sarge?' Mike blurted out. 'Your face is really badly bruised.'

'I took one day off and that's it. I'm not giving in to such villains. The ones who attacked me were foreigners, must have been. I'd have recognised such big, strapping chaps if they'd lived in our valley. And they had a different accent to our folk here. Which means a certain person brought them in purely to attack me.'

He scowled at the memory, then nodded more happily. 'I did recognise the young lads who saved me from worse injuries, and I've sent a message asking them to come to the station today because I want to thank them in person. In the meantime, I hear you coped well yesterday.'

There was a tap at the station door shortly afterwards, and Cliff shouted, 'Come in. It's open.'

Two lanky young lads peeped in, looking rather uneasy. 'Sergeant Deemer sent for us.'

Cliff beamed at them from behind the counter. 'He'll be delighted to see you. Come this way.'

Deemer took over as soon as they entered his office. 'Come over here and let me shake your hands, lads. I can't thank you enough for coming to my aid.' He pumped their hands up and down, then looked at them very earnestly. 'You may even have saved my life, and I won't forget that.'

They both flushed slightly and wriggled uncomfortably, then one nudged the other to speak.

'Those men spoke funny so we reckoned they come from somewhere else, Sergeant, and they'd have to leave town by the main road. We kept watch on it overnight.'

'Did you now? Go on.'

'We saw them leave this morning just as it started getting light,' the other added. 'They were still wearing them knitted hats pulled down, so you couldn't mistake 'em. We could see the big black car clearly by then. It didn't have any lights on, but I've got good eyesight an' here's its registration number.' He passed over a piece of crumpled paper with the number written on it in pencil.

'Eh, you're a smart pair of lads!' he said warmly. 'There's not many clever enough to work that out. I think you two should join the police force when you grow up. You're exactly the sort of young chaps we need.'

They gaped at him, smiled shyly, but shook their heads, looking sad.

'I'm not good enough at reading,' one said.

'An' you have to be good at sums too,' the other added. 'I can't seem to get the hang of that long division stuff, an' the master says I'm stupid.'

'We'll find help for you with that once we've sorted out the present troubles,' the sergeant said gently. 'Reading isn't hard. It's just practice. The master is probably too busy to help you, but I'm not. Sums are the same, lots of practice and it suddenly clicks.'

They still shook their heads. 'I'd like to, I really would, Sergeant Deemer, but my mam wants me to leave school an' start earning as soon as I can. She says I'm eating her out of house and home.'

'My mam says the same. She's heard that new church gives lads clothing, for a uniform, like, so she's making us go there. We don't like that minister, though.'

'But you'd like to be policemen if you could?'

They both nodded vigorously.

'Then leave it to me and I'll sort that out for you with your mams once I'm better. Now, I want you to continue helping me. Keep your eyes open, and if you ever see anyone who looks like causing trouble, especially someone from outside the valley, you're to come to the police house in the evening and report it. Do not try to do anything except report it to me because we'll need to watch them first, to see what they do and where they go. You'll be special assistants to the police from now on.'

'Like in the *Boy's Own* comic?' one of them asked in a breathless, excited voice.

'I haven't read it lately, but that sounds about right,' Deemer said gravely. 'Now, I have to get on with my day, so give Cliff here your names and addresses, then any of us can find you again if we need your help. And tell your mams I'm coming to see them once I'm better to say how much you've helped me and how proud they should be of you. I'm a bit sore to move around much at the moment, but not as sore as I'd have been without your help.'

They exchanged quick grins. 'Yessir.'

'And in the meantime, buy yourselves a treat.' He slipped them a florin each and they smiled even more broadly.

Their clothes were ragged and they could have done with a wash, but they walked out of his office with heads held high and beaming smiles on their faces as if they felt like kings.

'Salt of the earth, lads like that,' he muttered and blew his nose to hide his emotions.

The two youngsters followed Cliff into the reception area and, when he'd taken their particulars, he saw them peering round, taking everything in, so gave them a treat by taking them to see the cells and locking them in one for a few moments, then showing them how handcuffs worked.

Once the two had left the police station, Sergeant Deemer called his two constables into his office. 'They give you hope for the future, lads like that do. Well done for showing them the cells, Cliff. Now, I promised to show you our valley, Mike. Cliff here can look after the station for us. He knows the ropes and I trust him absolutely.'

'I shall enjoy getting a good look round, sir.'

'You'll have to drive, I'm afraid. Who knows what rumours are spreading about the attack on me, so I want people to see that I'm all right. I shan't even try to get out of the car if I can help it, though, because I'm stiff as an icicle at midnight, to tell you the truth.'

'The bruises on your face are showing,' Cliff said hesitantly.

'I can't do much about that, so we'll ignore them. This isn't one of those seaside beauty pageants, after all.'

He left behind a beaming constable because the sergeant didn't give praise or express such absolute trust lightly.

And Deemer was driven by a man already won over by his new sergeant's kindness and integrity, not to mention his personal courage.

On the night of the attack on Deemer, Higgerson had been feeling happy. He'd been expecting the men he'd hired at considerable expense with the help of an acquaintance in Manchester to report to him that they'd got rid of Deemer.

He got so bored with his own company as he waited that he fell asleep on the comfortable armchair in his home office, waking suddenly when someone tapped on the window.

He beckoned the men to come in, asking eagerly, 'Did you manage to put him out of commission?'

'We did our best and got in a few good thumps, might even have broken a rib or two. He'll be sore tomorrow, I promise you.' He paused.

'Well, go on!'

'Unfortunately some damned passers-by rescued your sergeant before we could belt him to kingdom come.'

Higgerson felt furious. They might have got in a few good knocks, but he'd ordered them to do as much damage as possible to the old fool, and preferably put him out of action once and for all.

That meant his big scheme to get rid of Deemer had failed, which was bad enough, given how much it had cost him. But these were big men and he didn't quite dare shout at them. Truth to tell, he didn't dare do anything but pay them what had been agreed.

When they'd gone, the silence seemed to weigh heavily on him. He was fed up of having only an ignorant subordinate to chat to. Jem Stanley might obey his every command, but he was stupid.

The sight of Deemer being driven past two days later, with a badly bruised face, cheered him a little, but not much.

To his surprise, he was still missing his wife, damn her, especially in the evenings. It had been amusing to torment Lallie, and he'd found it a relief to thump her when things went wrong.

After fretting about it for a day or two, he decided to bring his younger son home from boarding school and start him in the family business. He'd teach him how to make money, which you didn't do by learning Latin.

It was doing the lad no good to keep his nose in his books and, as far as Higgerson could tell, Kit hadn't even used his schooldays to make worthwhile connections with lads from the better families. So the fancy school was a total waste of money.

Anyway Kit would be company if he were living here at home.

What the lad needed was to taste life, real life, and to start learning how to manage renting out houses so that they brought in steady money. You didn't get rich without some effort, and Kit could start at the bottom, by actually collecting rents, as Higgerson had.

He didn't want to give his son a chance to run away from school as his older brother had done, so he decided simply to turn up there and tell them Kit was needed at home.

When he gave orders for the car to be prepared for a longer journey, Stanley stared at him in shock.

'Where do you want to go to, Mr Higgerson?'

'To my son's boarding school in Cheshire.'

'Oh. Right. Um, have you got a map book, sir? I've never driven so far away from the valley before and I don't know the roads.'

'Isn't there a map book in the garage? I know I bought one a few years ago.'

'Not that I've ever seen, sir.'

'That sod who took my car probably stole it as well.' He thumped his clenched fist on the table.

Jem kept quiet. It was the best thing to do when his master fell into a rage.

After a short time Higgerson let out his breath. 'Well, go out and buy another map book, then. I shall want you to be ready to set off tomorrow morning early.' He fumbled in his pocket and handed over a five-pound note.

'Can I take the car, sir? It'll make it quicker to buy the map book, and I'll need to fill it up with petrol if we're going on a long journey.'

Silence, then, 'Yes. Put the petrol on my account. And don't forget that I check every entry!'

Jem smiled as he drove away. Higgerson always said that, but Jem had a little arrangement with the owner of the garage which added a few pence to every bill and his share was handed over after each purchase. He'd learned from watching and listening to Higgerson that even tiny amounts of money mounted up if you didn't spend them. He now had a Post Office savings bank account and so did his wife.

He wasn't looking forward to going into the bookshop, though. He'd never been in one in his life, but he knew where the one in Rivenshaw was. He didn't dare ask for more information from his master about exactly what to buy because that would show his ignorance. Surely the man at the bookshop would know what he needed?

He drove into town and parked the car, then walked towards the bookshop, stopping before he went in to stare in the window, which was chock full of books for those stupid enough to waste their time staring at squiggly lines on little squares of paper.

He stared inside, wanting to see what it was like before he went in. He wasn't pleased by what he saw, not at all.

There were two elegantly dressed old ladies chatting to an equally old man behind the counter. What was the fellow called? He checked the sign above the door. Oh yes, Mr Twomer.

Jem hesitated for a moment, then decided to stroll along to the end of the street and back, hoping the ladies would be gone by then. Posh old females who were fancily dressed like these two terrified him with their mincy-pincy way of speaking and their habit of looking down their noses at chaps like him.

He walked up and back, then came to a halt outside again, sagging in disappointment. Oh, hell! They were still there, and Mr Higgerson would get furiously angry if Jem took too long. Should he go inside now or take another walk?

He looked at the clock hanging over the entrance to a nearby shop and sighed. He'd have to do it now. Taking a deep breath, he pushed open the door.

The three people inside stopped chatting to stare at him, then Mr Twomer asked, 'May I help you, sir?'

'Yes please. I need a book of road maps.'

'For where?'

'Huh?'

One of the ladies tittered and Jem could feel himself flushing.

'For which part of the country, sir?'

'We need to get from here to Cheshire.'

'Ah. North of England. This way, sir. I have just the thing.' Mr Twomer set off for the back of the shop and Jem followed.

'Here you are, sir. Just check that it's what you want, and if it's suitable, come and pay for it at the counter.'

Jem opened the big floppy book and fumbled through a few pages, trying to look as if he knew what he was doing. None of it made sense to him. He'd never been out of the valley till he went to prison, and they didn't teach you map reading in there. He wasn't good at normal reading, let alone understanding this set of chicken tracks.

He'd just have to hope it was the right map book and that Mr Higgerson could understand it and explain which roads to take as they went along.

He was halfway home before he remembered the petrol, so he had to turn round and drive back into the town centre to fill up the car.

When he got back, he went to find Mr Higgerson and held out the parcel. 'Mr Twomer says this is the one you need, sir.'

'It's you who needs it if you're going to drive me there.'

What would be worse, confessing his ignorance now or tomorrow? Better get it over with now, then his master might be calmer tomorrow. Jem took a deep breath. 'I ain't never used a map book before, sir, and anyway, I'll be keeping my eyes on the road while I'm driving. It's important to keep you safe. It'll take longer to get there if I have to keep stopping to look at that book.' He held his breath and waited.

He thought Mr Higgerson was going to explode and got ready to leg it, but the high colour in his master's face gradually faded and a grumpy expression took its place.

'You're an ill-educated fool, but we don't want to crash or take for ever to get there, so I'll do the map reading. Go and get the car ready for an early start tomorrow. And make sure there's a rope in the car in case we have to tie my son up. I'm not having him run away as well. And I'm going to make sure he learns to do as he's told and also how to look after himself. I want you to teach him how to fight once we get him started.'

Jem's heart sank. This was sounding worse by the minute. If someone who was nearly a grown man didn't know how to defend himself by now, he'd probably have grown up too soft to learn.

He was getting more and more worried at Higgerson's increasingly strange behaviour, and it was getting worse. Tie up his son? Who ever heard of such a thing?

However, Jem had learned from what Dobbs had done. He had a bag packed so that he could take off and head somewhere else to live at the drop of a hat. His wife had helped him pack it and he'd promised that if the worst happened, he'd send for her when he found somewhere else to live. He'd meant it too. She was a capable lass, and why buy another mare when you had a good one to ride already?

He had a better understanding now of why his predecessor had run off. Dobbs had had enough of being treated like dirt. Jem smiled as he always did when he thought of Dobbs not only stealing Higgerson's car to make his escape, but getting away with it.

Pity he didn't have connections with people who sold cars, or he'd do the same one day down the track as well. In the meantime making money was the main thing he and his wife cared about.

★

Since Higgerson wanted to set off early the following morning, he told Jem to be there by seven o'clock sharp and not to turn up with a hangover, thank you very much. He'd need to be alert. Also, he should make sure he was wearing clean clothes that didn't smell of sweat if they were going to be shut up in a car together for a few hours.

Jem put on his Sunday best and got there just before seven. He soon had the car ready to leave, with the spare can of petrol in the boot. He then had to wait half an hour for his master to be ready to set off.

He didn't whistle as he'd like to while he did a bit of pretend tidying because his master might arrive at any minute and he said the noise of someone whistling hurt his ears. He got angry if he caught any servant idling around, so Jem tidied up the same things twice, moving them about, trying to look busy.

Never mind, it was worth putting up with the fussing about because Jem loved driving even when, as today, he didn't know where the hell he was going.

He enjoyed the driving except when his master read the map wrongly and directed him to turn down a narrow lane anyone could see wasn't a main road, yelling at him to do as he was bloody told. When the road came to a dead end in a muddy little village, his master blamed him, naturally.

Jem got out of the car and asked directions, finding it hard to understand the way the locals spoke, but to his enormous relief, the pointing fingers did the trick and he got them back on the main road.

Once there Higgerson took over giving directions again and they managed to get to the fancy school without any more detours and only a little later than he'd wanted to arrive.

They stopped in a wide open space in front of a huge building. There were two big doors up a flight of steps. Higgerson snapped, 'Get out and open the car door for me, you fool. What would it look like, me opening it myself?'

Jem did as he was told and to his relief, his master vanished into the building. First thing he did was go and find a wall and have a nice long pee behind it.

Kit Higgerson was standing by the window of the classroom, ignoring the other boys and wishing he were outside, wandering through some woods. They were waiting for the teacher to arrive for this lesson, and this particular master was always a little late.

When he saw a car draw up and his father get out of it, his heart sank. What on earth did *he* want?

Soon after that, the teacher came in and the lesson began. It was interrupted almost immediately. One of the junior boys knocked on the classroom door, came in, and handed a folded note to the teacher.

He dismissed the child, read the message and crooked one finger. 'Higgerson!'

Feeling dread in every fibre of his being, Kit went out to the front of the class. 'Yes, sir.'

'You're wanted in the headmaster's study. Your father's come to take you away from school permanently, it seems. Any idea why?'

'No, sir. It's the first I've heard of it.' And he didn't want to leave, let alone go and live at home again permanently.

'Better go and find out, then. Don't keep them waiting. See if you can persuade him to let you stay on. You're bright enough to go to university.'

As he walked slowly along the corridor, the thought of being taken home to live with his father, without his mother to help him stay out of trouble, made Kit feel sick. He'd been dreading the next holidays, absolutely dreading them after the horrors of spending Christmas alone with a drunken father who'd lashed out at him with a heavy fist several times.

He perfectly understood why Felix had run away, and was planning to do the same before he had to leave school at the end of next year. Had the time come to do that?

He slowed down still more, then stopped at the end of the corridor and took a few deep, shaky breaths. Before he could have second thoughts, he turned towards the sleeping quarters instead of towards the headmaster's study.

He rushed up the stairs and into his sleeping cubicle, relieved that there was no one around. He threw a couple of changes of clothing into his sports bag, including some old clothes they used for painting classes so as not to get paint on their uniforms. Grabbing the last of the Christmas money that he'd hidden among his underwear, he shoved it into his pocket and crept down the servants' stairs.

His heart was pounding and he felt literally nauseous with fear. If anyone caught him and realised what he was attempting, he'd be in more trouble than at any time in his whole life. But he had to try to escape, had to at least try.

Luck was with him and he managed to get out of the school the back way and slip along the narrow muddy space behind the lavatories, getting to a nearby copse without being seen. There he quickly shed his uniform and put on the old clothes.

He'd better get off the school grounds before he did anything else.

He walked quietly through the copse, with an anxious moment when he nearly bumped into one of the gardeners. Luckily the man was smoking a forbidden cigarette and had his back to the school, wasn't paying attention to anything but the pleasure of puffing away. He didn't even notice the noise Kit made darting behind a bush.

Once the man had finished his cigarette and moved away, Kit ran to the back fence, hurled his sports bag over the top, and clambered after it.

He snatched up the bag and started running then, not stopping until he reached the quiet lane that led past the village towards the main road. He knew where his mother was living now because his brother had written to him. If it was at all possible, he was going to seek refuge with her.

But first he had to get to her. He'd walk all the way to Wiltshire if he had to, even though it'd take him days. He wasn't going back to his father, whatever anyone said or did.

He was in luck again, had only walked a mile or two, heading south, when a truck carrying some large cardboard boxes stopped and a man leaned out of it to shout, 'You look weary, lad. Where are you going?'

'Swindon.'

'Long way, that. I'm going in the same direction. Want a lift down the road a bit?'

'Yes, please. Thank you very much.'

'Hop on board then.'

When Kit was settled in the cab the man set off again. 'I hope you're an interesting talker. I get bored on long journeys. Tell me about yourself.'

No way was he going to tell the truth, so Kit made up a story about a sick grandparent. It must have been good enough to keep the man entertained, because he not only bought Kit a pie and a cup of tea at a café, but said he could take him as far as Reading if he didn't mind sleeping in the cab for a while when the driver got tired and took a nap.

'Who are you running away from, then?' he asked as they set off again. 'The truth this time, mind, though you do make up entertaining stories, I must admit.'

Kit stared at him in terror and nearly flung himself out of the lorry.

'Don't try it,' his companion warned. 'Now, let's start again. My name is Monty Norton. And your real name is?'

★

Higgerson sat in the principal's office, in a damned uncomfortable chair which stood with two others in a draughty bay window.

The principal made polite conversation about the weather and the fine display of crocuses for a few minutes, then frowned as a clock struck the quarter hour. 'It's taking your son longer than I'd have expected to get here. Let me just go and check that he knows where to come.'

He vanished, leaving Higgerson alone and rapidly running out of patience, even though he usually kept his temper under control when he was with the nobs.

The principal's secretary came in, a fat older woman who seemed to be suffering from a head cold.

'Would you like a cup of tea while you're waiting, Mr Higgerson?'

He held back his anger. 'Yes, please, but could you hurry up with it. I have a long drive home after I leave here.'

She forced a smile and nodded.

It was ten minutes before she brought in a tea trolley, followed shortly afterwards by the principal.

'I'm afraid your son can't be found. We don't understand it. He did get my message. I've sent people out to search the grounds.'

Alarm bells rang in Higgerson's mind. Surely Kit couldn't have run away? How could he have known what was intended today? There was only one way. These idiots must have told him his father had come to take him away.

It was a full hour later that the principal was forced to confess that Kit couldn't be found and they'd looked everywhere in the school and its grounds.

'We'll have to call in the police,' he said.

Higgerson rose to his feet. 'I'm not hanging around while you dither with them. If my son isn't returned to me by tomorrow teatime at the latest, you'll be hearing from my lawyer and I'll be suing the school for every penny I can get out of you. You're not paid annual fees as high as that to *lose* people's sons.'

'But sir—'

He pushed the man out of the way and strode out of the building, finding his chauffeur leaning against a wall chatting to a gardener. 'Stanley! Get over here, you lazy sod!'

'Yes, sir.' He ran across the gravel and stopped by the car, glancing towards the school. 'Has Master Kit been found?'

'No, he damned well hasn't and I'm not hanging around here waiting. They're a bunch of effeminate fools. Drive me home as quickly as you can.'

'I'd appreciate it if you'd remind me which roads to take as we go, sir.'

'Heaven help me! I live in a world full of morons!'

Jem set off, not speaking in case he said the wrong thing. He wondered if Kit had run away like his brother Felix. A voice boomed out suddenly from the back seat, making him jump in shock.

'I've told those lazy sods that if they don't find my son and return him to my care by tomorrow teatime, I'll put the matter in the hands of my lawyer and sue them for a large amount of money.'

'Yes, sir. Quite right, sir.'

Higgerson continued to talk angrily about ungrateful sons and stupid women, then went on to give his views on how lads ought to be educated. But he didn't forget to yell out directions and curse other motorists as they went.

Jem could see in the rear-view mirror that his master was nearly purple in the face with anger and he worried that Higgerson might have a seizure. What the hell would he do then?

It was a huge relief to get back to Rivenshaw, and since his master didn't tell him to stay and do anything else, he locked the car away, sent the key in to his master, and hurried home.

He changed out of his best clothes, told his wife what had happened, then grabbed a cheese sandwich and went off to drown his sorrows in the company of his friends at the pub.

13

Arthur telephoned Charlie Willcox from Maisie's house to say that the pieces of furniture were finished. He thought he saw a little girl vanish up the stairs, just the back of her skirt and skinny little legs still showing. That made him feel sad, reminding him of how long it was since he'd spent time with Beatie.

'I can't come round till tomorrow to check that the repairs are all right,' Charlie said. 'I expect they will be. You sound as if you know about wood. And there's another piece I remember seeing in the dining room that might suit a client of mine, that small bookcase over by the window, so we'll look at what needs doing to that while we're at it.'

Arthur thanked Maisie for letting him use the phone and went to re-join Biff, who was waiting for him outside. As the two men went back to Number 25 he told his companion what Charlie had said.

'If he likes what you've done, and I must say the pieces look perfect again to me, I think we should nip into town and buy you some better clothes,' Biff said.

'I don't have the money to spare, so I'll manage with these. They've still got plenty of wear in them if I'm careful.'

'Those clothes are worn out, suitable only for wearing when you're at home working on mending stuff, not for going outside the house and looking decent. Trust me, what you're wearing will matter a lot more to other people now you're living here.

If you're short of money, I can lend you some till Charlie sells some of your better furniture.'

Arthur went to look at himself in the nearest mirror and pulled a face at what he saw. Biff was right, the clothes wouldn't have attracted attention in a slum area, but he had to look better, not only because of inheriting the house, but also to keep showing people that he was respectable again.

Only, he was so worried about the money needed to run this big house he'd already grown to love that he hated to spend a penny if it wasn't absolutely necessary.

'We can go to Charlie's other shop, the one where they sell better quality second-hand clothes,' Biff said quietly. 'You won't have to spend as much money there.'

'Good idea. Just one or two things, eh?'

Biff went to tell Phil they were going out and remind him to keep his eyes open for any attempts to break in.

'Do you think they'll try that?' Phil asked. 'They know by now that we keep a careful watch here. And people don't usually break into houses in the daytime anyway, not if someone's inside them.'

'Word is that Higgerson is in a tearing rage about something, and even I know that he's famous for lashing out blindly at people when he's angry.'

'I'll be careful who I open the door to. I always am,' Phil assured them.

Biff and Arthur drove off and Phil went round the house, making sure as he went that all the doors and windows were indeed locked.

Ten minutes later he heard the sound of glass breaking in the kitchen, and went pounding down the stairs to find out what the hell was going on.

Gwynneth was in the bedroom she shared with Beatie when they heard the sound of glass smashing somewhere nearby. She rushed to the window that looked out over the backyards. 'Oh, no! There are two men breaking into Number Twenty-five.'

Beatie came to stand beside her just as one man looked up and Gwynneth shielded her from view. Surely the burglar had been too far away to see the child clearly?

She hesitated about going to help, but she couldn't leave these men free to steal things. She was alone in the house with Beatie, so yelled, 'You stay in our bedroom. Bolt the door till I get back, and don't stand near the window where you can be seen.'

She ran downstairs and grabbed the telephone, calling the police number and telling them what she'd seen, asking for immediate help. Then she went into the backyard and stood on a stepladder, trying to get a glimpse into Number 25. Only, she couldn't see the men now. Had they got inside already?

Bella had also come out of the middle house, and called across. 'What's going on? I heard glass breaking.'

'Two men looked to be forcing their way into Number Twenty-five by breaking a window, and there's only one of the Becksleys there at the moment. I've rung the police.'

'If they think they can break into these houses in the daytime, it won't be long before they're coming after us all.'

Gwynneth stared at her for a moment, then said, 'Are you game to go and intervene. There would be two of us, plus one of the Becksleys, and surely they'll run away if someone else turns up.'

'I suppose we could always run away again ourselves if they don't, and look like they're going to turn violent.'

'I'll go in if you will. But get something to defend yourself with. It always makes me furious when burglars get into houses and steal things decent people have worked hard for.'

Bella still hesitated. 'Dare we?'

'Dare we let whoever it is think it's easy to break into these houses? We'll go in the back way.'

She clambered down the ladder and grabbed the big mallet from the yard, one that her son used for breaking up pieces of coal as he loaded the scuttle from the coal shed. Hefting it in her hand, she nodded. As she hurried out of the back gate, Bella came out of the next yard, carrying a poker.

'We should hide our weapons in our skirts,' she called. 'Surprise them if necessary.'

As they opened the end gate cautiously, they heard yelling and shouting coming from inside.

'Sounds like Phil's in trouble. We can't leave him on his own. Let's scream for help before we go in, though.'

They spent a minute proving there was nothing wrong with their lungs, and to their relief someone yelled from down the back alley. 'What's wrong?'

'Burglars in Number Twenty-five!' Gwynneth yelled back.

A man called, 'I'll bring help!'

'That makes me feel better about going in,' Bella said.

'Come on, then. Let's give 'em what for.'

As Gwynneth led the way into the kitchen they saw Phil rolling about on the floor fighting with a stranger. Then there was a crash from the hall. No one seemed to have noticed them.

Bella whispered, 'You stay here. I'll find out what's happening in the hall.'

She found one of the intruders raising a short metal bar as if to smash the hall mirror, and let out an involuntary cry of protest. He must have already smashed a chair lying in pieces to one side.

'Put that down!' she yelled at the top of her voice.

He swung round, lowering the bar briefly, then laughing confidently. 'Ooh, I'm scared,' he mocked. 'A woman is so frightening.'

She backed into the kitchen, still hiding her makeshift weapon in the folds of her skirt. As he followed her and reached out to grab her, she caught him by surprise, walloping him across the lower arm with her poker.

He yelled out hoarsely in pain.

'You'll regret that, you bitch.'

As she backed away again, Gwynneth saw who the man was and stepped forward. 'Let me deal with this one, Bella. You see if you can thump the other one.'

She smiled at the man. 'Haven't you learned your lesson yet, Fred Shorter?'

He stared across at her, looking shocked at hearing his own name.

Phil and his assailant were still tussling on the floor. Bella kept an eye on them, but watched the man who'd just followed Gwynneth in from the hall. He looked frightening to her, but her neighbour suddenly seemed to have lost her fear of him.

She pulled out the mallet and stopped moving. 'I hit you where it hurt most last time you tried to grab me, Fred, and I've a fancy to do it again.'

'Shut up, you bitch!'

'Idiots like you can't make me.'

The man didn't seem to have noticed Bella and was watching Gwynneth as if he really was nervous about tackling her, so she darted forward and used the poker on his nearest leg, taking him by surprise and causing him to stumble backwards.

Gwynneth immediately carried out her threat and managed to kick Fred in his most vulnerable place. He yowled in anguish and clutched himself, bending over protectively.

She stepped back, smiling. 'I learned to do that when I was living in the worst part of Backshaw Moss.' She held her mallet ready, but he was in too much pain to continue the fight.

Phil was still holding his own, but with Fred disabled, his opponent rolled nimbly away and ran towards the back door.

He ran straight into another man coming into the kitchen from the yard, and jumped back again, trying to grab

Gwynneth who was nearest to him. But she wielded her mallet again, and then a second neighbour came into the house, looking furiously angry.

The intruder looked round, as if trying to see another way out, but before he could move the newcomers jumped on him.

Gwynneth smiled down at Fred, who was clearly in agony, raising her mallet again. 'Stay where you are.'

A car screeched to a halt outside the back gate, and a minute later two young policemen rushed into the house.

'Nice to see you, gentlemen,' Bella said with a smile, letting her poker hang down by her side.

The injured intruder winced as he moved incautiously, trying to get up, and one of the constables said, 'Stay where you are.'

The other intruder spread out his hands in a gesture of surrender.

Deemer followed his constables through the back door, moving more slowly than usual. He paused to study the people in the kitchen. 'Having a bit of trouble, Gwynneth love?'

'We were, but I know where to hit a man. I was just wondering whether to kick this one again. What do you think?'

'Don't let her touch me, Sergeant,' Fred begged, edging across the floor away from her, still looking as if it hurt to move. 'She's a wild one, she is. I won't give you any trouble.'

Deemer chuckled openly. 'Beaten by a woman, eh?' He turned to his constables. 'Handcuff them, lads. If they give you any trouble, just ask Gwynneth to help you deal with them.'

The one called Fred shrank back visibly, shuddering and putting one hand protectively in front of his vital parts.

'Fasten their handcuffs to the rails in the car and take them to the lock-up, then one of you come back and collect me.'

He watched them handcuff the two men inside the car before turning back to the group now standing in the kitchen, all of them laughing.

'Folk aren't usually so amused about catching intruders,' he said mildly.

One of the neighbours chuckled. 'It was the daftest fight I've ever seen. Heaven help me if ladies as fierce as these two ever come after me.'

Gwynneth shrugged. 'I'd met that Fred before, yes, and bested him the same way. He looks fierce, but he's never keen to fight unless his opponent is much weaker, the coward.'

Biff and Arthur arrived back just then, and had to be told what was amusing everyone. Soon they too were smiling broadly, though Arthur's smile faded quickly as he assessed the damage.

'What's it going to cost to have those windows repaired?'

'The lawyer will pay for it and I know a glazier who'll fix the windows as quickly as possible,' Biff whispered to him, guessing what he was worrying about.

Deemer was still smiling. 'The best of it is that when the details get out about how you two ladies dealt with them, that sort of chap will keep out of your way for a while, so your houses should be safe.'

'I'll still keep something to defend myself handy,' Bella said.

'I expect these two will get a couple of months in prison. And a certain person will be furious about their failure.' He hoped Higgerson would hold back on causing trouble for a while till the general amusement died down, but it was hard to guess about that lately, the way the man had been behaving.

What upset him most about this incident was that when he questioned the men at the police station, no threats would persuade them to tell him why they'd chosen to try to burgle a house full of broken furniture, or why they'd deliberately smashed several panes of glass.

He could guess they'd been told to make a mess, and was quite sure who had hired them, but as usual he had no proof.

His biggest regret was that he'd not seen Gwynneth vanquish Fred Shorter. What a redoubtable woman she was.

While they were waiting for Mike to come back, Arthur offered the visitors a cup of tea.

'Thanks, but I've got a stew simmering on the stove, so I'd better get back to give it a stir,' Bella said.

'And I've left Beatie locked in the bedroom,' Gwynneth said. 'Another time perhaps.'

As she turned to leave, Arthur grabbed her arm. 'Did you say Beatie?'

'Oh dear! I didn't mean to say her name. Please don't tell anyone she's staying with me.'

'Beatie Hicks?'

'Yes.'

'She's my granddaughter.'

It was a few seconds before this sank in fully. 'I hadn't realised – well, I haven't had much to do with your family. You can't know the family details of everyone in the valley, can you?'

'Is Beatie all right?'

He was still clutching Gwynneth's arm and looked so anguished she patted his hand to comfort him. 'I'm afraid not. She's been badly beaten and ran away from that Hicks woman. I'm hiding the child, trying to give her time to recover, and then, well, I haven't worked out what to do afterwards. She can't go back to that life.'

Arthur closed his eyes, still not letting go of her arm. 'The law will send her back to that harridan if they find out where she is. I have – a bad reputation, so they won't give her to me. I used to drink, you see.'

'I did hear something like that. But you haven't done it for a while, if I remember correctly, have you?'

'It'll still count against me and Mrs Hicks not only has the money to hire a fancy lawyer, she has the support of the minister of her church, who deals with the world as harshly as she does. Please tell me, how is the child?'

'Badly bruised with a few lacerations, all from a vicious caning, I'd guess.'

He sucked in a breath. 'Dear heaven, I'd like to cane that woman and give her a taste of her own medicine, except I've never hit a woman or child in my life. Sergeant Deemer was going to ask the doctor to check Beatie's injuries, but she'd run away and they couldn't find her. The law would probably force him to take her away from you. Can you keep her safe till we can work out what to do? Or even, find a way to let the doctor see her before the wounds heal?'

'I don't know. Let me think about it.'

'You'll go on hiding her?'

'Oh, yes. We even have somewhere clever to hide her if they come searching.'

Arthur looked thoughtful. 'I don't think Sergeant Deemer would search very hard. Everyone knows he can't abide children being hurt.' Then he sighed and added, 'That woman would keep searching, though, and the minister at her church would help her. Even if we kept Beatie safe from them, she'd never dare go out again, and what sort of life is that?'

They were still standing close together, looking at one another, and he suddenly went a bit red and let go of her arm. 'Eh, I'm sorry. I didn't mean to manhandle you.'

'You didn't hurt me.'

'Can I come and see her? I've sometimes been able to watch her from a distance, but haven't been able to speak to her since her parents were killed.'

Biff had been watching and listening with interest, and now judged it time to join in. 'You'd better not go next door till after dark, Arthur lad.'

Both of them seemed startled when he spoke, as if they'd forgotten he was even there.

'He's right. Come around tonight, Mr Chapman. About eight o'clock. It'll be fully dark by then and most people will be indoors. Come the back way and I'll leave the gate unlocked.'

Arthur smiled in relief. 'Thank you, Mrs Harte.'

There was a pause, then she said, 'Call me Gwynneth.'

'And I'm Arthur.'

'I'll tell Beatie to expect you.'

After staring at one another for a moment longer, they both stepped back at the same time.

Arthur spoke bitterly, looking at Biff this time, 'My daughter would have thrown a fit at the mere thought of her mother-in-law taking the child. She fell in love with Peter and they married quickly, but she wouldn't have anything to do with her mother-in-law once she got to know her because Mrs Hicks tried to come between her and her husband. Peter only went round to see his mother once in a while, out of duty.'

'I've heard Mrs Hicks can't keep maids for long and doesn't have any real friends.'

'That'd be right.'

Gwynneth took a step towards the back door. 'I'd better go and tell Beatie what's happened. She'll be anxious.'

'I'll see you to your house,' Biff said.

'My son's wife's house, actually. I've had to move out of the place where I worked because of the fire at Wilf's. I'm going to try and find a new job, as well as somewhere to live, though. I miss my independence, even though Gabriel and his wife couldn't have made me more welcome.'

When Biff came back he found Arthur brushing away tears.

'Sorry. I'm being a fool. But it was so good to hear that Beatie got away. I can't wait to see her again.'

'You love that child. I knew that the first time I heard you speak about her.'

'I might not have gone on the drink if I'd been allowed to look after her. I'd lost nearly everyone I cared about, and my daughter was dead. The drink didn't help, on the contrary, and because of it my son has stopped speaking to me. Ah, who knows anything? I can't blame others for my own weakness.'

'You've got over it now, looks like.'

'I have that! I shall never touch another drop of alcohol as long as I live. In the meantime how are we going to keep Beatie safe from that woman? I'd emigrate to Australia with her to do that if necessary.'

'I don't think you'll need to go that far away. And we also have to keep you safe from Higgerson too, don't forget. Eh, your life's in a right old muddle, isn't it?'

'In one way. In another there's hope crept into it again, what with this house and Beatie. Real hope.' He caught sight of himself in a mirror. 'But if I'm going to see her tonight, I'd better change into my new clothes. You were right about these being on their last legs. I don't want to look like a rag-and-bone man, do I?'

Biff watched Arthur stride up the stairs briskly. It seemed to him that every day the other man was growing stronger, more determined to make a new life. It was good to see, exactly what Jane Chapman had intended the bequest to do.

But how they were going to sort out the problem with that child long-term was more than Biff could see. Surely they'd find a way?

The trouble was, Mrs Hicks had a powerful supporter in the minister from her church. Biff suspected that was because she donated generously to the church. And Arthur had blotted his copybook badly after his wife died. Plus, everyone would say a girl needed a woman to look after her properly.

The first step they could take would be to let the doctor see Beatie before the wounds healed. He'd accompany Arthur next door tonight, and tell Gwynneth that, then suggest she pretend the doctor was coming to see her.

14

Kit sat in the cab of the lorry, gave the driver his real name, and explained what had been going on in his family and why he'd run away. This time he told the absolute truth.

Monty let out a long, low whistle when he stopped. 'You sound so sure your father's that bad.'

'I am. He's probably worse, for all we know. He used to beat my mother, so I was glad for her sake when she managed to run away. I knew I'd have to escape from him too eventually, but I wanted to continue my education for as long as I could. I'd really like to become a doctor, you see, only I don't suppose there's any hope of that now. I've been reading books from our school library about first aid and anything else medical, and of course we've studied the human body in science classes. It's fascinating.'

'Good for you, lad. Just a minute!'

Kit stopped talking to allow Monty to put his full attention on driving carefully through a busy junction.

'There are some idiots driving around,' Monty muttered once the traffic had thinned out a little. 'That sort of family must make life very difficult for you.'

'You believe me, then?'

'This time, yes. There's something about the way people talk about what's happened that shows whether it's the truth or not. Well, it does to me, and I've not often been wrong.'

'Please don't hand me over to the police, then. I'm sure they'll have started looking for me by now. My father and the headmaster will have made sure of that.'

'No, of course I won't. I will have to speak to your mother when we find her, though, just to be absolutely sure I'm doing the right thing helping you, and perhaps her as well.'

'We're going to find her?'

'If we can. Who else would you turn to?'

'I know where she's gone, well, I think I do. My brother said something in a letter, not openly, but I knew what he was talking about. My father never thought to tell the school that Felix wasn't to be allowed to write to me, you see.'

'Go on.'

'So I'm trying to go to them.'

They drove on, and after a while, Monty said, 'It's getting late so if it's all right with you, I'll take you home with me tonight and we'll go and look for your mother and brother tomorrow.'

'Will your wife not mind me turning up without warning?'

'Bless you, no. She'll be quite happy to give you shelter. I've taken in a few waifs and strays in my time.'

'I'd be very grateful for your help.' Kit had to concentrate and dig his fingernails into the palms of his hands to stop tears of sheer relief escaping his control.

They drove on for a while and were nearly at Monty's home when an accident happened so quickly that Kit was never afterwards sure how it could have come about. Another lorry suddenly drove out of a side road and hit their lorry at speed. They spun around so rapidly that Kit was thrown from one side of the cab to the other.

Monty was flung about too, but the window of his door was smashed by a pole outside. To Kit's horror, shards of glass whirled around everywhere in the cab of the lorry. One of the larger pieces sliced into his companion's arm and blood immediately began to pump out through the torn clothing.

The trucks had both stopped moving, but the blood didn't stop pouring out, and Kit guessed that an artery had been hit. He pulled away the shreds of cloth around the huge gash, dragging off his tie and fastening it tightly around the arm in a makeshift tourniquet. He'd never even seen this done before, but he'd read about it and could only hope he'd got it right.

As people came running to help them get out of the twisted wreckage he yelled, 'An artery in the driver's arm has been cut open. Don't loosen the tie.'

The bystanders got Monty out and then helped Kit.

'I've got to help him.' He pushed his way through the group, shouting to let him take over the tourniquet again till they could get help.

Another man came across, calling, 'Someone's gone for a doctor. He says there's one lives nearby.'

Kit continued to keep an eye on Monty, who was still losing blood, but at a much slower rate thanks to the tourniquet.

'That lad seems to know what he's doing,' one woman commented.

He so hoped she was right.

The crowd around them parted suddenly and a man carrying a small leather bag elbowed his way through, calling, 'I'm a doctor. Is anyone hurt?'

'The driver's got a big cut!' Kit yelled back.

The doctor quickly checked the tourniquet and said as he worked, 'The person who did this has probably saved this man's life.'

'It was the lad here who did it.' A man clapped Kit on the back.

'I phoned for an ambulance and it's on its way,' someone called out from a nearby garden.

When it arrived, Kit was told to go in it as well to have his own cuts tended. He hadn't even noticed them, and looked down in surprise at the bloody gashes made on his hands by flying glass, feeling blood trickling down his face as well. He'd read about a new sort of safety glass for car windows that didn't splinter and had thought it a good idea at the time. Pity the lorry hadn't had that sort of glass fitted.

'I'll take over the tourniquet now,' the nurse in the ambulance said gently. 'You've done really well. Just sit in that corner and hold tight to the strap.'

At the hospital Kit told them he was Monty's nephew because he was terrified of being taken away from him. To his relief someone had found the driver's home address in his wallet, so Kit wasn't asked for it.

They took Monty away, tended to his so-called nephew, and left him sitting to one side of the reception area. He felt sick with worry about that kind man.

Half an hour later a lady arrived and she turned out to be Monty's wife. The people at the reception desk were so eager to tell her that her clever nephew had saved her husband's life that they didn't notice the puzzled look she gave Kit.

The hospital doctor came back and took the two of them into a small room further inside the building.

'Your husband will have to stay in overnight, but your nephew can go home with you now, Mrs Norton. You should be extremely proud of him. He definitely saved his uncle's life today.'

Kit had been watching her warily. She didn't say anything to him, but she put one finger briefly to her lips when the doctor wasn't looking, which he took to mean he should be quiet, so he nodded and said nothing more.

Once they got out of the hospital, she led the way across to a car where a neighbour was sitting behind the wheel waiting. 'Say nothing till we get home,' she whispered to Kit as they walked.

'Yes, ma'am.'

Once they were in the car, she explained the situation to her neighbour, and the man marvelled at what had happened, then drove them to her home, which was outside a village along a winding road, with him the only person living nearby.

'Thanks, Tim.' She left the neighbour to put his car away, assuring him that she'd be all right. Then she led the way into the house via the kitchen.

'What's your name, lad?'

'Kit.'

'Sit down and tell me all about it while we wait for the kettle to boil.'

He tried to do so, but suddenly began weeping. 'S-sorry.'

'Shock.' She put her arms round him and gave him a long hug till the sobbing tailed off, then handed him a big handkerchief when he couldn't find his own.

'Right. We both need a nice, sweet cup of cocoa. Are you able to talk now?'

'Yes. And thank you for bringing me back here, ma'am.' He then managed a jerky explanation.

'Ah. That's all right, then. You've told me enough for me to be happy to take you in, because that's what Monty would have wanted.' She chuckled suddenly. 'He's a great one for gathering waifs and strays and sorting out their problems. And you've already more than paid him back for his help, so I'm very happy to give you a bed for the night.'

'I can't tell you how grateful I am, ma'am.'

'Then drink your cup of cocoa and we'll sit quietly for a while. My name's Chrissie, by the way. It'd better be Auntie Chrissie to you from now on, and you can call my husband Uncle Monty when he comes home. We'll work out what to do with you once he's better. He'll figure something out. He's a clever chap, my Monty.'

It was her turn to brush away a tear or two, and she suddenly plonked a kiss on Kit's cheek. 'Eh, if you hadn't been there, I could have lost him. What would I have done then?'

He let her persuade him to go to bed early. He didn't expect to sleep much, comfortable as the bed and hot-water bottle were, but to his surprise he didn't wake till morning.

He found the bathroom as a matter of urgency, then made his way downstairs.

Chrissie smiled across the kitchen at him and gestured to the teapot. 'I heard you moving about and brewed a fresh pot of tea. Would you like a cup?'

'Yes, please.'

As she poured it, she asked, 'Did you sleep well?'

'Like a log.'

'Get that down you and I'll make you some breakfast. Are you hungry?'

To his further surprise he was.

They had a telephone, so she was able to phone the hospital at the time they'd told her to, to check how her husband was, and to her relief they said that Monty could come home as long as he took things easy for a few days.

'You won't run away while I'm gone?' she said to Kit as she got ready to leave with Tim, the neighbour.

'No, ma'am. I have nowhere to go and very little money. And anyway, I've never had an aunt or uncle before. It feels nice, even if it is only pretend.'

'Bless you, we can carry on pretending afterwards, if you like. You've earned a place in our family by what you did yesterday.'

He smiled shyly, not having expected that. 'Thank you.'

'And remember, whatever the rights and wrongs of what your father's been doing, as far as I'm concerned you can come here any time you feel you need shelter, and I know Monty will say the same.'

Kit watched the car drive away and went to sit and read the newspaper. But soon he felt sleepy again so let himself slip into a doze.

Safe. He was safe for a while. How marvellous that felt!

*

Arthur sat and watched the clock until it was five to eight, then stood up and looked pleadingly at Biff. 'I can't wait another minute.'

'Let's go, then.'

'They only live two houses away, so I don't need to trouble you. I can find my own way over that short distance, even in the dark, and surely there won't be anyone else hanging around?'

'Sadly, anyone might be waiting nearby in the darkness, and we'd not like you to get murdered or to lead someone to Beatie, would we? Two good reasons for putting up with my company.'

A shrug was his only answer.

They crept out the back way, putting the lights out before they opened the door, and leaving both Becksley brothers on watch. Biff insisted they stand quietly near the gate and listen for a couple of minutes before going out into the alley. By the time he opened it, Arthur was literally twitching with impatience.

It took only a couple of minutes to slip into Number 21, and when Biff tried the back door, he found it unlocked. Their eyes were used to the darkness by now, and there was enough moonlight filtering in for them to see a man standing inside with a knob-topped walking stick upside down in his hand, ready to defend himself if necessary.

When he saw them he gave a nod of recognition, set the stick down on the kitchen table, and gestured to them to come inside. He locked the back door again before taking them through the house into the sitting room.

Beatie was sitting on the sofa next to Gwynneth.

She and Arthur stared at one another for a moment or two, then he held out his arms and she ran across to fling herself into them, sobbing, 'Grandpa! Grandpa! Where have you *been?*'

He didn't know what to answer, but shame ran through him as it had so many times during the last few months. 'I've been lost,' he managed at last. 'But I've found myself again now, and I've found you, too.'

No one interrupted as they gave one another a long hug, rocking to and fro. He showered kisses on her, and the joy on her face was lovely to see.

After they'd all sat down, Arthur introduced Biff to the child and was about to speak when someone hammered at the front door.

A voice called from outside, 'Open up! Police!'

'Damnation!' Biff muttered. 'They must have found out that Beatie's here.'

Gabriel slipped out of the room and came back almost immediately. 'There's someone knocking at the back door as well. We've got a hidden cellar, though, and you can all three hide down there if you hurry. Follow me!'

He took them down to the normal cellar, fiddled with something, and an opening appeared to one side, showing stone steps leading down. He grabbed a box of candles and a box of matches from a nearby shelf and thrust them into Biff's hands, then the three of them clambered down the steps into the darkness.

The door they'd come through started shutting immediately.

'Stand still,' Biff whispered. 'I need to light a candle.'

When he'd done that he held it up and they stared around.

Arthur's voice was equally hushed. 'I was right about these tunnels. The underground passage from our cellar does lead past all three houses.' He pointed to the left. 'Our house is that way.'

'I don't know how you can tell that in the darkness,' Biff said.

'I'm fairly sure of it, but if you give me another candle I'll go and check, in case we need an escape route. Stay with Biff, Beatie love, and keep very quiet. We don't want them to find you and take you back to your grandmother.'

She nodded, shuddering visibly at that thought.

He was annoyed at himself for upsetting her further. 'Don't worry. We'll keep you safe, love. I'll be back in a minute.' He lit another candle and held it up as he moved to the left.

The other two watched the bobbing light, saw it stop, and then start moving back towards them.

'We can go into my house if we need to. I've worked out how to open it from this side. Eh, it's chilly down here, isn't it?' he said as he joined them again. 'We'll leave some blankets at the top of our steps from now on, Biff, in case anyone has to hide again. There are plenty of spares in the linen cupboard.'

When he put his arm round his granddaughter and gave her a quick hug, she hugged him back.

'I didn't think there'd be secret passages in real life, just in books,' she said. 'I hope no one finds this one.'

Biff smiled across at her. 'I don't think they will. The entrances are very carefully hidden.'

'I'd better not waste candles. We don't know how long we'll be here.' Arthur extinguished his and sat down on the steps. 'Why don't you sit on my knee, love. It'll be warmer than stone steps. Eh, you've grown a lot taller since last time I held you like this.'

But she had never been so thin, and he was quite sure she was undernourished because she had that starveling look to her face. He'd learned to recognise it in other children whose families couldn't afford to feed them properly. Why hadn't she been given enough to eat, though? Mrs Hicks wasn't short of money. Was that woman trying to kill her?

'We should stay quiet in case they come down into the cellar of the house,' Biff murmured. 'Even a faint sound could start them searching.'

The other two nodded and, as they waited, the silence seemed to hug them tightly. They listened very carefully, but didn't hear any sounds from inside the house, so could only hope any noises they'd made earlier had been muffled as well.

Sergeant Deemer was annoyed at being dragged out so late in the evening, because he was still aching all over and he didn't believe what he'd been told anyway by Vanner, the minister from Mrs Hicks's church. He took his senior constable along to drive, and in case there was any physical effort needed.

When they got there, it seemed to take a long time for them to be let into the house. He left it to the younger man to search the place, but Vanner and the two young men whom he'd brought to help search insisted on being involved.

Deemer sincerely hoped they'd find no one hiding. He didn't like or respect Vanner, but unfortunately he couldn't always avoid the man, even though he tried to have as little to do with him as possible. Truly religious people, whatever place of worship they attended, weren't like this arrogant fellow; they were kind and helpful to other people. Vanner was always complaining or scolding or looking for faults in others.

However, there had been no choice about the police being involved because there was a child missing, and it was Sergeant Deemer's duty to look for her.

The minister had sworn very dramatically on a Bible that there had been a sighting of the little girl at one of the bedroom windows in this house by one of the young men from his congregation.

Sadly, the law was on Mrs Hicks's side about who had custody of Beatie. Deemer was worried about the child's safety now, but would be even more worried if he had to return her to her grandmother after what he'd seen in the park several times.

When they were allowed inside, the three occupants of the house denied that anyone had come to visit them that night.

'It was probably someone taking a shortcut along the back alley,' Maisie said.

The minister pointed his forefinger at her. 'You're lying, woman! The child was seen at a bedroom window. Put your hand on the Bible and deny her presence again if you dare.'

She smiled sweetly at him. 'No.' Then she turned back to the sergeant. 'I'm not speaking to him. I prefer to deal with you.'

Vanner actually choked with anger, coughing and spluttering.

Deemer found it hard to keep a straight face as they waited for him to calm down, serious as the situation was. 'Shall we make a start? I'll stand at the rear of the hall, from where I'll be able to keep an eye on both the kitchen area and the back door as well as the front door and the entrances to the various downstairs rooms.'

He could only give Gabriel and the two women a swift, regretful glance as he went to stand there and hope they'd realise that he hadn't wanted to do this to them.

It seemed to take a long time to search the house, and there was so much banging of what sounded like cupboard doors and drawers from upstairs that Maisie went over to Deemer and said angrily, 'I'm going up to find out what they're doing. This is my house and I don't see why they need to search the drawers and cupboards with my underclothes and other personal property in.'

'I'll come with you,' Gwynneth said at once, looking even angrier than her daughter-in-law. 'It sounds as if they're searching my room at the moment.'

Gabriel was about to say he'd go with them, but Deemer grabbed his sleeve and held him back. 'Leave it to your mother, lad. She won't take any nonsense from them. I've seen her get furious at people before.'

He smiled. 'Yes. I have too. Has Vanner had her confront him, do you think?'

'When he arrived, and he's about to feel her anger again. Let's go and stand at the foot of the stairs and listen, in case she needs help.'

'I doubt she will.'

While they were speaking, Maisie had led the way upstairs with Gwynneth close behind. They found the two young men in Gwynneth's room going through her drawers.

'Stop that at once!' she yelled in a very loud voice.

They turned round and stared at the furiously angry woman in shock.

Footsteps sounded behind her on the landing, but she didn't turn, only stepped sideways so that she was completely blocking the doorway.

'What do you think you're doing, going through my underclothing?' she demanded.

'They're looking for children's clothing, on my orders,' the minister said from behind her.

'In my drawers? Are you mad? Do I look like a child?'

'We found some children's clothes in the top drawer. Where have you hidden that little imp of Satan, and what have you done with the rest of her things?'

Jabbing her elbow hard into him when he tried to push past her into the room, she looked across at the small pile of clothes on the bed and laughed. This clearly took all three men by surprise.

'Those belong to Maddy next door, who sometimes stays with me.'

Vanner looked down his nose at her. 'I don't believe you, woman.'

'I don't care what you believe, *man*. You said you were searching for a missing child, not coming here to fumble through an old woman's underwear. Does it titillate you, make you feel shivery here?' She patted herself on a roughly appropriate part of her body.

The two younger men flushed and stepped hastily away from the drawers.

The minister gaped at her open-mouthed.

She raised her voice and called loudly, 'Sergeant, can you please come up here?'

Deemer sighed and made his way with painful slowness up the stairs. He smiled as he heard Vanner start to say something and Gwynneth tell him sharply to be quiet and wait for the man in authority here to join them.

When he got to the landing, he gave Maisie a quick glance full of suppressed laughter, but it was Gwynneth he addressed. 'Is there some problem, Mrs Harte?'

'These young men have been pawing through my drawers. Do they think I've got a child hidden in them? Of course not. Even they can't be that stupid. You couldn't even fit a baby in there. They're just being nosey. Or they like fiddling with women's underwear, or—'

Vanner tried to speak over her, but she just carried on speaking even more loudly than him. '—or else they're stealing things. If there's anything missing, I'll know, and I'll be reporting the theft to you, believe me.'

The minister once again tried to push her away, and she shoved him back even more forcefully with both hands, so that he stumbled a couple of steps backwards. 'Stay out of my room, you dirty old man!'

It was a couple of moments before he righted himself, then his voice was shrill and loud. 'You know very well there's no theft going on, woman! But I still can't see why you'd have a little girl's clothing here if she lives next door.'

'Well, you're even more stupid than I'd thought, old man, and it shows how much you know about real life. Neighbours actually help one another; they don't just talk about it from a pulpit like you seem to do. Maddy from next door stays the night with me now and then to give her mother a rest. She stayed with me in my former home, too. Now that I'm living here, it's even easier for me to help them that way.'

'Is there a little girl next door?' the minister demanded of Sergeant Deemer.

'There are two little girls, actually, and a boy. I know from my own experience that Mrs Harte is friendly with the whole family and is a good neighbour to everyone.'

The minister scowled at the sergeant as if he didn't like this information. 'That's as maybe, but we must be free to search everywhere.'

'I'm afraid not,' the sergeant said. 'I agreed to let you search for a child, but as Mrs Harte says, a child couldn't fit into those drawers, so you have no reason whatsoever to go through them. And since you've had more than enough time to search the whole house, I'm calling a stop to this farce straight away. You were, as I suggested when you came to see me, mistaken, and that's been proven. I'd be obliged it you didn't waste my time again. It's obvious that there is no child hiding here or you'd have found her by now.'

'But we—'

'What's more, I've been called from my sickbed to accompany you tonight, or I'd have taken a more active part in this search, believe me, and it'd have been over and done with in half the time. Nor would you have been allowed to intrude on this lady's privacy in that disgusting way.'

He turned and limped back to the top of the stairs and pointed, 'Go downstairs immediately, if you please. This has been a wild goose chase. Mrs Harte is a law-abiding lady, a regular attender at her own church, and I have the utmost respect for her.'

'But I know she—'

'A recent arrival in Rivenshaw, like yourself, can't know as much as I do after years serving here. You should ask advice before accusing decent folk and behaving indecently with their possessions.'

As this speech progressed the two young men turned scarlet with embarrassment, edged their way to the top of the stairs, and ran down them.

The minister stopped at the top, next to Deemer, to say, 'I shall complain to the local JP about this lack of cooperation on your part.'

'And I'm going to be complaining to him about your false accusations and your damned intrusive way of searching. If those young men are the sort who mess around with women's underwear, perhaps you are too.'

The minister gasped in outrage, gobbling like a turkey as he sought in vain to control his anger and speak calmly. 'You can't! I won't let you—!'

Deemer again jabbed one forefinger towards the stairs. '*Downstairs, sir! Now.*'

The minister glared at him. 'You haven't heard the last of this.'

'Nor have you.'

Sergeant Deemer made his way painfully down the stairs after him and gestured to the constable to open the front door. 'Leave this house at once. There's no little girl here.'

The two young men went out quickly, but the minister moved with exaggerated slowness, turning to have a final word with Deemer from just outside.

The sergeant slammed the door in his face before he could speak, muttering, 'And good riddance to bad rubbish!' loudly enough to be heard by those outside.

Gwynneth came down to join him in the hall, but when she would have spoken to him, he held up one hand to stop her. 'I'm sorry, but it's the other Mrs Harte I need to speak to.'

She stepped back and waited as Maisie moved forward.

'Since you're the owner of this house, I shall report my findings to you. As far as I'm concerned a search has been carried out of your premises with no sign of the child they're looking for being found. I apologise for any inconvenience caused.'

When he finished, Gwynneth would again have spoken to him, but he said firmly, 'And that's all I need to know about your situation here, ladies.'

He stared at each woman in turn, and there was no mistaking the meaning behind what he'd said, so each nodded.

'We'll leave you in peace now.'

The constable led the way out, and Deemer followed, shutting the front door quietly behind him.

He looked along the street. 'Damn me! They're still there.'

'I don't like that man, Sarge. He's . . . nasty.'

'Neither do I. But it's a free country, and we can't stop him parking in public areas and watching this house without a very good reason. Now let's get home.'

'My goodness, I'd not like to get on the wrong side of Mrs Harte,' Mike said as he got into the driving seat of the police car.

'Neither would I. But she makes a very good friend, and has helped a lot of people during these hard times.'

Gabriel had been peeping out of the window and wondering what the sergeant and his new constable were talking about. They sat in the car for a few moments, but eventually he heard the sound of the engine starting up. He waited for the other car to drive away too, but it didn't move.

In the end he let the edge of the curtain fall. 'The police have gone now, but the others are still there.'

Maisie blew out a long, shaky breath. 'That was . . . worrying. Thank goodness for the secret cellar.'

'Yes. And for our sergeant. He'd have done more to help us if he could,' Gabriel said quietly.

'That minister is a nasty creature,' Gwynneth said. 'I'd never go to his church. No wonder his congregation is growing smaller. I know of a family that left them last month and then came to worship at our church instead. Nice people they are, too.'

They went to sit in the living room to wait, continuing their conversation in low voices.

After a while, Gabriel went to peep out of the window again. 'That other car is still there. I wonder if they're going to stay all night. I think we'd better wait a while before we open up the lower cellar.'

'The poor things will be chilled to the marrow down there,' Maisie protested.

'Better chilled than have to go back to Mrs Hicks,' Gwynneth said. 'I warn you now: I'll run away with Beatie if anyone tries to return her to that torture.'

'And I'll help you,' her son said.

'Don't worry. I'm completely on your side,' Maisie said.

15

Arthur was almost sorry when the secret cellar door opened. He looked up to see Gabriel beckoning to them from the top of the stairs. But when he looked down again, he saw that Beatie had fallen asleep and didn't want to give her up. He could have sat there all night with his precious grandchild nestling in his arms if it hadn't been so chilly down here.

Biff went up to the exit and whispered to Gabriel, pointing to the sleeping child.

'Do you want me to carry her up to her room for you, Arthur?' their host called down.

He couldn't deny what Biff had noticed. 'Yes, please. I'm rather stiff and cold. May I suggest that you leave a couple of blankets down here in future, in case anyone has to take refuge in the tunnels again?'

'Good idea. We weren't expecting them to find out so quickly where the child was, but Gwynneth told me it was Beatie's own fault. She'd peeped out of the bedroom window earlier and must have been seen by someone from that church of theirs. They're getting a reputation as a nosey lot since this new minister was appointed.'

'Damn them for interfering in what's not their business!' Arthur said with feeling. 'Is it safe to put her to bed, do you think?'

'I hope so.' Gabriel told them about his mother's confrontation with the unwelcome visitors after their intrusive search.

'It's not really safe here then,' Arthur said in a flat, unhappy voice. 'Why don't you keep her downstairs for the rest of the night in case they come back, then you can whip her down into the hidden cellar if necessary?'

Biff looked at Gabriel. 'I think Arthur's right. Why don't we all sit near the fire with her for a while and warm ourselves. I need to explain about our entrance to the tunnels.'

After they'd rested by the fire for a while, Biff took Gabriel and the two women down to show them how their tunnel entrance led to another one under Arthur's house, pointing to the left from the bottom of the steps.

When they rejoined Arthur in the sitting room, Gwynneth looked at the sleeping child and grew angry all over again. 'If I need to get her away, can I come to your house, Arthur?'

'Of course you can. She's my grandchild, and I love her to pieces.'

'I love her too. I hope you don't mind, but I feel as if she were mine.'

'Why should I mind? You can't have too much love. If it starts to feel even slightly unsafe here, don't hesitate to come and stay with me. Even if they're watching all the houses, they won't know how she gets into my place.'

'Thank you. I shall feel better for having an escape route and another possible hiding place. Just let that horrible minister come near me again while I'm out and about, and I'll give him what for. I won't put up with him interfering in my life in any way, and he can keep his stupid opinions to himself.'

Gabriel gave her a worried look. 'Be careful what you say and do, Mum. You don't want to get into trouble with the law.'

'I'll do what I have to if that child needs help. I feel furiously angry every time I bathe her wounds.'

'Are you sure you can manage to get out of this hidden door on your own?' Arthur asked.

'Oh, yes. I'm sure of it now that I've practised doing it myself.'

'Then let me take you along the tunnel to show you where to go once you're down there and how to open our door from the outside.'

'Good idea. Put Beatie on the sofa. We'll keep an eye on her,' Maisie said.

Arthur watched Gwynneth in admiration. He didn't think he'd ever met a woman as determined as this one. She was magnificent when she was angry. His granddaughter couldn't have found a more caring protector.

He took her downstairs, and they went along to the very end of the tunnel system. He showed her the entrance to his house. She practised opening and shutting it several times, her expression intent.

They did no more than peep into the cellar of Arthur's house, and even that brought Phil rushing down to see what was going on, which was good to see. He knew Gwynneth, but Arthur told him about the child and said the two of them could come and take refuge here if it were ever necessary.

'If they do, it'll be more important to look after them than the house,' he added.

Phil nodded. 'I'll make sure my brother knows.'

Afterwards, as the two of them walked back, Arthur said quietly, 'Thanks for what you're doing, Gwynneth, protecting that child.'

'She's a little love. I wish I had grandchildren. None of my sons have produced any, and they're all over thirty.'

'I'm sure Gabriel and Maisie will give you some one day.'

'I'm hoping so. But I can't see Lucas ever marrying. He's more interested in books and studying than he is in women.'

'You can't tell them how to live their lives. My son won't even speak to me. I didn't blame him when I was drinking, but

I wish he'd give me a second chance now.' He added in a softer voice, 'And I daren't even approach him.'

She patted his hand. 'I'm sure he will come round to it. Do you ever drink these days?'

'No. I'm never going to touch a drop of alcohol again as long as I live.'

'I'm glad to hear it.'

He got another pat for that, which pleased him. Some women were like that, touched other people often. His Susan had been the same.

When they rejoined the others, Biff stared at them, then turned to smile slyly at Gabriel, who had also, from the thoughtful way he was gazing at them, realised how strongly his mother and Arthur were attracted to one another.

The two people in question didn't seem to have realised it yet, or perhaps hadn't dared admit it to themselves. Well, they'd both had some hard years, from what people had told Biff.

He wondered what they'd do about it when they did work it all out. Get married, he hoped. People weren't made to live alone, and from the sadness in her face when she talked about Lucas going off to university, he reckoned she'd miss her son greatly. All things considered, these two seemed well suited to one another, as well as linked by their love for the little girl.

After a while, the two women said they'd better put Beatie to bed now. Gwynneth let her son carry her upstairs, and the child didn't wake up.

When Gabriel came back, Biff said, 'Arthur, we should follow the women's example and get some sleep now.'

He went to the window and peered out. 'Their car is still there, Biff. We'll have to use the cellar route.'

Gabriel peeped out as well. 'Do you think any of them will dare try to come inside here again tonight? Our good sergeant was very stern with them.'

'Trouble is, Vanner has those two young men as obedient as a pair of well-trained sheepdogs. What I don't understand is why he's so antagonistic towards your mother.'

'That's easy to work out,' Gabriel said with a grin. 'She dares to answer him back and argue with him. I'd guess he thinks a wife should act like a mouse and not open her mouth, and believes firmly that all men are superior to all women.'

'None of my family or friends believes that these days,' Gabriel said. 'Yet even Mrs Hicks seems to do as that man tells her.'

Biff sighed. 'There are still plenty of men around with that bossy attitude, unfortunately. When you think what women did during the Great War, it's ridiculous.' He glanced at the clock on the mantelpiece. 'Look at the time. We'd better leave you in peace.'

'I'll come to the cellar exit and make sure you get through all right.'

'Thanks.'

When they got back into Number 25, Phil came to check who it was, smiling when he saw them. 'You're going to and fro between the houses like yo-yos tonight. No need to worry. Everything's peaceful here.'

'Good. The minister and his tame sheep are still out in the street, so we came back via the cellars.'

They'd agreed to explain to their watchmen how the cellars of two of the houses were connected. But they didn't know where all these tunnels led and why they'd been dug out further than the older ones that had led to the quarry. It must have cost someone a fortune.

'I prefer to stay above ground, personally,' Phil said.

'It gives us some extra storage space, if nothing else.'

Rob Becksley rolled his eyes. 'I don't own enough to need extra storage space and I'd not like people to be able to creep into my cellar. Anyway, you go and get some sleep now, Arthur. We'll keep a careful watch, I promise you.'

'I've noticed. Well done, lads. We're grateful.'

The following morning Maisie phoned the doctor and when his wife answered the phone, as usual, asked if he could come to the house to see her mother-in-law, who had a problem that made it embarrassing for her to go out.

When he arrived later that day, Gwynneth greeted him, looking the picture of health, and took him up to her bedroom. She followed him inside, shutting the door behind her.

He smiled knowingly. 'Our good sergeant told me about the situation here. Where's the child?'

'Hiding till we're sure you're willing to help us. She's utterly terrified of being sent back to her grandmother, and you'll see why when you examine her. If you'll wait here a moment, I'll fetch her.'

She brought Beatie back, helped her undress, and he stared at the partially healed wounds in shock. 'Mrs Hicks did this to a child?'

Gwynneth nodded, keeping Beatie's hand clasped tightly in both of hers.

'The child is rather thin. Don't you get hungry, dear?'

Beatie nodded vigorously but seemed nervous of opening her mouth.

Gwynneth said it for her. 'She loves to eat, but she's been half-starved.'

After another astonished look, he asked, 'Why? Mrs Hicks is not short of money.'

'Tell him why, dear,' Gwynneth coaxed.

'My grandmother didn't let me have any tea when she said I'd been naughty, which was most days.' Tears welled in the child's eyes. 'But I wasn't naughty. I didn't dare be naughty in case she hit me again.'

'Dear God, the woman must have gone mad!' The doctor's exclamation was barely above a whisper.

Gwynneth looked across at him, feeling close to tears as she did every time she saw the child's injuries and thin body. 'Well, thank goodness Beatie is eating well now, aren't you, love? She's even asking for seconds, and I love to see her clear her plate.'

Beatie nodded vigorously.

'I'm not letting Mrs Hicks get her hands on Beatie again, Doctor. I'll do whatever it takes to keep her safe.'

'I'm glad you sent for me.' He smiled down at the still-anxious child. 'I won't tell her where you are, dear, I promise.' He made the sign of crossing his heart to emphasise this and saw her relax and sigh in relief.

'I'm prescribing plenty of good food, and keep asking for seconds if you're still hungry.' He turned to Gwynneth. 'Don't just give her bread and butter, but fruit and vegetables, eggs, and cheese.'

'Why did my grandmother say I was greedy and ate too much?' Beatie asked suddenly.

'I don't know. She seems to have forgotten that children need good food so that they can grow bigger and stronger adult bodies.'

The child nodded, as if that made sense to her. But what Mrs Hicks had done didn't make sense to the doctor or Gwynneth.

When he got ready to leave, Beatie snuggled down in bed, and Gwynneth gave her a loving kiss before escorting him down to the sitting room to speak to Maisie and Gabriel.

'She's taking a nap because of her disturbed night, Doctor.'

'My main prescription is for love and good food. And if you ever need me to bear witness that she'd been kept dangerously short of food and beaten savagely by Mrs Hicks, then you have only to call on me.'

'That's what we hoped when we sent for you today. We shan't hesitate to ask for your help.'

'I'll speak to our good sergeant and tell him what I found but pretend officially that you brought her to see me so we don't have to talk about where she is.'

'Thank you.'

When he'd left, Gwynneth went back to check on the child, relieved to find her fast asleep.

'I'm still worried about what that woman will do next,' Maisie admitted to her husband.

'And I'm worried about how deeply my mother will get involved,' Gabriel said. 'She can't bear cruelty, especially when children are involved, and she has a bit of a temper when she thinks something is wrong or immoral.'

'She and Arthur both love Beatie.'

He smiled. 'And they're getting on very well with each other, don't you think?'

'Are you thinking what I'm thinking?'

'Yes.'

'And good luck to the pair of them. I feel so lucky to have you, my darling.'

So he had to kiss her. He couldn't seem to get enough of loving her.

16

Later that afternoon Charlie Willcox arrived to check Arthur's furniture repairs. 'Sorry to have had to postpone my visit,' he said cheerfully as he came in.

He examined the two pieces carefully and nodded in satisfaction. 'You did a beautiful job on these. I knew you would, somehow. You handle furniture like a lover.'

Arthur shot a delighted glance at Biff.

'Can I look at that little bookcase near the window now, see if it's as good as I remembered?'

'Of course.'

Arthur had set it out on the dining-room rug, but it was clear it needed mending. 'I was going to fix it before you came, but we've had some other problems to solve.'

'Oh?' Charlie looked at him inquiringly.

'We should tell him about what's been going on, since he's a town councillor,' Biff said. 'Don't worry, Arthur lad. He can keep a secret.'

Charlie nodded vigorously at that.

So they went through the incident again, though every time they talked about it, Arthur felt anger rise at the minister.

When they'd finished the tale their visitor looked thoughtful. 'I'm surprised Vanner's even got involved.'

'We all were. He's very arrogant, isn't he? Looks down his nose at everyone.'

'You're not the first person I've heard complain about that. Yet he's only the minister at a small chapel that was set up recently. What has he to be arrogant about? As everyone knows, the congregation there has gone down in numbers since they got to know what he's like. I'm surprised anyone donated the money to him to set up a chapel, and that he chose an out-of-the-way place like Rivenshaw to do it in, especially as he seems to hate the area and people.'

Arthur sighed. 'The trouble is, I now have a bad reputation, so even if we could do something legally about Beatie, I doubt the authorities would let me look after the child.'

'I'm afraid you're right. They prefer a married couple when they're placing orphans, and if that's not possible, an older woman. So even without your, er, troubled patch, you'd still have difficulty getting custody of her.'

'My utterly stupid patch, you mean!' Arthur said bitterly.

'Well, you're over that now. I'll keep my eyes and ears open about that Vanner fellow. I don't want newcomers to our valley causing trouble. We have enough of that with a certain local person.' After a brief pause he said, 'Anyway, let's get back to the furniture. How much do you want for the bookcase once you've repaired it, Arthur?'

'Whatever you think fair. I have no idea what it'll be worth. And I trust you.'

Charlie beamed at that, then tapped the side of his nose slowly as he had a think. 'You do the repairs then leave it to me to get the best price I can. It'll bring at least five pounds, I should think, minus my commission, probably more if your repairs are as good as those you've done on the other two, because this one is an eighteenth-century piece. Is that all right financially?'

'Fine by me.'

'Can you lend a hand getting the other two pieces out to the van?'

'Of course.' Arthur stepped forward.

Biff put out his arm to bar the way. 'I'll do that. For the moment, it'd be better if you stayed out of sight.' He didn't say it, but he wouldn't put it past Higgerson to arrange an attack on Arthur – as he had on Sergeant Deemer.

'I can't hide away for ever.'

'Just for a week or two longer. Let me sort the problems out first,' Biff coaxed. 'We need to know exactly who is doing what. Someone has set out to harm you, that's for sure. And we have other folk to think of. I may be able to help them as well.'

Charlie looked from one to the other in puzzlement.

'The Hartes at Number Twenty-one are being annoyed and targeted too.' Biff told him about that house still being watched, this time by Vanner's followers.

Charlie gaped at him for a moment, then said firmly, 'Nice people, all of the Hartes. They can't have done anything wrong. I've bought a lot of pieces from Maisie, good ones too. Her house was so full of furniture when she inherited it, you could hardly get into some of the rooms. There were some really good pieces, and yet others were clumsy cheap rubbish. But even they had a value, and it's better to earn a few shillings than nothing.'

When his visitor had gone, Arthur settled down to do some more repair work. He felt he was marking time till solutions could be found to the problems darkening his life, and that was annoying. But if he could use the time productively and earn some extra money, it'd not be so bad. He was certainly going to need it to look after his house and pay his way in future.

Besides, he always found working with wood soothing. It seemed to set his mind free, and he had a lot to think about. His granddaughter's well-being was the first problem that needed solving. He smiled, as thinking of her immediately brought to mind the way Gwynneth had cuddled her. Lovely woman, Gwynneth. She'd look after his grandchild, he was sure.

He sat very still as it slowly sank in that he was growing rather fond of Gabriel's mother. Too fond? He didn't know.

He'd thought he'd never find another woman who was as 'special' as Susan had been, but maybe he had.

He didn't dare use any other word about the situation yet, so 'special' would do for starters. No use thinking beyond that till he found out what she thought of him, and they sorted out Beatie's problems.

After that he proceeded to think about Gwynneth and Beatie in about equal amounts, as a result of which, his work was slower than usual.

He couldn't help wondering what Susan would have said about all this. She'd have liked Gwynneth, he was quite sure, because he and his wife had always liked or disliked the same people.

He shook his head ruefully. In the past year he'd gone from despair and living mainly on the streets to making his life decent again, then he'd inherited a big house, and hope for the future had blossomed brightly. What a turn-up for the books that was.

You couldn't know what was going to happen to you next in this life, but if he had to choose what he wanted most, it would be to save Beatie from that wicked woman. That child was the most important factor of all to him.

But maybe there was one solution that could help solve two problems at once? He gulped and swallowed hard, feeling his cheeks go so warm he was thankful there was no one nearby to see him.

Did he dare hope for that solution to happen? He didn't deserve it, oh no – but a man could dream, couldn't he? And she didn't have a home, had just lost hers so maybe she wouldn't reject the idea.

As if fate intended to prove it hadn't done with giving Arthur a series of shocks, he had another visitor that afternoon. When the door knocker sounded, Biff called out that he'd answer it, which was good, because Arthur was in the middle of smoothing down and blending in a scratched spot on the bookcase and had to judge very carefully indeed how far to go.

When the door to the small room he'd taken as a workshop opened, he didn't look up at first, thinking it was Biff coming back. Then when no one spoke he did lift his head, only able to stare in shock because his son was standing in the doorway. His son, who had refused to speak to his father for most of the past two years!

Lewis was studying him carefully.

Even after he stopped drinking, Arthur hadn't dared try to see his son and risk another rebuff, not even now that he was getting his life in order.

Their last encounter had sent Arthur hunting frantically for a bottle of something to drown his sorrows, Lewis had been so scathing about his way of life.

'How are you, Dad?'

'Much better than last time you saw me.'

'So I hear. And you look a lot better too. I'd not have come here else.'

'I'm glad you did. Would you like to sit down?'

When his son did so, relief ran through him. He gestured to the bookcase and looked back at the spot he was dealing with. 'I can't leave this even for a few moments because I'm in the middle of doing my preparations for re-polishing it, and it's a valuable piece. I don't want to lose track of even the tiniest detail of how the grain runs, but after I've finished I could make you a cup of tea. If you have time?'

'I do, and I'd like that.' He looked around. 'This is a lovely room.'

'You must have heard about me inheriting this house.' He was hoping desperately that Lewis wasn't here only because of that.

'Several people told me. You're a bit of a nine-day won-der in the town. But I also heard that you'd not have inher-ited it unless you'd stopped boozing and settled down to live decently, which was far more important to me. I hope you don't mind, but I checked that with your lawyer.'

'I don't mind at all because it's the simple truth.'

'Let's get one thing straight, Dad: I'm doing quite well in my job, so I'm not after your money. But it's sad when family fall out, and if the cause of our quarrel has been mended, well then . . . ' His voice tailed away.

'I behaved shockingly, I know, but my world fell to pieces after your mother died. I'd known her since I was a little lad kicking a football around the streets. I didn't feel alive at first without her. And she died so suddenly.'

'Yes, I understood that. And then we lost my sister on top of it all. People who drive cars dangerously fast should be shot! I still miss Dulcie, and I lost my niece completely as well, because Mrs Hicks won't let me see her and sent me a lawyer's letter when I persisted in trying to.' He hesitated, then added gently, 'I also saw for myself that my niece looked unhappy, and then heard that she'd run away from that hor-rible woman. I've been hoping you've given Beatie refuge. It's another reason for me coming here today. Did you? Is she safe?'

'No. I wouldn't dare do that, much as I'd love to. I'm the first person they'd come to see about it. Sergeant Deemer asked Biff about it. But I don't want anyone dragging her back to her grandmother, so if I had to snatch her and run far away from here to keep her safe, I would have to try.'

'Haven't you even seen her?'

'I'd rather not talk about that.'

Lewis frowned and opened his mouth to speak.

'Leave it till another time, eh?' Arthur said gently.

'Can you just tell me Beatie's safe, at least?'

'No. I can't tell you anything. You must be able to swear in court that you haven't heard anything about her from me, except that I denied she ran away to me.'

After a long, thoughtful look, Lewis nodded. 'I suppose you're right. If you're involved, it's better for others not to know about it. And if you're not involved, then I don't want to rub a sore spot in your life.'

'Thank you.' Arthur bent over to inspect the bookcase, nodded and put down his sandpaper. 'It's ready for the glue now. I'll do that tomorrow. Would you like a quick look round the downstairs of the house before I make your tea?'

'I'd like that very much. And you must come outside and see my van. I've got my own sales territory now, selling haberdashery into shops all over south Lancashire.'

Arthur shook his head. 'I wish I could, but Biff, the man who opened the door to you, doesn't want me to go outside. Mrs Hicks's minister has men waiting to get at me, you see. They've been sitting in a car just down the street all day.'

'What in heaven's name has it got to do with him?'

'He claims he's helping Mrs Hicks because she's a pillar of the church, apparently, and he wants to save the child from a wicked man like me. I think it's because she gives the church a lot of money.' He paused, then added, 'Biff is acting as a sort of bodyguard. Jane Chapman's lawyer hired him to keep an eye on me for a while. And I'm very grateful for that.'

His son looked puzzled. 'Do you really need a bodyguard to protect you from churchgoers?'

'Not only from them, but because all the people who've inherited these houses from her have had trouble from Higgerson, who wants to buy the houses for far less than their value and is prepared to hire bullies to persuade us all to sell.'

His son nodded with an instant understanding of the explanation. 'That man is a disgrace! How he gets away with things in the valley is disgusting.' He shook his head in bafflement, then followed his father round the house in near silence.

Holding a conversation was like treading on eggshells, with awkward silences in between what they said, but Arthur consoled himself with the thought that they were both trying to communicate.

After they'd shared a pot of tea Lewis said abruptly, 'I've met a lass, Dad. She's called Edith and I've asked her to marry me. We're hoping to do that next year.'

'Eh, I'm glad for you, very glad indeed. I hope you'll be as happy in your marriage as your mother and I were. No one could have asked for a better wife than I had.'

His son's expression softened and he touched his father briefly on the shoulder in a gesture of comfort. 'I know. It was so obvious how you two felt. If things continue to go well between you and me, I'll bring Edith to meet you. I'm not in Rivenshaw all the time, though, because I have to go out taking orders from shops in my area.'

'I'd like to meet Edith very much. A good marriage makes for a rich and satisfying life and is more important than money.'

When his son said he must be going, Arthur walked with him to the front door and looked at the new van from the safety of that position, admiring it and bringing a proud little smile to Lewis's face.

Biff stayed with him, then hurried Arthur inside and locked the door again even before Lewis had driven away.

What a way to live! And all because of one greedy man and a chapel minister who seemed to Arthur to be a big bully, which was not what you'd expect of a person in his position.

He had to be patient, till everything could be sorted out. But it was hard.

17

When a message was sent to confirm the 'tea party' with His Lordship, though it would actually be a regular meeting in the rocky cavern, Sergeant Deemer asked Dennison Peters to drive him there because his ribs were still sore, and changing gears was particularly painful.

'You're still moving stiffly,' his friend said as they set off, this time late in the afternoon.

'I'm lucky to be moving at all, but it's a lot easier than it was.'

'Well, I've got a bit of good news to share with you today, not group business, a local police matter. I've managed to plant a spy in Higgerson's household: a gardener. That should help us keep an eye on him.'

'Who is it?'

'Jack Webster. He's moved back to the valley to look after his widowed father.'

Sergeant Deemer looked at him in surprise. 'Webster's a good chap. I'm surprised he agreed to do it.'

'He'd be delighted to help trap Higgerson, who drove a cousin of his away by violent means.'

'Will Webster be working for him full-time?'

'Just three days a week. He's working for that new minister to keep the grounds at his chapel tidy for the other two days.'

'Rather him than me, with both of them.'

'You're not kidding. You wouldn't believe what a tight-fisted devil Vanner is when it comes to payment, though. He tried to fine Webster the very first week and take money from his wages for some imaginary fault.' He chuckled. 'Vanner backed off when Webster threatened to quit that very minute if he wasn't paid the full amount agreed, and then sue him for non-payment of wages.'

'He would have done it, too,' Peters said. 'If he'd been born to an upper-class family, Webster would have become a member of parliament or a successful lawyer by now. As it is, he's just bought that small but thriving corner shop in Castrill Street, which his wife and her sister are going to run. That'll bring them an income, in addition to his work as a gardener. And he's going to buy a field and set it up as a market garden. I admire him greatly.'

'He sounds a clever chap. I can't stand that Vanner, though. He's mean spirited in every way.'

'Neither can I. As a JP, I've grown used to liars and thieves claiming that they're honest citizens and have done nothing wrong. I'm not used to feeling suspicious of a church minister who clearly isn't true to his calling. I mistrusted this chap from the start, for no reason except gut instinct.'

'Me, too. Though there's nothing happened to *prove* him a bad 'un, and most people wouldn't even consider that a possibility for a man in his role.'

'Well, I'll continue to trust my instincts and we'll both keep an eye on him. I'll tell Webster to keep his eyes on both his employers, just on principle, but I'm more interested in him providing us with some useful information on Higgerson.'

'Don't count on it. Higgerson has broken the law and escaped retribution for many years now. He's only too adept at doing it, damn him, and still has friends in useful places!'

They fell silent. It was a major frustration to both of them what that man had got away with.

They were among the last to arrive at the cave where the meetings were held, so didn't manage to do much chatting to their fellow conspirators, as the final two members arrived soon afterwards. His Lordship immediately cleared his throat and the group fell silent.

'I'll go straight to what I consider to be the most important item: our local traitor is, it seems from certain correspondence, still happy to welcome a German invasion of our country, but is demanding payment for his services as well as a high position afterwards before he reveals who he is.'

'Hasn't there been any clue to his identity?'

'Unfortunately he has continued to conceal it. I don't know what he's said or done to convince them that he has enough influence to be worth listening to.'

'How do we know about his ongoing efforts?'

His Lordship spread out his hands in a gesture of helplessness. 'I can't reveal my exact source without destroying another project we're keeping an eye on. I'd been hoping one of you might have heard something about who the fellow is.'

He looked around, but people shook their heads.

'Well, I'd be obliged if you could continue making efforts to discover this traitor. It's one way we can serve our country.'

His Lordship let them nod and continue murmuring for a moment or two, then said loudly, 'We come now to the other important item on the agenda: we need to decide whether to push the tunnels further out in case of any future need to accommodate larger groups who might have to live in hiding for a while.'

Peters raised his hand. 'If you do that, you'll have to take into account Higgerson's latest project.'

'What do you mean?' His Lordship asked.

'He's digging out new cellars under some of his rental properties in Backshaw Moss.'

'Is that allowed? It wouldn't be in our local area.'

'It shouldn't be allowed anywhere, but he got three more cellars given special approval when we had two of our group on the council fall ill at the same time with severe food poisoning.'

There was dead silence, then a woman asked, 'Do you think someone poisoned their food on purpose?'

'Highly likely. I'd advise you all to be careful what you eat, and to warn whoever does your cooking not to leave any visitor delivering food in your kitchen on their own from now on.'

The woman who'd asked the question looked horrified.

A man said slowly, 'It can't be safe to dig out cellars if preparations weren't made and foundations laid when the houses were originally built, surely?'

Peters let out a scornful sound. 'When they were built, there were very few regulations, and some people employed rather haphazard building practices.'

'I remember my grandfather telling me about a house collapsing on his street when he was a lad,' one man commented.

'I heard about a similar problem in Backshaw Moss from my grandmother,' a woman said.

'We may have got rid of Higgerson's majority on the council, but regrettably we can't change all the regulations at once or remedy lacks from the past, especially the distant past. Some of those houses have stood there for a hundred years or more, even if they are badly built and maintained. Our group of councillors would lose a serious amount of support in the valley if we tried to have them demolished, even on safety grounds.'

'What about new tunnels, then?'

'I think we should leave things as they are unless we come to a time when war is imminent and the government is still skimping on its preparations.'

'Do you think we'll ever need the present set of tunnels, let alone more of them?' one of the female members asked. 'I just can't see Britain being successfully invaded, not by anyone.'

Others murmured agreement with this patriotic sentiment.

His Lordship raised his voice. 'And yet you come here and help plan for that very possibility, Mrs Farson-Greene.'

She shrugged. 'Better prepared and not needed than not prepared at all, after the last war. And I like to keep busy, do my bit for the valley. If *you* feel it's worth doing, Your Lordship, I'm certainly not going to disagree with you.'

Sergeant Deemer didn't allow himself to smile when His Lordship winced at this fulsome flattery. This woman was known as someone who liked to be in on anything that was being organised by someone important, if only out of sheer curiosity. How she fitted all the various activities into her life amazed him. But she had a good heart in spite of being a snob, and had helped a lot of people during the bad times since the Great War.

He was glad when the meeting ended. It hadn't been an important one, His Lordship's main purpose being to remind people to keep watching out for the traitor, he'd guess, and rightly so. They had to put a stop to that potential betrayal, however, in case the chap infected others. Deemer felt fairly sure that the villain would turn out to be Higgerson. Who else was there with both adequate money and consistently evil intent?

His body was still aching and stiff, but he managed to keep a smile on his face till he got back to the car, then he let himself sag, leaning back in his seat, eyes closed. He was grateful that Peters didn't comment on this or try to make conversation.

There were some jolly decent people in this area of the county. He hoped the services of their group would never be needed, but was glad they were standing ready.

On the way home he had a thought, and asked Peters suddenly, 'Why haven't we asked Charlie Willcox to join our group?'

'If I remember correctly, Mrs Farson-Greene protested against it.'

'Well, she can damned well unprotest. It's wrong to leave him out. He can be a very useful chappie.'

Peters sat frowning, clearly lost in thought, so Deemer left him to it and was rewarded eventually by a sly smile on his friend's face.

'If she were made aware that he's likely to be our next mayor, perhaps she might change her mind. What's more, I think I know how to approach her.'

'How?'

'Through my sister.'

'She is another person who ought to have been invited to join our group. Very capable woman.'

'I agree. I've been wondering whether to . . . Look, leave it to me. I'll have a quiet word with Veronica and with His Lordship. We definitely need more women in our group. And those who've been running Women's Institute groups, as my sister has, have developed some excellent skills at organising people and activities. The country has owed the WIs a lot from when they were first founded during the Great War, and they've quietly gathered strength all across the country since then.'

Kit felt rather shy when Monty returned from hospital, but he was given a beaming smile and invited to join him and his wife in the sitting room.

He watched anxiously as Monty sat down carefully, easing his arm a little in its sling. When he found a soft cushion to set under the injured arm, his host smiled at him.

'Thank you. Do sit down with us. I'm not used to being out of commission. I gather I owe you thanks for saving my life, Kit.'

He could feel himself flushing. 'I just happened to know how to make a tourniquet.'

'I'm very glad you did, lad, believe me. Some would have panicked and messed things up, however much they knew in theory. I'm supposed to spend a few days resting, and I shan't be able to drive for a while, so I can't take you to find your mother yet, I'm afraid. I must admit to feeling rather weak.'

Kit dared say, 'If you could lend me some money, I could take the train, sir. And I promise I'd pay you back.'

'I think we should look into your mother's situation first. We don't want you leaping from the frying pan into the fire. Do you know the name of the people she and your brother are staying with in Swindon?'

'Yes. Tillett. He's a merchant of some sort.'

'I wonder if he's the Tillett who sells rugs and carpets both to the public and to shops. They sell other things too. I've delivered all sorts of items for a company run by a gentleman of that name over the years. Eh, we should all be so successful!'

'I don't know any details, just that my brother works for someone of that name and because of his protection my father hasn't been able to get at Felix, which makes him absolutely furious.'

'If he's the Tillett I think, he'll have the money to protect them both, and he's well thought of as an honest trader. But the more you tell me about your father, the less I like the sound of him.'

Kit couldn't help shuddering. 'I'll be happy if I never see him again as long as I live. I think if he managed to capture me and take me back to Rivenshaw, I'd be in serious trouble, not to say in danger of losing my life. He can be vicious when crossed.'

'To the extent that he'd kill his own son? Surely not?'

'Oh, yes. If he got into one of his blind rages he'd do anything. And he'd hurt his own wife too, for running away from him. I know Mum was in fear of her life towards the end. Only desperation would have given her the courage to leave.'

'Shame on him. Well, I'll not be able to do anything to help you today, because I'm a bit tired. I don't know how any patient ever manages to get a good night's sleep in a hospital, because people are making noises around you all night long, not to mention nurses waking you up to check on you.'

Monty fell asleep a few minutes later and his wife put her forefinger to her lips, so Kit sat there quietly, enjoying the peace.

His host didn't wake up until his junior partner in the haulage business came to the door and refused to go away, insisting loudly that he knew Monty was home, and he absolutely had to speak to him today about the damaged lorry if they were not to lose money hand over fist by it being out of commission.

Fortunately Monty had woken feeling a little better, and was able to deal with the matter of repairs and hiring a stand-in driver to keep deliveries going until he was better.

When his wife quarrelled cheerfuly with him afterwards about what he was and was not fit to do, Kit watched in amazement. He had never seen people arguing and smiling like this because of wanting the best for each other.

It ended when Monty grabbed his wife and gave her a smacking big kiss, agreeing reluctantly to take a day or two off work, adding, 'If only to stop you nagging me, woman!' in such a teasing voice that it made the lad smile.

It also made him wish yet again that he'd had a decent father, and his mother the loving husband such a kind and caring person deserved.

When Monty fell asleep again, Kit asked in a whisper whether he could do anything to help his new 'Auntie Chrissie'. She set him to filling the coal scuttles in the downstairs rooms, then doing a few other small jobs around the house. She had to show him how to do some of the tasks because his father had always refused to let his boys do any 'women's work'.

They all went to bed early, and to his surprise Kit had no trouble falling asleep. In fact, he could hardly keep his eyes open.

It was such a lovely, comfy home, seeming full of love and he felt so safe there.

18

A few nights after Vanner had insisted on Deemer searching Maisie and Gabriel's house, a small group of men gathered just after midnight in the laneway behind the three houses on Daisy Street. They couldn't get inside Number 21 the back way because the gate was padlocked, but their minister had told them he would hire someone to help them gain entrance to the house, all in the name of justice. Finding the child would prove the people inside guilty.

So they waited, as rain poured down and the minutes ticked slowly past.

After a while a couple of men slipped away to the comfort of their own homes. 'Justice be damned!' one of them said to the other. 'I don't intend to catch my death of cold.'

'Me neither. We don't know for certain the child is there, whatever he claims.'

Grumbling about the weather, the rest tried in vain to find more sheltered spots nearby as they waited for the locksmith.

'Why isn't Vanner here braving the weather with us?' one man whispered to another.

'He damned well ought to be. This was his idea in the first place.'

'My wife said I shouldn't have listened to him.'

'So did mine.'

Before they could talk themselves into leaving, the locksmith turned up, escorted by a church elder, who indicated the gate he needed to unlock.

The men all moved closer and waited, shoulders hunched against the downpour.

Seeming oblivious to the weather, the man clambered up on to the top of the gate to look over it and check how it was locked.

'It's only an old padlock. Useless, that one is.' With a soft chuckle he leaned over and began to fiddle with it.

The street lamp at the end of the back alley shone on him and one man nudged another. 'Who the hell is he? There's no locksmith like him in Rivenshaw.'

'Look how far he's leaning over it. He'll fall head first into the yard if he doesn't watch out.'

The elder turned around and said in a low voice, 'Shut up! Do you want someone to hear us?'

'I just want to get out of the damned rain.'

As the men shuffled to and fro in a vain effort to warm their feet, the grumbler moved back to stand near the gate of the next house, which was at least out of the worst of the wind. He bumped into it, setting it rattling slightly.

'Stand still, you fool.'

'You're even more of a fool. I don't know why I let you persuade me to come here.'

'*Shut – up!*'

Inside Number 21, Gwynneth was having trouble getting to sleep. She hadn't done more than doze, jerk awake, then doze again, because she couldn't stop worrying about what Mrs Hicks and her horrible minister might try next.

The sudden rattle of a gate caught her attention and that alerted her to other faint sounds. She sat up in bed, trying to work out what was going on. That sort of noise hadn't been made by cats or the wind.

She slid out of bed and went across to peep through the window in time to see the back gate of their house open slowly and several men shuffle through it into the yard.

Letting out a small, muffled whimper she ran along the landing to wake Gabriel, whose room was at the front of the house, going up to the bed and shaking him.

'Come quickly and look through my bedroom window. Some men just came into our backyard. They must be intending to break into the house.'

He ran to look, shocked at what he saw, 'Oh, hell! You stay upstairs with Beatie.'

He pulled trousers on over his pyjamas and went downstairs.

Maisie shrugged into her dressing gown and followed him.

Gwynneth hesitated for a moment, then took a decision. This incident showed that Mrs Hicks and the minister were not going to give up trying to get Beatie back, so she wasn't waiting any longer to move the child across to Arthur's house. He'd want to save his granddaughter, she was sure, and he had such a kind face, she trusted him absolutely.

She shook the child awake and told her to get dressed quickly and quietly, explaining that some men were trying to break into the house. 'We'll have to escape through the cellar to your grandfather's.'

'But—'

'No noise or lights. Hurry!'

She slung on her coat over her nightie and picked up the bag of Beatie's clothes that she had set ready 'in case'. Beatie didn't have many garments, poor lamb, so Gwynneth was able to stuff some of her own clothes in from the top drawer as well, and bundle the few remaining items into a pillow case.

Another peep out of the window made her thank her lucky stars that she'd planned ahead. There were half a dozen men down there, but only Gabriel and two women to protect the house.

'Come on, love. They've not got in yet, so you and I have time to move to your granddad's house. We'll be safe there.' She pulled on a skirt over her nightie as she was speaking.

'Has my grandma sent them after me?'

'I think so. Hurry up.'

'I'm frightened of her.'

'I won't let her take you again.'

While the child finished dressing, Gwynneth made the bed, then looked around. The moon was dipping in and out of the clouds, letting her check that nothing showed anyone had been sleeping there.

'Come on, love. Move as quietly as you can and don't try to switch on any lights.'

Gabriel heard someone try to open the locked back door and peered out through the pantry window, shocked at how many men there were. Too many for him to fight. He'd have to fetch his mother and Beatie, then help them down into the hidden cellar.

He turned to go upstairs, praying he'd have time to hide them before the would-be intruders forced the door. Men coming out in the middle of the night in the pouring rain wouldn't knock and stand around trying to negotiate. They'd do whatever it took to break down the door and get at the child, he was sure.

Thunder rolled loudly across the sky. Would the neighbours hear any calls for help if the storm continued?

To his relief, his mother had already come down.

'I'm going to stay with Arthur. Can you help me get the hidden door open, then close it after me, Gabriel love?'

'Yes, Mam. I'll get you away first, then I'll phone Sergeant Deemer.'

Maisie moved forward, barefoot and wearing her warm woollen dressing gown. 'I'll phone the police, love. You help your mother and Beatie to get away.'

Gwynneth blew her daughter-in-law a quick kiss, then she and the child followed her son down into the cellar. Once they'd shut the door to the hall behind them, he switched on the light.

He was in the middle of getting the secret door open when they heard a big thump from the kitchen area. He glanced upwards, frantic with worry for his wife. 'Hurry up, Mum. Take this torch.'

As he thrust it into her hand, the two fugitives crept out on to the stone steps that led to the hidden tunnel. The door closed above them, leaving them in utter darkness.

As Beatie whimpered and clutched her with a hand that trembled, Gwynneth fumbled with the torch and managed to switch it on. 'There, that's better.'

'I don't like it so dark.'

'Neither do I. Good thing we've got this torch.'

'It's not very bright.' Beatie flung her arms around Gwynneth's waist. 'I'm frightened.'

'Don't be. It's bright enough to show us the way, and it won't take long to get to your granddad's house.'

She dropped a kiss on the child's forehead and gave her a quick hug. 'There's nothing to be afraid of now we're down here, love. Come on. Let go of me and start walking.'

She thrust the pillowcase at her. 'You carry this bundle and I'll take the big bag.'

'You won't walk too fast and leave me behind?'

'Of course not. I'd as soon leave my own head behind as leave you.'

That brought a faint giggle from Beatie, and they began moving carefully down the steps.

Gabriel ran back up to the kitchen, relieved that Maisie was safe in the hall, speaking into the phone. The back door was a heavy one and the windows not only had bars across them but consisted of small panes set in solid wooden frames, making it difficult to break into the house that way.

These people seemed to be hurling themselves against the door now, grunting with the effort. Were they trying to batter it down? They'd have trouble getting it open. It had huge, old-fashioned hinges, with big bolts top and bottom, as well as the lock in the middle.

He disliked fighting and violence, but tonight he'd do whatever he could to protect his family. He heard his wife speaking to the sergeant as he went through to the kitchen.

Furiously angry now, he yelled at the would-be intruders more loudly than he'd ever shouted in his whole life, 'What the hell do you want? There's nothing worth stealing here.'

The banging on the door stopped.

Someone yelled back, 'We're not trying to steal; we're honest folk and we're here for that poor little lass that's been stolen away. She should be in her grandmother's care, not a stranger's.'

Another man called, 'Be a sensible chap and open this door, then you won't get hurt!'

He didn't recognise either voice and he didn't believe they wouldn't get hurt. These men had already damaged his property, and he bet they'd do the same to the rest of his house. Besides, he wasn't stupid enough to open the door to any group of strangers in the middle of the night.

He looked around and picked up the poker to defend himself, then yelled, 'We've called the police and reported burglars trying to get in.'

'We're not burglars, damn you, we've come to free the little girl.'

'What little girl? There's no child here.'

'Liar!'

They rattled the door again, and Gabriel was glad for the iron bars on the windows.

'You're a liar, Harte. We know she's there. *Open – this – damned – door.*'

It rattled several times but held fast, then someone shouted, 'Move back. I've found an axe.'

His heart sank. 'I'll thump anyone who tries to come inside.'

Maisie came into the kitchen. 'The sergeant will be on his way after he's called his senior constable, but neither of them will be able to get here for a few minutes.'

'Go and lock yourself in our bedroom, love.'

'No. I'll fight beside you, if necessary. This is my home.' She brandished a big meat hammer.

The noise the group of men made as they continued to yell and hammer on the back door of Number 21 woke everyone in the other two houses, in spite of the thunder.

In the middle one, Ryan got up and stumbled into the back bedroom to look out of the window. His wife joined him.

'What's going on?'

He put an arm round her. 'I don't know. Some men seem to be trying to break into next door. I'd better get some clothes on in case, then go and help Gabriel. You keep an eye on them while I do that.'

In Number 25 Arthur yanked some clothes on over his pyjamas and joined Phil Becksley, who was keeping watch that night, to peer out of the landing window.

'There are people outside at the back. I can't see very clearly but I think they're trying to get into Maisie and Gabriel's house.'

'We'll see better from Biff's bedroom at the back. Sounds like he's up.' They found him looking cautiously out of his bedroom window, half hidden by the curtain.

He gave them a quick glance, then turned back to watch. 'A group of men have got into Maisie's yard and are trying to force their way into the house.'

Lightning lit up the scene. 'Looks like they've got an axe now.' Phil frowned.

Arthur went to stand behind the other curtain. 'They must be after Beatie. I reckon Gwynneth will bring her to hide with us here as we arranged.'

'She's bound to. Let's go down to the cellar, open the secret door and check whether she's on her way.' Biff began moving towards the door. 'Phil, if you think they've got inside and Gabriel needs help, run down and let us know, then be ready to go to his aid. I'm sure other neighbours will help them too. But you stay here in case they come after Arthur.'

'I'd rather go outside straight away and punch them good and hard. Have they run mad?'

'Hold on a bit. See what happens.'

Biff followed Arthur downstairs. In the cellar they switched on the light, then fell silent and listened intently at the panel that led to the tunnels.

'We won't be able to hear any sounds from here,' Arthur said impatiently.

Biff pulled him back. 'Other intruders might be waiting in the tunnels, for all we know.'

Arthur shook off his hand. 'I doubt it. The sergeant said no one in town knows about the passages and I'm not to tell any-one. It's Beatie and Gwynneth I'm worried about, not myself. I can fight if I have to.' He began to open the secret cellar door.

Looking at his determined expression, Biff nodded, pleased to see the man he was guarding find the courage to deal with whatever life threw at him.

Arthur got the door open and saw only darkness. 'I still can't hear anything. I hope they're on their way here.'

'Let's hope those men don't come to your house next. They might remember that you're the child's grandfather.'

'If someone tries to break in here, they'll meet my fists,' Arthur said sharply, then added slowly, 'This can't be bur-glars, surely. People who break into houses do it quietly.'

'Well, even if they do get into Number Twenty-one they won't find that child.'

'*Shh.*' Arthur nudged his companion and pointed to the right where there was now a faint gleam of light in the distance. 'Look! Someone's coming.'

'Be careful. Don't rush into danger.'

'To hell with careful! It can only be Gwynneth bringing my Beatie here.' He didn't wait, but went down to stand a few steps lower to get a better view.

Gwynneth and Beatie started making their way along the dark passage, moving slowly and carefully, shining the faint beam of the small torch to and fro across the ground in front of them. Beatie was still clinging to Gwynneth's arm, which further slowed them down. Eh, it hurt to see a child so terrified.

The middle house didn't have a hidden cellar, so there was no flight of stone steps to mark its existence, but it seemed to be taking longer than Gwynneth had expected to get to the third house. Surely she hadn't turned the wrong way?

Then she stopped dead because a light shone suddenly in the dimness ahead. It took her a moment or two to make out two men standing part way up the stone steps. One man was shining a torch down the steps and the other was shining his light on his companion as if trying to show them who he was.

Beatie let out a little squeak and suddenly ran ahead, leaving Gwynneth standing alone in the near darkness.

'Granddad!' The child hurled herself at him, and Arthur picked her up for a quick hug before shining his torch back down towards the solitary figure.

'Let Biff take you into the house, love. I have to wait for Gwynneth.' He nudged Beatie gently towards the other man. 'Look after her, lad.'

Then he hurried down the steps calling, 'Well done, Gwynneth!'

As they met, he took the bag off her and put one arm round her shoulders. 'Are you all right, lass?'

'I will be if we can stay with you.'

'Of course you can. I'm glad you brought her to me.'

She looked back into the darkness.

'Is someone else coming?'

'No, I'm worried about my Gabriel. He closed the entrance to the tunnels behind us, but now he and his wife will be facing those men on their own. Maisie had just phoned the police when we left, but it'll take them a few minutes to get here.'

'Who was trying to break in? Could you tell?'

'It was too dark to see their faces. They were shouting that they'd come to rescue Beatie. *Ha!* Taking her back to her grandma would put her in danger again.'

'They must be from that nasty little so-called church. Careful up these steps.'

Once they were safely inside the cellar of the house, he said to Phil, 'Can you keep watch over our yard? I don't want them coming here and taking us by surprise.'

'Yes, of course.'

Biff smiled down at the child in his arms. 'Let's all go up to the bedroom your granddad got ready for you. It's got lovely comfy beds.'

She leaned her head against him with a tired sigh.

He waited to say to Arthur, 'You'd better check that all the downstairs doors and windows are locked before you follow us. You can never be too careful about such details.'

He started up the stairs without waiting for an answer, smiling slightly even at a time like this at how close Arthur and Gwynneth had been standing to one another. They looked like a couple already.

When Biff had gone ahead, Arthur saw how anxious Gwynneth was looking and said gently, 'Let's check all the doors and windows, then we'll go and join Beatie.'

When they'd done a quick check, she stopped at the bottom of the stairs. 'I've not heard any cars arriving, Arthur.'

'There hasn't been time yet for the sergeant to get here. But he'll have a clear road at this time of night, and his new constable is in Birch End, so he'll get here even sooner.'

He saw tears shining on her cheeks and pulled her into his arms, holding her close. 'We'll look after you and Beatie, lass.'

'I don't know why I'm crying. We're safe now. Only, I was so afraid we'd lose our way or they'd find the cellar and snatch Beatie from me before I could get her to you.'

He kept hold of her, rocking her slightly, and couldn't resist dropping a kiss on her forehead.

She looked up at him, startled, and for a moment they didn't move or speak, then they pulled apart self-consciously.

She gave him an uncertain smile, but a smile nonetheless, and somehow he found the courage to say, 'It's not the time for you and me to get to know one another better *yet.*'

'No. I hope we can do it later, though.'

'Be sure of it. Let's join Beatie for now.' Still smiling, he picked up her bag and took her hand. Eh, it felt so right in his! She'd said 'later', and she wasn't trying to pull her hand away! He felt hopeful.

They went to join the others upstairs. The only light came from moonlight shining through the various windows because the thunder and lightning seemed to be fading away now, but their eyes were used to the dimness.

They could see Biff sitting on the bed next to Beatie, but as Arthur and Gwynneth came into the room, the child ran to fit herself between them, taking hold of a hand from each.

'We'll be all right here, won't we, Granddad?'

'Of course you will, love. I don't think they'll even try to get into this house. Why should they? There are no lights showing, and they don't know about the tunnels.'

'Are you sure they don't?'

'Very sure of it, love.'

'Good.' She yawned suddenly and sagged against him.

'I think the best thing we can do is get you into this nice warm bed. Will this room be all right for you two, Gwynneth lass?'

'It'll be perfect. We'll each be snug as a bug in a rug with such lovely thick quilts.'

Beatie sighed out her breath in a big whoosh, but when he turned back the covers, she looked around with a frown. 'I can't see very clearly what the bedroom's like, Granddad. If we drew the curtains first, we could put the light on.'

'Better not. The curtains wouldn't be enough to hide the light completely. We don't want to show even a tiny glow. You'll be able to see every last detail in the morning.'

Gwynneth pulled the covers back. 'Never mind getting undressed. Get into bed as you are, and your granddad will pull the covers up. You'll soon be as warm as toast.'

'Oh, lovely.'

'Here you go.' As she lay down, Arthur tucked the covers right up to her chin. 'Can I give you a goodnight kiss?'

She held up her face instantly and he kissed first one soft little cheek then the other.

Gwynneth added kisses of her own. 'I'll wait with you till you get to sleep, Beatie love, but then I might need to talk to your granddad. If you wake up later and there's no one here, don't panic and don't put the light on. We'll only be downstairs.'

She sat on the end of the bed, while he stayed by the door, watching them both. It didn't take long for the exhausted child to fall asleep, then he said quietly, 'You'll be all right in this house, lass. I'll make sure of it.'

'I know. I feel safe with you already.' She couldn't hold back a yawn, she hadn't been sleeping well lately.

'Do you need a drink or anything?'

'No. I thought I did, but it's mainly sleep I'm short of.'

'There isn't a bathroom, I'm afraid, but there's a chamber pot under the bed and a jug of water on the stand.'

'Thank you.' She was a bit embarrassed to be discussing the presence of what she'd always called a 'po', though she'd had to use one for much of her life rather than stumble across dark yards to outdoor lavatories in rain and snow.

'I'll leave you to it, then. There'll be at least one of us three men on watch at all times.'

'Good. And Arthur? I'm glad you're here.'

'I'm glad you are too.'

He felt ten foot tall as he walked down the stairs to think how she trusted him. He wouldn't let her and Beatie down, not in any way. He seemed to have found his old self again.

Biff and Phil were waiting for him in the entrance hall.

'We should take it in turns to keep watch till the police have sorted out that lot of idiots along the road. Trying to break into houses, indeed! What is the world coming to?'

'You two could get some sleep,' Phil said. 'Believe me, I'll notice it if anyone tries to get into this house.'

'I doubt they'll even try,' Biff said. 'Why should they? There are no lights switched on. But until the police have got rid of those pests, I'll keep watch from my bedroom at the back as well, and you can watch the street at the front from your window, Arthur. Better be sure they're not coming to get us as well because of you being the child's grandfather.'

'I'd expected the police to be here by now.'

'They won't be long, I'm sure.'

19

When Mike Grafton arrived in Daisy Street, the storm was starting to abate. He took a brief detour and parked his motorbike further along from the house in question. As he walked slowly along the street, he wiped rainwater from his face with his forearm. There didn't seem to be anyone around except for whoever was making a noise at the rear of Number 21.

His sergeant's instructions were to wait for him before confronting the men, unless there was an emergency, in which case he'd have to use his own judgement on what to do.

A man stepped out of a gateway and said, 'Glad to see you, Constable.'

He jumped in shock and moved back a step, annoyed at himself for being taken by surprise, but with the wind rattling anything movable it was all too easy to creep up on someone.

'Don't worry. I live on this street and I'm on your side. So is my friend.' He pointed to another man peeping out of a gateway further along his side of the street.

'What are you doing out here?'

'We were just going to find out who's making that racket and if our neighbours need help, Constable. The noise must have woken the whole street up.'

'The lady from Number Twenty-one called the police to say that a group of men is trying to break into her house at the back.'

'A *group* of men? Why?'

'I don't know yet. I'm waiting for the sergeant to arrive.'

'I never heard of such a thing. Have these chaps run mad? This is England not the wild west!'

'I'd like to go round the back to have a peep at the situation. Will you wait here, in case I need help?'

The man nodded and beckoned to the other one to join them.

'Tell him what's going on, then you two wait here!' Mike ordered.

As they both nodded, he crept along the side wall of Number 21, moving carefully from shadow to shadow. But though there was still a group of men at the rear, they didn't seem to have got inside, and two of them at least were arguing about how best to proceed. They weren't even attempting to keep watch.

A regular thumping sound began suddenly and he hesitated, wondering what exactly it was and whether or not to intervene.

Then he heard a cry of '*ouch!*' and the noise stopped.

'What the hell are you playing at?' someone called out.

'The damned axe slipped an' I banged into the door frame.'

'Can't you do better than that?'

'This is the hardest wood I've ever tried to chop,' the axeman complained.

The thumping began again, but more slowly this time. Mike wondered if he should intervene to protect the property, when he heard a sound in the distance. He strained his ears. It sounded like a car engine and was coming closer, so he went back to the front of the house. It could only be the sergeant.

He kept an eye out for any of the would-be intruders following him, but the men stayed at the rear. Not only were they making a lot of noise, but thunder was rumbling from time to time. They might not have even heard the car. He was puzzled. They didn't seem to be at all experienced at breaking in. And why were there so many of them?

Headlights played along the street, showing up every bump and puddle-filled hollow as the police car rolled slowly to a halt in front of Number 21.

As Mike moved towards it, Sergeant Deemer eased himself out stiffly. 'What the hell is going on here?'

He explained what he'd seen so far, then indicated the two neighbours.

They moved forward to join them. 'Need some help, Sergeant?'

He turned and squinted at them. 'Indeed we do, Fred. And Sam. Thank you for offering.'

'We live here, Sergeant. This end of the street is respectable, and we're not letting anyone from the other end start damaging our homes and putting our families at risk.'

His companion nodded agreement.

'Thanks, lads.' He turned and listened, frowning. 'Eh, it sounds like amateur night at the opera back there, doesn't it?'

Another quarrel seemed to have broken out.

'They're not your usual burglars,' the sergeant said. 'They'll probably run away when they realise I'm here, but if you lads can catch any of them it'll be a big help.'

He turned to Mike. 'Let's go round the back. I will not have riotous behaviour taking place in my town. Who do these people think they are?'

Their two helpers nodded agreement to that.

The intruders did indeed try to run away when he got to the back and roared, 'Police! Stop that at once!'

Three of them were caught, one because he tripped and obligingly fell over Fred's outstretched foot. With his help, Mike managed to handcuff two of them together while Sam kept hold of the wildly struggling third.

'What the hell did you think you were doing?' Sergeant Deemer asked loudly.

After a pause, during which two of them looked at the third, who was older, the man said, 'We were trying to rescue that little lass that's gone missing. You police should have been here doing that job.'

'Are you talking about Beatie Hicks?'

'Who else has been kidnapped by that wicked Harte woman?'

The sergeant grabbed a fistful of the man's jacket and anger gave him the strength to shake him like a rat. 'I'll have more respect when you talk about that lady.'

The man glared at him, but didn't say anything else.

Deemer turned to their two helpers. 'Don't I remember that you've got a van, Fred?'

'Yes, Sergeant.'

'Can I have the use of it to take these criminals to the police station?'

'Definitely. I want them punished so that they won't do this sort of thing again.'

'We're *not* criminals,' one muttered.

Sergeant Deemer poked him good and hard in the chest. 'You are when you break the law.' He turned to his helpers. 'Let's take them round to the street. We'll wait there while you fetch your van, Fred.'

'Won't take me a tick.'

He got his handcuffs out of the police car as they waited. 'I think we'll handcuff the third one to the others, Mike, so that they'd find it hard to run away.'

'What about the child?' the man yelled as he was dragged off to join his companions and the handcuffs clicked on. 'Surely you're going to rescue her?'

A voice came from the front door of the house. '*There's no child here,*' Gabriel said.

'There must be. You can't have got her away because we've been watching the house.'

So Gabriel said it again, 'I didn't need to get anyone away. *There is no child here.*'

The prisoner scowled at him. 'I don't believe you.'

Fred came back with the van just then and they shoved their three protesting captives roughly into the back, then Mike set off for the police station squashed up with their two helpers in the front.

Sergeant Deemer joined Gabriel at the front door and asked if he would take Mike's motorbike into his backyard and keep it safe till he came for it.

'Happy to do that, Sergeant. Thanks for coming to our aid. Do you have to leave straight away or would you like a cup of tea or cocoa? It's a chilly night.'

'A cup of cocoa would go down well,' Deemer admitted as thunder rumbled again, but much further away this time. 'It'll do that lot good to wait for me to charge them.'

'I'll look after the bike. You come inside. Maisie will you lock the front door after you.'

When they were all three settled at the kitchen table, Sergeant Deemer asked quietly, 'Is Beatie here?'

'No. I swear she isn't.'

'Then what the hell has got into those men?'

'Their minister seems to have decided that she is here and also that she has to be returned to her grandmother. Though why he thinks he has the right to send people to break into my house, I do not understand.'

'And he didn't join in the attempt to find her, did he, the coward?'

Deemer didn't pursue the matter of where the child was any further. His Lordship had impressed it upon the members of their group that the existence of the tunnels should not be revealed to anyone except the people who owned the properties the tunnels led to – *not under any circumstances, as a matter of national security.*

Besides, the sergeant had seen for himself how badly Mrs Hicks had treated her granddaughter, and the doctor had told him how dangerously thin the child was, definitely not fed properly. He'd not be responsible for taking her back to that harridan if he could help it.

He didn't mention Beatie again, but enjoyed his cup of cocoa and a gentle chat about how the improvements to the house were going and who would have to pay for this night's damage.

When he got back to the station, he found that Mike had locked up the men they'd captured and left them still hand-cuffed to one another. He'd made cups of tea for his two help-ers, who deserved them, but not for the prisoners.

Mike and the other two were grinning at Sergeant Deemer expectantly.

'I'm not charging them till I've spoken to Mr Peters, and I'm too tired to interview them till the morning. Let them stew.'

He went and told the men that. They seemed to have lost most of their defiance now and were standing in a miserable huddle.

'Can we have the handcuffs off, please?' one asked.

He jerked his head to Mike, who undid the cuffs, then locked the cell door again, saying, 'See you in the morning.'

'There's nowhere to lie down,' one complained.

'Then you'll have to sit up, won't you? That's what you get for breaking the law.'

The sergeant didn't wait for an answer, but walked back out to the reception area.

'We'd better be going,' Fred said. 'My wife will be worrying.'

'Just a minute. Bear with me, Sergeant.' Sam went to the door that led to the cells and raised his voice. 'Those villains had better not come disturbing me again, let alone damaging property in my street or I'll really give them what for.'

There was not even a rustle of clothing from the cell after he'd finished.

Deemer winked at him, then asked his constable, 'Can you stay the night, Mike, and keep an eye on them? Gabriel's put your bike into his backyard. I'll drive you up to Backshaw Moss tomorrow morning to retrieve it.'

'Yes, of course I can stay. I doubt that lot will give me any bother, though, from their miserable expressions. I think being locked up is already making them realise how much trouble they're in.'

'I hope they're absolutely panicking,' Deemer said with relish. 'I'll question them tomorrow about what's going on at that chapel of theirs, and ask for the names of the others who took part in tonight's fiasco. Then I'll discuss charges with Mr Peters, not to mention payment for repairs.'

He smiled at Fred and Sam, and walked with them to the door. 'Thanks again, lads. I'll make sure you get a letter of commendation from the senior police officer for this district, and if you ever need a character reference to get a job, don't hesitate to come to me. I can't thank you enough for your help.'

Sam grinned. 'It made a change. Nothing like a bit of excitement for stirring the blood.'

In the morning, Sergeant Deemer gave the prisoners some bread and water, then left Cliff in charge and went to have a chat with Peters, who then came back with him to speak to them in his capacity as a Justice of the Peace.

He asked them why they had tried to break into Gabriel and Maisie's home.

'We told the sergeant that already,' one protested.

'And now you can tell me,' Dennison said sternly. 'I'm probably going to be the one who has to decide whether to send you to jail or not.'

One of them gasped and turned white, another said earnestly, 'It was to save the little girl, your honour. She'll be brought up godless if we don't get her away from that woman.'

'What makes you say that?'

'Because that Harte female used to live in the worst part of Backshaw Moss. That shows you what her morals are like.'

Peters held up one hand to prevent Sergeant Deemer from reacting angrily. 'Who told you that?'

'Our minister.'

'Well, he hasn't been here long enough to get his facts right. A couple of years ago her three sons had to sell nearly everything the family owned to pay for an operation to save her life, and that's why they had to live in one room in Backshaw Moss for a while.'

'Serve her right. Women in that line of work do get certain diseases,' one man said darkly.

Peters stared at him in shock. 'And did your minister tell you that, as well?'

'Yes.'

'Why is he telling such lies? She's an honest, hard-working woman who has raised three sons, all decent young men. And her illness needed an operation due to complications with her appendix, as you can check for yourselves. It was *not* due to an immoral way of life. Only, people need money to pay for some of the fancy modern operations, and then there's recuperation time needed afterwards.'

They looked at him as if they didn't believe a word he said, so he went into the sergeant's office and phoned Dr Mitchell, explaining the problem of persuading the men what had really happened to Gwynneth Harte. 'And you'd better check them out too while you're here. I don't want any complaints being made about ill treatment.'

'I'll call in shortly on my way to do my rounds.'

'No hurry. They'll be here for most of the day, believe me, if not longer.'

Deemer went back and told the prisoners that the doctor was coming to see them.

'I am still undecided whether to charge you formally or not with breaking and entering. It might be better to send you to prison and protect honest citizens if you're going to act wildly just because someone else tells you lies. Maybe a few weeks in prison would make you realise what criminals are really like.'

They stared at him in obvious terror at that remark.

'And there will be the question of repairs to Mr Harte's house. You've damaged the place, so you'll be responsible for paying for the repairs.'

When the doctor arrived, bringing his wife with him to corroborate what he said, the men listened in utter silence and didn't protest.

The doctor then checked them quickly, asking if they'd been injured. 'What's this bruise.'

'That's where the axe slipped.'

'And your hand was grazed recently. How did that happen?'

'I tripped up trying to run away,' another admitted. He shot a quick glance at Deemer and added, 'My own fault.'

After the doctor had left, Dennison gave the trio another severe talking-to, then said, 'This is what I'll do. I'll bind you over to keep the peace, but you must make good the damage to Gabriel and Maisie's house at your own expense. If you break the peace *in any way* during the next twelve months you will be sent straight to jail. Do you understand?'

They stared at him, then nodded slowly.

When he dismissed them, they walked out in silence, not speaking till they were well away from the police station.

'We were too eager, rushed in without there being any proof,' one said when they got outside.

'The minister himself suggested we do it. He wouldn't lie to his congregation.'

'Not knowingly. He must have been misinformed by someone he trusted. I'm sure he'll change his attitude towards Mrs Harte from now on, and help us get the rest of the congregation to chip in for repairs to that back door.'

They went straight to the minister's house, but his housekeeper told them he was busy and couldn't see them at the moment. She didn't meet their eyes as she said this, and tried to close the door on them straight away.

'But this is important,' one of them protested. 'He'll want to know what happened.'

'He says he's very disappointed that you've got yourselves in trouble with the police, and he'll see you at the Sunday service as usual.'

They walked away together and stopped at a public garden nearby. It wasn't raining now, thank goodness, but everything was too wet to sit down, so they stood under a tree to discuss their problem.

'I don't know what to think,' one said.

'It's clear the minister is avoiding us, and yet it was he who sent us to rescue the child. That's not fair. And why is he so interested in that child, anyway?'

'I reckon he wants to keep in with Mrs Hicks. She gives a lot of money to his chapel.'

Silence, then the third one said, 'I don't think my wife will want me to go back there. She didn't want to change our place of worship in the first place, and she's already told me she's going back to our old church where people care about one another and help out in times of trouble.'

'Mine feels the same. She gets angry at the way Vanner talks to women, says he treats them as if they're all stupid, unlike our other minister. And what's more, she says she knows why Vanner isn't married.'

'Why?'

'Because no woman would have him.'

In the end two of them went home and meekly agreed to go back to their old church, but the third insisted to his wife that they had to give Vanner a few more days to make things right. It wouldn't be fair otherwise.

'And in the meantime you and your friends will have to pay for a new door, which means dipping into our savings. That's not fair either. How stupid can you get, believing him about Gwynneth Harte? I could have told you she's a decent person.'

'There is a very good reason why: Vanner was trying to get the child back. Don't forget that poor little girl is still missing.'

'And if he proves to be a liar about the rest of this affair as well as about her?'

'In that case you and I will go back to our old church. I do miss the music there, I must admit. They have the best organist in the valley.'

'And I miss the true friendship they offered, instead of a minister who berates us for imaginary sins and tries to make us put more money in the offerings plate on Sundays.' She glared at him. 'I'm not going back to that chapel, and you can't make me. What's more, you can look after yourself this week while you think about things. I'm going to stay with my parents.'

When Beatie woke in the morning, she didn't recognise her surroundings and gave a little squeak of shock.

Then she saw the woman sleeping peacefully in the next bed, and would have settled down again only she needed to wee.

She went across to the other bed and shook Gwynneth.

'Oh, my! I slept so soundly.' Then she noticed how the child was wriggling, and smiled. 'I can see what's woken you up.

You'll have to use a po because we daren't go to the outside lavvy in case someone sees us. Have a look under the bed. They said they'd left us one.'

Beatie knelt down and sighed in relief. 'Yes, they have.' But she still hesitated to use it.

'We'll put it behind that screen over in the corner, shall we? And don't worry. I'll empty it.'

Beatie looked undecided about all this, but need drove her to ignore her shyness, and Gwynneth turned over in bed till it was her turn.

'Last night was a real adventure, wasn't it? I'm so glad we're here. Let's tidy ourselves up a bit and see if we can find some breakfast.'

'Yes, please. I'll try not to eat too much.'

'You must eat plenty. I'm sure your grandfather isn't short of food, and the doctor said you were too thin.'

Beatie beamed at that.

Downstairs, Arthur drew the curtains in the kitchen as soon as the two of them came in, saying cheerfully, 'We don't want anyone seeing you, do we?'

It all felt so blessedly normal, Gwynneth thought. What a nice man he was. And what a lovely house this was, too.

20

The attack on Gabriel and Maisie's house was a nine-day wonder in the valley. Jem Stanley, who was good at picking up the latest news early, told Higgerson about it almost as soon as the news broke.

His employer snorted in disgust. 'Stupid fools. Who cares about a child? Unless— there isn't a reward posted for finding her, is there?'

'No, sir.'

'Then why bother to look? Daughters aren't nearly as useful as sons anyway – or as sons *should be*.'

Jem nodded and tried to look interested when the other man started ranting on yet again about ungrateful lads who knew nothing about the real world and who sorely needed teaching a lesson or two.

'What I can't understand,' Higgerson finished up, 'is where Kit has disappeared to. The chap who's observing things for me in Swindon says he hasn't turned up there, though *she* is still living in the same house, damn her to high hell.'

He thumped one meaty fist down hard on the desk. 'I'm just biding my time, waiting for the right opportunity to pay her back. You'll see. They'll all see.'

After a while, Jem decided it was time to change the subject. He was getting better at distracting Higgerson, who might be clever enough to make a lot of money, but wasn't clever enough to keep a wife, unlike Jem.

Fancy thumping a woman and then expecting her to care about you and your interests! Plain stupid, that was. She'd rather see you dead.

He waited till there was a break in the complaining and changed the subject abruptly. 'There's something else to sort out, sir. What do you want me to do about those two cellars?'

'Cellars?'

'The new ones you said you wanted digging out under them two Clover Lane houses on the corner. Ty Baker won't do it, not for anything. I even offered him double, an' he still turned the job down. Says he can't abide closed-in spaces and he's got plenty of work without putting himself through that sort of misery.'

'What? Well, don't use him again for anything else. We'll see how much work he has without my jobs. Find someone else to do the cellar and don't pay him double, either. Any fool can dig a hole.'

'I'm afraid you'll need to pay a bit more than usual for having that sort of hole dug, sir, and buy some big planks to hold the new walls back. Ty says it isn't safe to dig too deep in that part of Backshaw Moss, an' he's got other folk afraid to do that sort of work there.'

Higgerson gaped at him. 'Even if I pay double?'

'Even so. I'm sorry, sir. I did try, but most of the fellows who usually work for you won't touch that sort of job. I was speaking to Calum Baxter, though, and he might be interested.'

'Aha! I knew we'd find someone.'

'He can be a bit careless. Leaves a mess behind him, an' people complain.'

'What does a bit of mess matter when you're digging a hole? Let them complain all they like. It won't make any difference to me.'

'All right. But he'll definitely need to be paid double.'

Higgerson scowled but after a few seconds shrugged. 'We'll make up the difference in a few months' rent, because the first house will give me two extra rooms.'

'Two, sir? I thought there was only going to be one under each house. Is there enough space for two?'

'We'll be making the space, won't we? Why be content with one rent payment when we can squeeze in two rooms under the bigger house and get twice the money?'

Jem hesitated but abandoned the idea of arguing. It'd do no good. Once Higgerson had made up his mind to do something, it got done one way or the other. 'I'll speak to Calum tomorrow, shall I?'

'Yes.' He waved one hand dismissively. 'That's all for today. I've not had time to read anything but the front page of my newspaper yet. See that you speak to Calum first thing tomorrow morning. I want to get those new cellars started before some pea-brained fool on the council manages to change the rules again.'

When Jem had left, Higgerson settled down to his newspaper, chuckling. He'd fettled those stupid fools on the council about their damned rules, hadn't he? Some judicious bad food had given him a majority of votes for once, and he'd seized the opportunity to amend the rules to cover what *he* wanted to do.

He might try getting rid of fellow councillors again when he wanted some new by-law to be passed. He'd save that for something important, and anyway, he'd need to work out a different way to incapacitate some of them. An idea would come to him, it usually did.

Meanwhile, he needed a rest. He was run ragged, had far too much to do. His smile faded as he wondered yet again where the hell Kit was if he wasn't with his mother. Dammit, he had to find someone else to help in the central business. There was a limit to what an uneducated fellow like Stanley could do, however willing. The better sort of person didn't like to deal with rough types like him.

He'd find Kit. Oh, yes. Whatever it took, he'd get his son back and teach him to be obedient and useful. He'd lost one son; he wasn't losing the other.

And if he couldn't get his wife back once he'd lulled that Tillett fellow into a false sense of security, his name wasn't Higgerson.

He was paying a fortune to a local chap down there who was a skilled watcher, so he knew where she was and who was with her.

He'd teach Lallie a few sharp lessons. Or maybe he should just get rid of her once and for all. She'd given him two sons, but had never been much fun in bed. He'd have to think about it.

The new gardener worked very busily on the flower beds, readying them for the better weather and planting some seedlings. Jack Webster was well aware that his new master was keeping a careful watch on him. Well, he did his work properly, whether anyone was watching him or not.

After a day or two, Higgerson stopped bobbing up nearby and left it to Stanley to superintend and pay him, which amused him. A dishonest chap who knew nothing about gardening watching an honest, experienced gardener, that was.

Jack worked steadily and found to his surprise that he really liked this garden. Someone had put a lot of thought and effort into planning it. Gardens like this didn't just happen. But when he asked the cook who'd done it, she looked over her shoulder before answering and spoke nearly in a whisper.

'The mistress did it. Loved her garden, she did. She could grow anything. Nice woman, she was, but too gentle for her own good.'

She didn't have to explain that. A gentle person would have no chance against a bully like Higgerson.

'No one has ever said why she left. Do you know?' He saw the cook close her mouth and start to turn away, so said hastily, 'I'm only asking because I don't want to put my foot in it and lose this job.'

'Well . . . the master used to beat her and she was terrified of him. In the end he hurt her so bad, it gave her the courage to run away, though she couldn't have managed it without the help of her maid.'

'Ah. Some men are like that.'

Her expression grew fierce. 'Well, they shouldn't be. If I had a husband as did that sort of thing, I'd wait till he was asleep and take my rolling pin to him every time he touched me. Oh, yes. If someone started to hit me for no reason, I'd give him one or two good reasons to stop.'

He laughed. 'I bet you would. So would my wife. She's a grand lass, my wife is.'

The cook smiled at that. 'I like to hear men say that. It shows their hearts are in the right place.'

'Isn't the master's heart in the right place? Didn't he care for her at all?'

Another of those checks that no one was nearby, and then she whispered, 'He hasn't got a heart that one, and you shouldn't trust him an inch.'

After that they got on very well together and he managed to wheedle explanations out of her about what was going on, not to mention pieces of cake and extra cups of tea. Well, she was normal enough to enjoy a chat, unlike Jem Stanley and his new master, both of whom were surly devils.

Webster found things very different at the Samson Street chapel. No one talked to him at all there if they could help it, let alone offering him a cup of tea to help him through the day. They didn't chat much to one another, either. Miserable bunch, they were.

He shrugged and got on with the work, using his eyes and ears to gather information. He didn't clear up all the shrubs in the graveyard behind the chapel, instead using them to create places from which he could eavesdrop on conversations without being noticed, with the excuse of kneeling down to do the weeding.

He saw the minister doing things that upset him, browbeating women and weaker parishioners, viciously caning children, taking home food donated for the poor, even. No wonder the minister looked as if he ate well.

Jack was glad he'd stood up to Vanner from the beginning about fines and punishments. Fancy extra hours of work being 'required' for no pay, on the pretence that he hadn't done things as well as the minister wished. He'd do what the plants needed or they'd die, and he wasn't working any extra hours for no pay, not for anyone.

He also continued to refuse point blank to attend this chapel.

'No thank you, Mr Vanner. I'll continue to attend the church I was brought up in, which suits me and my wife just fine.'

'But—'

'I've been going there since I was a little lad, and I'm never, ever going anywhere else.' He folded his arms and stared back defiantly.

'Well, you're an ungodly fellow, but you have a way with the grounds and the graveyard, I will admit. Perhaps you'll come to see that what I preach is the right way to worship and live after you've worked here for a while.'

Jack was quite sure he wouldn't change his mind. He was only staying in this pair of jobs to oblige Mr Peters, whom he greatly respected, because he'd quickly come to despise both his new employers.

Once he had found out some information that might trap Higgerson, he'd leave and take a more congenial job. He might even have enough saved by then to buy himself the suitable field he'd noticed, with a stream at one side. It'd make a fine small market garden. He and his wife had been saving for something like that for a while.

Kit enjoyed living with Monty and Chrissie. Monty was teaching him about running a small business. He was rightly proud of his own, which he'd started from scratch.

Chrissie was knitting her guest a sleeveless pullover for the cooler weather later in the year. She also often chatted to him about her grandmother's herbal remedies, a subject he found fascinating.

She looked at him one afternoon and said softly, 'No adult has ever spent time with you chatting and reminiscing, have they? You don't seem to know much at all about what life was like when my generation and that of our parents were young.'

'No, my parents didn't chat to me. I think my mother would have liked to, but she hardly said a word, in case my father was eavesdropping, something he often did or set others to do. I really like to hear your stories. Please don't stop.'

Another time she said abruptly, 'Does your father know you want to become a doctor? I'd have thought he'd have been proud of that.'

'I never talked to him about it. He'd not have let me do it and he'd mock the mere idea, trying to make it sound silly, which it isn't. He wants me to follow in his footsteps and run his business with him. But I won't cheat and ill-treat people like he does, I just won't. He cares more about money than people.'

'Well said. Would your mother let you become a doctor?'

'I think she would, but she's never had any power to allow or not allow things, and she has no money of her own.'

'Well, I think you ought to have a taste of what doctoring is like before you decide for certain. I'm quite friendly with our doctor's wife. Shall I ask her if he'd let you spend a day or two observing what her husband does?' She smiled to see the blaze of joy light up his young face.

'Really?'

'Yes, really. She and her husband like to encourage clever young folk to become doctors, even girls sometimes. Modern medicine is so much more advanced than things used to be, and women can't always talk to male doctors about their troubles.'

'Some men are good listeners, surely?' he protested.

'Yes, but they don't have the same shape of bodies, do they? So they can't truly understand.'

'I never thought of that.'

'You should open your mind to all sorts of modern ways and ideas once you settle on medicine as a career. We'll help you if we can but first we have to get you completely clear of your father.'

Kit didn't say anything, couldn't, because he wasn't at all sure he could ever really get away. His father was so tenacious when he wanted something.

The lad had even thought of emigrating to Australia. It would be so wonderful to be sure you were free. Only then he'd lose his brother, and he and Felix were close.

The next morning Aunt Chrissie came home from her shopping and beamed at Kit. 'I ran into Dr Irving at the market so I seized the moment. When I told him how you'd saved my Monty's life and desperately wanted to become a doctor, he said he'd be happy to let you observe what he does for a day or two. He agrees with me that it's important to see what the life of a doctor is like before you decide.'

Without thinking Kit flung his arms round her, saying in a muffled voice, 'I can't thank you enough.'

She patted his back gently and didn't move till he'd calmed down because young men didn't like to be caught weeping for joy. 'I can't thank you enough, either, Kit, for saving my Monty.'

The following day, she took him to the doctor's house early in the morning and introduced them, then left him to spend the happiest day he could remember for years.

When he came back that evening he couldn't stop talking about what he'd seen and done, not telling them any patients' names or details, of course. And what's more, his new aunt and uncle seemed truly interested.

'It only made me want to become a doctor more than ever, Auntie Chrissie. I can't thank you enough for arranging it. And guess what? Dr Irving knows of scholarships which help pay the university fees for poorer students. I shall have to work extra hard to study for the examinations if I'm to get one of those.'

'Will your mother be able to help at all with the cost of clothes and lodgings?'

'I'm sure she will if she can, only I don't know whether she's got access to money in her new life or not.' Or whether she would manage to stay free of his father. He was quite sure she'd be as worried as he was about that particular danger.

'Well, if she can't do anything for you, we'll see if we can help you find a way.'

He gave her another hug then looked at her sadly. 'I don't know anything about how my mother is living. I do wish I could see her.'

'My Monty is going to phone this Mr Tillett tomorrow. He didn't want to do that till he was well enough to take you to see him, just in case something goes wrong and he needs to bring you back here.'

'That will be wonderful! You're the kindest people I've ever met.'

That got him another lovely hug.

As Kit lay in his bed that night, he felt as if the world was opening up to him like a big, beautiful flower showing off its bloom. He might have a chance, he really might, of achieving his dearest ambition.

How wonderful that would be!

21

Kit's mother was enjoying life with the Tilletts. She particularly liked using her maiden name now that she'd left her husband. Being addressed as Mrs Fennell made her feel more her own person. She never wanted to see her husband again, or her own parents, whom she blamed for her previous unhappy life because they'd forced her to marry him.

Gareth Higgerson was a dreadful person. He was evil through and through, not only in his business dealings, but towards his family too. She had several scars he'd given her over the years, the first one when he'd thrown her down the stairs. Most of the marks were now faint, but still served to remind her to be careful.

Since she'd come here, if she forgot to have a good look around before going outside the house, even if only into the garden, John Joe would remind her gently.

She'd never met a man with dark skin before, and had a lot of time for him. He was kind, clever and a hard worker. Kindness was one of the most important qualities to her and who cared what colour anyone's skin was?

She smiled at the thought of how well he was getting on with Pansy, who had been her maid and who had helped her escape from her husband at some risk to herself. She now counted Pansy as her dearest friend and would love to see her happily married to a good man.

Just before their evening meal there was a tap on the door of her small private sitting room at the rear of the house, and she called out to come in.

Felix joined her, with the solemn expression she saw on his face when he was seriously worried about something. Her heart gave a little skip of fear, because that was usually caused by something his father had done.

She gestured to him to sit beside her on the sofa. 'What's wrong, dear?'

'You can always tell when I'm upset, can't you? It's Kit, I'm afraid. I write to him from time to time, as you know, but the school has just returned my last letter. They'd opened it, though, so I hope they don't tell Father about its contents.'

He paused and took her hand, so she knew it was something really disturbing this time.

'Apparently my brother is no longer a student there and they're surprised that I didn't already know that he'd run away rather than go with Father, who had gone there to take him home permanently, it seems. Here. Read the note they sent.'

She did so, then stared at Felix in dismay. 'What can have happened to him? Surely if he was running away, he'd have come here to join you? And he's had plenty of time to do that.'

'That's what I'd have expected too. I did mention in my letters that "we" are still here, without naming you of course. Kit's very quick-witted and would have picked up on that, I'm sure.'

She reread the note, then looked at him again, not hiding that the information had made her feel seriously worried too. 'Your father will be hunting for him.'

'Yes. That's what I thought. He might even have caught him by now.'

'I pray not.' The mere thought of that made her feel sick.

He took back the letter and stared down at it as if he hadn't read it several times already. 'I think we should tell John Joe, Mr Tillett, and Eleanor about this.'

'I agree. Though we all know that it's likely to be John Joe who works out what's going on and keeps an eye on things.'

'The man's a miracle. I don't think he ever forgets a piece of information. No wonder Mr Tillett thinks so highly of him. Shall I ask them all to join us here as soon as convenient? We don't want to spoil the meal by breaking the news. Perhaps dinner could be a little later this evening?'

'Good idea, Felix. Could you ask cook to delay dinner by half an hour? I need to – pull myself together.'

She'd be shedding a few tears, he guessed.

Would this nightmare caused by his father never end?

Since everyone was home by this time of day, the rest of the family came at once, crowding into the cosy little sitting room.

When Felix told them what had happened, they passed his letter and the headmaster's note from one person to the next, studying them, frowning.

John Joe was last, and held them for longest before handing them back to Felix. 'I don't think there's anything in your letter that will give your father more information about your mother.'

Felix shrugged. 'No. He already knows that she's here and that watcher of his has been seen near here regularly. Does he think we don't notice? But I don't think he knew that I was in touch with Kit regularly, and if the school has told him what I said in my letter, that will make him even angrier.'

'Your brother will be welcome to stay here if he turns up,' Mr Tillett said. 'But I'm sure you all knew that already.'

Lallie smiled at her kind host. 'Yes, Mr Tillett. We did know we could turn to you for help. I can't thank you enough. You're the kindest of men.'

He smiled back at her in a way that made Felix feel sad that she hadn't married a man like him. Even though the two of them always addressed one another formally, you could see the attraction between them.

He frowned down at the letters. 'Where can Kit have got to, though? He won't have had much money to pay for travelling, because my father always kept us short, and it's too far to walk.'

Felix looked across at his mother, worried by how pale she was. Her smile had completely gone now.

'If he can be found, we'll do it, my dear Mrs Fennell,' Mr Tillett said.

'I know. But what if he can't be found? What if Gareth has already captured him and locked him away somewhere?'

'We'll check that out,' John Joe said. 'It isn't easy to make some-one vanish completely, not if there are people still keeping an eye on them. There would have to be someone guarding him.'

She stared down at her tightly clasped hands and forced herself to put her worst fears into words, 'Unless he's dead and buried.'

'Even *he* wouldn't do that to his own son, surely?' Mr Tillett protested.

'I think he'd do anything he decided would benefit him financially. He has no morals. His god is money.'

She didn't join them for the evening meal, sent Pansy to tell them that she was indisposed.

When Mr Tillett and Felix sat chatting after Eleanor had gone to bed, the older man said, 'I don't like to see your mother so pale and anxious.'

'Neither do I. I think she'll cry herself to sleep tonight.' Felix stole a glance at the man who was going to become his father-in-law and saw how tightly his hands clenched on the arms of his chair.

'I hope we can find your brother, Felix lad. Your mother has had far more than her share of sadness and trouble in her life. She deserves something better.'

Felix thought again how unfair it was that his mother was legally tied to his horrible father, who would never stop trying to punish her for leaving him.

★

As the three of them gathered for breakfast the following morning in the Nortons' dining room overlooking the garden, Monty declared himself fit to take Kit to his mother as soon as it could be arranged.

'You couldn't wait another day?' his wife asked.

'I think it needs doing now I'm much better. They'll be so worried about him.'

'We could phone to say he's all right.'

'And they'd come for him straight away. No, I'd like to finish what we started and take Kit to his mother myself, just to make sure he's all right. I'll contact Mr Tillett straight away, and then, if he's happy about me taking you to him, lad, I'll drive you there.'

'*We* will take you there,' she corrected. 'If you get over-tired, I can take over the driving.'

Kit couldn't hold back a deep breath of relief. He'd not only been worrying about his own safety, but that his father might trace him before he could get to his mother and then harm his kind hosts for helping him.

It seemed a miracle to him that his mother had managed to stay out of his father's hands for this long. It was thanks to Mr Tillett, and he was almost certain that he would be allowed to join her in that safe refuge until he could work out what to do with his life.

He'd talked with the Nortons about getting a scholarship to study medicine, and it was his most treasured dream, but you had to face facts: it was unlikely to happen, because if he came out of hiding to study, his father would come after him.

He stood next to Monty while his friend made the important phone call, straining his ears to hear every word.

A woman answered, informing them that Mr Tillett had not yet come into work.

'Can you contact him, do you think, and ask him to tele-phone me as soon as possible? I have some very important news for him, something he'll want to hear straight away.'

'Certainly, sir.'

He put down the phone and nodded to Kit. They'd agreed not to say more than that.

After ten minutes – which felt more like forty – the phone rang.

Monty picked it up. 'Montague Norton here.'

'Edmund Tillett.'

'Thank goodness! Look, the younger son of your guest is here with me and wishes to join his mother. Is that possible?'

He winced and held the phone away from his ear as the man at the other end let out a loud, bellowing hurrah. That seemed such a positive sign that the three of them exchanged smiles.

'Definitely possible. Tell us where you are and I'll send John Joe to collect him.'

'I can bring Kit to you. I'd have done so before now, but I was in a road accident and had to wait to recover.'

'Are you aware of the possible dangers from his father?'

'Unfortunately yes.'

'My deputy, John Joe, is a very clever chap, and it might be safer for him to come to you.'

'Very well.' Monty gave him the address.

'His mother and brother will be very happy to hear that he's all right. My man will set off straight away and he'll be with you in a couple of hours.'

John Joe took one of his employer's faster cars and headed north.

So did another car, whose skilful driver was costing Gareth Higgerson a great deal of money. The driver didn't betray his presence, or that of another man he'd taken with him. The passenger wasn't visible because he was deliberately lying down on the back seat.

John Joe didn't at first notice the car behind him. There were, after all, a lot of Wolseleys on the road.

At one stage he did notice vaguely that one car seemed to have been following him for a while, but it vanished soon afterwards.

The next time he saw another Wolseley, he looked more carefully, but there were two men in the front of this car, so it wasn't the same one. Like most other vehicles today, its number plate was splashed with mud. When he arrived at the turnoff to Mr Norton's house, the other car continued along the main road.

John Joe was surprised at how modest the house was, and he was more than a bit concerned about its isolation. The car standing outside was modest too, a Morris 8, though quite a recent model. He couldn't get the lad away from here quickly enough. He could only see one other house nearby, so if there were trouble, help wouldn't be easily available.

He was glad Kit didn't come running out to greet him. The man who did appear stood at the front door for a moment and waited for a neighbour from the next house to walk across and join him before going across to John Joe.

'Tim will sit in the car and keep an eye on it while you come inside with me, if that's all right.'

'Good idea, sir.'

John Joe recognised Kit at once because he looked so like his brother. 'Your mother sends her love, Kit, and can't wait to see you. She'd have come with me, but we didn't think it safe.'

'Is she still in danger?'

'We fear so. There are men watching our house from time to time. Do you think your father will ever give up trying to get her back?'

'I'm sure he won't. He boasts about always paying back any-one who crosses him, even if it takes him years to do it. He is utterly vicious.'

'So we'll continue taking care of her.'

They heard the sound of a car driving past and fell silent, but it continued into the distance, so they relaxed again.

Mrs Norton came to stand by the lad, her hand on his shoulder. 'We think a great deal of Kit. You will take care of him, Mr— um?'

'Just call me John Joe. Everyone does.' He grinned. 'I don't like my surname, so I keep it to myself.'

'You can change it legally,' she said in surprise.

'Or simply not use it. Anyway, we'll take great care of Kit, I promise.' He glanced towards the window. 'I think we should set off straight away, if you don't mind, so that we can get back before dark. Good idea to ask your neighbour to keep an eye on my car.'

'Can't be too careful. We look after ourselves and our neigh-bours here in the country, more than townies do, I think.'

Monty gave Kit a cracking hug, then stepped back to allow Chrissie to do the same. 'Let us know how you get on, lad.'

'Of course. And thank you for everything.'

Monty smiled. 'Thank you for saving my life.' He turned to John Joe. 'Which road will you be taking?'

'The most direct one I can find. I wish the government would hurry up and finish sorting out the road numbering system. They keep changing it, and it's hard to keep up, even when local authorities bother to put up road signs. I had to wind along a few minor unnumbered roads for the final stretch on the way here, missed my way once and had to ask for directions.'

'In my job, properly numbered roads would be a godsend,' Monty said.

'Well, at least there won't be many vehicles on the country stretches for the first part of our journey. There were very few coming here.'

'Thank goodness. I read somewhere that there will soon be two million vehicles on Britain's roads. Amazing, isn't it?'

They both shook their heads at the thought of that much traffic as they walked towards the front door.

'Let me check first.' John Joe stood at the threshold on his own and listened carefully as well as looking around. But he couldn't see any cars parked nearby, nor was there any sound of cars in the distance, so he told Kit to get into the vehicle quickly.

Monty and the neighbour waited for them to drive off before going back into their own houses.

Another man, who had been hiding nearby watching the group, cursed under his breath as the two men stayed outside until the Ford drove away.

The watcher then moved quickly back to his own vehicle, which was parked off the road in among some trees.

'I thought we were going to get hold of him here once he got outside,' the other man said.

The driver started the car and set off before he answered. 'It wasn't worth risking it. There were two other chaps there as well as that sod John Joe, and the lad's big enough to join in a fight, too. Pity.'

'Aye, it's nice and quiet round here. We could have got hold of the lad without much likelihood of interference if there had only been John Joe. I'd have enjoyed giving him a good thumping in return for the one he once gave me a few years ago.'

'We'll have to push their car off the road at a quiet spot. They won't be able to go fast along these narrow lanes.'

'We'll need to continue taking precautions to stop them noticing us following them though.'

The driver smiled. 'I brought some bits and pieces. You don't need to change much to disguise yourself, as we've learned.'

They exchanged smug grins at that.

They set off and soon caught up with the Ford, but stayed well back from it.

Monty watched John Joe drive away. His neighbour went home, but Monty didn't move for a few moments, because he thought he'd heard another car start up nearby.

Yes, he had! A large black Wolseley drove past his gate almost immediately. He thought it was the local police car for a moment, because they had one of the same model, but he quickly realised his mistake.

Where the hell had that car come from?

A feeling of unease crawled up his spine. Something was wrong. He knew it. And his gut instinct was usually right.

There wasn't a minute to waste.

22

Arthur and Gwynneth introduced Beatie to Biff and assured her that she could trust him completely. She listened solemnly as he explained exactly what a private detective was. Then she was introduced to the two Becksley brothers, who were taking it in turns to keep watch on the house.

Even so, she asked hesitantly afterwards, 'And my grandmother definitely can't get inside this house?'

Gwynneth gave her hand a squeeze. 'Not easily. Even if she did, we'd have taken you down to the hidden tunnels, so she still wouldn't find you.'

'Good. How long will we be staying here?'

'I don't know, dear. As long as is needed to work out how best to help you make a better life with your grandfather, I suppose.'

'And with you, too?'

'Would you like that?'

Beatie nodded vigorously. 'I feel safest of all with you.' She'd been staring longingly at the fire and now moved towards it, holding out her hands to the warmth. 'Is it all right if I warm my hands?'

'Of course it is. Fires are there to keep us warm.'

A happy sigh greeted that, then, 'It's a lot better here than at my grandmother's house. She only has a fire lit in her sitting room and the kitchen, and I used to get very cold.'

Gwynneth could feel her hands clenching into fists at this further evidence of deliberate cruelty to the child.

When they'd set out food for breakfast there was another moment of hesitation and doubt, then Beatie whispered, 'How much is it polite to eat?'

'Good heavens, we're not short of food. You should eat as much as you wish, till you're not hungry any more. The doctor said you needed to eat more, remember? That's why we all serve ourselves at breakfast. We all need different amounts of food.'

The child's eyes went wide with astonishment at this, and she licked her lips involuntarily.

'I don't think you've been eating enough for a while, so dig in. Your body is trying to grow from a girl into a woman, and for that it needs plenty of food to build good bones.'

Arthur had been listening to this conversation with pain in his heart for the child's miserable life. 'Personally, I always start my day with a hearty breakfast. How about we all have two boiled eggs each and soldiers today?'

She looked at him in puzzlement. 'Soldiers?'

'We butter some toast then cut it into narrow strips so that we can dip them into the egg yolk. I don't know why they're called "soldiers", but they make a very nice breakfast, I promise you.'

'I'd forgotten about them. Mum used to make them.'

'You can make the toast for us all. See. There's a nice toasting fork, and the fire's hot.'

'I'd like that.'

He cut some slices of bread, handed them to her, and turned to Gwynneth. 'I'll cook breakfast today. You don't know your way round my kitchen yet, and anyway you look tired.'

'Aren't you tired as well?'

'I'm too excited at having my granddaughter here with me to feel tired today.' He winked at Beatie and she gave him a shy smile in return.

'What do you like to do to pass the time?' Gwynneth asked her as the child carefully watched till the bread was golden, then turned it and threaded it back on the toasting fork to cook the other side. They waited for the eggs to boil and Arthur showed his expertise with the kitchen range.

'My grandmother told me to read the Bible whenever I had nothing else to do, but I couldn't—'

She broke off, looking as if she expected them to be angry.

'You couldn't what?'

'There were so many long words, I couldn't understand a lot of it. I can read other books, but that one was too hard.'

'We'll have to see whether there are any children's story-books in the house. Do you have any favourites?'

'There's a book called *Anne of Green Gables*, and my mother used to read poetry to me. She had a lovely voice. But my grandmother said I was too old to be read to now.'

'Well, I don't think I shall ever be too old to enjoy stories and poetry, however old I get, so if we can find some books, I'll be able to help you read the longer words and read to you sometimes.'

Then the food was ready and they all enjoyed a hearty meal.

A short time after they'd cleared away the breakfast things, Beatie fell asleep in a big armchair. Arthur beckoned to Gwynneth. 'Come over here and sit next to me. We can chat quietly without waking her, and still keep an eye on her.'

She sat down beside him, feeling at ease, as always.

His hand twitched, moved slightly towards hers, then stilled again. She didn't let herself smile. She preferred a man who didn't grab her like a greedy child.

Since he seemed to have difficulty starting a conversation, she took over. 'What a bleak life the poor child must have led in the past year or two.'

He grimaced. 'I agree. That grandmother was always a kill-joy. She wasn't this bad when my daughter married her son, though. As for that new minister of hers, he's worse, somehow. I can't work out what there is about him.'

'He's a wicked creature who takes pleasure in wielding the power he has to make other people's lives a misery. He's not as bad as Higgerson, but he's not a good man, for all his religious platitudes. And he seems to bring out the worst in people like Mrs Hicks. She sounds to like bullying people.'

She let the silence continue and waited, seeing him take a sudden deep breath and watching him screw up his courage visibly before taking hold of her hand. He held his breath as he waited for her reaction, so she gave his hand a squeeze.

'About time, too, Arthur Chapman.'

He relaxed visibly. 'You don't mind?'

'No. I've missed having a hand to hold and someone to share my life with. Besides, I'm too old to waste time pretending, and I never was a flirt. I enjoy your company and would like to get to know you better, Arthur Chapman.'

'I don't want to waste time either. Eh, I've missed having a wife and family around me, missed it sorely. I nearly went mad at first when I lost them. Only you can't marry any woman you happen to meet. You're the first woman I've met in my whole life with whom I'm as comfortable as I was with Susan.'

When he raised her hand to his lips and gave it a lingering kiss, it made her catch her breath.

It was his turn to smile knowingly.

'She sounds to have been a lovely woman, from the way you talk about her.'

'She was. And I'm quite sure she'd have liked you.'

'There have only been me and my sons for a long time, because I haven't met a man I felt attracted to. You know my son Gabriel.'

'And like him.'

'You'll like the other two as well, I'm sure.'

She sighed and let go of his hand. 'That was nice, but for the time being the child has to come first.'

'Yes, but you'll come a very close second for me if I have my way.'

She didn't hesitate. 'So will you for me.'

His smile after she'd said that warmed her to the core, filling an aching space that had been empty for too long.

Monty turned to his wife who was standing in the doorway watching him. 'I'm going to follow them, Chrissie love, just to be sure they get there safely. I've got one of my feelings that something's not right.'

'What made you think that?'

'A car drove past just after they'd left. Where did it come from? It appeared suddenly, didn't approach slowly from a distance'.

'I wondered about that too. And since you're not usually wrong when you sense trouble brewing, I'm coming with you.'

He didn't try to dissuade her. She was a capable woman, stronger than many men. She'd had to learn to defend herself as a girl growing up in a rough area, and she'd never given in to threats or bullying that he'd seen – which had been invaluable in their early struggles to make a living. She'd been his wife and partner in every way possible.

They hurried to and fro, putting on warm hats and coats, and picking up a few other items. In less than five minutes, they were out of the house and he was driving as fast as was safe along the narrow lanes. There was only one route John Joe could possibly have taken from here to start heading south towards Wiltshire.

Monty didn't have to tell his wife that he'd put a small cosh in his pocket, any more than she needed to tell him that in her handbag she now had the small, weighted weapon that looked at first glance like a torch. This was something he knew she took with her when he was away overnight if she wanted to go out after dark to visit a friend.

He didn't let himself think of what might happen if the other man had taken a wrong turn. No, surely a chap as capable as John Joe wouldn't have done that? Surely they had a good chance of catching up with them?

Monty and his wife didn't chat, but watched the road carefully, both of them alert for the slightest sign of trouble.

After a few miles, driving as quickly as was safe, they crested a rise and he sighed in relief as he saw John Joe's car a couple of hundred yards ahead of them, going up another shallow rise. He caught up a little before slowing down and staying two or three cars behind him. To his annoyance, as one small Austin turned off the road, a larger van turned on to it before he got there, which made it harder to see clearly what was happening ahead.

However, he knew this road well, so he didn't worry too much. John Joe wouldn't come to a suitable main road for quite a while, and he was hardly likely to turn down a narrow farm track, so it was safe to stay a good way behind them.

After a while he said, 'Is it my imagination, or has that black car that passed our house been behind them all this time?'

'Yes. And it's a powerful car, so could have overtaken them in a couple of places.'

'That proves I was right to worry.'

'I never doubted you.'

They watched for a while, and at a bend they saw the driver put a hat on without even slowing down. When they were held up by a few cows, a passenger who must have been lying down out of sight on the rear seat got quickly out and moved into the front of the vehicle.

'Whoever is in that car is trying to change his appearance so that he doesn't appear to be following them,' she said. 'Can you overtake them and signal to John Joe to stop?'

'I'm not sure that'd be a good thing to do, Chrissie love. Anyway, I wouldn't risk overtaking anything on such narrow roads.'

'We have to do something.'

'Not till those following them make a move. If we got John Joe to stop now, it might leave us all vulnerable to attack. There are two chaps in that car, and the one who changed seats looked to be a big fellow. I bet they'll be carrying weapons of some sort, bound to be when you think about it. No, it'd be better for us to stay behind so that they don't realise we're following them until we're ready to act. It's my guess that if something happens, it'll be on a quiet stretch of road without houses or farms nearby.'

Ten minutes later they were driving along a winding road from which they could only get occasional glimpses of the cars ahead. There were still a couple of vehicles between the Wolseley which they suspected of going after their friends, and John Joe's car, thank goodness.

Then one of those cars turned off to the left down a farm lane, and a few hundred yards further on the van turned off as well. That left the Wolseley directly behind John Joe's vehicle, and their own car quite a way behind the two of them.

At a particularly sharp bend further up a hill, the Wolseley speeded up suddenly and vanished from sight.

'Oh, hell! Here we go.' Monty put his foot down on the accelerator and began to catch up as quickly as his smaller car would allow.

Before they even got to the bend they heard the sound of metal crashing into metal, so he slowed right down as they came to the corner, stopping where their car was half hidden by some trees to get an idea of what they would be getting into.

They could see that the two men had left the second vehicle, which was only slightly damaged. John Joe's car was smaller and in a much worse state. The men went to try to get its doors open.

Monty drove forward openly and as he stopped, one of the men ran over to him. 'I'm glad to see you, sir. The folk in that car aren't hurt, but after this accident it won't be fit to drive. Could you please stop at the next garage and ask them to send someone back to tow it in for repairs? We'll stay here and see they're all right till then, and afterwards we can take them somewhere to catch a train.'

The man tried to stand between Monty and the two cars as he was speaking, but he couldn't hide all that was going on. Did he think they were stupid?

Kit was now yelling for help and struggling with the other man, who had managed to get the passenger door open. The man who'd been speaking to them said, 'Please fetch help quickly! That lad must be injured to yell like that.'

Monty nodded as if agreeing to do what was asked, but he had no intention of leaving the scene of the accident. To his relief another car came along the road just then, and he flagged it down, shouting, 'Stop! Stop!'

But the driver of that vehicle was a woman on her own, and when he shouted to tell her what was happening and asked her to go for help, she looked at him in alarm and drove off rapidly.

He couldn't tell whether the sound she made was a 'yes' or simply a grunt of shock.

'Damn!' he said, and turned back to study the crash scene.

23

Cursing under his breath, Monty saw both men from the car that had knocked John Joe's vehicle off the road coming towards them, smiling confidently, not attempting to hide the knives they were now holding openly in their hands.

They stopped for a moment, and the one who was closer said loudly and slowly, 'As you've just seen, no one's going to stop and help you, so if you want your lady to stay safe, sir, you'll get back into your car and drive off quick smart.'

Monty shot a rapid glance at his wife, who was holding one hand close to her pocket. 'We mustn't anger these men, dear, so we'd better take care.' He tried to sound as if he was intending to leave but by this time he'd slipped his hand into his own pocket in a way she couldn't fail to notice.

He could see Kit on his knees by the car. He'd put up a good fight, but had been outweighed by his opponent and looked half stunned.

Why had John Joe not joined in to help the lad?

Monty's wife let out a brief, high-pitched scream, as if terrified. It was a signal they'd agreed upon in their early years of driving together on long-distance trips.

They waited for the usual count of ten after it, during which time he prayed she'd have retained her old skills, then they each attacked the nearest man.

He didn't like having to let her face the other one, didn't like it at all, but he hoped the man would be so shocked at being attacked by a woman, he'd hesitate to hit out at her. As he'd expected, the man going after her let out a yell of shock when she hit him. She was always very quick to seize any opportunity to best an opponent.

And as they'd often found, men like these didn't expect women to be able to defend themselves, let alone even try to go on the attack.

And he had no trouble whatsoever in dealing with his own opponent.

The woman who'd driven past the scene of the crash didn't have to go far before she saw a van she recognised coming along the road towards her. She flashed her headlights, stopped, and leaned out of her car to speak to the driver.

'Something wrong with your car, Mrs Peak?'

'No, Gordon. There's a fight going on just down the road. Two men in a big car have run another vehicle off the road. I think they must have been going to rob its occupants, only another car stopped to assist them. It looks like the rescuers need a bit of help now as well.'

He gaped at her. 'Good heavens!'

'They need help quickly.' She stepped back and made a shooing movement with one arm.

He waited to say, 'You go and fetch Mr Warth. I've only just left him. He was planning to drive into the village.'

She nodded. She'd been going to fetch Mr Warth anyway because his farm was the next one down the road.

Gordon didn't wait for her answer but drove off, quickly gathering speed.

When he got to the scene of the crash he saw a woman standing over a semi-conscious man holding what looked like a weapon in her hand, which made him blink in surprise.

Two other men were struggling, and a lad with blood on his face was hovering nearby, looking for an opportunity to help one of them, though which one Gordon couldn't at first tell.

He got out of his van, removing the ignition keys and picking up the knobbly walking stick he carried for defence. He was still trying to work out who was the villain in the fighting pair, when the woman yelled, 'The man in the black overcoat is my husband and he's not long out of hospital. He needs help. Be careful, though. That chap he's fighting has a knife and he's already tried to use it on my Monty.'

Gordon moved forward purposefully just as the man she'd indicated as the villain punched his opponent, sending him staggering backwards. He then turned abruptly away from the fight trying to run across to the Wolseley.

It looked as if the chap was attempting to escape, but the lad managed to drag him away from it until his former opponent could get to him. The woman stayed where she was, standing over the man who was lying on the ground groaning.

When the latter tried to crawl away from her, she threatened to hit him again. As he flinched back, Gordon smiled. She had a very determined expression and must have already used her weapon. He didn't think he'd challenge her either if he were lying on the ground half-stunned by a blow and she was still holding a weapon.

By hell, she was a handsome woman! Sturdy and rosy-cheeked. Reminded him of his sister. Dolly would have fought back, too.

Seeing that she was all right, he turned his attention back to the man who'd been trying to get away.

Just then another van pulled up, boxing in the two crashed cars. The driver got out and looked across at Gordon. 'What the hell is going on? Mrs Peak said you needed help. I was just about to go down to the pub.'

'I think this is an attempted robbery, Warth. You're in time to help us secure these two, then after the police have taken them away, I'll buy you a drink.'

The newcomer, a muscular man more than six foot tall, said loudly, 'I hate thieves. I'd enjoy a chance to teach you two a lesson. My wife will have phoned the police by now. If either of you tries to resist arrest, I shall get very angry indeed.'

Gordon watched with a confident smile. He'd seen before the effect Warth's size had on people who were trying to cause trouble. 'You wouldn't want to make my friend angry, believe me,' he called out as they hesitated. 'He put the last chap who tried to rob his farm in hospital.'

Which was a lie, because Warth was a gentle giant, relying mainly on his size to prevent trouble rather than getting into fights.

The two scowling attackers hesitated, then allowed themselves to be tied up with some ropes Warth produced.

Chrissie was attending to John Joe, who was only now coming fully to his senses. 'He must have been thrown forward and knocked unconscious when he hit the windscreen,' she called to the others.

'Kit,' John Joe muttered.

'It's all right. Kit is safe,' she said soothingly.

'I let myself get caught out,' he groaned. 'I knew by then that the car was following me, but I couldn't do much about it on these narrow lanes.'

'We watched him drop back and change hats, and when they were held up, the second man, who'd been hidden in the back, moved into the front seat. You probably weren't looking at the number plate but checking the people in the car.'

'You're right. You're sure Kit's not hurt?'

'He's fine.'

'Good thing you two came after us. Come to think of it, why did you?' He rubbed his head as if it was aching, and he was still speaking slowly and jerkily.

'Just after you set off from our place, my Monty had one of his feelings that something wasn't right.'

He looked at her suspiciously. 'I don't believe in that sort of thing.'

'Well, you'd better change your mind because his intuition saved you and the boy today. My Monty doesn't get such feelings often, but he has never been wrong about trouble brewing that I've seen, so I came with him to help. Now, sit still and rest. I think you must be concussed. Your eyes aren't focusing properly. We'll speak to the police when they arrive and get your car taken to a garage, then we'll drive you both to Mr Tillett's house.'

'Thank you.' He moved his head involuntarily to look as another car drew up, and groaned as pain jabbed him.

'It's the police. Do as I told you: sit quietly and leave everything to them and us.'

'I should phone Mr Tillett.'

'All in good time. You can't call him till we get to a phone.'

With a sigh he leaned back and closed his eyes.

They were allowed to make a brief phone call to Mr Tillett from the small country police station to which everyone was directed or taken. However, it was dark by the time they'd finished answering questions and proving who they were.

Monty insisted he was going to drive them to the Tilletts' house, though truth to tell, he was feeling exhausted now.

His wife looked at him, rolled her eyes, and barred the way to the driving seat before he could get into it. 'You've been driving for hours, and you're still recovering from injuries, Monty. Be sensible, love.'

'I can manage,' he said.

'Only if you have to, and you don't. I can manage better than you at the moment. I believe I'm the only one of us three adults who isn't recovering from an injury.' She opened the rear door of the car and pushed him gently towards it, taking his ignition key out of his hand, then getting into the driving seat.

The two men exchanged resigned glances, and John Joe got into the front of the car so that he could give her directions.

Kit was watching all this, fascinated. He took a seat in the back with Monty and whispered, 'I've never been driven by a lady driver before. My father didn't believe in women getting behind the wheel.'

His companion gave him a wry smile. 'You've never met a lady like my wife, either. Wonderful woman, she is.'

'I couldn't believe it when she knocked that man down. You're both wonderful!'

He patted the lad's hand and leaned back with a weary murmur. 'I'm not fully up to scratch yet. She was right to take over.'

No one was in a mood to chat, so the rest of the journey passed in near silence, with occasional instructions as to which road to take from John Joe.

When they reached Mr Tillett's house they found the gates open and a man standing outside the house like a sentry on duty. They parked on the drive and he nodded when he saw John Joe, then closed the gates behind them.

'He'll just have to open them again when we drive off,' Chrissie muttered.

'Better safe than sorry,' John Joe said. 'We have to take care at night since we became a target for Higgerson's malice. He's had a few goes at getting his wife back.'

Inside, the house was a haven of light and warmth.

Lallie and Felix were peeping into the hall to see who'd arrived, and with a shriek, she rushed to hug Kit. It was a while before she let go of him, by which time they'd been shepherded willy-nilly into a big sitting room with everyone else, and she could introduce her younger son properly to the Tilletts.

'You all look exhausted,' their host said. 'We've got plenty of spare beds. You will stay, won't you?'

Chrissie said, 'Yes! We'd be most grateful,' before her husband could speak.

'I think we all need to freshen up before we eat anything,' John Joe said.

Lallie stood up and moved back towards the door. 'I should have thought of that. Let me show them up to their bedrooms before we settle down, Mr Tillett.'

As she led the way up the stairs, she added, 'I'll get hot-water bottles put into the beds and find you some clothes to sleep in, Mr and Mrs Norton. We have all sorts of odd-ments in the linen store, because Mr Tillett seems to collect waifs and strays. Kit can borrow some pyjamas from his brother.'

By the time they'd used the bathrooms and had a quick wash, the meal was ready. After sandwiches and pieces of pork pie, they ate bowls of rhubarb crumble with custard.

Once the food had been cleared away, Mr Tillett said abruptly, 'It'll be Higgerson yet again who arranged the car and men to follow you. These attempts to get hold of Kit must be costing him a fortune.'

'He's not short of money,' Lallie said bitterly. 'And he doesn't mind spending it on his own wishes.'

'Well, this can't be allowed to continue. Now that Kit's free, we can do something to stop him once and for all without worrying too much about him taking out his anger on the lad. I'm going to discuss it with one or two friends. There has to be a way to stop the man, even if we need to bend the law a little. This is England, and we don't usually tolerate bandits.'

'If there is a way to do something, the police sergeant in Rivenshaw will be delighted to help you as much as he legally can,' Lallie said. 'He hates my husband too.'

'I'll bear that in mind. Now, you're all looking exhausted, so bed seems to be called for.'

No one protested.

In the morning, Tillett insisted on ordering a car to escort them and make sure no one was trying to follow them, let alone attack them on the way home.

He then discussed with John Joe and the family how best to proceed, because until Kit was over twenty-one, Tillett was fairly certain the lad would be legally subject to his father's authority, not his mother's.

Everyone began to look glum as that sank in.

'How can I stay out of his way for all those years?' Kit wondered aloud. 'He won't stop trying to get me back, you know.'

'It won't be easy, which is why I'm going to propose sending you to live with a friend of mine in Scotland. If the authorities come looking for you here, I'll claim you ran away.'

'That's a long way from here,' Lallie said with a catch in her voice.

'Which is a big advantage. And also, it's a small village, and any strangers coming after him would stand out a mile. I own a farm there, which I usually visit in the summer. It's a beautiful part of the world.'

After a pause to let that sink in, he added, 'Moreover, my friend there is a doctor, and Kit could act as a sort of apprentice and learn a lot from him. It's important to find out whether he's truly suited to what can be a rather demanding profession. My friend has tutored lads interested in becoming doctors before, so his arrival won't look at all strange to the locals.'

As Kit brightened up a little, Mr Tillett watched Lallie force a smile, and his heart went out to her.

She seemed to feel his eyes on her and looked across at him as she said, 'He'd be safe, which is the main thing.'

'And you'd be able to phone him regularly, and write to one another. There would be far more freedom for you to stay in touch with him than you've had in the past few months. I'll phone my friend tomorrow.'

Tillett could see that Lallie was upset by that suggestion, but there was no choice if Kit was to be kept safe.

24

When the phone rang the next afternoon, Sergeant Deemer was on his own while his constables were out on small jobs up in Birch End and Ellindale. 'Rivenshaw Police Station.'

'Are you alone, Gilbert?'

'Hello Dennison. Yes, I am, will be for an hour or two.' He didn't ask if something was wrong, because you could never be quite sure the operator or someone on a party line wasn't able to overhear. Anyway, he didn't need to ask. His friend wouldn't phone him during working hours for a mere chat.

'I'll see you shortly.'

Dennison arrived a few minutes later and joined Deemer in his office at the rear of the building.

He didn't waste time on greetings. 'I've two important things to tell you, Gilbert, and I don't want anyone else hearing them, which is why I've come in person instead of telling you on the phone.'

Deemer nodded. He'd have done the same.

'Firstly, I heard from a friend of mine who's also a JP that the police in his part of the Midlands arrested some villains yesterday who were operating a long way out of their normal territory.'

'Oh? How is that of interest to us?'

'The two men they apprehended refused to admit anything, but the people they'd attacked and who helped capture them, did volunteer some information. One of these people was Higgerson's younger son, and he was quite sure the chaps had done this on the orders of his father. One of them had even taunted him with it apparently.

'The other people backed up the lad's story, saying the men had deliberately caused the accident by pushing a car off the road suddenly. They too were sure it could only have been arranged by Higgerson. Which is why I'm letting you know about it. But this is off the record.'

'Do go on. It sounds interesting. I'd give a lot to trap that sod.'

'It seems the younger son ran away from school a week or so ago to avoid being taken back to live with his father. He headed south, trying to get to his mother and brother. Higgerson has been hunting for him and seems to have spent a surprising amount of money on it, too.'

'If the lad is under age, shouldn't the police have returned him to his father?'

'He, um, slipped away while they were busy with the two attackers.'

Deemer grinned. He'd have let the lad 'escape' too, if it was that or handing him over to Higgerson.

His friend returned the smile. 'Of course, no one can prove who's behind the attack, but it sounds highly likely to me that it's Higgerson.'

'It's definitely the sort of thing that fellow would do, especially as his older son ran away from him a couple of years ago. He'll be desperate to save face about the other lad doing the same. Hardly anyone in Rivenshaw includes him socially these days, for all his money. Go on.'

'The best of it is that the man who has given refuge to Mrs Higgerson and her older son is one of those chaps who live comfortably but modestly, yet are rolling in money and have very widespread influence. Not many people know about that.

Higgerson certainly won't. Tillett has friends and acquaintances in upper circles all over the country, including around here. In fact, the man we refer to only as "His Lordship" is one of them. It seems the two of them have had enough of Higgerson, and are intending to do something unofficial but permanent about him.'

Sergeant Deemer was startled. 'Kill him, you mean?'

'No, of course not. They aren't murderers!'

'He probably is though.'

'They haven't decided exactly what to do yet, because there's a complication come up. They said to ask you whether it's all right to contact you if they need your help to bring him to justice.'

'I'd sell my grandmother to do that!'

'I hadn't realised till I came back to live in Rivenshaw how much Higgerson's power has grown over the past few years. I'd just about sell my own grandmother as well to put a stop to his antics. I do believe in the rule of law.'

Deemer waited, but Dennison didn't continue. 'What's the complication?'

'It's to do with the second piece of news, and it's a matter that must remain strictly between you and me for the time being.'

'Of course.'

'An acquaintance has contacted His Lordship because they've been having trouble in their area with a minor group of fascists who are trying to follow the example of Mosley and his damned Blackshirts. During their investigations they discovered a connection to an even smaller group that has started up recently in our area.'

'*What?* Now that *is* news to me. I thought organised fascism had declined everywhere since the violence connected with that Olympia Rally of theirs a couple of years ago.'

'It has mainly, but there are some patches of support still here and there, as you no doubt know, hence this group's willingness to give some minimal financial support to the odd "affiliated" group, like this local one, to build up their numbers.'

'How did I miss that happening in Rivenshaw?'

'It's only started recently, and it's not going well apparently. Unfortunately the man leading it has managed to keep his identity secret until recently. Now they suspect who it is, but they're holding back on taking action until they obtain rock solid proof.'

Deemer let out his breath in a whoosh of angry air. 'Well, thank goodness it's not going well for him! How do these people get away with it at all in a country like ours? I blame Hitler partly, for setting a bad example to lunatics like them, and unfortunately he's a lot more successful than Mosley.'

'I gather the new group's main success in gaining members comes because they're providing lads who join up with uniforms – well, part uniforms. It's only dark shirts, leather belts and neckerchiefs, but you know how some fools love to put on a uniform.'

'And there are folk so short of clothes for growing lads that they'll say or do anything to obtain garments without paying for them. I wonder, sometimes, where the world is heading, I do indeed.' The sergeant frowned, trying to remember where he'd seen lads dressed like that. Somewhere in the valley, for sure, and only recently. It'd come to him.

'There's more information, but remember this needs to be hush-hush till we have incontrovertible proof.' Even though they were alone, Dennison lowered his voice to give further details.

Deemer listened in amazement, and when his friend stopped, whistled softly. 'Are you sure?'

'The chap who's infiltrated the main national group of fascists is sure, but he can't prove to the satisfaction of the law that the person in question is doing anything wrong legally.

And the members of the top group might even kill this chap if they find out he's spying on them.'

There was silence as both men contemplated the situation, then Deemer sighed. 'Well, you can be sure I'll do my very best to help catch the traitor.'

'I never doubted that. Remember, no word to anyone else yet, Gilbert. This is just between you and me till we have proof.'

'I shall be keeping my eyes open. I know who my main suspect would be, only he's never been into politics before.'

'You do that. Good thing I've got my chap working for Higgerson, eh? You can rely on Webster absolutely, I promise you, if you need help. He's a smart bloke, not easily fooled. If there's anything to find, he'll find it.'

'I'll remember that.'

When Dennison Peters left, the sergeant sat thinking for a while. Was this going to be a breakthrough with the struggle against Higgerson? He fervently hoped so. But that doubt still lingered. It was so unlike the man to get involved in something that didn't bring him a good financial reward.

His constables came back soon afterwards, and Cliff was scowling. 'That group of lads in Backshaw Moss who've been causing trouble is bigger than we thought, Sarge.'

Deemer stared at him. 'Is it, now? Were they wearing anything that looked a bit like a uniform?'

'Could have been, if you count dark shirts and neckerchiefs as a uniform. Could also have been just a batch of cheap shirts for sale at the markets that got snapped up by all the mothers. I've seen that before.'

'Who's been supplying them? Do you know?'

'I'm not sure.' Cliff went on to tell him what he'd overheard one saying, and the situation got even more confused.

Deemer would bear everything in mind. It was all needles and haystacks at this stage, nothing proven. As he got older, he sometimes dreamed of gathering together all the villains in his valley and dumping them on an island far out to sea, with only bread and water supplied. And he'd leave them to build their own shelters, too.

Sadly, he had to play by the rules, and the villains didn't. And a major villain like Higgerson was even more free to act than Deemer was because the chap had money behind him. It could make dealing with some situations very difficult, as the sergeant had discovered over the past couple of years.

He'd been getting very upset and frustrated about it till Dennison came back to Rivenshaw as their local JP. He felt he'd turned a corner once he'd found himself a clever ally like his friend.

He'd discuss the latest piece of information he'd acquired with Dennison the next time they got together, and in the meantime, he'd keep his eyes open.

Jack Webster had been kneeling down for too long. He was about to stand up and stretch when he heard the minister approaching, talking loudly, as usual. The fellow was either going deaf or was in love with the sound of his own voice.

'We'll arrange a meeting for tomorrow evening, out near the reservoir might be best.'

'Are you going to be there?'

'Yes. But I shall wear my mask. I don't want to reveal who I am yet.'

'You do realise that some of them have guessed, sir.'

'Guessing is one thing, proving it in a court of law is quite another. Make sure you don't say anything, not even to your wife.'

'No, sir.'

Webster waited until they'd passed by to stand up and stretch, nearly jumping out of his skin when a voice nearby said, 'I'm glad you heard that too.'

He turned to see Judge Peters, of all people, standing behind a large bush that had just come into leaf.

'I didn't hear you approaching, sir.'

'I'm rediscovering skills I learned as a lad, one of which was to move around unnoticed. It was a game then, but it can be deadly serious sometimes. What was all that about, do you think?'

Webster frowned. 'Vanner seems to have got a group of lads together to act like a gang, or like the military, he'd say. But I call it a gang. Some of them have already started attacking anyone who says anything bad about the minister or that so-called church.' He jerked his head towards the ugly red-brick building behind them, which had been a bakery before it had been purchased by a religious group. They might have put a big cross on the roof, but it still looked more like a bakery to him.

'I'm very interested in what this group of lads does. Any chance of you watching that meeting tomorrow without them knowing, Webster? I'll pay for your extra time.'

'I thought it was Higgerson you wanted watching, sir.'

'Oh, I still do. But I'm starting to get interested in Vanner too. How do you find him as an employer?'

'He's an out and out bully, especially towards women. I had to make it plain that if he tried to bully me I'd leave. Can't abide that sort of chap. I'd normally have found other work, but I only need the two extra days till we've finished with Higgerson, so it's not worth bothering to change.'

'Bear with both your employers for a while, if you can. I'm hoping the situation with Higgerson won't continue for too long. Got enough saved yet to buy that field?'

'Not quite, sir.'

'How much are you short?'

'About ten pounds, sir.'

'Buy the field now, while you can. I'll lend the money to you and you can pay me back in vegetables over the next year or two. I'm very very fond of fresh vegetables and fruit, especially strawberries in summer.'

Webster's face lit up. 'Are you sure, sir?'

'Very sure. Go and buy it straight away.' It was a pleasure to see such joy on a man's face.

'And if you can report back to me tomorrow after their meeting, Webster, no matter how late it is, I'd be most grateful. You should come to my back door, though.'

They shook hands on that.

The following evening various lads slipped out of Backshaw Moss and Birch End in ones and twos and gathered behind the reservoir, unaware that a hideout had been created nearby and an observer was already in place.

A rather short man wearing a mask strutted to and fro, giving them commands to march tidily.

The observer smiled. Did Vanner really think no one had recognised him? Even his voice gave him away, rather shrill for a man, with an edge to it when he got angry. But why was he doing this? It seemed a lot of fuss that was leading nowhere.

When he reported what had happened, Mr Peters seemed similarly puzzled as to the reason for all this pseudo-military prancing around.

'Perhaps he has a fantasy about being a military commander.'

'Or perhaps he admires that Hitler chap in Germany and wants to imitate his strutting around.'

'That's more likely.'

They knew why the lads did this, for the uniform and the mild excitement, but where was Vanner leading them? Into trouble, Webster feared. And he'd seen a neighbour's son among them. She'd throw a fit if she found out about this.

25

Jem Stanley had never seen his master as furious, or as unreasonable, about a situation. He counted himself lucky that he'd managed to avoid being the target of Higgerson's bad humour for the past few days. One man was now sporting a broken arm because he'd upset their master.

'Are you deaf? I asked if you'd got those basement rooms sorted out yet.'

Thank goodness he'd got Calum Baxter working on the new cellars. 'We've made a start, sir, but I'm afraid we're going to need stronger supports to hold the walls in place than we'd anticipated. Calum went back the second day to find part of one wall had collapsed. He said we were lucky it hadn't brought the others down with it.'

Higgerson breathed deeply, containing his anger with difficulty.

'No use spoiling the ship for a ha'porth of tar, is it, sir? After all, you'll make up for it long term with the rents you'll collect.'

'I suppose you're right. Part of a wall collapsed, you said?'

'Yes, sir.'

'Well, see what he needs and get it for him. But make sure you find the best price.'

'Yes, sir. I always do.'

He went back to Calum, and together they worked out what was needed and went out to order it.

It cost more than Jem had expected, but he was assured by the owner of the new building supplies yard that had opened up recently in Rivenshaw that these materials might be second-hand but they were sound and would do the trick. He knew from his own checking that the prices at this new yard were the best in town, so he bought them.

He told Calum to start work and to get as much done as he could. 'Make it look like more's been done, if necessary, if you want to keep the job.'

Calum sighed. 'I wish I'd not taken it on, and that's the truth, but I daren't leave now.'

'Why do you wish that?'

'It's fiddly work and it's hard to find men who can stand being shut up underground. Oh well, I expect it'll feel better down there when we get the new rooms fully dug out and proper supporting walls made.'

Jem didn't tell his master that, of course, just said Baxter had made a good start and was a hard worker.

'He'd better be. I want those cellars completed as soon as possible.'

'Yes, sir. Definitely.'

But his master remained grumpy, and nothing was right today. Jem was glad when it was time to go home. He'd thought himself in heaven when he got this job. He now considered it more like in hell, the way Higgerson blamed him if anything went wrong.

He hadn't sacked him, though. Well, who would take his place? Jem knew most of the petty crooks in the valley, men who'd do anything if you paid them enough. He was more efficient than them by far and his employer knew it.

Higgerson watched his foreman walk off down the street, then moved away from the sitting-room window, wondering how to pass the evening.

When the maid served his evening meal, which he ate in the small breakfast parlour now he was on his own, he looked at it without much interest. He looked at her the same way too. Old and ugly, she was nothing to tempt a man. It was beginning to worry him that since Lallie left he wasn't getting the urge for a woman very often. Probably because he'd been too busy.

Damn Lallie! She'd had a comfortable life, hadn't she? Always plenty to eat, warm clothing, and a big house. And he'd not hit her very often. All men hit their wives, for heaven's sake.

And damn his sons as well. Ungrateful brats.

He read the evening paper from cover to cover, whether the articles were worth reading or not, then saw that it was eleven o'clock. Time for bed.

But once again he found it hard to get to sleep.

He didn't like living alone, he admitted to himself. He had to work out a way to bring his family back. Trouble was, that Tillett fellow seemed to have some very good chaps protecting them. And the two men Higgerson had hired, who'd given him the most hope of success and who'd cost him a fortune, were now behind bars, the stupid sods. Good thing the police didn't know who had hired them.

At least Jem Stanley was proving his worth. He was a bit rough, but would do anything and was a fast learner.

Higgerson turned over again, trying to get comfortable.

He'd give that new fellow a few days to work on the cellar, then go and check how it was going. It paid to keep an eye on the details and let those working for him know it.

Gwynneth settled happily into Arthur's house – well, she would be happy here if she could live a normal life. But as things stood, she couldn't risk going out at all. She had to leave the purchasing of food to Biff, Arthur, or her daughter-in-law.

Maisie and Gabriel came to see them a couple of times in the evenings, using the tunnel route because they didn't want anyone to wonder why they kept going to visit a man they hardly knew. They didn't want to bring anyone here to investigate that anomaly.

She spent a lot of time playing with Beatie, gentle games at first as they built up her strength with good food. Gradually she started to teach her the things she should be studying at school: the more advanced reading, writing and arithmetic. She was surprised how much she enjoyed that.

Beatie seemed to love learning anything and everything, especially when her efforts won her praise. She devoured any children's storybooks they could find for her, rereading them several times for lack of new ones.

Gwynneth grew as fond of the child as if she were her own, taking particular pride in her rosy cheeks, now that Beatie was eating properly.

Arthur continued to repair the furniture, and encouraged her and Beatie to spend time with him as he worked, explaining what he was doing and why, and smiling at them frequently. Ah, she loved that smile of his!

He might not be formally qualified, but he seemed to have a feel for wood, and when you watched the way he stroked a piece with gentle fingertips you could see his love for it. And the finished pieces were truly beautiful.

She sat with him and Biff in the evenings once Beatie was asleep, and enjoyed their company, the three of them discussing everything under the sun.

But she had to admit to herself that she enjoyed the evenings most of all when it was just Arthur. Biff seemed to have grown rather fond of his former landlady, and called in to see her occasionally. He was also looking for premises to start a business once this situation was resolved, so he sometimes went out in the early evenings now that the days were getting longer. Of course either Rob or Phil Becksley would still be on duty, just in case of trouble, but they didn't intrude.

'Will poor Beatie ever be really free of that woman?' she wondered aloud one evening.

'We'll make sure of it, one way or the other,' Arthur said firmly. 'And if we have to leave the country to do that, I'm willing to emigrate.' He hesitated, then added, 'Would you go that far away with me to help her?'

'Definitely, though I'd rather not, because it'd mean leaving my sons.' She smiled at him, had known he'd say that, then saw Biff look from her to Arthur and open his mouth as if to speak, then close it again.

She guessed he'd been going to comment on their growing closeness and was glad he hadn't done so. Arthur was a rather shy person and it might have upset him. Anyway, they didn't need interference. They were getting to know one another quite nicely, thank you very much, and were old enough to manage their growing friendship in their own way.

She smiled and corrected herself: it was a courtship, really, even if it was a quiet one. No flowers, no fancy words and pro-testations, just a lovely feeling of growing closeness as they got to know the smaller details about each other's lives and hopes for the future.

Well, life was mostly made up of small things, wasn't it?

After some consideration, Vanner went to call on Mrs Hicks in his role as minister of her church. She was one of his most important parishioners and was generous in her contributions to the Sunday collections, and he knew she was fretting about not having found her granddaughter.

'My dear lady, is there any news of that poor child?'

'None at all, Mr Vanner.'

'I was thinking about your situation. She hasn't been seen with her grandfather, I know, but I noticed in the village shop that he was buying more food than I consider necessary for one man, even though he has Mr Higgins living with him.

And there was a Fry's chocolate bar too. Who was that for? The shopkeeper sounded surprised when he bought it, asked if he'd developed a sweet tooth lately.'

She looked at him in puzzlement and he realised he'd have to be more specific. She was not the cleverest of women, though actually he preferred that. Clever women were an abomination as far as he was concerned.

'Do you suppose Arthur Chapman has somehow managed to get the child into his house without our watchers noticing?'

'Even if he has, I can do nothing about it. Mr Peters won't authorise a search of his house or any other without good reason, and no one has actually seen Beatie there.' She sighed.

He wasn't going to let her drop her search because it had occurred to him that the child would likely be Mrs Hicks's heir. Beatie might also inherit a share in Chapman's house if anything happened to him and his son. Money was the one thing Vanner had never managed to accumulate, he couldn't understand why. He had to turn to the church in desperation for financial security.

Maybe he should arrange something else to deal with Chapman. It'd make a useful diversion, taking some of the attention away from his corps of young men. Training them to act in a more military manner was something which gladdened his soul. That was what young men should be doing with their lives. Look at how things were being organised in Germany.

'My dear Mrs Hicks, I think you should get another JP to authorise that instead of the Peters fellow, who is far too friendly with Chapman. Perhaps Mr Forester?'

'I've heard the name, but don't know him.'

'He lives in the country just south of Rivenshaw and they tell me he's strict in his application of the law.'

'Do you think Mr Peters would allow this to happen?'

Vanner took a deep, happy breath. This was exactly the opening he'd been hoping for. 'I don't think he can prevent it, especially as I am a little acquainted with Mr Forester and can explain the situation to him. If you'd like me to help you, that is?'

Her expression brightened considerably. 'Would you do that? I'd be so grateful.'

'You don't have a telephone at home, do you? We can telephone Mr Forester from my house tomorrow, if you like, and find out when he'll be free, then I could drive you over to see him.'

'You are most truly the shepherd of your flock.'

He smiled at her. She was almost literally correct. He had attracted a group of sheep who liked to be told exactly what to do, how to run their lives, and these included men who deplored the modern way of women working outside the home and not obeying their husbands as was only proper. He might not be married, but he sympathised with them. The Great War had led to a sorry situation in this country if you asked him.

If only there was a man of Herr Hitler's calibre to lead them here in England.

Still, if things turned out as he expected in Germany, and some of the covert activities of the remaining English fascist groups paid off, there might be hope that England would be forcibly brought to heel when the inevitable happened, even if it all took longer than they'd hoped.

And in his small way he, Osbert Vanner, intended to contribute to this necessary change, and of course, to benefit from it afterwards.

But at the moment, he wished to reveal Arthur Chapman for what he was, a drunk, an incompetent, and a child abductor.

It was abominable that such a person would inherit a big house like that while a godlly man like himself could so lack money. Chapman didn't deserve it. Most definitely not.

But if something happened to that fellow, and the child inherited under the grandmother's guardianship, well, that might be a very lucrative situation for Osbert to step into.

26

Higgerson had told Jem he intended to visit the new cellars to check that they were being dug out properly, so Jem in turn went to see Calum while he was out on an errand for his master.

'You need to push ahead with the work,' he warned. 'It doesn't look at all near to being finished.'

'We're at a crucial stage,' Calum said. 'You can't hurry this sort of job. You have to dig the foundations properly and put in strong supports for the walls.'

'Can't you just make it look good, then go back and do things properly afterwards? You know what *he's* like. He wants to see progress.'

'He must be a right old sod to work for. Don't know how you stand it.'

Jem shrugged. 'He doesn't bother me too much. He knows there isn't anyone else in the valley who can get things done the way he wants.'

'How does someone who spent a good part of last year in prison know that?'

'Before I slipped up, I worked for Dobbs, and watched how he did things. Smart fellow, Dobbs.'

They both chuckled at the thought of him stealing Higgerson's car. It was still talked about and laughed over.

Calum rolled his eyes. 'I suppose you're planning to get away with his new car, too.'

'I'd rather stay here and make money.'

But his friend's joking words lingered in Jem's mind as he walked home after he'd put the car in the garage and handed the keys to his employer. He didn't know anyone in the valley who dealt in stolen cars, but he'd shared a cell with a chap who had been a used-car salesman in Bury. Cortonby hadn't spent all his working life on so-called honest selling, but had confided in him that he'd also dealt in stolen cars, which brought in a lot more money.

And to tell the truth, Jem was finding it very tiring kowtowing to Higgerson day-in day-out. He would love to get the better of him.

Could he do the same thing as Dobbs, run off in his master's car? He'd have to think about it. No harm in working out how to do something if an opportunity arose, was there?

When he got home that night, he said abruptly to his wife, 'I think you should have our bags packed, ready to take off suddenly. In fact, we should live out of them from now on.'

She clutched his arm tightly and gave him a little shake. 'You haven't lost your job?'

'No, of course not, but you can never be sure of anything with Higgerson, and if I see a chance to do what Dobbs did, pinch his car and run off in it, well, we could make a nice chunk of money. You've always wanted us to set ourselves up in a little business like a shop somewhere, haven't you? Maybe it might be worthwhile keeping our eyes open for an opportunity.'

She let go of his arm but didn't say anything. He cocked his head and waited. You couldn't push her into doing something, only hope she'd agree.

'All right,' she said at last. 'We'll think about it and keep our eyes open. But we'll make sure we work out properly how to do it this time. I don't want the police catching us and putting us both in prison.'

He shuddered at the mere thought of that. 'I don't want to be locked away ever again. I couldn't seem to breathe properly in that place.'

'How are you coping with going down them new cellars, love?'

He shuddered and said nothing. He hated it, absolutely hated it. Which was another reason to get away.

Could he really do it?

Higgerson had told him to be ready at ten o'clock sharp the following morning, to go and look at how the cellars were coming on, so Jem got to work a bit early. When his employer came in, a quarter of an hour later than he'd said, he was yawning.

'If you're tired, sir, we could go another day,' Jem ventured.

Higgerson stared at him. 'Well, it's nice to have someone to notice how I feel.'

'Yes, sir.' He waited.

'I said we'd go today and that's what we'll do. Bring the car round and we'll be off.' He handed over the keys.

It was such a nuisance to have to wait till he handed them over each day, Jem thought as he drove carefully up the hill from Rivenshaw. That was going to be one of the big problems about finding a way to run off with the car.

When they were driving through Birch End and approaching Backshaw Moss, Higgerson said suddenly, 'Stop!'

Jem did as he was told, and waited. What now?

'Look at the damned place! I'd been forgetting what a slum it is. I'd hoped to be out of this sort of business by now if I'd got those three houses, but at least there's money to be made in slums if one is careful. As you'll see today.'

'Yes, sir.'

More silent staring, then, 'Drive on.'

Jem stopped the car opposite the houses with the pile of dug-out muck outside them. 'I'll not arrange for that to be taken away until after all the digging is finished.'

'Yes. Hmm. I think I'll get out here and you can park the car further back in Daisy Street. There seem to be fewer urchins around back there. Find a strong lad and offer him sixpence to keep an eye on the car.'

'Yes, sir.'

Jem chose to pay a hungry-looking man to watch the car rather than a lad. Grown men were more reliable, he'd found, and more grateful if you needed a favour from them one day.

He rejoined his master, who was standing staring round, his eyes darting here and there. He did this sometimes when he was considering how to make money from a place.

After a few moments Higgerson nodded to him. 'Right, then. We'll go inside now. No, wait a minute. I'll take my jacket off. It's a new one and I don't want to get it messed up. Here, you can run back down the street and lock it in the car for me. Look sharp!'

Jem took it, surprised at this order, even more surprised to feel the wallet still in it. His master was in a strange mood this morning, that was sure. He hurried back to the car, then returned to find Higgerson staring round again. He sighed and waited. You did a lot of waiting when you worked for Higgerson, and you did it in silence if you had any sense.

'What are you standing there like a fool for, Stanley?'

Waiting for another fool, he thought, but of course he couldn't say that. 'I was wondering if I should go inside and tell Baxter you're here, sir.'

'No, don't. We'll just walk in on him. You learn more when you take people by surprise.'

Jem prayed that Calum had had someone watching out for their arrival, or at least looked to be working hard.

To his relief, Calum was there in the cellar, digging busily, together with a man he'd employed throughout this job to share the heavy work.

Higgerson walked slowly and stiffly down the new cellar steps that were formed temporarily of wooden planks. He stopped almost at the bottom to look at the progress.

The two men stopped digging to watch him.

For some unknown reason, a shiver ran down Jem's spine and he stayed at the top of the steps. At least there was more space down here, now that the rooms were just about finished. It had been hell forcing himself down the narrow hole formed when Baxter first started.

'I thought the work would be further on. How much longer do you expect it to take?' Higgerson asked Baxter.

'Another two weeks at least, probably more like three, Mr Higgerson. This isn't sand, you know, so it's not simple to dig through it. Luckily it's soil from the original swamp Backshaw Moss was built on. That's how it got its name. But we do have to shore up them walls properly.'

'They look all right to me.'

'If you want to risk them caving in, sir . . .?' He waited, a questioning look on his face.

'Of course I don't, you fool. I suppose you'd better shore them up.'

'That's why I found a man with some bricks for sale, second-hand, which are cheaper but just as strong. I'm going to use them as piers to support the walls. They'll last longer than wooden panels would.'

Jem watched Higgerson open his mouth to protest. He knew that expression and sighed. Why did the man always want the impossible?

Calum held up one hand. 'If you want years of rental money from these cellars, *sir*, you'll need to make sure the walls are held firmly in place and stay that way. I thought you agreed about that when you gave me the money for the materials.'

'Well, do your best to keep the costs down.'

'I always do.'

The other man stopped digging to listen intently as if he could hear something outside, then left the cellar. He came back a few seconds later to call down, 'The bricks are here, Calum. They won't unload them till they've been paid.'

Calum moved forward. 'Excuse me a moment, sir. I need to see the bricks are unloaded into the backyard, so that no one can pinch them.' He paused at the top of the steps to add, 'I'd be obliged if you'd not touch anything down there, sir. Some of the panels are only put up temporarily.'

Higgerson watched him leave, then turned to Jem. 'Go back outside and wait till I call you. I want to pace these cellars out, see if I can get three rooms out of it.'

Jem did as he was told, glad to get back into the fresh air. It always seemed harder to breathe down in that cellar. He couldn't understand why Higgerson would want to spend more time down there than he needed.

He hurried outside, sucking in big mouthfuls of air. Wonderful, that felt. You could almost taste the difference.

In front of the house, Jem found Calum helping a man unload some second-hand bricks into wheelbarrows and then taking them along a narrow path at the side of the house to the backyard. They were all sorts of colours, but they'd not be on view if the walls were going to be plastered over, so that didn't matter.

Calum came to stand beside Jem and left the man delivering the bricks to carry on. 'What's *he* doing down there?'

'Mr Higgerson is pacing it out, trying to work out whether he can fit three rooms in. He wants us to wait outside till he calls.'

Calum scowled. 'Well, I'm not going to extend that space, not for anything. It'd be asking for trouble. He's already had me go further than I wanted.'

'Ah, never mind him. Fancy a fag?' Jem asked.

'Yes, please.'

'He usually takes a while when he's figuring something out, so we might as well enjoy a break. It's no wonder he's made a lot of money. He certainly thinks hard about what he's doing. I sat waiting in the car for two hours once when he was planning something. Only that idea didn't come off. Here.' He held out the packet and they both got a cigarette out and lit up.

'What did he want that didn't work out?'

'To buy them three big houses at the end of Daisy Street. He's still furious about not getting them.'

'He gets angry easily.'

'Yes. Used to treat his poor wife badly when something happened that he didn't like.'

'Well, she escaped, poor woman. Even I heard about him thumping her.'

'He's still sending men to try to get her back.'

'Stupid waste of money, that. He's rich enough to find another woman, one who's more willing like.'

'Ah, but his wife is *respectable* and another woman wouldn't be. He likes to pretend he's respectable, but the other business owners aren't fooled, and they don't have much to do with him outside work.'

They puffed contentedly for a while, then Jem reverted back to today's job. 'Who'd have thought you could get two more rooms under the house?'

'He'd have been better leaving it at one.'

'I'm telling you straight: if he says he wants two, or even three new cellars, don't argue with him.'

'Well, he'll have to find someone else to make more space if he does decide he wants more, because I won't do it. The ground there isn't right for it.'

Left alone in the cellar, Higgerson slowly paced it out. He couldn't see any reason why there shouldn't be another cellar space dug out. It had gone all right so far, hadn't it?

Mind, it was a bit damp and stuffy down here, but that'd be the tenants' problem, not his.

He poked his walking stick into a gap between the temporary wall panels opposite the wooden steps and it slid into it with no problem.

'See!' he said aloud. 'It could easily be dug out further.'

After he pulled the stick out, a trickle of soil ran down from the narrow hole it had made, and only gradually stopped. 'Piece of cake to dig that,' he said scornfully.

He moved along a couple of yards and tried the wall there. Once again, his walking stick could be pushed in easily. '*Ha! ha!*' he said triumphantly as he began to walk up and down the dimly lit space, poking holes here and there, and thumping one of the panels, wondering why he was bothering to pay for bricks.

He calculated how much rent three cellars would bring in as opposed to two over the course of a year, pleased with the amount, and started to work out what use he would put the money to. Another house to rent rooms in or a better house to rent out the whole?

Another trickle of soil ran down the wall, but he was too engrossed in his calculations to bother with that. When one hole started to get bigger he stared at it and thought again how easy it would be to dig out further.

'I'm going to be the richest man in the valley before I'm through, and I'm well on my way,' he added in a loud voice, thumping one clenched fist on the wall panel next to him for emphasis. 'And I'm going to get Lallie back and—'

There was a sudden loud brushing noise, followed by a low rumbling, not like anything he'd ever heard before. He swung round to find out what had caused it, only to see the wall next to the steps bulge outwards.

He moved towards the steps, but it all happened so quickly the way was blocked before he could start to go up them, and he had to jump back out of the way of the tide of muck.

One of the lamps had been tipped over by the movement of the earth, leaving only one still burning, and the cellar had become darker, feeling threatening. He didn't like it, not a bit.

'Help! Stanley! Help! Get me out of here!'

Then the wall behind him turned into a stream of soil and minor rubble, burying his feet to his ankles. As he began to kick his way out of it, more of the wall caved in, and suddenly he was buried up to the waist and couldn't move.

He yelled again for help at the top of his voice.

Then he couldn't seem to find the breath to yell, was having trouble breathing as the soil continued to grip more tightly and the pile moved up his body.

When the earth shook beneath them, Calum tossed his second cigarette aside. The solid wall they'd been leaning against suddenly seemed to be pushing them forward and with a shout of 'Get away!' he dragged Jem forward into the road and they turned to stare as the wall of the house began to collapse slowly, spreading outwards like a flood, pouring some of the house's contents with it.

'What the hell's happening?' Jem demanded.

'It's all caving in, the whole sodding house. An' it's pulling down the next house with it. I told him it wasn't safe to dig that cellar out, but he insisted, didn't he? It's not my fault. You'll tell them that, won't you?'

'Why should I tell anyone anything about this cave-in?'

Calum pointed towards the front door, or where the front door had been. 'Because it'll have collapsed on him and killed him, so the authorities will have to look into it. You surely don't think he's going to come out of that cellar alive, do you?'

Jem could only goggle at him.

'Look at it. Everything has collapsed, and he hasn't run out, has he?'

'We have to get him out, then.'

'I'm not going in there. I like having air to breathe. Anyway, he'll have been crushed to death by now, and serve him right.'

'You mean—' Jem couldn't finish his question because the rest of the house was subsiding as they watched, and they had to move backwards again.

People were running along the street now, calling out, asking what was happening.

'Stay back!' Calum yelled. 'It's a cave-in.'

The man who'd been helping with the digging appeared from one side. 'It's giving way at the back too! We had to jump over the wall to save ourselves. People have run out of the other two houses. I think they all got out.'

The whole world seemed full of dust and strange noises. Jem couldn't form a single word, couldn't move, only watch in horror. He could have been down there, under all that.

Higgerson was down there still.

'Any chance at all that he could be alive?' he asked Calum.

'None. Look at it, all piled up on top of whatever's in the cellar. We hadn't strengthened the walls properly down there yet.'

'It'll have crushed him to death?'

'Of course it bloody will. How many times do I have to tell you?'

Even the people who'd come to gawp were staying well back, whispering to one another and pointing.

'The council or somebody will hold a big inquiry after this, and we'll be called as witnesses,' Calum said. 'Happened to me once before. I'm leaving town before they start all that fussation here. They're bound to blame me, even though I was only doing as *he* ordered. I'll find work in the south, change my name.'

It didn't take Jem long to decide that he wasn't going to stay around for any damned inquiries, either.

Then he realised what this was – his big chance. He sought for an excuse to leave Clover Lane. 'I'd, um, better go and fetch Mr Higgerson's lawyer.'

'What can he do?' But Calum was talking to himself, because Jem had set off running down the road towards the car.

If no one could have lived through a bad cave-in like that, Jem thought, Higgerson wasn't going to need his car, was he? And no one else would notice for a while that it was missing. It'd be simple to drive off in it, easiest thing in the world if he did it quickly before anyone realised what he was doing.

This was meant to be.

People were coming out of houses and shops now to look at what had happened.

'Keep back!' he yelled as he passed them. 'More of the ground may cave in yet.'

'Was anyone caught inside?' one man shouted.

'Higgerson.'

That shut them up for a few moments.

Jem fumbled with the car keys.

A man came over to ask, 'Is he really dead?'

'Bound to be. The whole house has fallen down on top of him.' He thumped one clenched fist down on the other to illustrate this, and saw one woman standing nearby smile as if that was good news.

A man shouted, 'Higgerson was in there. He's likely dead!'

Someone at the back of the crowd cheered, and others joined in. They were all smiling.

Jem shook his head. He hoped when his time came people weren't happy to see him go.

He got into the car and started the engine. The sooner he got away from Rivenshaw the better.

This was his big chance, and if his wife wasn't coming with him, he'd go on his own.

27

When the phone rang at the police station, Sergeant Deemer picked it up.

Whoever was on the other end of the line made no sense, so he said loudly and clearly, 'Start again. And speak slowly. You're not making any sense.'

'A house has fallen down. We think a man's been killed. It just . . . collapsed on him.'

'Where is this?'

He took down the particulars, not surprised that it was in Backshaw Moss.

'And who is missing? Do you know?'

'Mr Higgerson.'

It was the sergeant's turn to struggle for words. It couldn't be. His valley couldn't be so lucky as to get rid of their major villain.

'Are you still there, Sergeant?'

'Yes. Sorry. I was just – um, a bit surprised. Have you called the fire brigade?'

'No.'

'I'll do that, then set off. Don't let anyone try to go inside.'

He didn't put the phone down, but cleared the connection and dialled what he knew to be the fire chief's direct number. He explained what he'd been told, ending, 'I'll meet you there.'

'And they said Higgerson had been killed?'

'Yes.'

'Bloody hell!'

Sergeant Deemer put the phone down and yelled for Cliff. 'Where's Mike?'

'On an early lunch break.'

'Where did he go?'

'Round the corner to the café, said he was fed up of sand-wiches.'

'Go and fetch him back quick as you can. There's trouble in Backshaw Moss.'

'There usually is.'

Deemer got the emergency kit out of the cupboard, the pack of items designed to rescue people on the moors. It hadn't been used for a long time, and he wasn't sure it'd be any use today, but it was all he could think of.

He stopped dead, standing motionless as he realised how ironic it would be if he used it to rescue Higgerson.

He couldn't seem to believe that the man was really and truly dead.

You shouldn't hope for someone's death, but Higgerson had done such harm to the people of this valley, the poor ordi-nary people struggling to put bread on the table, watching their children grow up spindly and stunted. He'd done more harm than anyone Deemer had ever known and — He cut that thought short, carried the kit outside and put it into the car boot, just as Mike and Cliff came racing round the corner.

'You can drive us up to Backshaw Moss, Mike. Go as fast as is safe. I'll tell you all I know on the way.'

The news left two more people stunned into silence.

When they got to the place where the houses at the corner of Clover Street usually stood, they all exclaimed in astonish-ment at what they saw. There weren't any houses left, just piles of rubble with all sorts of building materials and household items poking out. Everything looked higgledy piggledy, as if a child had thrown a tantrum and destroyed its toys in one fell swoop.

'I've never seen anything like it.' Deemer's voice came out scratchy.

'What should we do, Sarge?'

'To tell you the truth, I'm not sure. I've never had to deal with a house collapse before.' To his relief the fire engine came racing along Daisy Street just then, stopping nearby.

The fire chief and three men tumbled out as if ready to grab their hoses, but then froze, staring in shock, like most of the people nearby.

Deemer hurried across to the chief. 'Where do we start, Nigel lad?'

The chief shook his head. He echoed the sergeant's words. 'I don't know. I've never dealt with a collapsed building before.'

'Neither have I.'

So that made two of them treading new ground, Deemer thought. 'Well, we can only do our best. I'll get my constables to move people back, shall I?'

'Yes. I'll, um, examine the scene.'

A man came across to them before they could put this plan into operation. 'I was outside it when this happened. Sergeant. It wasn't my fault. Higgerson had insisted on digging out another cellar. I told him it wasn't safe to touch the walls till they were braced properly, but he went down there on his own and he must have started poking about.'

'Where's Jem Stanley? He usually drives Higgerson round town. Is he trapped down there too?'

'No, he was outside with me when it happened. He drove off to fetch Higgerson's lawyer.'

Deemer frowned. 'Do you know who that is?'

'I think he's gone to that new chap: now, what was his name? Oh yes, Littleproud, that's it. Why do lawyers always have strange names? Anyway, Jem will be bringing him back to look at this, I suppose.'

This puzzled Deemer. Why hadn't Jem Stanley simply phoned the lawyer, who would have his own car to drive here in?

He looked across at the bystanders. 'Can someone make a phone call for me?'

A young woman stepped forward. 'There's a phone at the village shop in Birch End. I can go, if you like. Only take me a couple of minutes if I run through the back alleys.'

'Thanks. Ask them to phone Littleproud, the new lawyer. Tell him his client Higgerson has probably been killed and there aren't any of his family around, so we need him to take any actions necessary legally.'

That made him wonder what provisions if any Higgerson had made for his death, given that his wife and both his sons had left him. 'And just check that Stanley's with him.'

He frowned. He had a strange feeling about this. Had Stanley gone off to see the lawyer, or had he copied his predecessor and run off with Higgerson's car? No, surely not?

In spite of the seriousness of the situation, a smile escaped Deemer's control. He couldn't help hoping Jem Stanley had done that. It'd be poetic justice, and it'd get rid of another nuisance from the valley.

The smile quickly faded and he turned back to the mess, waiting for the fire chief to decide how to start dealing with the wreckage.

His mother had always said, *If in doubt, do nowt.* He had no idea what the correct procedures were for a situation like this, so he would definitely do nothing without a good reason.

Jem drove down into Rivenshaw as fast as he could. He was going to do it. By hell he was! You didn't often get a chance to make a lot of money. Well, it'd seem a lot to him.

He knew the name of the place where his former cell mate had gone back to work because he'd been there when Cortonby got a letter offering him his old job back and started boasting about it. In Bury, it was. Maybe Cortonby would help him sell Higgerson's car on the quiet in return for a share of the profits. Otherwise he'd just have to dump it.

When he got back home, he pulled the wallet out of Higgerson's jacket and told his wife what had happened.

They looked inside it and found over thirty pounds.

'All that money,' she whispered.

'Get the bag. We're leaving.'

She stared at him, looking terrified.

'It's our only chance to make a lot of money. I'm going whether you come with me or not. Make up your mind. We need to act quickly.'

She steadied herself with one hand on the table, as if she were feeling dizzy at the thought, then said, 'I'm coming with you.'

She had gone so pale, he asked, 'You all right, love?'

'Yes. No. Well, I've never broken the law before. It makes me feel strange even to think of it.'

'We won't break it again after this, but it's our big chance,' he said soothingly. 'We'll see my friend, find out how much money we can get for the car, then change our names and head off somewhere to start a new life.'

She ran upstairs to the bedroom and he followed her, watching her stuff a few more things into the battered suitcase, then fill a pillowcase with their best shoes and some other bits and pieces.

He stopped her getting anything else. 'That's it. We have to go straight away if we want to escape.'

'All right. You carry the case down, Jem.'

He did that, then glanced at her. She was looking better now, had got her colour back, was more like her usual brisk self. He loaded the things in the car, she grabbed their hats and coats from the hooks in the hall, and off they set, just like that. Excitement ran though him.

Even before they'd got through the town she said, 'Stop at the next place with a post office and we'll draw our money out. If we're going to change our names, we won't want to give ourselves away by where we draw money out.'

'Eh, I never thought of that.'

'Which is why you need me.' She was smiling now. 'It might work, Jem love. If it does, we'll go and live in Torquay.'

'What? Why there?'

'I've always liked the seaside and I've got an old auntie there. Auntie Mary. We'll go to her. She'll take us in till we can find a place of our own.'

'We can't tell her what we've done,' he warned.

'We can, you know. She's the black sheep of the family. Her husband made money really quickly one year. My dad always said they couldn't have done that honestly. When they moved away in the middle of the night without telling anyone, we were quite sure he was right.'

'We're not telling anyone where we've gone, either.'

She nodded agreement. 'My auntie didn't get in touch with anyone in the family till she sent me a birthday card with a postal order for five shillings in it three years later. It had her address on a bit of paper.'

'She's the one you send Christmas cards to.'

'Yes. And I've always kept the address. I was her favourite, you see, and I got on really well with her. I always wished she was my mother.'

He still didn't like the sound of it. 'That's all very well, but I thought it was going to be just the two of us from now on, with new names. She'll know who we are.'

'She'll not give us away and she'll help us build a new life. And I'm giving you notice now, Jem Stanley: after you've sold the car, I'm going to be the one who handles the money and does the planning. You're useless at it. Don't worry. I'll make us comfortable – and through honest hard work this time, without having to worry about the police knocking on the door. That's the only way I'm staying with you.'

He looked at the expression on her face and realised he might be getting away from Higgerson but he was still going to be ordered around. Maybe she was right, though. Maybe he should have listened to her more. She was a clever woman, he'd give her that. Probably as clever as Higgerson had been.

Had been! It amazed him to think of his employer as dead. Just went to show that you never know what might hit you next.

Well, as long as he got rid of the car without getting caught, he didn't really mind what they did from now on. It couldn't be worse than working for Higgerson. The man had got more and more unreasonable, and look where it'd led him: he'd lost his wife and now his life.

Jem grinned suddenly. He was doing better than his former employer, still had a wife who was a tidy armful in bed and liked her cuddles, so it wouldn't all be bad, would it?

And it'd be wonderful not to see Higgerson again. Jem had earned more money than ever before in his life working for him, but money wasn't everything.

Then a dreadful thought occurred to him. Was Higgerson definitely dead? They'd assumed it, but no one had seen the body.

If he wasn't, he'd come after them.

Oh, he must be dead, surely! The whole house had collapsed on him, hadn't it? It'd have crushed him as if he were a black beetle crawling out of the wall.

The firemen worked hard under Deemer and the fire chief's supervision, first putting up markers to warn people the area was dangerous, then dealing with the problem of whether any of the tenants from the two houses had been trapped and killed.

It was not at first known who exactly had lived there, and who was there to ask now, with Higgerson, the landlord, missing presumed dead? It was all a big muddle.

They heard someone calling for help and found two women and a baby trapped at the rear of one house. They were able to hand them over to a group of women from the local chapel to be cared for, not Vanner's chapel, whose members didn't seem to help anyone unless they belonged to the same congregation.

The other tenants came home one by one as the day passed, from shopping or work, or just simply visiting friends. All were the poorer sort of people, so were shocked and in despair at losing all their possessions.

In the end Sergeant Deemer and the fire chief commandeered the hall at the Birch End chapel. They sent out a call for blankets and clothing for those who no longer had a home by asking people to phone friends and pass on the message in any way they could about what people were now calling a disaster.

There was no chance of anyone retrieving their possessions, and it was completely out of the question to try to retrieve Higgerson's body.

'We need some miners,' the fire chief said thoughtfully as the afternoon wore on. 'They know about shoring up dangerous places and making tunnels.'

'I don't like leaving a dead body in there,' Deemer confessed. 'Even Higgerson's.'

'We don't have any choice.' The chief paused, then asked, 'Do you have any idea where his wife is? We ought to let her know. In fact, she ought to come back. She will presumably be the one who inherits, her or one of the sons?'

'Who knows what that sod has arranged? I have the phone number of a gentleman who's helping her.' He caught the look on the fire chief's face and added firmly, 'A very respectable gentleman, and I gather Mrs Higgerson has been staying with his daughter who is engaged to marry her older son. There's nothing immoral going on there, believe me.'

'Ah. I see. Rumour said otherwise.'

'Rumour is often wrong, especially when Higgerson is— *was!*— involved. Anyway, I'll phone this gentleman when I get back to the police station and he can find out what she wants to do. In the meantime we have people to house and feed, and a guard to be set on the property in case anyone is stupid enough to try to dig out possessions that might still have value. We don't want any more deaths.'

28

It was eight o'clock before the sergeant was able to pick up the phone and get through to the Tillett household. To his relief it was Mr Tillett who answered, so he explained the situation to him, impressed by the way the man quickly recovered from his shock and started being practical. He suggested the family discuss what had happened and get back to the sergeant in the morning to let him know what they wished to do about the situation.

'You'll have to call me quite early, I'm afraid, because there will be a lot to do tomorrow and I'll have to be out and about. Eight o'clock is the latest I dare leave it to get to the site of the disaster.'

'We'll discuss it and have an answer for you by seven o'clock in the morning about what we wish to do.'

'That'll be very helpful. Perhaps that poor lady can have some peace in her life now,' Deemer said gently, wanting to show that he understood the situation between her and Higgerson.

'I certainly hope so. She's suffered a lot. You're sure about him being dead?'

'I don't think there can be any doubt about that, Mr Tillett, even though we haven't seen the body yet. Three storeys of house came down on top of him, and it was a bare cellar without anywhere to shelter and only wooden support walls. No one could have survived that.'

'Thank goodness. All three of them need to feel safe again.'

★

Edmund Tillett went to join his family, who were starting their nightly ritual of a cup of cocoa and piece of cake as a prelude to going to bed.

His face must have betrayed the seriousness of the news he was bringing because they immediately stopped talking, put everything down, and waited for him to explain what the phone call had been about.

'I have to tell you, my dear Mrs Fennell, that there has been a serious accident in Rivenshaw and it is feared that your husband has been killed.' He gave them brief details, then waited.

'Can he really be dead?' Felix asked in a whisper, as if afraid of saying it too loudly.

'It seems highly likely.'

It was Kit who said bluntly what everyone must be thinking. 'We would all be free if he were. We could build decent lives for ourselves without always having to look over our shoulders and worrying about what he might try next.'

'And you won't have to be sent away from us now,' his mother said.

He beamed at her.

'And you can become a doctor.'

'Oh, Mum!' He gulped audibly.

'You have no good feelings whatsoever for him, do you?' Edmund asked gently.

'No, none. All we feel for him is hatred and loathing.' Kit looked across at his brother for confirmation and got an immediate nod, the same reaction from their mother.

'How can we like him?' Felix asked. 'We've both felt his fists times without number, and we've had years of seeing him thump Mum, and been helpless to stop him. I still get nightmares about him.' His voice came out choked as he said the last few words.

Lallie took over. 'We've all seen him lie, cheat, steal, and, we suspect, arrange for people to be killed or else have to flee from their homes and families to escape his wrath. No, we shan't grieve for him at all, Mr Tillett. The only good thing he's ever done for me has been to give me two wonderful sons.'

Both her sons went to sit on the arms of their mother's chair, each wrapping one arm around her shoulders and kissing the nearest cheek gently.

Tillett gave them a minute or two to pull themselves together, then said, 'I promised to phone Sergeant Deemer tomorrow morning at seven to let him know what we wish to do about the situation, so we'll need to decide on our first steps before then. Do you want to work that out now or get up very early in the morning?'

'I'd rather decide now,' Lallie said. 'I doubt I'll sleep well whatever we decide, but I'd like to have something definite to plan for while I'm wakeful. I'll start the discussion by saying I think I ought to go back to Rivenshaw straight away.'

'You're sure?'

'Who else is there to deal with things? I'm still his wife legally, and he doesn't have any other relatives that I know of, and no real friends. I've sometimes wondered if Higgerson is his real name and where he actually comes from.'

'To whom will he have left his property, do you think?'

'I have no idea. To one of the boys, probably. I hope so, anyway.'

They discussed it for an hour, but she remained adamant that it was her duty to return.

Edmund saw the relief on her face and those of her sons when he said that he was going with them. 'And what's more, I'll take John Joe and a couple of his men, just to make sure you three stay safe. If this is a trick, and he is still alive, he'll not get away with harming you.'

When Biff heard the news he hurried straight home to tell the others in Number 25.

'Higgerson's dead?' Arthur stared at him. 'Are you sure?'

'The houses at the corner of Clover Lane collapsed on him and he's buried under the rubble. He can't have survived that.'

'I shan't truly believe it until they find his body,' Gwynneth said bitterly. 'How that man has survived this long is a miracle, he's hurt so many people. It'd be just like him to crawl out alive.'

'Sergeant Deemer says it's not at all likely anyone could have survived.'

'His death would mean I felt safe in this house,' Arthur said. 'Maybe I wouldn't even have to hire guards.'

'We'll still have the problem of keeping Beatie safe from her grandmother,' Gwynneth pointed out.

He sighed. 'Yes. Poor little love.'

'I'll go out first thing tomorrow morning and find out what's happening,' Biff said thoughtfully.

Phil Becksley, who was on guard duty that night, beamed at them when he heard the news. 'I feel as if there is some justice in the world if Higgerson has been removed from it in such a way. Now, if someone would just deal with that horrible Mr Vanner, people round here could get their lives back again, without him haranguing them in the street.'

His eyes went to Beatie as he said this, and the others nodded slightly. Everyone in the household had quickly grown fond of the child and even in the short time she'd been with them she was looking healthier.

Biff waited till the little girl had gone to bed to tell them something else. 'I didn't want to say anything while Beatie was around, but I heard that Vanner had called on Mrs Hicks and come out of her house looking smug. No one seemed to know why, but you have to wonder what mischief he's planning now.'

'No doubt we'll find out. We must remain ready to get Beatie down into the tunnels at a minute's notice.'

★

Jack Webster watched the minister drive away, then went back to weeding at the back of the chapel. Eh, the place had been sadly neglected. He had got as far as a small shed, and then stopped. Mr Vanner had told him it was to be left strictly alone because it was used to store important religious articles.

As usual the arrogance with which he spoke had irritated Jack, and he wondered why the minister had made such a point of threatening him about the loss of his job if he tried to get into the shed. Usually sheds were used to store garden tools, and surely that's what this one had originally been intended for?

He had to keep the tools they'd provided for him in a small lean-to at the other side, with a cheap padlock on the door that a child could have broken apart.

Naturally he wondered what the minister was hiding inside the shed and decided to see if he could find out. Mr Peters might be interested. And what better time than the present? He'd get warning of Vanner's return when he heard the car engine.

The wood at the bottom of one rear corner had rotted, and he'd brought a few worn pieces of wood from home that would match that of the shed, with a vague idea of repairing it out of sheer pride in doing his job properly.

He always picked up pieces of wood if he saw them lying around, because he didn't like to see things rot when they could be saved, if only to use for firewood. If he opened up the corner of the shed and got caught inside, he could claim he'd only been trying to repair it.

And if the minister sacked him, he wouldn't care. He was finding this job tedious because no one at the small chapel talked to him, not even to pass the time of day. That was strange, against human nature as far as he was concerned. He was only staying at this job for Mr Peters' sake, because now that he'd used the judge's money to buy the field, he was itching to work full-time on preparing the ground.

Besides, with Higgerson killed, who would pay his wages for the other half of the working week, that was what he wanted to know? He'd have to sneak in a visit to Mr Peters and have a private discussion about that.

The rotten wood came away easily, and with a little care he managed only to pull away enough to allow him to crawl inside. It was a very tight fit.

To his amazement he found some weapons stored there, a pitiful collection of daggers and rather old-fashioned revolvers just lying in an old chest of drawers.

What on earth did a minister of religion want with those? And why so many?

Inspection of another drawer showed letters received and copies of letters sent in a folder that had been wrapped up in oiled paper, presumably to keep it from rotting in the damp or being nibbled by mice or insects. The package and folder didn't seem to have been touched for a week or two, judging by the lack of recent dates on the letters at the top of the pile.

Why hadn't Vanner kept these at home?

On an impulse he removed a few letters, choosing a selection of different dates and stuffing them into his inside waistcoat pocket where he kept a few coins and a clean handkerchief when he was working out of doors. He didn't have time to read them now and could always put them back if they weren't of interest. But he'd pass them on to Mr Peters and hope they'd show something that was worth following up.

What on earth was that pitiful excuse for a minister of religion up to anyway?

Webster crawled out and replaced the rotted wooden bits with pieces he could pull in and out of that corner as needed, standing back to admire his own handiwork.

29

The following day it seemed as if the main topic of conversation in every corner of the valley was Higgerson, and how to prove that he really was dead. An anxiety to be sure of that was displayed by people from all levels of society, and revealed how much he had been feared.

People strolled past the two adjacent houses that had collapsed, stopping to stare from the other side of the street. However, there was nothing to be seen except a huge pile of rubble and two workmen keeping watch. It didn't take much persuasion for people to stay clear, and the guards themselves stayed out in the middle of the street. No one wanted to be caught in further collapses.

Was Higgerson really under all that? many asked, and the guards simply shrugged. Who knew?

Later in the afternoon interest shifted to his house in Rivenshaw when a large luxurious car and a big van drew up at the front. Neighbours peeped out of windows, passers-by stopped to stare.

A strong-looking man got out of one of the vehicles and began to walk around the house on the garden path.

Those who had seen them arrive later confirmed that the man seemed to be checking that everything was in order and he was definitely not attempting to break in.

The housemaid had also been noticed staring out of the front window, but she made no attempt to open any of the outer doors, let alone ask him what he was doing.

Another car drew up in front of the house a few minutes later, and a man in a dark suit got out, carrying a worn brief-case and looking flustered.

Only then did John Joe get out of the big Ford and start to walk across to him, then sigh and wait as the man stopped and stared. He was used to this reaction from some people when they first saw his dark skin, and he merely waited patiently for the man to finish staring and move closer.

He held out his hand. 'Good afternoon, sir. I'm John Joe. I work for Mr Tillett and deal particularly with the safety of his family.'

The new arrival hesitated, then shook the hand briefly. 'Oh, er, yes. I'm Stanley Littleproud, Mr Higgerson's lawyer.'

John Joe turned and beckoned to Mr Tillett, who got out of the car and also introduced himself. He was accorded a much longer and visibly more enthusiastic handshake, which amused John Joe.

Mr Tillett took over. 'Shall we go inside and discuss the situation, Mr Littleproud? Mrs Higgerson is waiting in the car to do that. I'm helping her at this difficult time because her older son is engaged to marry my daughter.'

John Joe watched the lawyer nod and glance towards the car as if reluctantly accepting the respectability of the lady. He didn't like the looks of the fellow, who was wearing a cheap suit in a rather loud pinstripe and a shirt that had been badly ironed.

When the lawyer rang the doorbell, the front door was opened by the elderly maid, who nodded to him. 'I'm so glad you've come, Mr Littleproud. I haven't known what to do today and that's the truth. I hardly slept a wink last night, with only me and cook in the house in case of trouble, because Mr Higgerson's man has disappeared as well.'

She obviously thought some respect was due to John Joe and Mr Tillett, so gave them an awkward jerk of the head.

However, when Lallie got out of the car, the maid darted forward, beaming. 'Oh, Mrs Higgerson, it's so nice to see you again!'

'Nice to see you too, Dora. Let's take everyone inside, shall we? It's a bit chilly to linger out here.'

Lallie led the way in and John Joe noticed how she braced herself and took a deep breath before she stepped across the threshhold. Her two sons followed the others into the house.

Two other men slipped out of the rear of the van and went across to speak to the chap who had originally done a circuit of the building. After a quick word with them, he went into the house as well, leaving the front door wide open. One of the men stood outside at the front, arms folded, expression watchful, while the other went round the house to the rear.

Inside the hall Lallie paused for a moment, feeling a strong urge to run out again, shuddering at being back here. She had hoped never to return, but felt it was her duty to be with her sons. She didn't know what her husband had done about a will, but was determined to guard her boys' inheritance to the best of her ability, because quite a large amount of the money had come from her family originally. She couldn't imagine that Gareth would have left anything to her, even so.

It took a while to get everyone except John Joe settled in the big sitting room, which had a forlorn air, as if it hadn't been used much lately.

Dora brought in a trolley with tea things on it.

Lallie made no attempt to speak to the sleazy-looking lawyer. She'd leave him to Mr Tillett.

When the maid had finally left them alone, John Joe came back to join them and said quietly, 'I did a quick check of the house and it seems unoccupied except for the two female servants. Definitely no sign of anyone who shouldn't be here. I've got three men on duty, so we should all be quite safe, day and night.'

'Thank you, John Joe. I don't know what we'd do without you.'

When Mr Tillett looked at Lallie to see whether she wanted to say anything, she waved one hand to indicate that he should continue to manage the proceedings.

'Mr Littleproud, perhaps we can start by finding out about Mr Higgerson's will? Since he seems to have been killed, it'll be up to the heir to manage things from now on.'

'He hasn't left a will, not with me at any rate, and he assured me that he had taken all business away from his previous lawyer. He, er, did say once that he wasn't old enough to need a will yet.'

'In which case, would the property go to Mrs Higgerson or to the eldest son?'

'I don't want it,' Lallie said. 'Let's carry on as if he'd left it to Felix.'

The lawyer looked from one to the other, shrugged, and said, 'As you wish, Mrs Higgerson. Actually, I think my client would have preferred that.'

'Has there been any word about retrieving Mr Higgerson's body?' Tillett asked.

'Not that I know of. The police say that since there seems no chance of him being still alive they don't want to risk anyone else's life searching the rubble.'

'I'll go up to the accident site with John Joe after we've finished our meeting with you. I'd like to see the situation for myself. As for your fees, I can guarantee you payment of any reasonable demand, on the family's behalf, if that makes you feel better about continuing to act as their lawyer.'

'Thank you. That would be entirely satisfactory, Mr Tillett.'

'I think we shall all stay in this house for a few days, given that Felix is likely to be the heir, if you see no problem with that, Mr Littleproud?'

'No problem at all, sir.'

There seemed little else to be done until there was confirmation of Higgerson's death, so Mr Tillett got rid of the lawyer, doing it so adroitly that Littleproud went away convinced that he had made a good impression and would be asked to continue working for the family.

Not until the lawyer had left the house and driven away did Mr Tillett turn back to the others. 'John Joe and I will go and see what's happening in Backshaw Moss, if you'll be all right here, Mrs Higgerson?'

'I suppose you have to call me that while we're in Rivenshaw.'

'Unfortunately, it would be prudent.'

She sighed. 'Very well.'

'I'll come with you, Mr Tillett, if Kit will stay with Mother,' Felix said abruptly.

'Two of the men will stay here as well. You'll be carefully guarded at all times, Mrs Higgerson.'

Lallie nodded acceptance of this.

When the others had left, she confessed to Kit how much she hated being here.

'So do I, Mother. I have no happy memories of my father, only of you trying to keep us safe.' He came across and gave her a hug and she clung to him for a moment or two.

She could do it, she told herself, stay here for her sons' sake.

But she wasn't coming back to live here permanently.

That same day, Vanner picked up Mrs Hicks in the early afternoon and drove her to visit Mr Forester, a very elderly gentleman who was a JP in a nearby village.

When Vanner told him why they were there, he looked at them with a disapproving expression. 'It's rather unusual for someone to ask for another JP to intervene. Are you sure that's necessary?'

'The situation is rather unusual, but it's the child's morals we're most concerned about if she lives with her grandfather.'

'You said you didn't know where she was.'

'We don't know for certain, have no proof, but who else can she be with? And to add to the worries, there's an elderly widow who has also been involved with the child, a Mrs Harte. The two of them were seen with this Arthur Chapman, so it's rather worrying, not to say possibly immoral, that they are cohabiting.'

Forester frowned and stared at them. 'Hmm. Well, all I can promise you is to visit my colleague, Mr Peters, and discuss the situation with him. He may know something you don't.'

'Oh dear. We'd hoped you'd help us to rescue the child straight away. Who knows what she's seeing going on in that house? On top of everything else, the grandfather has been a known drunkard for several years.'

When Mr Forester said nothing, he spoke more forcibly, 'Surely you can authorise me to go into the house and search for her? The members of my church would be prepared to come with me to force an entry.'

'I cannot give you the authority to do that without more proof than just your word. And as I told you, I need to discuss the matter with my colleague before I can do anything.'

He stood up. 'Let me show you out.'

That put Vanner in a very bad mood as he drove back. He dropped Mrs Hicks off at her home and went back to his own to have a think about how to proceed. Apart from anything else, it would make a useful little exercise for him in guiding his flock. He needed to get them used to acting forcefully, ready for when the time came to change Britain.

Sadly it seemed likely it'd be years before that happened, because things were not going as well here as in Germany. But Vanner was certain that reason would eventually prevail against these loose modern attitudes, and men like him would be needed to guide people back to proper ways – and especially to deal with women who had grown morally lax and abandoned their rightful place in society since the last war.

★

That evening Dennison Peters received a phone call from a colleague who lived just outside the valley, asking him if he could visit him the following morning to discuss an urgent matter.

'You'd be welcome any time, naturally. May I ask what is so urgent?' And if it was urgent, why was Forester waiting till the following day to deal with it? He asked that too, as tactfully as he could manage.

After some humming and hawing, Forester told him there had been a complaint that he'd been biased in carrying out his duties as defender of the law of the land.

'I beg your pardon?'

'I really don't care to discuss this over the phone. I'll see you about nine o'clock tomorrow morning.'

Dennison put the phone down, grimacing. Not his favourite colleague, Forester. Very old-fashioned in his ways. And who could have complained? He had never let bias skew the way he carried out his duties, never had and never would.

When the phone rang again, it was His Lordship, asking if there was any progress on recovering Higgerson's body.

'Not yet, I'm afraid. We're trying to find someone with mining experience to come and assess how to do it.'

'Well, I can help you there. I know just the chap, the one who was in charge of extending the tunnels. I'll bring him over to see the site tomorrow morning. We'll be at your place just after nine. Got to go! I've a meeting about to start.'

Dennison sighed. Typical of His Lordship. Well, he'd see if he could sort out Forester's business before His Lordship arrived tomorrow.

Trust Higgerson to continue making life difficult even after he'd died. It was going to be hard even to retrieve his body safely.

Dennison had heard that Mrs Higgerson had arrived in town and had meant to call on her first thing in the morning, but that would have to wait till later now.

★

In Derbyshire a small car chugged up a hill and Jem Stanley nodded to his wife. 'Nice little runner, this. We did well to get this and some money for Higgerson's car.'

'*You* did very well.'

He beamed at that compliment. 'We'll make a little holiday of the journey, shall we? Two or three days on the road. Stay at bed and breakfast places.'

'No, we won't.'

'Eh?'

'You're already trying to spend that money, Jem. Well, it's not enough to make us rich, so we have to eke out every penny and make it do the work of two.'

'But—'

'We're still going to Torquay, mind. I've always wanted to live there. It looks so lovely in the photos other people have shown me.'

He tried to take charge. 'Who got this money, eh? Me, that's who. So I'm the one who says what we do with it.'

'You are if you want to sleep alone and cook your own meals.'

She'd threatened this before, yes, and carried out her threat, too. He tried a softer approach. 'I was thinking of making this into the honeymoon we never had.'

'No, you weren't. And we're not doing it. Do you want to go into the poorhouse when you're old?'

'They don't call it the poorhouse these days.'

'I don't care what they call it. That's what it is. And we're going to do better for ourselves. So when you get tired, we'll stop and have a nap in the car. Yes, and when we get settled in Torquay, I'm going to learn to drive.'

'I am *not* going to be driven around by a woman.'

'Oh, yes, you are, Jem Stanley.'

Nothing he said would make her change her mind. She wouldn't even allow him one night in a bed and breakfast place.

He tried sulking. She slid down in the seat and said, 'If you're not talking to me, I think I'll have a nice little nap.'

'Aw, don't be like that.'

'I am like that. I nearly left you when you were locked up. Did you realise that?'

He was shocked rigid. 'You wouldn't do that to me!'

'I still will if you waste our big chance in life.' She patted her handbag. 'And I have the money here. You'll have to fight me to get it back at all because I know you'll only waste it.'

He stole a quick glance at her. She had *that look* on her face, worse than he'd ever seen it before. His heart sank. Not only had he exchanged one boss for another, but she could be every bit as determined as Higgerson. More determined, sometimes.

Only, he needed her to help him if they were going to start up a little business. She'd always been able to make one penny do the work of two. And he'd miss her in bed.

Another glance showed she'd folded her arms and was sitting rigidly in the passenger seat.

She turned to stare at him and he tried a smile, seeing her smile back after a moment or two. He started hoping he'd softened her a little.

'Our future will be good, Jem,' she said in that soft, come-to-bed voice he loved. 'Hard work, but a good life. I promise we'll do well.'

'You're a bossy bitch,' he said, resignation making him speak more softly now.

'But I stuck with you, didn't I? So you stick with me now.'

It took him a while to face the fact that he would have to do things her way. He couldn't bear the thought of losing her, and had never seen her this determined. 'You'd better make us a lot of money, then.'

'I shall do, love!'

She patted his knee and gave his thigh a squeeze that promised more later. He let her have her way. 'Oh, very well.'

Then something made him smile and he shared the joke with her. 'You'll be more fun in bed than my last boss, that's for sure.'

She grinned. 'Count on it.'

30

Mr Forester arrived just before nine o'clock the following morning. Dennison answered the door himself and
took his visitor straight into the small sitting room.

'I'm expecting His Lordship to visit me shortly on rather
important business that's cropped up suddenly, so I hope
you'll forgive me for not offering you any refreshments and
getting straight down to your reason for coming here.'

'Of course.'

'Then I shall start by saying how outraged I am that anyone
should claim I have not applied the law properly and equitably
to a case.'

'Well, I must admit I was surprised myself. And I didn't take
to the fellow who made the complaint, only, well, I felt obliged
to investigate.' Forester paused to shake his head sadly.

'Go on.'

'The complaint is about how you dealt with a child who
had been kidnapped from her grandmother's home, a certain
Beatie Hicks, to be precise. It was alleged that you had shown
a bias in favour of the kidnapper and deliberately let him get
away with it.'

'That's ridiculous.'

'The person who spoke to me does not wish to be named,
so—'

'It's Mr Vanner, I suppose?'

'Ah. He was afraid you'd guess who had made the complaint and treat it less than seriously. How did you know?'

'Because I found out he'd been poking his nose into the upbringing of that particular child and been encouraging ill-treatment of her.'

'What? You're sure she was being treated badly when she was living with her grandmother?'

'Oh yes. And I can prove it. Vanner has very harsh rules for bringing up children, like depriving them of food if they displease him, or beating them viciously enough to draw blood.'

Forester looked at him in patent shock, so he nodded and carried on, 'Precisely. Not only is the grandmother totally in that man's thrall but I'll tell you frankly, he isn't like any minister of a church that I've ever met, whatever the so-called religious denomination. What did the grandmother actually say about it?'

His companion frowned. 'Well, now I come to think of it, she hardly said a word. He did nearly all the talking. What made you so certain the child had been ill-treated?'

'The woman who took her in when she ran away is a very decent person, a widow well respected in this town. She was so worried when she found signs of a severe beating, she called in the doctor to check her injuries. He was horrified at both the beating, which had drawn blood quite a few times, and how emaciated the child was. He said she'd been starved to a dangerous extent, and offered to bear witness to that in a court of law, if necessary.'

'*Starved?* But the grandmother was a well-dressed woman and, to put it bluntly, she shows every sign of eating rather too well.'

'Well, the child was not only dangerously thin but had that starveling look I've seen all too often among the children of the poorest families, the ones who haven't been eating properly for a good while. I felt this child must have acquired that look the same way.'

'I know what you mean by that, Dennison. My wife calls it the hunger look. We do our best to help some of the local families who're struggling, but there are so many. We've been living in sad times ever since the Great War, have we not?' He fell silent, then resumed with, 'Even so, I have to ask whether you know where this child is now?'

'No. I authorised one search of a house indicated by Vanner, but she wasn't there, nor was there any sign of her having been there, so I'm not going to allow invasion of every house because he has a grudge against its occupants.'

'Was it the grandfather's house you searched?'

'No. One nearby. While we searched it, however, Vanner's own men kept watch on the outside of the grandfather's place, and the child definitely wasn't sneaked into it. In fact, no one went in or out.'

'I think we ought probably to check that house now. Vanner told me about the man. He has a very bad reputation, for drunkenness among other things. If someone like that has the child, she really does need rescuing.'

'Chapman has mended his ways and been sober for nearly a year now. He only started drinking a couple or so years ago, after his wife and daughter both died tragically within a few months.'

'Ah. That's sad, of course, but a man on his own isn't usually awarded custody of a child of that age, whatever the other circumstances.'

'And I don't deem it safe to return her to the custody of a grandmother who starves and beats her.'

'Hmm. You have a point there. This Beatie must be put into an orphanage, then.'

'There are decent families here in the valley who would take her in.' Dennison hesitated, then said, 'I want your word not to tell anyone about what I'm going to say. It's a matter of national importance.'

Forester looked startled, but murmured a promise.

'This Vanner is one of the subjects of a secret inquiry in which His Lordship is involved, and I am assisting. In short, we have traitors among us, and Vanner is a suspect. Certain matters have to be kept secret for the time being, even from you, including where Beatie could possibly be and how she got there.'

'How on earth can His Lordship or our nation be involved in the disappearance of a child?'

The doorbell rang just then, and Dennison stood up to peep out of the window. 'Here he is, so you can ask him yourself. His main purpose in coming here today is to help us with the problem of retrieving Higgerson's body, but I'm sure he'll spare you some time to discuss the other matter. I'll let him in.'

Sadly, he'd known it wouldn't be easy to sort out what should be done with the child if he did find her, Dennison thought, which was why he hadn't pursued it.

His Lordship stood in the hall, listened to Dennison's whispered explanation of the other JP's presence, and rolled his eyes. 'That old fusspot.'

'You can't doubt his patriotism, though, unlike Vanner's.'

'No. I suppose not. Well, let's send my chap up to Backshaw Moss to make a start on working out how to get to the body. I'll talk to Forester, then we can both join Harris up there. The car can come back for us.'

In the sitting room His Lordship scowled across at the older man. 'Frankly, I wish you'd waited to raise this matter, Forester. Or mentioned it to me before you've been seen to come here. If the child is safe, we can surely leave her be for a few days?'

'She's nine, needs a woman's care.'

'Sounds to me as if a woman is already caring for her.'

'A woman who is living with a man to whom she isn't married is hardly a respectable guardian.'

'Nonetheless, the child is in no danger, which is what really counts, and this can surely wait a day or two?'

Forester frowned and fell silent, then shook his head. 'I'm afraid Vanner made it plain that if I don't intervene, he'll take the matter to a higher authority.'

'Who could be the very person we're trying to catch out. Leave it with me, then. If necessary I'll take the child home with me after I've finished today's tasks. I am surely respectable enough for your purposes?' He glared across at Forester as if daring him to disagree.

'Oh, definitely. Very well. I'll wait a day or two.'

When Forester had left, His Lordship said, 'If only we had proof about Vanner's involvement with these people further south. I'm wondering now whether he is using this alleged concern about the child to probe into our affairs, find out our weaknesses, and report them to his fellow fascists. What do you think?'

'I think it's surprising that he's making such a fuss, so perhaps there is something else behind the way he keeps causing trouble.'

'Hmm. Well, first things first. Let's go up to Backshaw Moss and see what my man Harris says about this house that's collapsed. If anyone can find a way into it, it's him.'

As they sat in the car, he said thoughtfully, 'I think nearly everyone in the valley would be glad to verify that Higgerson is dead. His fame, or rather infamy, has spread further afield too.'

Beatie let out a shriek when she saw a man she knew only too well walking slowly past the back of the house, studying it.

Both Gwynneth and her grandfather went running up to the bedroom and found her hiding under the bedcovers, shaking with terror and sobbing. 'He's found me. I saw him walk past, looking at the house.'

Arthur held her close. 'I won't let him anywhere near you, my little love. Can you check the back alley, Gwynneth?'

After staring out of the window for a few minutes, Gwynneth said quietly, 'Vanner is walking up and down at the back, deliberately making a noise and showing himself. I wonder what he's plotting now.'

Beatie let out another whimper of fear, so Gwynneth went across to sit on the edge of the bed next to them, and put her arm around the child. 'Let's plan for the worst, Arthur.'

'What do you suggest?'

'Beatie dear, try to calm down and listen to me: would you like to spend the day in the tunnels? You and I can make ourselves comfortable, and that horrible man will not be able to find us there, even if he breaks into the house.'

The child clutched Gwynneth tightly. 'Yes, please.'

'Then we need to collect all our clothes and other things and take them with us so that they can't find any sign of us being here if they come to search. Can you put all your toys and books into a pillowcase?'

'Is this necessary?' Arthur asked in a low voice as the child immediately began to gather her things.

'It won't hurt, and will make her feel safer, which is the main thing. And Arthur – I've been feeling anxious today, too, I don't know why. I think that accident has unsettled everyone in the valley. Better safe than sorry with such a precious possession, eh?' She nodded towards Beatie to show her meaning.

'Yes. I'll tell Biff and Phil what you're going to do.'

She walked to the bedroom door with him. 'I'll pack my own things and we'll leave most of them in the tunnels from now on, except for what we need each night. I don't fancy trying to sleep down there, though. It'd be too uncomfortable.'

He leaned closer to whisper, 'I hate to see that poor child so anxious. Is there anything else I can do for her? Or for you?'

'I don't think so. That Mrs Hicks has a lot to answer for. I'd like to starve the stupid woman for a while, see how she feels about going without food, not to mention whipping her bare legs till it draws blood, as she did to Beatie. I'm filled with rage every time I see those bruises and scabs, and the child never complains about the discomfort, though I see her change how she's sitting sometimes to ease it.'

'Well, she's looking a little plumper already, with some good food inside her.'

They took blankets and pillows into the tunnels with them, not to mention two packets of sandwiches wrapped in grease-proof paper and an old Tizer bottle full of water, plus another one of the special ginger beer made in the valley, for a treat later on.

Only after they'd made themselves comfortable on the steps in the tunnel did Beatie start to relax.

Arthur stayed a short time, then said he'd better return to his woodworking in case anyone came to the house.

After he'd gone, Beatie sat quietly, twice asking if Gwynneth was quite sure her grandmother couldn't find them here. Then she fell asleep suddenly with her head on her companion's lap.

Tears she'd held back until now began to trickle down Gwynneth's face at the thought of what had been done to this little girl for the past few months. She couldn't abide cruelty to man or beast. If she had to leave her family and run away to Australia to save Beatie, she would. They were adults and could manage on their own, but this vulnerable child couldn't.

Those dreadful people were not getting their hands on her again, not as long as Gwynneth had breath in her body.

And she knew Arthur felt the same. Eh, he was a gentle, lovely man.

A smile gradually replaced the tears at the thought of him and the easy conversations they'd had.

The chauffeur opened the door of the big limousine, and His Lordship and Dennison got out.

Harris was standing at the front of the collapsed buildings, and turned to call that he'd be with them in a couple of minutes. He and another man were still poking around in the remains of the lower part of the front doorway and the inner wall beyond it, some of which was still left and was helping hold back the tide of debris.

While they waited, the two men studied the rubble where houses had previously stood.

'I've never seen anything like this,' Dennison said. 'It must have been very badly built in the first place. We're lucky it happened at a time when most of the tenants were out at work or shopping, so only one person got killed.'

'And that's a chap no one will miss,' His Lordship added quietly.

Harris clapped the man he was talking to on the back and came across to join them. 'I'll have to come back tomorrow with the proper equipment to dig a tunnel down to the cellar where they think Higgerson was trapped, my lord. You can be sure I'll make everything safe as I do that.'

'But you'll be able to get down there?'

'Oh, yes. It'll be very straightforward, actually, once we have the right equipment and some very solid planking and metal struts that chap is going to provide. We'll go carefully, testing each area as we move forward till we find where the body is. It's my guess he'll be as far as he could get from the stairs. They must have been very poorly constructed stairs or they'd have helped hold back more of the wall.'

'Well, it's a relief that you can do it. Once the body has been retrieved, can you fill it in and make the whole area safe?'

Harris nodded and looked at Dennison. 'I don't suppose you know what the heir wants to do with the site afterwards, sir, whether he'll build again or leave the ground bare? They could do with a few open spaces around here. Terrible place, this Backshaw Moss, isn't it?'

They all stared in disgust at the tumbledown dwellings crammed against one another, and the ragged people who slouched past occasionally.

'The council is trying to get rid of the worst slums little by little,' Dennison said. 'This will give them added impetus and support from the ratepayers, I'm sure.'

'Have you heard officially who the heir is?' His Lordship asked.

'No. It'll be one of Higgerson's sons surely. But it'll take time to work out what to do.'

'So I'll just make it safe for the time being,' Harris said. 'We don't want any urchins daring one another to go inside and getting buried by miniature landslides of debris.'

His companions shuddered at the thought.

'We'd better have an undertaker standing by to remove the body, which might look a mess,' he went on. 'It'll probably be retrieved the day after tomorrow at a guess. This will be quite a short, shallow tunnel, compared to the mine tunnels I've worked on.'

'I'll speak to the family and help them arrange the under-taker,' Dennison offered.

'I'll be ready to leave when you are, then.' Harris left them and got into the big car.

After a pause Dennison asked, 'Are you really taking the child home with you tonight, Your Lordship?'

'Of course not. Neither of us have been able to find her, have we? I only said that to keep Forester at bay for a day or two. I can take her to my place if it's absolutely necessary, but she's with people she knows, who care about her from the sounds of it, so I'd rather leave her with them for the time being. Don't worry, I shan't let her grandmother have her again.'

He winked at Dennison. 'It's my guess that they've hidden her in the tunnels, which gives us a valid excuse for not revealing where she is.'

'That'd be my guess too.'

'If she can bear to stay there, we may have time to get the proof we need and sort out that damned traitor.'

'Amen to that. More than one traitor, if we're lucky.'

'I'll be off, then.' His Lordship joined Harris in the car and it left at once.

Dennison went to see Arthur before he returned home.

'Let's stand at the front door to talk. I gather Vanner has watchers keeping an eye on this place day and night.'

'So my neighbours have told me.'

'Well, we can be seen by anyone who passes, so they'll know I've not spoken to anyone except you, and haven't been inside to see the child. No one will be able to eavesdrop if we stay here.'

'Fine by me.'

'One of the things I want to suggest is that you employ both your guards for the next few nights. Vanner may get desperate.'

'Isn't there any news at all from those people in the Midlands who're hunting for traitors?'

'I'm afraid not.'

Dennison worried all the way home about what they'd do if proof of Vanner's perfidy wasn't found.

When Peters got back he found Jack Webster waiting for him in the kitchen, and sighed. He'd been looking forward to putting his feet up for an hour or so, hoping to indulge in a refreshing nap because he hadn't slept at all well last night.

However, the man had been doing him a favour working as a gardener for two unpleasant people, so it was only fair to find out what he wanted.

Webster stood up as he went into the kitchen.

'Have you been waiting long?'

'A couple of hours, Mr Peters. But your cook has kindly furnished me with cups of tea and something to eat. Best fruit cake I ever tasted it was, too!'

The cook flushed and tried not to look gratified. Dennison managed to hold back a smile till he'd taken Webster up to the morning room. All the good gardeners he'd ever known had made friends with the cook or lady of the house where they were working, and usually displayed hearty appetites.

'Do sit down. I presume there's some news?'

'There may be. I broke into the shed behind that so-called church and found some weapons.'

'*What?*'

'Surprised me too, sir. Rubbishy old stuff, guns mostly from the Great War, if not earlier, but they'd still kill you.'

'What exactly did you find?'

'Daggers, guns, and some letters. I took a few out of the bundle in case they were of interest, but I doubt he'd notice they've gone because there were quite a few. I can't read that fancy handwriting very well, so I brought them to you.'

He pulled them out of his inner pocket. 'Oops! I'm afraid they got a bit crumpled.'

'Never mind that. Would you give me a few minutes to read them?'

'All right if I glance at your newspaper while I wait, sir?'

'Of course.'

Ten minutes later, after scanning them quickly, Dennison looked across at Webster. 'You've more than repaid me with these for helping you buy that field.'

'I have?' Webster tried in vain to hide his pleasure at this compliment.

'Yes. You don't owe me a penny. In fact it's I who owe you my deepest gratitude.' And so did His Lordship and the whole county, but he couldn't tell Webster that.

'Can I ask what's in them, sir?'

'I'd rather keep that to myself. It's important, but you're better off not getting involved.'

Webster shrugged. 'All right. Good to know it's useful, though.'

'You'll be working at Higgerson's house tomorrow, won't you?'

'I would normally, sir, only I wondered if you'd want me to go there any longer, seeing as he's dead? I'm itching to get started on my field.'

'Bear with me a little longer, if you don't mind. Higgerson's wife and sons will probably be staying there, and they'll want the gardens kept up to scratch. I'm more concerned to keep them safe. You can help keep an eye on them.'

Webster looked puzzled. 'Will Vanner be likely to harm them as well? He's been a bit chancy-like lately. Flies off the handle for nothing. Even the folk who worship here seem surprised by his behaviour.'

'I want to make sure he doesn't hurt anyone, so it would still be good to have you there. In my opinion he is unhinged and may lash out at anyone he feels threatened by. You could just carry on as normal in the garden there for the next day or two and leave the rest to me, but keep your eyes open. I'll make sure you're paid for any work you do.'

'Very well, Mr Peters.'

'Good man.'

Once Webster had gone, Dennison picked up the telephone, intending to leave a message for His Lordship to call him as soon as he got home, then put it down again with a sigh. This was too important, so he'd better not use the phone. An operator or someone on a party line could easily eavesdrop and leak information. This discovery needed to be kept very quiet indeed till their allies further south worked out how best to use the information to identify the traitors.

His Lordship had a special phone line set up at his home, one on which the operator was a special government official not likely to share what she heard with anyone except the authorities.

Talk about treading delicately. Dennison put on his outdoor clothes again and set off to see His Lordship, which meant at least an hour's driving each way.

At least His Lordship had returned home by then, so there was no need to hang around waiting. The information pleased him just as much as Dennison had expected, so it had been well worth coming here. He listened as his host immediately phoned his contact in the Midlands.

The man asked to speak to Dennison directly, but he couldn't give him all the details he wanted. Only Webster would be able to do that. But Dennison could guarantee Webster's honesty at least, and the truth of what he had been able to share.

'You've done well and so has your man.'

His Lordship took over the phone again, holding it between them so that Dennison could listen in.

'We'll get back to you within a few hours, once we work out how best to deal with this Vanner fellow. It's clear that he's a traitor. We can do without fanatics of any sort in this country, especially those who're fascists as well. He sounds to me to be – well, almost deranged. Better locked away in prison on all counts, I should think.'

'I hope no one gets hurt sorting this problem out.'

'I hope *he* gets hurt.'

'They wouldn't do anything to Vanner, would they?' Dennison muttered after the call ended.

His Lordship shrugged and gave him a very direct stare. 'They'll do what they have to. We weren't prepared for a big war last time. If that Hitler chap starts another one, some of us will be a lot better prepared this time. And that doesn't mean leaving proven traitors free to do more harm.'

Dennison nodded reluctantly.

Later that afternoon Arthur left Biff in charge and went down into the secret tunnels on the excuse of taking Gwynneth a big, enamel mug of tea. In reality he simply wanted to see her, be with her. Each time they chatted, he felt they were growing closer.

She looked up, her face sharp with anxiety, as the secret door slid open, relaxing visibly when she saw him.

He clambered down and saw that Beatie was asleep beside her, so handed her the mug and went back to close the cellar door again.

There was just enough light from the single candle for him to see her, and barely enough room for him to sit down on the step next to her unless he put his arm round her shoulders. Which he was happy to do – and which didn't meet with any protests.

'I thought you might like some company as well as a drink of nice hot tea, my lovely lass.'

She nestled against him. 'I want some company most of all, especially when it's you, Arthur love. It's seemed a tediously long day down here.'

Her face was so close to his he couldn't resist kissing her cheek, only she turned her head so he kissed her lips instead. Which he didn't mind at all. And she didn't seem to mind it, either, because she gave as good as she got, and it was an extremely satisfying kiss.

In fact, it felt so wonderful that as he caught his breath again, he risked saying what was in his heart. 'I love you, Gwynneth.'

'I love you too, Arthur.'

'I'm glad you're not acting coy, because I can't pretend any longer.'

'We're too old to waste time pretending, don't you think?'

'Yes. And old enough to realise when something is right for us.'

They kissed again, after which they simply sat there, with his arm round her shoulders and her hand in his, chatting intermittently, falling silent just as comfortably, close in every way that mattered.

When he started feeling that his joints were growing a little stiff, as older bodies do, he stretched carefully and slowly, noticing that she did the same.

He quoted one of his favourite pieces of poetry, not remembering where he'd found it or who had written it, or even if he'd quoted the words accurately, only that he'd found its basic idea so very true of this time of life. 'Old age gives no quarter, though spears spare us.'

'I like that. And it's so right. Even if you don't always show your age, you feel it sometimes.'

'You don't show your age, lass. You're as bonny now as you must have been when you were younger.'

She chuckled. 'Your eyesight is failing you.'

'No, it's not. I've heard other men say you're a good-looking woman.'

Her smile was glorious. 'I don't care about what other men think, just you.'

They sat down again and continued to chat quietly. After a while they inevitably discussed the child. 'How has Beatie been?'

'Fretting. She's absolutely terrified of being sent back to her grandmother.'

'Is it any wonder? I'm terrified of what I might do if I ever got my hands on Mrs Hicks. How she produced a son as nice as my daughter's husband, I'll never know.'

'Perhaps him getting killed soured her. It made even you turn to alcohol, losing your wife and daughter did.'

He scowled. 'Aye. I'm ashamed of that, and I promise you I'll never do that again. I don't touch the stuff now, as I told you, and I never shall. But though her loss might have made Mrs Hicks worse, she was always sharp-tongued. I overheard her tell someone once how badly her son had married and that we were a useless family.'

'How disloyal of her! I'm so lucky that my two older sons have married wonderful women. I think my youngest is married to his books. I can't believe Lucas has gone off to university. I thought only rich people did that.'

'He must be very clever.'

'He is.'

'But he still loves you.'

She gave him another of her glorious smiles. 'They all seem to, and I certainly love them. They'll love you and your grand-daughter too, Arthur. Unreservedly. Never doubt that. We don't ration love in our family.'

After a while she began yawning and he found himself joining in, so he took his leave. 'Are you sleeping down here tonight?'

'I didn't want to, but she's so upset maybe I'd better. It'd be a shame to wake her.'

'Instead of which you'll be uncomfortable and won't sleep well.'

'I'll survive.'

'I'll light a fresh candle for you before I leave. That one's got less than an inch to burn. Do you need anything else to eat?'

'No, thank you. But the warm tea was lovely. We brought plenty of sandwiches and cake. I'm not very hungry, actually.

Thanks for sorting out the candle, though. I'm not afraid of the dark, but Beatie is, poor dear.'

'Can I kiss you again before I leave?'

'I've been hoping you would.'

Such loving moments are beautiful, Gwynneth thought as the door to the cellar closed behind him. Knowing you're loved helps see you through the bad times and makes the good ones even happier.

As she remembered the way he'd said he loved her and how tender the expression on his face had been, she smiled all the way into sleep.

31

The phone rang in the middle of the night and Dennison Peters jerked awake. 'I'll answer it,' he called as he heard his sister stir.

He ran downstairs and picked up the telephone receiver from the hall table. 'Yes?'

'I'm sorry to disturb you, but can you come over straight away. And bring our mutual friend.'

'Yes, of course.'

As the receiver was put down at the other end, he grimaced at the thought of another hour's drive to His Lordship's house. It must be important, though.

He got dressed hurriedly and telephoned Sergeant Deemer. It rang a few times, then a sleepy voice said, 'Police station.'

'It's me. I'm coming across to take you to see our mutual friend. Group business.'

'I'll be ready.'

When he got to the house at the rear of the station Sergeant Deemer must have been watching for him because he came straight out and got into the car.

'Something wrong, Dennison?'

'His Lordship wants to see us. But before we set off, I'm wondering if I've been followed here. I'm sure I saw the glow from car headlights above the roofs of some houses further up the hill.'

'We can go to a place I know and get rid of any followers there. I set it up for myself years ago and use it once in a while.

It'd be better if I do the driving, and we'll switch off the head-lights.'

They changed places and Deemer drove them a few streets, then stopped at the rear of a business whose owner he knew. 'I've got a key. He doesn't mind me going through his ware-house. If we go in by this delivery entrance, you'll find the place is bigger than it appears and we can use a different exit into another street. I'm afraid you'll have to hop in and out, opening and shutting doors. I'm not as spry as I used to be. Good thing there's a three-quarter moon tonight and not much cloud, eh?'

As they drove away from the warehouse by an exit in another street without using the headlights, Deemer stayed at the wheel, driving slowly and trying not to let the car engine make more noise than necessary. After a while he stopped and switched the engine off. They sat in the car with the windows down, listening for about ten minutes. At first they could hear a car driving to and fro along the streets lower down the slight slope, presumably looking for them, but the noise gradually faded away into the distance.

Deemer returned the task of driving to Dennison and they continued out of town, still not using the headlights.

'I hope the information you received gets that chap out of my hair for good,' the sergeant said at one stage. 'And soon. Minister of religion indeed! He's nothing like a real clergyman. He's a lunatic who is basing his life on fixed ideas of what he thinks the world should be like. He wants it run by superior folk like himself and is trying to force others towards that way of living, hence the group of lads he's training.'

Dennison murmured his agreement. 'It's not likely he'll suc-ceed, but he's being encouraged by a bunch of more senior traitors, probably fascists who're using him and other similar little groups as a distraction to cause trouble for the author-ities. Well, that's how I see it, anyway. They didn't succeed in their big push for power in this country, so they're trying to edge forward, relying on Hitler to cause more trouble for our country in the future.'

When they arrived, they saw that His Lordship had the lights on in a room at one side of his large, sprawling family home. They took that as a signal to park nearby and as they got out of the car they saw one of the French windows open, so went straight through it into the library.

His Lordship beamed at Dennison. 'You and your man have done very well, Peters, very well indeed. That information couldn't have been more timely. This is how our friends in the Midlands want us to deal with it . . .'

They stayed for half an hour, first discussing the details, then drinking a glass of excellent port each, before setting off back to Rivenshaw.

'Good man, Webster,' Deemer said. 'We could do with more chaps like him in the world, instead of wicked fools like Vanner. If Webster hadn't taken the initiative, you and I would still be fumbling around for evidence.'

The following morning Harris arrived in Backshaw Moss at seven o'clock in a big lorry, and three men got out of the back and began to unload tools. They immediately followed his directions and started work on the remains of the two houses, taking it in turns to dig and tip the debris from one area into the back of the lorry till he said to stop and brace the walls of the narrow tunnel they were making before allowing them to continue.

People came to watch at first, but they didn't linger for long because there wasn't much to see after the first brief push. Most of the digging was being done inside the newly-created opening.

Harris took great care with the panels and carefully braced them with metal struts.

At one stage a child's rag doll emerged whole from the debris and was perched outside further along the pavement as if overseeing the work.

When a child edged towards it, hand outstretched, one of the local men keeping folk away shouted, 'Is it yours?'

'No. It's my cousin Patsy's doll.'

'Then leave it alone for Patsy and her mum or dad to claim.' His voice softened as he added, 'Why don't you go and tell your cousin about the doll?'

She backed away, scowling. 'Why should I? She never lets me play with it.'

'If you don't care about helping others, I don't have the time to speak to you.' He gave the mother a dirty look and she glared at him as she dragged her sobbing daughter away.

When John Joe turned up just before noon with an urn of tea and a tray of meat pies for the diggers, they fell on them hungrily.

'Eh, that's good,' one said, wiping his mucky sleeve across his lips. 'Thanks, lad.'

'I try to help folk when I can.'

'Aye. Decent folk do. That chap whose body they're searching for was a thief and worse, from what I hear.'

'Far worse.'

It was harder going during the afternoon, and progress was slower. At intervals Harris got out a long thin piece of metal and poked it gently into the loosely packed debris before they put up more panels, trying to see whether there was anything softer and more solid that might be a body. But there was nothing.

By teatime the new tunnel had gone down part way into the cellar. They hadn't managed to find the body yet, and Harris wasn't surprised. He'd always reckoned it must be at the far side of the new part. He set guards for the night, and watch lanterns were placed on the street in front of the entrance to keep cars and pedestrians away from the mess of rubble.

Then he and his men got directions to the tip so that they could dump the debris from the back of their lorry, after which they left for the lodgings His Lordship had booked them into.

There, a hearty meal was waiting for them and they followed that with a drink at the pub, just one pint of beer each.

'I reckon we'll find the body tomorrow,' one man said as they strolled back to the lodgings.

'Morning or afternoon?' another asked.

They all guessed what time it'd be found, winner to buy the drinks, then sought their beds.

Harris smiled as he lay down in his room. He was the one who'd be buying the drinks tomorrow, whoever had guessed correctly. Good lads, they were, hard workers, and they'd more than earn a bit of encouragement.

Lallie chose not to use her former bedroom, but she slept badly even in a single bed in another room, and felt restless when she woke.

Since she could do nothing until her husband's body was found, she spent the first morning sorting through the clothes she'd had to leave behind when she ran away. To her surprise they were all still there in what had been her bedroom.

She'd have thought Gareth would have burned them or given them away. Then she realised he'd probably expected to get her back again, one way or the other, and shuddered even to think of that.

Mr Tillett came to find her when luncheon was ready.

She was sitting on the bed, staring into space, and jerked in shock when he spoke to her.

'How are you?'

'A bit upset at the horrible memories this house brings. I know coming back was the right thing to do, but I hate it here.'

'I'm not surprised, Mrs – oh, hell, now that you're a widow, may I call you Lallie when it's just the family?'

'I'd like that . . . Edmund. Only we're not sure yet that I am a widow, are we?'

He saw the traces of tears on her cheeks and stretched out one hand to wipe the moisture away with his fingertips. 'It's been hard.'

'What has?'

'Not saying how fond I've grown of you.'

'Oh.' She blushed a rosy pink.

'Can I say it now? Or are you too upset?'

'I'm not upset at all about Gareth, if that's what you mean. I feel as if his death will take a huge burden from my shoulders. He can't be alive, can he?'

'I doubt anyone could be alive in those circumstances, but if the impossible has happened, I'll get you away, I promise.' He took her hand in his and raised it to his lips.

She gasped but didn't pull away. 'We'd better be careful.'

'I don't want to be careful.'

'Nor do I.'

He sighed. 'But I don't want to destroy your reputation. When he's buried and his heir has taken over the business, will you marry me and come back to Wiltshire with me permanently?'

'Oh, yes. I'd like that very much. As long as Felix is safe here I shan't stay in Rivenshaw. Gareth tainted it for me even more than I'd expected.'

'Well, your Felix has a good head on his shoulders, so you can leave him to look after things. Felix has talked to me about righting some of the wrongs his father inflicted on people. If he and my lass marry quickly, she'll be able to help him do that. She has a good business head on her shoulders, my Eleanor does. I've had her working with me for years and not fiddling around with housework and embroidery.'

'I've noticed how capable and intelligent she is. And it's wonderful to see how much they love one another.'

'And we can make sure that Kit can go to university and become a doctor. I think he'll make a good one.' He gave her one of his lovely smiles. 'You won't make me wait too long to set our own lives in order, will you, Lallie? I'm an impatient chap when I want something.'

'Of course not. I have years of misery to make up for. Only I don't want a fancy wedding, if you don't mind. I had that last time.'

'Just the family will suit me.'

The smile she gave him was brilliant, and the warm feeling and joy it left behind lingered in his heart for the rest of the tediously long day.

The next morning they found Higgerson's body and it was Harris who'd made the closest guess. The men who dug it out shuddered at the expression on the dead man's face.

'He died in a rage, this one did,' one said in a near whisper.

'People hereabouts have nothing good to say about him. You should hear the things they mutter when they come to look at what we're doing. Anyway, that's not really our business. I'd better tell Mr Harris.' He yelled up the narrow tunnel that they'd found the body.

'Bring it out, then. What are you waiting for?'

When they'd hauled it up, he too stared at the dead face and shook his head. 'Nasty chap. You can often see it in their faces after they've died when they've been bad 'uns. Put him over there and cover him with that old tarpaulin. I'll send someone to phone for the undertaker and the police, too, just to check things out.'

'Do we go on digging, or is that all you want done down there, Mr Harris?'

'I think that's all. No one else is missing, and anyway, we're near the end of the recent excavations they stupidly made. The family have already said to fill in the hole once we find him. They're not sure what they want to do with the land, but they definitely don't want that cellar leaving.'

He stretched, glad not to be going down there again. A bad feeling seemed to linger in the excavation. 'I'll go and make the phone calls from the village shop in Birch End.'

'The sooner they take that body away, the happier I'll feel,' one man muttered after he'd left. 'Fair gave me the shivers, it did, the look on his face.'

When the phone rang, Mr Tillett answered it, then went to find the others. 'They've found his body and they've sent for the undertaker and Sergeant Deemer. I think we should let Mr Peters have a look at the body as well, so that he can confirm it was really him if it's ever necessary. Then you can arrange a funeral.'

'We're not having a funeral, just a burial,' Felix said quietly. 'None of us want any fuss made. All we wanted was to be certain he was dead.'

'Are you sure you won't regret that? He was your father, after all.'

His voice was harsh. 'Quite certain, Mr Tillett. He wasn't much of a father.'

His mother laid one hand on his shoulder. 'Don't let him sour the rest of your life, dear.'

'You're more forgiving than I can ever be.'

'I don't forgive him, but I shan't let thoughts of him spoil the rest of my life. You can't change the past, only take advantage of what the future brings.' Her eyes went to Tillett and the way he smiled at her made Felix stare in surprise. Eleanor had said her father was fond of his mother, but he hadn't realised how fond.

'If it's all right with you,' Tillett said, 'I'll set John Joe to make the arrangements for a quiet, speedy burial. He's the best assistant I've ever had. I'm going to give him a share of the company officially when we get back to Wiltshire. He's more than earned it.'

'It'll be good if he can arrange the burial. I don't want anything to do with it. I think I'll go and walk round the garden for a while, if you don't mind. I need some fresh air.'

She held up one hand. 'On my own, please, Edmund. It'll be so wonderful to be outside and not afraid, and it looks like being sunny all day, even if the weather is still cool.'

Tillett waited till she'd gone outside to ask Felix and Kit if she'd be all right.

'She'll be fine. She loves being out of doors. That garden was her main refuge from *him*. She designed it, you know. She's probably saying goodbye to it.'

They watched through the window as she stopped to chat to Jack Webster and let him show her some groups of plants.

Already she was looking younger, more alive, wearing her freedom like a warm cloak.

32

Sergeant Deemer sent a message to the two lads who'd helped him when he'd been attacked and with whom he'd kept in touch. He asked them to come secretly to the back door of his house.

When they arrived, his wife let them in and handed them a big bun each, which brought beaming smiles to their rather gaunt faces. She then went across to the police station to tell her husband that Alan and Griff had arrived.

'Just going home for my tea,' he called out to Mike, who was on duty at the desk, then he strolled across to his house.

The lads were both sporting the shirt and belt that said they were members of Vanner's squad.

'How's it going with that lot?' he asked.

Alan grimaced. 'I'd only do this for you, Sarge. Vanner's a nasty chap. Makes up for being short by shouting loudly, whether it's needed or not, and loves to march us up and down. If it weren't for the shirts and the food he provides each time we meet, not many lads would have stayed in his stupid squad.'

'Well, it's been very useful for me to have you two telling me what's going on and when you'll be holding meetings, so I'm grateful to you for putting up with it.'

They shrugged. 'It's something to do, at least.'

'I want you to tell him you saw two strangers arrive at this house, a younger one with red hair and an older man who's bald with just a bit of grey hair around the edges of his skull.'

They looked surprised but repeated what he'd said.

'And tell him you managed to eavesdrop and hear that I'm meeting them and someone else tonight at the Methodist chapel hall in Birch End around midnight.'

'Will he believe that, Sarge? You've never met anyone before at midnight that I've heard.'

'That's why he'll believe it. It's going to sound like something special. And your tale will be confirmed when he sees someone with red hair during the day coming and going at the police station. Got all that?'

They nodded, accepted his sixpenny bits, and slipped out again.

He went to find his senior constable again and told Mike to drive over to His Lordship's house and tell him everything was being arranged in the way their friends from the Midlands wanted.

'I'll have to be careful how I drive out of town,' Mike said. 'Maybe take a detour or two to lose anyone who's trying to follow me.'

'On the contrary, you are to let them follow you and pretend not to notice.'

'Really?'

'Yes. Be ready to come on duty again later tonight, and you don't want anyone to follow you then. We'll get to the hall well before midnight.'

When Mike had left, Deemer called Cliff in. 'I want you to call on some of our special constables this afternoon.' He named them and got Cliff to repeat the list and the message without writing it down.

'Vanner's men will try to follow you, so once you're part way to the first place, give the followers the slip by going through Mr Willcox's shop. I'll warn him you're coming, and take those old clothes you keep at the station for doing mucky jobs with you. You can change into them there and leave your uniform with him for when you get back.'

'Good chap, Mr Willcox. Folk are saying he'll be the next mayor.'

'I hope so. He'll get things done, especially sorting out those slums in Backshaw Moss. He's got a bee in his bonnet about them now.'

The next people Deemer called on were Higgerson's wife and sons, just to keep in touch and also to look as if he was doing his normal sort of work.

Vanner went to call on Mrs Hicks to see if she'd heard anything more about the child, but she hadn't.

'We'll find a way to get her back for you. She's the only close family you have left now, and you'll want to train her to do things your way, won't you?'

She stared mournfully at him. 'I'm beginning to wonder if it's worth it, Mr Vanner. She was always a naughty, disobedient child, and I'm not as young as I was. I get tired more easily.'

'Oh, it is worth it, Mrs Hicks, believe me it is. You must hold firm to our belief in where the future of our country lies.'

He had a thought. In one sense tonight was do or die for him, and if things went wrong he could at least make sure the child was taken away from those people. Not that he thought anything would go wrong, because he'd made careful plans, but he always liked to be prepared for every possible outcome. It gave him confidence.

'If anything happens to me, you must be sure not to leave that child in Arthur Chapman's keeping, even if he does have a bigger house than you.'

That sparked the ongoing anger in her, that the man she hated and despised should have inherited such a large house.

'I won't let him keep her,' she said. 'Definitely not. I know my duty.'

★

When the men sent from the Midlands arrived in Rivenshaw, Sergeant Deemer met them openly at the station in the town centre and made no attempt to hide their presence, walking back to the police station with them.

Then he got out the revolver he kept in a special locked cabinet in his office at the station, in preparation for tonight's trap. Just in case things went wrong. He didn't like using a gun, but they might be armed, from what Jack Webster had found in the shed.

All of those coming with him tonight were grimly determined to catch Vanner out. They'd already got a name that they thought was his main contact in London from the few letters Webster had stolen, but hoped to get more definite proof tonight.

As dusk fell, they prepared for the visit to Birch End and drove off, pretending to take care not to be followed, but allowing the small, shabby Austin 7 to stay behind them even after the Morris that was also following them turned off the road.

Deemer produced a key to the Methodist hall, and the three men slipped inside, finding Mike already there waiting for them. He didn't say anything, but pointed to the small room where religious equipment was stored.

They all grinned, since Deemer had been informed by telephone that someone had gone into the hall much earlier, and his watchers had later informed him that no one had come out, he'd guessed that Vanner had planted someone there.

Alan and Griff were very good at following people and had been thrilled to be involved in setting this trap.

The men who'd come with him went across to drag the man out of the cupboard in the room Mike had indicated. He struggled in vain against three men well trained in personal combat, and they managed to muffle his attempts to yell for help. They smiled as they tied him up and gagged him.

'We have other plans for tonight,' one of them said to him. 'Let's put you away again. You'll be nice and warm in that cupboard.'

He could only glare back at them as they stuffed him into it again.

'Parcel to be retrieved later,' one of them said, and they all laughed.

Knowing his man was already positioned inside the hall and would have let the others in, Vanner watched with a sneering smile as Deemer and the two newcomers to the town arrived there.

He walked briskly across to the shed near his own church and unlocked the door. Locking it carefully once he was inside, he took out one of the guns and caressed it lovingly. He'd loaded it carefully this afternoon and was now about to put the hours of practice he'd put in over the years to good use.

When he came out again, with the gun inside his overcoat pocket, he went to the Methodist hall where he intended to prove himself fit to play a more senior role in the on-going preparations for a time when order would prevail, and Britain would be governed by heroic men who knew how to lead people.

The place was in darkness as he crept round the back. He'd asked the most trusted men from the church to meet him here, but there was no one waiting for him.

He found the back door that led into a small kitchen at the hall unlocked, and realised they must have misunderstood his instructions and gone inside without him. The man hidden there shouldn't have let them in, and they'd better not have started anything yet. It was for him to fire the first shot in this operation, literally and symbolically.

That police sergeant was a fool, was so sure of his own safety in this valley that he hadn't even made any attempt to keep the building secure tonight. Eagerly Vanner pushed the door open and crept inside, then stopped again.

There was still no sign of the men he'd expected to find waiting here. Had something gone wrong? Surely not. There would have been some noise if they'd been attacked.

Should he be cautious and not do anything till he'd found out what had happened to his men? No, not now he'd come so far. His time had come and he was relishing the feeling of warm anticipation about killing Deemer.

He peeped into the hall and heard the sound of someone talking quietly from the far end. It just showed how well careful planning paid off that he'd drawn his main enemy here at a time of his own choosing. And he wasn't going to waste this opportunity. After all, he had a man in hiding ready to come to his support, and he would be the only one armed since the British police only carried truncheons.

Holding the gun ready to use, he moved silently forward. He had several bullets, could kill more than one man if necessary. He had to pause for a few seconds as excitement made his heart leap about in his chest.

Calm down! he told it.

It was dim in the hall, but his eyes were used to the darkness and there was enough moonlight for him to see the sergeant's hat poking above a high-backed pew at the far end. There were faint outlines of others, whose boots were showing under their overcoats as they sat near the sergeant.

No, there was no trouble here. He'd been right to continue even without his men. He took out his gun and crept forward so that he could take aim at the sergeant's overcoat. Taking care to stay in the shadows, he raised the gun and fired, feeling jubilant when the sergeant's body jerked as the bullet hit it and toppled slowly sideways.

Suddenly the hall lights came on and someone grabbed him from behind in a stranglehold that made him struggle for breath. He couldn't work out what was happening.

Then someone else twisted his hand backwards into a painful hold that made him drop the gun. As it clattered to the floor, he felt sick with disappointment, but at least he had shot that damned sergeant.

'We have the intruder, Sergeant.' It was a voice he didn't recognise. 'Can you please identify him?'

Deemer stood up on the other side of the hall from the shadows behind which the figure had fallen sideways. Looking grim, the sergeant strode across to stand in front of the prisoner.

Vanner stared at the man he hated. Who had he shot, then? Had he wasted this important opportunity to get rid of the main person blocking his path to his eventual control of the valley?

'Osbert Vanner, I arrest you for attempted murder.' Deemer continued to recite the usual words that accompanied an arrest, then pulled out some handcuffs and clipped one of them on Vanner's wrist.

He struggled again, but in vain. There were three of them and only him, and no man came out of the back room to help him. The other handcuff was quickly clicked into place by the constable.

Someone was feeling in his pockets, pulling out the contents, and of course they found the letter that had arrived today. His heart began to thump irregularly in panic. He should have left it with the others in the drawer in the hut. He'd meant to, but had been so excited about using the gun and disposing of Deemer that he'd forgotten a mere piece of paper.

One of the men read the letter and laughed softly. 'Fine conspirators these are, Sergeant. This time we have the envelope and the fellow who sent it's full name and address. We shan't even have to go and search that shed for the letter. This fool has been carrying it close to his heart.'

'If he has a heart,' the other man said. 'I can't abide murderers.'

'I'm not a murderer,' he croaked. 'I've killed no one.'

'Not for lack of trying,' Deemer said. 'As I said, you've only been arrested for attempted murder, because you failed.'

They all laughed at him, laughed! He couldn't bear it. Rage erupted in him like a red hot geyser, blinded him, set his heart thumping in great jerks of painful fury.

The room spun around him and the floor rushed up to meet him.

'He's fainted, Sarge,' Mike said suddenly.

'Pick him up and sit him on that bench. Shove his head between his knees.'

But when they did that Vanner fell slowly sideways and still didn't stir. Deemer bent over him to feel for a pulse – and found none. He stared down in dismay. 'He's not breathing. Quick, we need to revive him.'

One of the visiting men put out a hand to stop him even trying. 'No. Better to leave him like this. He has no future but jail, and he's a traitor. Let him go. He's died of rage, if you ask me. Must have had a weak heart.'

'As well as a weak and warped brain.'

It went against the grain, but Deemer picked up the letter and the sight of it made him not attempt anything further. In a sad way, it was the most merciful release for this bitter, twisted man.

Mike shot him a questioning look and he shook his head. 'Leave him be, lad. Go and wake the lady at the village shop and tell her it's urgent that you make a phone call for me.'

As his constable set off at a run, Deemer went to the back door and beckoned.

Two lads appeared from the shadows and came to stand in the light flooding out of the hall.

'Has anyone else come out and tried to join him?'

'No, Sarge. Those special constables you sent warned everyone from the church and they all stayed home. Did you catch Vanner?'

'Yes, but he just dropped dead.'

'Really?'

'Yes. He seems to have had a seizure.'

'Can we see him?'

'No, lads. Let him lie in peace. And well done for acting as messengers and observers for us tonight.'

'Does that mean we don't have to go to those silly marching meetings any more?'

'It certainly does.'

'Good. They were driving us mad. But can we still keep our shirts?'

'Yes. And from now on you'd better study a lot harder in your final year at school. You'd be the perfect sort of lads for joining the police force.'

'All right, Sarge.' But their tone was markedly less enthusiastic about that prospect.

'It'll be worth paying attention to your schooling,' he said quietly. 'There's only a year to go now, after all. You'll make good policemen and you'll like wearing the uniform.'

They brightened visibly at that thought. He loved to see young faces like these filled with hope and excitement as their future beckoned.

'Again, thank you.' He slipped them another shilling each, knowing they'd pass it on to their mothers, then went back inside.

The body was now lying to one side, covered by an old curtain. The two men standing there smiled at him. 'Good night's work, eh, Sarge?'

'I suppose so.'

Maybe he was too soft-hearted, or maybe he had seen too much death in the Great War. That had sickened him to the core and only his return to police work had more or less healed the sad memories. Nothing would ever fully erase them, though.

Still, Arthur Chapman could now bring his granddaughter out of hiding and continue to court Gwynneth Harte.

That would be good news for all three of them. They'd make a lovely little family.

For the time being there would be peace in his valley – though a lot of paperwork to deal with before this case, and Higgerson's doings, were laid to rest officially.

33

Three days later, Lallie confessed to Felix that she couldn't bear to stay in this house any longer. 'I can't sleep properly and I still keep expecting to see Gareth coming through the door. Can you manage without me if I go back to Wiltshire?'

He stared at her pale face and the dark circles under her eyes. 'Yes, of course, Mum. I'll see you at our wedding anyway. Only a month to wait. I'm sure Kit will stay and help me here, if that's all right with you, because he's enjoying working with Dr Mitchell part of the time to get some experience.'

Edmund came up to her and put one arm around her waist. 'Let's sort out a few other things while we're chatting. Your mother and I would like to make it a double wedding if that's all right with you, lad.'

Felix beamed at them, his pleasure in that news obvious before he spoke. 'About time you two were able to bring your feelings out into the open. Wait till Eleanor hears. She'll be delighted. And yes, a double wedding will be wonderful.'

'It's not too soon?'

'No. He's dead and gone, thank goodness, and she hasn't lived with him for months anyway. We can all live in safety now and shouldn't waste our time. I'll feel a lot better, though, when I've remedied some of the wrongs he's done to people.'

'Did John Joe tell you what I suggested?'

'Yes, sir. It's very kind of you, and I accept with deep gratitude.'

Lallie looked from one to the other questioningly.

'I offered to let John Joe stay here for a month to help Felix settle into running the business. He'll help him go through any records and check anyone who used to work for your husband. I'm sure some of them will be suitable to stay on once they accept the changes.'

She beamed at them. 'Oh, that's wonderful. John Joe is such a capable man. I shan't worry about my sons if he's here to help them. And if they're going to help those who've been robbed and wronged, well, I can't think of any more suitable way to mark the change to an honest business.'

Felix grinned. 'Well, I'll help all those except Jem Stanley, who seems to have helped himself to my father's car. I can't get over the cheek of that.'

'John Joe told me you're not intending to pursue the matter,' Edmund said.

'No. I like to think of our father being cheated again that way just before he died. He fully deserved it.'

They were all smiling at the thought.

'Stanley doesn't deserve to have the car,' Lallie worried.

'No, but wouldn't it be funny if having that car made an honest man of him from now on?'

Even she couldn't help a quick smile at the thought. 'We can only hope.'

Edmund took over again. 'I think your mother needs to get away from here as soon as possible, so she and I will plan to leave first thing tomorrow morning.'

Four days later, Mr Forester turned up at the police station without warning. 'I've come to ask that you help me take that child to safety.'

Sergeant Deemer looked at him in shock. 'Beatie is safe with her grandfather and Mrs Harte.'

'As I said last time, an unmarried man with a record of drunkenness is not a suitable guardian for the child. And moreover, the man is living in sin.'

'He is not living in sin.'

'He and the woman are not married, and are living together in the house.'

'To look after the child. They're not sharing a bedroom.'

'That isn't good enough, Sergeant. You can't guarantee it to be true. And if you will not help me, then I must go to your superiors.'

Deemer looked at him in dismay. 'Very well, sir. If you insist, I shall help you to do this. Where will you be taking her?'

'Since no one got back to me about the child's current situation, I've had to make enquiries myself. The grandmother has been very helpful. She no longer feels able to look after the child herself, but she's helped me find Beatie a place in an orphanage on the road to Bury.'

'That place!' Why was that woman still making trouble for poor Beatie?

'The people at the orphanage will take care of her moral welfare, which I consider crucially important, and they'll also make sure she eats a good, plain diet, so her health will improve. Also, the place is kept spotlessly clean.'

And they'll chill the poor child's soul with their harsh rules, Deemer thought.

'I'll just get my overcoat and give my constable instructions.' He managed to tell Cliff to call Mr Peters and send him as a matter of urgency to Number 25 Daisy Street. Deemer wasn't sure their local JP could do anything to stop Forester taking the child away, but he had to try.

Then he went back to rejoin the severe-faced old man pacing the reception area impatiently.

★

When they knocked on the door of Number 25, Arthur answered and smiled at the sergeant but looked doubtfully at Mr Forester.

'May we come in?' Forester asked. 'I don't wish to conduct business as important as this on the doorstep.'

Beatie was sitting in the kitchen chatting to Gwynneth, but when Forester followed her grandfather in, she picked up on his solemn expression and huddled closer.

'The child cannot remain here,' he said baldly. 'You two are not married and it is simply not fitting.'

Beatie let out a wail of sheer terror. 'I'm not going back to my grandmother. I'm not!'

'She doesn't want you to. I've found you a place in an orphanage where you'll be with other children, and—'

'I'm not going anywhere!' She began to sob loudly. 'I'm safe here and they love me.'

Someone else knocked on the front door, and with a tut of annoyance Arthur went to answer it while Gwynneth put her arms round Beatie and cuddled her protectively.

Arthur came back with Mr Peters, who addressed Mr Forester. 'Out of sheer professional courtesy you should have informed me of your intentions.'

'You would have diverted me from what I know to be my moral duty, putting that child into a situation of decency. And no, it's not with Mrs Hicks.'

'It's the orphanage,' Arthur said. 'It's a cold harsh place, and everyone knows how unhappy those poor children are.'

'Let's sit down and discuss the best way to deal with the situation,' Peters said.

'She is *not* staying in a household in which two people are living in sin!' Forester roared, making no attempt to sit.

Gwynneth stared at him for a moment, then, as everyone tried to speak at once, she picked up the meat hammer and banged it several times on the table.

'Be quiet!' she yelled.

Everyone fell silent and stared at her in surprise.

She turned to Arthur. 'This is what comes of not telling people that we're engaged to be married till later! I told you it would be better to do it openly, but no, you're too shy.'

'Woman—' Mr Forester began.

'Don't you "woman" me in that odious way, you nasty, suspicious creature!' Bang went the meat hammer. 'Arthur?'

He moved to her side, waiting to follow her lead. But amusement was starting to twitch at his face muscles.

'Tell them now!' she demanded.

'Gwynneth and I are engaged to be married, and if it's so urgent to you, we can do it by special licence.' He looked sideways at her, hoping he'd said it how she wanted.

She took hold of his hand. 'There. It wasn't so hard, was it?' Then she glared across at Mr Forester. 'I presume it'll be all right for her to live here once we're married? We're going to open as a lodging house for single women once we've got the furniture sorted out.'

Arthur stared at her in such obvious surprise at this news that Sergeant Deemer hastily turned a chuckle into a cough.

'I told you I had a solution to earning our living. I've been looking into it and speaking to Mrs Tucker, who has been doing it for years in Rivenshaw, and she's going to help us set it all up. I shall enjoy the company, and you can continue to make money working with wood.'

Arthur gave her a glassy smile, then turned to look enquiringly at Mr Forester. 'So that's all right, isn't it?'

'That is a perfectly respectable way to earn a living,' Dennison said pointedly to his legal colleague.

'The child can't stay here till after they're married,' Forester insisted. 'And *she* should never have come here in the first place.'

'You are being ridiculous.'

'We can go and stay at my son's till after the wedding,' Gwynneth offered.

'Your idea of respectable and mine do not match, Mrs Harte. Your son lives too close to Mr Chapman.' Forester added sarcastically, 'Perhaps you will take them in, Peters?'

'Willingly.'

'Then more fool you, but I suppose it'll do.' Everyone was glaring at Forester, but he just stared coldly back at them, before turning to Gwynneth. 'Please go and pack your things and the child's, Mrs Harte. I shall escort you to your temporary abode.'

He folded his arms and went to stand beside the fireplace, scowling round the room. 'Though what the grandmother will say about this, I dread to think. She may even appeal to the local courts.'

Gwynneth stopped at the door to glare across at him. 'She won't dare. She'll be too afraid of Dr Mitchell standing up in court and offering his testimony about her ill treatment of the child. And you should be ashamed of yourself for causing this fuss, Forester.'

'*Mr* Forester to you.'

'Oh, no it isn't. I don't call people with a nasty, suspicious mind like yours "Mr". I have always been and always will be respectable, whatever you think. You clearly have an unpleasant view of the world, and it's no wonder you're thoroughly disliked.'

He made a gobbling noise, having difficulty finding a sharp enough response to this.

She reached out to pull the sobbing child up from her seat and drew Beatie into a close embrace. 'Come on, love. We're going to live with Mr Peters and his sister till after the wedding. That'll be fun, won't it? Will you be my bridesmaid?'

Beatie had stopped crying and now positively beamed at her, nodding vigorously.

'For your information, Forester, after we've moved our things, I'm going across to the town hall with Arthur to book a wedding by special licence. Feel free to come and breathe down our necks while we do that.'

He was looking thoroughly embarrassed at her sharp comments by now and didn't even try to answer.

The others watched her storm out, then Peters grinned at Arthur. 'She is magnificent, but I bet she rules the roost.'

Arthur was looking both shocked and happy. 'She can rule anything she wants as long as she doesn't change her mind about marrying me.'

He stared across at Mr Forester. 'Please leave my house now, sir. You and your suspicious mind do nothing but taint the atmosphere.'

Forester's mouth dropped open in shock at this further attack.

Dennison hid a smile and took his colleague's arm. 'I agree that it's time for you to go. And in case you're worrying, I promise not to allow them to jump into bed together while Mrs Harte and the child are staying with me.'

Forester stared at their two hostile faces and saw a third man, who looked equally hostile, standing in the hall holding the front door open. He pushed past Biff and went outside, pacing up and down while he waited to see Gwynneth and the child taken to the home of Dennison and his sister Veronica.

He was merely doing his duty, he told himself, as he'd been brought up to do. But he had a sneaking suspicion that he'd gone too far this time. Once he'd seen the woman move out, he'd leave them to it.

He didn't envy Chapman marrying her. She'd lead him by the nose. Which was why he'd never risked marrying.

When Dennison explained to his sister why he'd brought Gwynneth and Beatie back with him, she too was furious with Forester.

'There's just one good thing about it.'

They all looked at her in surprise.

'We can make sure we prepare for a very good wedding – to which we're not inviting that old fuddy duddy.'

Epilogue

Ten days later, Gwynneth woke later than usual after a restless night, to find Beatie's bed empty.

Her heart did a little leap of nervous fear at the thought of what today would bring. Her wedding day. And her kind friends were insisting on making a big fuss.

When she saw the time, she got up straight away. She didn't want all this song and dance, she just wanted to get the ceremony over with and start her new life. What she cared about was the people who would be most closely involved in it: Arthur and Beatie. She wanted to make a happy home and a family with them.

She hated, absolutely hated, the thought of being the centre of all this carry on.

Why did everyone, even Beatie, seem determined to make sure everything was done in a style that terrified her.

Her new outfit was hanging in the wardrobe, a gift from her sons. The dress and jacket were beautiful, a soft dusky pink that suited her. But they shouldn't have spent so much money on one set of what would be her Sunday clothes afterwards.

The only good thing about this fancy wedding was that it had brought Lucas home from Manchester for two days to take part in the ceremony. It had been lovely to see him again. They'd had a nice chat last night, and it made her feel a lot better to know how much he was loving his new life.

There was to be a fancy meal that was costing heaven knew how much after the ceremony at the town hall. Dennison was insisting on paying for that as his wedding present to them, but it was such a lot of money to spend on one meal. Three courses, they were having. What if she made a fool of herself and used the wrong cutlery?

There was a knock on the bedroom door and Veronica peeped in. 'Oh, you're awake. Thank goodness. I've brought up a cup of tea. I'll go and run your bath while you drink it.'

She set it down by the bed and whisked out of the room. She was like that, nice but always busy, didn't stop to chat till the late evening.

If Arthur had been by her side, Gwynneth would have felt better, but she wasn't allowed to see him today till they got to the town hall for the ceremony. Another stupid wedding custom.

She felt quite angry at it all.

No, not angry, terrified!

As she was getting out of bed, Beatie peeped into the room. 'Miss Peters said you were awake.' She looked over her shoulder, put one finger to her mouth in a shushing sign, and handed over an envelope.

'What's this?'

'From Grandfather. You're to open it when you're alone.'

So Gwynneth hid it in her towel and went along to the bathroom where a lovely warm bath was steaming gently as it waited for her.

Thank goodness she was allowed to do this on her own, at least. As far as she could see, she'd not be able to take a single breath on her own for the rest of the day.

She stared at the envelope: Arthur's handwriting. Carefully she opened it, trying not to tear it. Such a pretty envelope.

It was a very short note but it brought tears to her eyes.

After today, we'll not let them fuss over us, my dear. I know how you hate it, but they only do it because they're so fond of you.

To me, it's worth doing anything to marry you. I love you and I know you feel the same.

Your Arthur

PS I meant what I said. I'm never allowing that Forester into my house, if I have to toss him out of the front door myself. I am still angry at him for insulting you.

She smiled and found a tear tracking down her cheek. But it was a happy tear and it was followed by a chuckle at the last two sentences in the letter. Her shy Arthur threatening to toss a JP out of his house for upsetting her. That was love, coming from such a gentle man.

And the thought of his lovely little note carried her through the fussing over her hair and clothes, and the drive to the town hall.

Beatie's hand clasping hers helped too, as did the way the child stroked her own new clothes every now and then, and the sight of her rosy cheeks and shiny hair.

Gwynneth got out of Dennison's car and took the arm he offered her as he walked with her into the town hall and through to the rear of it and the registry office.

They stopped at the door and he whispered, 'You all right?'

'Yes, thank you.' Arthur's letter crackled in her pocket as she patted it for courage.

Then they were inside and she let Dennison lead her to a seat in the front next to Arthur, who looked so blissfully happy at the sight of her that the last of her nervousness about being the centre of attention fled.

He stood up and waited for her to sit, before taking his place again and grabbing tight hold of her hand beneath the folds of her new skirt.

'I love you,' she said, not caring who heard her.

'I love you too.'

Then someone called out their names and she let Arthur lead her towards the next room where the brief ceremony was to take place.

Beatie took her other hand and walked with them, clutching the box with the wedding ring in it, an honour that had thrilled the child to pieces.

Gwynneth must have acted automatically because she didn't become fully conscious of her surroundings again until 'Mr and Mrs Arthur Chapman' were walking out of the registry office and then into the open air.

Dennison's car now had white ribbons on it.

Some people were standing just outside the building and they tossed confetti over them.

It was a nice thing to do, but the nicest thing of all was holding Arthur's hand on one side and Beatie's hand on the other.

The three of them sat in the back and let Dennison and his sister sit in the front as he drove them all to the town's smartest hotel for a wedding meal.

She'd tried to tell them not to waste their money on such a fancy meal, but now, suddenly, she was glad of it, had found her appetite again.

She blushed a couple of times when it came to the speeches, but Arthur squeezed her hand and she got through it.

And then came the best part of the day.

Beatie went off to stay with Gabriel and Maisie, and Dennison dropped the two newly-weds outside Arthur's house – her house now as well. To her surprise, after Arthur had opened the front door, he scooped her up in his arms and carried her across the threshold.

'You fool!' she whispered.

'A very happy fool.' He set her down and turned to close and lock the door, while their friends and family cheered loudly outside.

'What do you want to do first?' he asked.

'Make a cup of tea, then get out of these fancy clothes and have my wicked way with you.'

He grinned. 'Your wish is my command, o princess.'

And darned if the butterflies didn't start dancing in her stomach.

'Never mind the tea,' she said in a husky voice.

'You're sure?'

She nodded.

'I wish I were strong enough to carry you all the way up the stairs.'

'I'd prefer to walk beside you.'

'In love and in life,' he said, and kissed her so beautifully she felt the warmth of his love run through her from top to toe.

There were flowers in the bedroom, a pretty new nightdress folded on the pillow – only he tossed it aside. So she tossed his pyjamas aside as well, and fell into his arms and life at the same time.

No woman had ever been as happy as she was today, she was quite sure of that.

Secret defences before and during World War II

This thread in the story was inspired by my ongoing reading about the era in which the Backshaw Moss series is set. If you're interested in the topic, you can read more about it in:

History in Hiding by Stewart Ross (Robert Hale, London, 1991) final chapter in particular.

Churchill's Underground Army by John Warwicker (Frontline Books, London, 2008) especially Chapter 18.

We all know about Bletchley Park these days, but I'm quite sure we don't know all the secrets involved in the past and ongoing defence of Britain or any other country.

Summer 1943 – my mother,
her cousin and me at two years old!

My husband and I at our graduation
ceremony in 1962 – we got married later that same year.

CONTACT ANNA

Anna is always delighted to hear from readers and can be contacted via the internet.

Anna has her own web page, with details of her books, some behind-the-scenes information that is available nowhere else and the first chapters of her books to try out, as well as a picture gallery.

Anna can be contacted by email at
anna@annajacobs.com

You can also find Anna on Facebook at
www.facebook.com/AnnaJacobsBooks

If you'd like to receive an email newsletter about Anna and her books every month or two, you are cordially invited to join her announcements list. Just email her and ask to be added to the list, or follow the link from her web page.

www.annajacobs.com

An invitation from the publisher

Join us at www.hodder.co.uk, or follow us
on Twitter @hodderbooks to be a part of
our community of people who love the very
best in books and reading.

Whether you want to discover more about a book
or an author, watch trailers and interviews, have the
chance to win early limited editions, or simply browse
our expert readers' selection of the very best books,
we think you'll find what you're looking for.

And if you don't, that's the place to tell us what's missing.

We love what we do, and we'd love you to be a part of it.

www.hodder.co.uk

@hodderbooks

HodderBooks

HodderBooks